A WATER WITCH COZY MYSTERY ANTHOLOGY

BOOKS ONE, TWO, AND THREE.

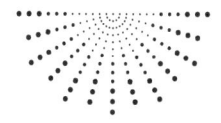

SAM SHORT

WWW.SAMSHORTAUTHOR.COM

Copyright © 2017 by Sam Short

All rights reserved.

No part of this book may be reproduced in any form or by any electronic or mechanical means, including information storage and retrieval systems, without written permission from the author, except for the use of brief quotations in a book review.

❧ Created with Vellum

For Louise. The best daughter a father could wish for.

Under Lock & Key

A Water Witch Cozy Mystery - Book One

Sam Short

Copyright © 2017 by Sam Short

All rights reserved.

No part of this book may be reproduced in any form or by any electronic or mechanical means, including information storage and retrieval systems, without written permission from the author, except for the use of brief quotations in a book review.

❧ Created with Vellum

*For Katie.
My love. My life. My all.*

CHAPTER ONE

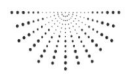

"I'll stick this onion so far up your backside, that your breath will smell like a Frenchman's!"

Sacré Bleu! That's not what I expected to hear just as I was about to take a big gulp of wine — or a little sip in my case — naturally. It's lucky that I hadn't managed to get any wine in my mouth — it would have been spluttered all over my clothes, and I knew from bitter experience that elderberry wine does not come out of a white summer dress.

The berries had been picked under a full moon, and the glass which contained the crimson liquid brushed my lips enticingly as the woman's voice echoed around the clearing. I took a last sniff of the fruity aromas and reluctantly placed the glass next to a pot of herbs on the flat roof of my boat.

"I'd better go and have a look," I said to Rosie, who was pacing on the roof behind me, nagging me for her evening meal. "It sounds like somebody's got a bee in their bonnet!"

It's sometimes lonely on a boat, and I unashamedly used Rosie as a surrogate person to talk to. Anyway, I wasn't one of those people who thought speaking to animals was crazy.

In fact, some of my most memorable conservations had been with Rosie. One sided as they were.

The cat gave me a look that I interpreted as a final demand, and mewled pleadingly, her black tail swinging in annoyance. "It's not time yet," I said. "Catch a rat if you're that hungry, I'm sure there are plenty along the canal bank."

Rosie looked at me with the disdain I deserved. She would chase rats off the boat, but kill them she would not — and eat them? No chance. I put it down to her being a pacifist, but my friends insisted she was just bone idle and a fussy eater. Maybe it was a mix of both. Either way, my boat was free of vermin, and I was never treated to the macabre gift-giving habits of other people's cats.

I clambered off the roof and stood on the bow deck of the *Water Witch* as the shouting female launched her next verbal barrage, this time a little less xenophobic. Or was it racist? I'd not spoken to Granny for sixteen weeks, so my knowledge of politically correct buzzwords was meagre to say the least. She'd soon jog my memory when I got around to visiting her. "You're an awful man, Sam!" the woman shouted. "A greedy man who should know better! You grew up here in Wickford, how could you do this to us?"

I deduced that the shouting was coming from the shared allotment gardens, which were at the top of one of the three footpaths that led up the hill from my secluded mooring. The woman's threat of using an onion as a highly intrusive weapon strengthened that theory.

The female voice wasn't recognisable, but I guessed who the person she was shouting at was — Sam Hedgewick, local businessman, and owner of the football pitch sized piece of land that was the allotments.

The shouting continued as I stepped ashore onto the strip of stonework which separated my boat from the grass, and skirted the mooring, reminding myself that I'd have to thank whoever it was from the hotel who'd mowed the grass for me. I'd been away for four months, taking my floating witchcraft shop on its first business trip along the canals and rivers of England, and it was nice to come home to freshly cut grass.

The Poacher's Pocket Hotel, hidden by trees on the hill above me, owned the mooring spot I leased, and I could access the hotel's beer garden using the second of the three footpaths. The final path gave me access to the town of Wickford which was a short walk away, and emerged on Bridge Street, near the *Firkin Gherkin* greengrocers.

The hotel had once offered canal trips, and the two picnic benches the customers had used while waiting for the boat, were still there, a few feet from the water's edge. The potted plants I'd left to fend for themselves still looked healthy, and the water and electricity supplies, housed in a green metal box, were the cherry on top of the cake. There'd be no more worrying about the boat's batteries going flat, or having to cruise a few miles to fill up my water tank — until I took my shop on its next trip at least. It was good to be home.

I'd been strangely lucky to have been offered the lease. When the hotel stopped offering boat trips, wealthy people had queued up to buy the unique mooring, but after a visit from my grandmother the hotel owners had offered me the chance to lease it — for a surprisingly affordable monthly fee.

I was convinced that magic had been involved, despite my grandmother's vehement denial. She vehemently denied everything she was accused of though, including the infamous incident of Farmer Bill's whole dairy herd working out how to leap a four-foot fence. It had coincidentally occurred just two days after he'd publicly spurned my grandmother's completely inappropriate sexual advances, and Granny had been seething with rage and embarrassment.

It was only when the cows had finished causing havoc in the town and reached my grandmother's cottage, churning up her lawn, that the herd had decided their field was a better option after all. The police who had escorted the animals home had never worked out why the cows had suddenly turned around and headed back to their field, just as Granny hurled a tirade of abuse at them. My grandmother had tried to blame the whole incident on a low-pressure weather front coming in from the east, but my sister was adamant she'd seen Granny brewing a potion that involved milk and an energy drink.

Impressed at how far away the shouting woman could make her voice heard, I climbed the steep hundred-metre-long footpath. The gate at the top of the hill which led into the shared gardens was open, and a group of gardening enthusiasts crowded around Sam Hedgewick and his angry adversary.

I paused for a moment before stepping through the gateway. Was I being nosy? No, I decided, I was being naturally inquisitive — a quality that any good witch needed — according to my mum.

Anyway, I'd recognised the shouting woman as Hilda Cox, a normally mild mannered woman, and certainly not the sort of person who routinely made vegetable related threats of violence. Something must have really made her angry, and I *absolutely* needed to know what. How could that possibly have been construed as nosiness?

I weaved a route between the beds of vegetables and bamboo frames which bean plants covered with bright red flowers, and joined the group of spectators. I recognised a lot of them, and some of their eyes lit up when they saw I was back in town. Now was not the time to catch up with them, though — now was the time to watch a woman clutching an onion twice the size of the ones you find in supermarkets, giving a sullen faced Sam Hedegwick a dressing down.

"How could you, Sam?" yelled Hilda. "You know most of us will be lost without our allotments. We can't all afford homes with big gardens." She looked Sam up and down. "Like some people."

"Hilda," said Sam, his business suit looking as out of place amongst the vegetable patches as a cow did in a horse race. And I'd seen that. Believe me. With a grandmother like mine, I'd seen a lot. "I don't want to sell it, but I have to. You'll all get your rent back for the remainder of the year, you don't need to worry about that, but the allotments are being sold next week. That's the end of the matter."

"It's not my rent that worries me," Bill Winters, a ruddy faced man with a full head of snow white hair, chimed in. "It's the fact that I was probably going to win the largest marrow contest this year. How can you do this to me? To us? You know I've been trying to win that competition for ten years, and this year I've got it right. It's going to be a monster marrow, Sam! A monster!"

Sam looked down at his shoes and shook his head. "I'm sorry, Bill. Really, I am. There's nothing I can do. The contracts are being signed next week, and then it's up to the developers to decide how quickly they start building."

"So, my beautiful cabbages will be buried beneath posh folk's fancy apartment buildings?" said another man, much to the agreement of the grumbling crowd.

"Can you dig them up before I sell?" asked Sam, looking somewhat flustered.

"They're not ready!" spat the man. He lowered his head, and his body slumped, his voice faltering as he spoke again, "my cabbages aren't ready. They're just not ready."

A woman placed her hand on his back. "There, there, Timothy. Don't upset yourself. You know what the doctor said, no stress, and no whiskey. Oh, and no fried bacon. I must remember that one." She turned her attention to Sam. "See what you've done to him? My husband is a proud man, who grows the best cabbages in this town —"

"Easy now, Marjorie," interrupted a tall elderly man with a stern face, leaning on a gardening fork which he twisted into the soil. "They're good cabbages, yes, but the best? I'm not so sure."

"See what you've done, Sam?" said Marjorie. "You've got us bickering amongst ourselves now!"

"I'm sorry all right!" said Sam. "I can't help you. Any of you. I'm sorry."

Several people spoke at once, and Sam's panicked face flitted between them. "What about our sheds? They cost money," said one. "And my tools. Where will I store them? I live in a tiny apartment!" pleaded another.

Sam dropped his head and turned his back to the crowd. "Sorry folks," he mumbled, and began making his way across the allotment towards the small carpark. "Really, I'm sorry."

He cut a sad figure as he meandered along the muddy paths, and I couldn't help feeling sorry for him.

"Watch your back, Sam Hedgewick!" yelled Hilda, brandishing the onion above her head like a gladiatorial weapon, her face beetroot red. "You've made a lot of people angry!"

Sam raised a hand in surrender and continued his lonely walk.

Fingers tightened on my wrist, and I turned to see the smiling face of Veronica Potter. Her make-up was as garishly applied as always, and I struggled to keep a smile off my face as I remembered my mother once referring to her as a pantomime dame. She had certainly put an awful lot of effort into getting prepared for a visit to an allotment. "It's good to see you back, Penelope!" she gushed. "I thought I heard a boat in the distance, and I said to Marjorie, 'Penelope's sister told me that she's due home this week. I wonder if it's her!'"

"It's great to be back, Veronica, but I wasn't expecting all this as I settled in for my first evening at home. I've only been back for an hour."

Veronica moved her head closer to mine. "Ignore it," she whispered. "They'll get over it. They can take up bowling or something when the allotment goes. It's only a hobby after all. It's not like they can't buy veg in the supermarket."

The other people had begun traipsing back to their plots of land since Sam had left, and I waved and said hello to the ones who greeted me.

"Why is he selling it?" I said, freeing my wrist from Veronica's surprisingly strong grasp.

"He didn't say. He just came here and broke the news." She moved her face even closer to mine. "He's a gambling man, and not a very good one, he's probably got himself in debt. Between me and you, Penelope. I don't really care. I only come here to flirt with the men. It's just a shame that most of them are at the age where they feel the cold more. It's summer, and I was hoping to at least see a few torsos."

I hid the shudder that traversed my whole body. "What about Ron? Aren't you and him still an item?"

"It's complicated, Penelope. The nursing home have a new rule in place stopping us from visiting each other's rooms after nine at night. We can get around it of course, but it's not nice to be sneaking around at my age, and then of course we're forced keep the noise down. And where's the fun in that?"

I wished I'd learnt a spell that would stop Veronica speaking, or at least one that would wash away the images that Veronica had conjured up in the darkest recesses of my mind. "It must be hard," I murmured, thinking of an excuse to get away from there. Quickly.

"Yes, well. It's not easy being old, dear. You'll see one day."

That wasn't *totally* true, but of course Veronica didn't know that. Not many people knew that real witches existed at all, and of those people, only a select handful knew about the existence of the haven. A place I was never going to get to if I believed my mother. Not that it bothered me too much at the age of twenty-three. I had plenty of time left to put in the work needed to ascend.

"Didn't Ron want to come to the allotment?" I asked. "He's usually here tending the nursing home's patch. He kept me well supplied with green beans last year."

The nursing home was not a run of the mill retirement home. It was for people who had been financially successful in life, and the allotment patch kept the kitchens supplied with the freshest of produce for the chefs to prepare outlandishly delicious meals with. The home encouraged its residents to get out into the open air and do a little gardening from time to time, and with the home being less than half a mile from the allotments, it was a relatively easy walk for the fitter of residents, and a minibus ferried the less mobile back and forth.

Last year had seen a record crop of green beans, and thanks to the kindness of the allotment owners, I'd practically lived off them — coated with a little melted butter and sprinkled with cumin seeds. It was handy having the allotment so close to my mooring, and to my shame, as well as accepting free offerings from people, I'd once or twice sneaked in under the cover of darkness and dug myself a potato to bake in the oven. To even out the universe and absolve myself from guilt, I'd cast a gentle fertility spell over the allotments which had been too late in the year to benefit last year's produce, but was certainly responsible for the size of Bill's marrows this year.

Veronica laughed. "Ron won't come here anymore, not

UNDER LOCK AND KEY

since they built a new gym in the home. He's always in there, pimping steel."

"Iron," I smiled, managing to swallow a giggle. "*Pumping iron*."

"Yes, that's it. You should see him though, Penelope. Big and buff, and with a line of muscles that takes the eye from his stomach, right down to his big old —"

"It's good to keep fit!" I interrupted. "Good for Ron."

"Yes, but Ron's not doing it for that reason, he's doing it to keep fresh for me, and to make sure I don't stray. I'm quite the flower amongst weeds in the home, and a lot of the men wouldn't mind walking into the breakfast room with me on their arm, and doesn't Ron know it!" Veronica giggled as my eyes widened. "He threw a pea at Wally during dinner on Tuesday because he looked at me for a little too long. He's got quite the jealous streak, but he's a real man, Penelope, and with his new muscles he struts around like a big old peacock."

Veronica gazed into the distance for a few moments with a twinkle in her eye, and I took the chance to change the subject and make my escape. "Well, it was nice seeing you, Veronica," I said. "But I have to get back to the boat. I rushed over here when I heard the shouting, and I think I...."

"Yes?"

Think Penny. Think. "...left the oven on?"

Veronica put her hand on my back and turned me in the direction of the canal. "Get back then, Penelope, hurry. I've never trusted gas. I've read too many stories about gas explosions. You don't want one of those on your boat. It would probably sink!"

I started my walk across the allotments with unwelcome images of Ron and Veronica imprinted on my mind. "See you soon, Veronica," I said, stepping over an abnormally large cauliflower. Maybe my fertility spell hadn't been gentle enough, there seemed to be some unfeasibly healthy looking vegetables growing everywhere I looked.

"Oh, Penelope!" she called. "Are you open for business?"

"I won't be opening for normal business hours, I need a break after the last four months, but if I'm home and someone stops by, they're welcome to come in."

"Oh good. All that talking about Ron has given me an idea. I need you to make me a special potion. A *very* special one."

I dodged an overturned wheelbarrow and hopped over a two-foot-long cucumber. "Pop in tomorrow if you like. I'm going into town in the morning, but I'll be home by six."

"Six o'clock it is!" said Veronica, stumbling over dried clods of earth as she headed towards a group of men, pruning her hair as she walked.

With a final farewell, I headed back the way I'd come, and paused halfway down the footpath to appreciate my piece of paradise. The canal sparkled below me, travelling east to west, and my mooring led directly off it at a right angle. It was a tight angle to negotiate in a long boat, but under the tutelage of a friendly fellow boat owner, I'd soon learnt how to make the turn.

My sister had insisted the man had only helped me because I was blocking the canal, but I liked to think it was my first introduction to the legendary community spirit of the people who made the canals their home.

The dead-end channel of water was large enough for two boats, but home only to my canal narrowboat, and grassy slopes rose on all three sides of the cutaway, giving way to the trees which gave me seclusion.

A towpath ran along the opposite bank of the canal, and trees shrouded the side of the waterway my home was cut into, dipping their lower branches in the water.

I shouted as I descended the footpath. "Mabel! Mabel!"

She'd failed to appear when I'd arrived home, but she'd show up soon enough. She wasn't the type of goose who got on with other members of her species. She preferred human company, and certainly wouldn't put up with the two swans which were feeding in the margins of my mooring.

Rosie was leaning over the edge of the roof, hissing at them as I climbed back aboard the boat. "Come on," I said. "It's dinnertime. It's tuna Tuesday!"

She leapt down with a happy mewl, and scurried through the open bow doors. Rosie ate tuna flavoured food on most days of the week, but I tried to make it sound more special on a Thursday and a Tuesday.

I ducked as I descended the two steps into the belly of my boat. The shop section of my boat, which had been the saloon lounge when I'd bought it, was packed with various incenses and herbs — along with all the other witchcraft paraphernalia that mortal witches enjoyed trying to make magic with, and the whole boat smelled deliciously herby.

Stepping past the tiny sales counter, I breezed through the purple curtain that acted as a door, and made my way into the middle section of the sixty-foot narrowboat, the part that customers never saw. Unless they were of the nosy variety — the type of person that would scare you half to death as you looked up from reading a book, or stirring a stew, and saw them peering in through one of the large rectangle windows that ran along either side of the steel hull.

The living quarters and galley kitchen area was compact, but cosy and comfortable nonetheless. With ample seating, a fully functioning kitchen, and minimally decorated in a way that I hoped said modern *and* traditional, it was my idea of perfect. The coal and wood burner stood in the corner, unused since winter, and the space on the wall where I had intended on hanging a TV was still bare.

Beyond the living area was my bathroom, and past that,

my bedroom, which was accessed by a narrow corridor. The bedroom was large enough for a compact double bed, and a pair of doors opened onto the stern decking, allowing me the pleasure of a breeze on my face as I slept on a warm summer's night. With a fire burning in the living area stove and the stern doors closed, the bedroom became a toasty warm haven on a cold winter's night.

The bathroom was small, but contained everything I needed. With white tiled walls, it boasted a full-sized shower, a sink, and a toilet. I'd decided to keep quiet about my composting toilet in the future. I'd almost been chased away from a village I'd moored up in, when I'd used it as a unique selling point to sell more of the potted herbs that dotted the flat roof of my boat. I'd never been back to the village, and I was beginning to understand how snake oil salesmen had felt.

I loved the *Water Witch*, and I loved living between walls that were just under seven-feet apart. Who needed acres of floor space? Especially floor space that you couldn't move from scenic village to bustling town, or even busy city at the drop of a hat. No, living in a house or apartment was not for me. I liked to imagine myself as a nomadic witch, like those of the past.

With Rosie's bowls filled, and the radio switched on and placed next to an open window, I reclaimed my position on the roof. After fishing the suicidal and drunk flies from my wine glass, I took a long gulp, closed my eyes, and lay back beneath the last of the evening sun.

An hour later, and with a warm tipsiness coursing through my veins, I climbed off the roof as the sun began setting over the canal, and went inside the boat. Rosie leapt onto me as I sat down, and with her curled up on my lap, I made a few phone calls to let people know I was home, and to arrange some meet ups for the following day.

It was good to be back in Wickford, and I looked forward to not having to negotiate canal locks or worry about finding a mooring spot in a busy town on market day. With the sound of water lapping against the hull competing with Rosie's snoring, I drifted off to sleep on the sofa, to intrusive thoughts of Ron and Veronica sneaking around the nursing home in just their underwear.

CHAPTER TWO

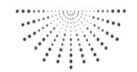

*R*osie woke me up at precisely eight o'clock in the morning by massaging my face and mewling in my ear. "Okay," I said, gently pushing her away, and promising myself for the fiftieth time that I wouldn't fall asleep on the sofa fully clothed again. "I know. It's breakfast time."

After topping Rosie's water and food bowls up, I put some coffee on, took a shower, and dressed in a short purple dress over leggings, with my favourite oxblood Dr Martens on my feet. The short boots were years old and beginning to show their age, but shoes and clothes shopping was almost at the top of my 'things I don't enjoy in life' list — directly beneath public flatulence — but a few spots above sporks. Whoever had come up with the idea for sporks was certainly not a fan of soup or a meaty steak. Too shallow for soup, and not strong enough for a nice piece of rump, a spork was just not fit for purpose.

With a mug of black coffee in my hand, and Rosie rubbing against my legs, I tossed some stale bread to the noisy congregation of ducks and swans that had gathered around my boat. They'd soon disperse when Mabel the goose made an appearance, but for the time being they were welcome to share my mooring with me. Several of them looked up at me sullenly as I threw the last piece of dry bread to a particularly shy looking duck on the edge of the group, and set about unstrapping my bike from the front of the boat. The red bike clattered as I threw it ashore, but I'd long ago stopped worrying about scratching it, and after locking the boat up and making sure Rosie's cat flap was open, I headed off up the footpath towards town to meet my best friend.

I was due to meet Susie at nine o'clock sharp, and when Susie said sharp, she meant samurai sword sharp. Just being half a minute late would have elicited a soul wilting stare from her — even if she hadn't seen me for months. It was a quick cycle into town, and I waved at the few people who recognised me as I negotiated the almost traffic free streets of Wickford. The morning sun was already warming my face, and the older building's light coloured stonework glowed in the golden light, like the crust on a particularly good clotted cream. The scent of the freshly watered flowers that bulged from the hanging baskets beneath every wrought iron street light made me strangely happy, and I even looked forward to visiting my mother later in the day.

The imaginatively named Coffee Pot Café stood on the corner of Church Street and High Street, and after leaning my bike against the post-box outside, I went inside to a friendly welcome from Mrs Patterson, the long-term owner and baker of some of finest pastries in town.

"Penelope!" she said, "Susie said you were coming! It's great to see you."

"It's great to be back," I said, looking over the heads of the other diners for my friend.

"She's over there," said Mrs Patterson, pointing. "At the

table in the corner. She's tucked away behind the Colonel and his massive newspaper. She's ordered a drink and some toast for you."

Susie was huddled at the table with a pot of tea for two, and two slices of hot buttered toast for each of us. She was well hidden by Colonel Bradshaw's newspaper, and her face lit up when she took her eyes off her phone and saw me. "Penny!" she squealed, standing up as I approached the table. "You're early! I was just about to phone you."

I gave her a wide grin and returned the bearhug she locked me in. "Pleased to see you too, Susie," I said, raising my eyebrows.

"Of course I'm pleased to see you, Penny. I just wasn't expecting you to be early."

After knowing Susie for as many years as I had, it was easy to let her obsessive time keeping go straight over my head with a smile. I sat down opposite her, wondering why I always got a seat that had one leg shorter than the others, and bit into the crispy crust of my toast while Susie poured us a cup of tea.

"So," said Susie. "How's tricks?"

It was a private joke we'd shared since we were eleven years old, when Susie had discovered my family were witches. Everyone had been using the trendy question at the time, but to me and Susie it had always had a greater meaning.

"Things are magic," I said, delivering the punchline, much to Susie's delight.

"I've missed you, Penny," she said, tucking into her toast. "Please tell me you're staying for good."

I narrowed my eyes and stared at her. "You've been talking to my mother, haven't you? She's recruited you into the '*get Penny to stop her ridiculous floating shop fantasy, and live a normal life'* team, hasn't she?"

Susie flicked a stray strand of blonde hair from her eye and tried to stifle a giggle. "Did you use magic to work that out, Penelope Weaver?" she said, keeping her voice low, as we always did when we spoke about witchy things in public.

I added another sugar to my tea. "I wish I *could* do mind reading magic, but as we all know, especially if you listen to my mother..." Susie laughed as I put on a voice, not a million miles away from my mother's high pitched whine, but closer to the sound a boy makes when he traps himself in his trouser zipper, "...I'm a witch who has absolutely no pride in her heritage, and has absolutely no chance of ascending if she continues to only focus on the element of water. A witch needs to feel the earth between her toes, just as much as she needs to be near water."

Susie did very well not to spit her tea across the table. "That's exactly what she says!"

I took another bite of toast, savouring the melted butter. Mrs Patterson sourced all her ingredients locally, and the butter was from the dairy on the outskirts of town, produced from Farmer Bill's errant cows. "Does my mother not know that a canal has banks? And occasionally I venture onto the aforementioned banks and walk around on dry land?" I said, smiling as I chewed.

"She just misses you," she said, "and Willow does. Speaking of Willow — you won't believe how tall she's got. It's like she went on a massive growth spurt the day she turned eighteen."

My heart sank. I'd wanted nothing more than to be with my sister on such a landmark birthday, but I'd been miles away, near London, moored up next to a music festival. It had been a great day for trade and I'd practically sold all my stock to the legions of women, and some men, who'd wanted to become witches. They'd have been shocked to know that the dark-haired girl who'd served them was a real witch. Not as shocked as they'd have been to find out that real witches existed, though.

"I'm gutted that I missed her birthday."

"She understands. She's really proud of you."

"I'm going straight there after breakfast to see them," I said. "I wanted to pick some flowers up for mum first."

Susie sipped her tea. "I hope she likes cheap flowers from the convenience store."

"Why?"

"There's a passive aggressive handwritten sign in the florist's window," said Susie, picking up her phone and showing me the screen. "Look, I took a photo. In my line of work, it pays to keep your finger on the pulse."

I took the phone from Susie and read the sign.

'It is with deep regret that I must inform my customers that this shop is closing down. You can thank the town's most successful businessman and all-round nice person — Mr Sam Hedgewick, for the inconvenience to yourselves, and the life altering change in my circumstances.

He has been kind enough to give me a full three days' notice that he is selling the property, and I must vacate it immediately. Thanks to an exceptionally well written contract, which Mr Hedgewick was kind enough to read aloud to me, I have no legal leg to stand on.

Please show Mr Hedgewick your appreciation when you next pass him in the street, or when he crosses the road in front of your car.'

I passed the phone back to Susie with a frown. "Sam's ruffling a few feathers."

Susie narrowed her eyes. "A few?"

I told her about the incident in the allotments, leaving out my conversation with Veronica. There were better places than at the breakfast table for talking about randy elderly folk.

"I wonder what he's playing at," Susie said. "I'm going to look into it."

I swallowed the toast in my mouth and took another bite. "Investigative journalism. At least some reporters still practice it."

Susie smiled. "I have to, I'm a freelance journalist. Not many newspapers will pay for a story about a vandalised bus stop in Wickford. Between this Sam Hedgewick thing and the car show, I'll probably be able to sell a story to The Herald."

"Car show?" I said.

Susie poured the last of the tea, sharing it between us. It was hardly worth adding sugar to the inch of liquid in my cup.

"You've come back just in time, Penny. It's a vintage car show, you'll see loads of old cars on the roads in the next few days, and the local businesses will make more money this week than they have in months. Some of the cars are real beauties, even to someone like me who can't tell a Rolls Royce and a Mini apart. They've hired the big camping field next to the canal on the outskirts of town. There's a big marquee too with a bar and live music. I think the whole things just an excuse to get drunk to be honest. You should moor your boat there. You'll make a lot of money."

I shook my head. "No. I'm staying right where I'm moored for now. I need a break."

"Fair enough," said Susie. "It will probably be more of a man thing anyway, maybe not your target customers."

"You'd be surprised," I said. "There's more men into witchcraft than people imagine."

"Probably trying to conjure up a few more inches down there," Susie laughed, her hair falling into her eyes. She waved it away and drank the last of her tea. "Or trying to magic themselves into some tarts underwear while their fiancée is at home planning their wedding."

I raised my eyebrows and gave a theatrical sigh. "I'd have thought an independent woman like you would have been over a waste of skin like him a long time ago."

Susie giggled. "Oh, I'm over Robert. Don't you worry about that. It doesn't hurt to laugh about him now and again though. I mean, what sort of man pays for tablets from China that promise to grow his pride and joy an inch or two overnight? And to think he was taking them to try and impress that tart!"

I laughed hard from my belly, and the table shook, nearly knocking the teapot over the edge. "I shouldn't laugh. It sounds like he was very poorly. God knows what was in those pills."

"Bath salts I imagine. Or some type of acid. He thought he had two heads at one point and tried to drown the imposter in the bath. It's a good job I found him, he was almost out of breath."

Our loud giggles drew the attention of some of the other diners, and we calmed ourselves down with deep breaths. I'd been on my canal travels when the Robert incident had occurred, and Susie managed to remember something new every time we spoke about it. The bath story was new to me, and possibly one of the funniest she'd told me yet. Not for Robert though. He'd spent a night in a mental health facility, and hadn't fully recovered for weeks.

When we'd calmed ourselves down, Susie asked about my trip, listening intently as I told her about all the people I'd met and the places I'd been. "I almost sold out completely last week," I answered, when she asked me about business. "I stopped off and restocked on my way home, so my shelves are full again."

"I'm so happy for you, I knew you could do it," said Susie reaching for the bag at her feet. "I'm really sorry I can't stay longer, but I need to go and do some work. Do you want me to take you to the florists in Covenhill first? My cars parked around the corner."

"No thanks," I said. "I'll buy some pastries from Mrs Patterson. Mum loves the cinnamon and raisin ones. She'll enjoy them more than flowers. She thinks flowers are for funerals and cheating husbands."

"You mentioned something about free steak when you phoned last night," hinted Susie with a grin. "Is the invitation still open?"

"Definitely! I'll pick up some meat from the butchers on my way back to the boat. I'm going to invite Willow and Mum too. Willow loves barbecues, but Mum will say no – she has a thing about accidentally eating insects. She has to inspect her bedroom every night for spiders. She thinks they lower themselves into people's mouths while they sleep."

Susie spoke in hushed tones. "And to think that woman is a powerful witch," she said. "I'd have thought she'd embrace spiders." She leaned down and gave me a hug. "It's great to have you back, Penny. I'll see you tonight, and I'll bring some wine."

"No need. I've got plenty of my homemade stuff left."

Susie smirked. "That's why I'm bringing my own."

CHAPTER THREE

With a bag of pastries in the small basket on the front of my bike, I took the narrow lane that led north-east out of the small market town. The mile-long trip to my childhood home was all uphill, and the tall hedgerows were alive with singing birds, with wild strawberry plants dotting the grass verges. Resisting the temptation to stop and pick some, I took the right turn onto the long gravel path that led through my mother's private woodland, and smiled as Hazelwood cottage appeared around the bend. The garden, and the climbing roses that crawled up the cottage's white walls, were in full bloom, and I sniffed the scented air happily as I wheeled my bike up the pathway.

The thick oak door swung open as I approached it, and my sister ran out to greet me, dressed in shorts, a tight white t-shirt, and a pair of flip-flops. "Penny!" she shouted, hugging me so tightly I nearly dropped my bike.

I returned her hug one with one arm, and looked her up and down as she took a step backwards. I gave a low whistle. "Wow," I said. "You've blossomed."

"So I'm told," she laughed. "Quick, come inside, Mum's going to be back soon."

Mum's little car was still parked beneath the large beech tree alongside the cottage, so I guessed she hadn't taken a trip into town. "She's in the haven?"

"Yeah, come inside quickly, we can watch her coming back."

Willow led me into the cottage, and a flash of silver on her wrist caught my attention as she closed the door behind us. "You got my present then?" I said. "I'm sorry I wasn't here for your birthday."

"You can make up for it next year," she smiled, "but I love my bracelet! Thank you!" The silver bracelet, complete with the cat and wand charms I'd added, jangled as she held it out for me to inspect. "Look, I bought another charm."

"A cauldron, it's lovely."

Willow narrowed her eyes. "Seriously though, Penny... did you put any *real* charms on it? Of the magical variety? I can't detect any, but I'm pretty sure you have."

I shook my head. "No, I promise. I wouldn't cast a spell on of anything of yours without telling you. Why do you ask?"

I followed Willow down the hallway towards the kitchen, fascinated by how her backside had filled out in the time since I'd last seen her. When I'd left four months ago, she'd been stick thin — nothing like the curvy young woman she'd become.

Willow sat at the large wooden table and pulled a seat out for me. "It's just that since I've been wearing it, I've had a lot of male attention, much more than normal. Something's not right. I thought you'd put an attraction spell on it."

I placed the bag of pastries on the table and pointed at my sister's chest. "I think it's got more to do with those than any magic tricks," I smirked. "Those are the only attraction spells you need. How did they get so big so quickly?"

My sister gazed down at herself, her cheeks blushing red. "Mum calls them my devil's dumplings."

My laughter echoed around the kitchen, and Willow joined in, her body shaking.

"Mum's just jealous," I said when I'd managed to stop laughing. "Granny told me she used to stuff her bras when she was younger."

Willow opened her mouth to say something, but put her finger over her lips instead. "Stop talking about Mum, she's back," she said, nodding towards the lounge.

I turned to face the open doorway. Although I'd seen Mum entering and leaving the haven hundreds of times, the trick never grew old. The crooked doorway quivered and creaked, and the edges began glowing white as a hovering light appeared in the centre. It spread outward until the space was filled with bright blue light, that made a low humming sound as it rippled like the surface of a pond on a windy day.

A large chocolate covered cake on a tray appeared through the light, held by hands on the end of arms that were cut off at the elbows by the shimmering sheet of blue. "Take care, Eva!" came Mum's voice, throbbing in time with the humming of the spell. "Don't do anything I wouldn't do!"

"You know me, Maggie, always on my best behaviour!" came the distant reply.

With her long hair standing on end, the tips sparking with flashes of red, the rest of my mother emerged through the doorway as the light faded and disappeared behind her. The humming stopped immediately, and my mother gazed at us in turn. "Penelope, you're home. I hope you're hungry. Aunt Eva made a cake."

"I brought pastries," I said, tapping the paper bag in front of me

Mum smiled. "How nice," she said, placing the huge cake

on the table next to my meagre offering. "Perhaps I'll try one later."

Willow giggled. "Mum, your hair's smoking."

Mum nodded. "Thank you, dear."

"No, I didn't mean it like that. It's actually smoking," said Willow, pointing at the smouldering strands of hair that framed Mum's plump face.

Mum frantically patted her head. "I'll have split ends!" she said. "It's because I brought the cake through. Eva put a little magic in it to make it taste better, bringing magic through the portal messes with the space-time continuum."

"Mum's been watching Star Trek re-runs," whispered Willow, as my mother extinguished the last of the embers that fell onto her shoulders. "It's not a space-time continuum, Mum. It's because there's too much of Eva's magic in the cake for this world. The portal just evened it out a little."

The type of magic that could be used in the haven was far older than magic in the real world, and any magic that came through from the other dimension was severely weakened by the portal. The safeguards were put in place after the portal wars of 1907, which left twelve people in our world transformed into toads. They now languished in a purpose-built pond in the haven, surrounded by only the most succulent of flies.

"I know that, young lady!" snapped Mum. "I'm just trying to make magic sound more exciting to you two girls. Today's young generation of witches don't care about magic like we used to when I was younger. You're more interested in boys and make-up."

My eyes widened and Willow's jaw dropped. "That's hardly fair," I protested. "I haven't had a proper boyfriend since I was nineteen, and when do you see me wearing more than a little lip gloss?"

Mum opened one of the large cupboards that lined the

kitchen walls. She retrieved four plates and took a large knife from a drawer. "Well maybe not so much you, Penelope," she said, placing a plate each in front of me and Willow and laying the knife next to the cake. "You're too busy floating around the countryside in that death trap of yours, selling fake magic to desperate people who can't find love the old-fashioned way. Your sister on the other hand..." She didn't finish her sentence, she just pursed her lips, raised her eyebrows, and shook her head gently.

"Yes?" said Willow, "go on, what about me?"

Mum turned to me. "Since your sister grew those fun pillows, she's been parading herself around town, pushing her chest out, and acting puzzled when men suddenly start wanting to give her their phone numbers."

"I do not!" said Willow, placing her arms protectively across her chest.

The two of them stared at me as I burst into laughter.

"What's so funny?" said Mum.

"It's just good to be back," I said truthfully. "Come on, let's have some cake."

Mum sat down and pointed at the fourth plate. "We won't cut it until your grandmother gets here."

"Fun pillows," muttered Willow under her breath.

"Granny's coming?" I asked. "How is she?"

"Your sister hasn't told you?"

Willow moved a finger towards the bulging layer of sticky chocolate that covered the cake. "You told me not to tell her," she said.

"When do you ever do anything I ask you to?" said Mum, knocking Willow's hand away. "It's not good news I'm afraid, Penelope."

My heart sank.

"She's got witch dementia."

My heart lifted again. "That's not too bad," I said. "She'll soon get over it."

Mum fixed me with a stern stare, the frazzled hair hanging around her face making her look far less imposing than she was trying to be. "That's not very nice, Penelope. Imagine having your spells mixed up. Last week she tried to make one of her chickens lay bigger eggs, but she accidentally used a spell meant for an ostrich. That poor chicken... and the ones who witnessed it."

"It got better," said Willow, gazing at the cake. "It still looks a little shocked though."

"It's dangerous for other people, and scary for your Grandmother," said Mum. "The sooner it wears off, the better."

"How long has she had it?" I said.

"Since the accident with that goose of yours."

I sat up straighter in my seat. "What accident? Granny told me she did that because Mabel stole her sandwich. She said she'd reverse the spell as soon as she'd learned her lesson."

Mum dropped her eyes and fiddled with the top button of her long flowery dress. "She was ashamed. She'd tried to cast a spell to clamp its beak closed for an hour or so, but.... well, you know what happened."

Didn't I just — and so did the other waterfowl that used to share my little piece of water with her. Any sensible duck wouldn't come within a hundred metres of my mooring spot these days when Mabel was around. I'd thought Granny's spell had been a little extreme for the simple crime of sandwich theft by waterfowl. It made sense now. Granny had gone very quiet after cursing Mabel, and hadn't stayed around for the fruit trifle, which was very unlike my food loving grandmother.

"Anyway," Mum continued. "She's very angry about the whole thing. She just wants to get back to normal."

Willow agreed. "She can't even get to the haven to be cured. She's forgotten her entry spell. She blew a door off a changing room cubicle in a clothes shop when she tried."

I frowned. "Why on earth would she use a changing cubicle door to enter the haven? It's a very public place to be doing magic."

Mum stood up and crossed the kitchen. She brushed some hanging bunches of dried herbs away from one of the cupboard doors, and got the teapot out. She added some teabags to the huge pot and filled it with water from the kettle that whistled on the old aga stove. "She was trying on a new dress and she wanted Aunt Eva's opinion. The changing rooms were empty. Until the explosion anyway."

Willow laughed, and I couldn't help joining in.

"It's not funny, you two," Mum scolded, her wide hips swaying as she carried the teapot to the table. "At least your grandmother got her entry spell when she was nice and young, the way you two are going, you'll be lucky to get yours before you die! You need to take your magic more seriously. You're getting too wrapped up with what's going on in this world."

Since each of us had turned ten years old, our mother had been insisting we'd never work hard enough to ascend. Mum had acquired her ascension spell at the age of twenty-one, and whenever she entered the haven, that was the age she'd be while there. She could live to be a hundred in the mortal world, but as long as she entered the haven permanently before she died, she would always be twenty-one in the magical dimension.

Aunt Eva had been aged eighty-nine when she'd decided to permanently move to the haven, and she now enjoyed immortality in the body of a nineteen-year-old. She could never come back to our world, but we could go and visit her. If we ever ascended that is.

Each person's entry spell was different, and when a witch had gained enough magical knowledge to ascend, the spell would be made known to them. When a witch had acquired their spell, they could use any door or entrance to conjure a portal.

Mum's chair creaked as she sat down. "I've got more hope for Willow than I have for you, Penelope. At least she practices, and she's getting to know all the elements. You're stuck in that floating tin, surrounded by water for most of the time. You're like a goldfish."

Try as I might, I couldn't work out how living in a boat could be equated with being like a fish. Perhaps if I lived beneath the water in a submarine... maybe. "Why am I like a goldfish?" I asked her as she poured me a cup of tea.

She tilted her head and adopted a smug expression as she explained her theory. "What happens to a goldfish when it lives in a small bowl? It never grows, that's what happens. If you took it out of the bowl and put it a pond, it would grow to its full potential. You're the goldfish and your boat is the bowl. You'll never grow. You're not getting to know all the elements, Penelope. You need to step into a bigger pond."

I sighed. This again. "I have plenty of air. I have a fire in my boat. I live on water, and I feel the earth under my feet every time I moor up. I do just fine with the elements, thank you very much."

Mum wouldn't give up, and I sipped my tea and rolled my eyes as I listened to her. "You can't concentrate on one element more than the others, Penelope. I'm just concerned that you'll never understand the spirit element if you stay on that boat. You need to embrace the four earthly elements before you understand the spirit element, and it's the spirit element that will get you into the haven."

The sound of a car outside caught Mum's attention, halting her lecture — although I was fully aware she'd probably never give up on getting me back on dry land. Willow stood up to look through the window. "Granny's here!" she said.

The front door opened and Granny's hurried footsteps clattered down the hallway. She may have had witch dementia, but she was still three times as nimble as most women approaching eighty. She breezed into the kitchen, smiling at me before staring at my mother intently. She peered over her plastic rimmed purple glasses, inspecting Mum's charred hair, and sat down. "You've burnt your hair, Maggie. You'll need to trim and dye it."

"I don't dye my hair!" Mum said incredulously. She waved a hand between me and Willow. "I'm as naturally dark as these two!"

"Enough of your problems, dear," said Granny, her blue rinse perm looking as perfect as ever. "Penelope's home. Come and give your grandmother a kiss, I've missed you."

Granny puckered her lips as I approached her, and the smell of moth balls grew stronger as I bent down and gave her a hug, the hairs above her top lip tickling me as she planted a firm kiss on my cheek.

"And you, Willow," said Granny. "There's plenty of my loving to go around."

I heaved a sigh of relief as Willow hugged her — Mum might stop trying to talk me out of canal boat living now Granny was around. Granny had been ecstatic when I'd bought a boat, and she'd come on my first day trip with Willow, asking dozens of questions about the *Water Witch*, and offering loads of suggestions as to how I could improve her. I'd taken her advice on a lot of points, especially her idea of installing wine making equipment.

Willow sat down and Mum began cutting the cake. It

bulged at the edges as the knife sliced through the thick layer of chocolate.

"A little smaller," said Granny, watching Mum cut the first slice.

"This is my piece," said Mum.

Granny smiled. "I know, dear."

Mum was about to protest, but Granny spoke over her. "So, Penelope. How's life on the boat? I hope you're remembering to grease your stern gland regularly?"

"Enough of that!" said Mum, sliding a cake laden plate in front of Granny. "You know we don't speak about women's problems at the table. It's uncouth."

"It's part of the boat!" I laughed. "It keeps the propeller shaft watertight. I kept forgetting to grease it last year."

Granny looked happy with herself. "You'd have known that if you took the time to go on a trip with her, Maggie."

Mum ignored her and bit into her cake as she watched me take a bite of mine. My head throbbed as the cake hit my stomach, and I knew right away that the magic Aunt Eva had added to the mix was not to enhance the taste. It was a spell. Aimed at me. Images of sunny meadows and frolicking lambs swirled through my mind, with happy people in the background walking in and out of cottages in a picture-perfect village. The pleasant images faded into blackness and were immediately replaced with images of ships and boats sinking, with vicious sharks swirling through the waves below them.

The portal had obviously removed most of the spell, because almost as soon as the images had appeared, they were gone, and I still wanted to live aboard my boat.

"How do you feel?" said Mum, a crumb of cake attached to her bottom lip. "Is the cake nice?"

"You mean did the spell work?" I said. "No, it didn't, although it was quite imaginative. You can tell Aunt Eva that sharks don't live in canals, though. Sorry, but I still want to live on my boat."

"You tried to hex your own daughter!" said Granny, although she was a fine one to talk. She'd once put a spell on my mother that had guided her to the weight loss aisles of the supermarket every time she went shopping.

"I didn't. It was Eva," Mum mumbled.

"Just because you won't do the dirty work yourself, doesn't mean you're not as involved as that sister of mine," scolded Granny. "Getting somebody else to do it doesn't make you any less guilty. Anyway, you should know magic won't fully survive the trip home from the haven. If it could you would have brought something back to cure me by now."

"Oh yes, Granny," I said, changing the subject. It was best to ignore Mum. My mother trying to get me off the boat was nothing new, and the use of a spell was not unprecedented. She'd once given me a chilli flavoured toffee that she'd brought back from the haven, and it had taken me a few hours to get over my newly acquired fear of the dragonflies that lived on the canal. "How are you?" I continued. "Mum told me about your... problem."

"I'm fine," she said, "I'm sure it will wear off soon. I don't really like talking about it to be honest, it's a nuisance. I had another little accident this morning."

"Are you okay?" Willow asked with concern on her face.

"Oh, I'm perfectly fine, dear. Boris is a little shaken up though. He's a tough old goat, but even he's got his limits."

Mum raised her eyebrows. "What have you done to Boris?"

"Not me, Maggie. It was the dementia. You shouldn't label a person as their disability. It's ableism."

"Okay," said Mum, looking perplexed. "What's the *dementia* done to Boris?"

"That's better, Maggie. It's never nice to be intolerant."

UNDER LOCK AND KEY

Granny took a sip of tea and adjusted her glasses. "I was mowing my lawn, the part that Boris won't eat due to the terrible smells those naughty cows left on it." She ignored our chorus of sighs and carried on talking. "I put a spell on the lawnmower, but the dementia got it muddled up. Instead of cutting the grass, it chased Boris in circles around his pole until the rope ran out."

"Is he okay?" I asked.

"He's fine, a little shaken up, but the big pile of hay I left for him is cheering him up." She stirred her tea. "The hair will grow back soon enough."

Willow and I exchanged glances, and my sister hid a smile. Poor Boris. It was true what Granny had said though – he was a tough old goat. He'd soon bounce back.

Granny continued. "Then I nearly got knocked down by an old-fashioned car in town when I went to the post office, there's loads of them, all heading out into the country for some sort of show."

"Yeah," I said, "Susie mentioned it."

"Well, they should be more considerate, driving around town like toad of toad hall with their hats and goggles on, they'll kill someone," said Granny.

I pushed my empty plate away from me, smiling as my mother offered me another slice. "The spell won't work any better if I eat another piece," I said, "anyway, I'm full."

"Then I witnessed an argument," continued Granny. "Sam Hedgewick was coming out of the lawyer's office and he was accosted by a badboy, he was using all sorts of naughty words. Even the bad one, and I don't mean f — "

"A *badboy*?" I interrupted. Granny must have been at Willow's contemporary romance books again.

"Yes, you know the type — tattoos, short hair, and lots of muscles. The type I'd have ended up with if I hadn't married Norman. Rest his soul." Granny's eyes widened.

37

"Maggie!" she said. "Did you check there were no nuts in this cake?"

"Yes, and for the last time, none of us are allergic to them, and Dad choked on a whole brazil nut. He wasn't allergic to them."

"Well, if dying from something doesn't make you allergic to it, I don't know what does," said Granny. "Anyway, Penelope, that young policeman who who's got a thing for you broke the argument up and sent them both on their way."

"Barney? He hasn't got a thing for me." Granny and Willow laughed, and my cheeks warmed. "He hasn't," I protested. "Maybe in school, yes, but not anymore!"

"I agree with Penelope, I don't think he's into her," said Mum, much to my surprise. "I know he doesn't speak like one, but with that fabulous hair, and the way he walks, I think he's..." she lowered her voice. "...One. Of. Them."

Tea flew from my mouth. "Mum!" I said. "You can't say that!"

"You're being very intolerant today, Maggie," mumbled Granny through a mouthful of cake. "I'm quite ashamed. I didn't bring you up to be like that."

"Especially considering that your brother is *one of them*," I said.

Mum looked wounded. "Brian's not Scottish!"

"I thought you meant Barney was gay," I said, confused by all of what my mother had just said.

"What do you mean, Mum?" said Willow, looking as bemused as I felt. "Fabulous hair, and the way he walks?"

"That bright red hair of his — it's fabulous, and very Scottish. And the way he walks with that cocky swagger, that's very, *very* Scottish."

"He's not swaggering," I said. "It's because of his height. It's hard for him to get trousers that fit properly, they dig into his... you know."

"Love plums," said Granny, cutting herself more cake. "He needs to take care of them if you and he are going to be an item."

"We're not!" I said. "I don't understand, Mum. What have you got against the Scottish?"

"I've got nothing against the mortal Scottish, but there's a reason Shakespeare wrote Macbeth. Those evil witch hags up there in the north give us all a bad name."

Willow giggled. "But why wouldn't a Scottish person be into Penelope?"

Mum stood up and began clearing the plates away. "Because they're fighters, not lovers. Have you neither of you watched *Braveheart* or *Trainspotting*?"

"What *are* you talking about?" I said.

Mum turned her back to us and took the empty plates to the sink. "I don't want to speak about it anymore. Haven't you two girls got something better to do than gang up on me with your grandmother?"

"No one's ganging up on anyone," I said, "but no, I've got nothing to do until later. I've got to make a potion for Veronica Potter, and then I'm having a barbecue which you're all invited too, naturally."

"What potion does that painted harlot want?" said Mum.

I bit my lip. "Veronica's lovely," I said. "She wants a potion for Ron, I'm not sure what yet."

"Don't you go putting real magic in it, Penelope," said Granny.

"Of course not, I'd never do that," I said. "I just give my customers what any mortal witch can give — hope, and a bit of a show."

"I'll never understand why a real witch pretends to be a fake witch," said Mum.

"She's hiding in plain sight," said Willow. "I think it's perfect, and yes, Penny, I'd love to come to a barbecue."

"Mum, Granny?" I asked.

"Not me," said Mum. "There are too many mayflies near the canal."

"They already hatched," I said, "and they only live for a few hours. They won't hatch again for a few months."

"My point precisely," said Mum, washing the plates, her arms deep in soapy suds. "If any *did* survive, they'd be monsters by now. I can't risk one of them landing on my burger, I might not see it, and you know how I feel about eating insects."

"Granny? Do you fancy a nice piece of steak?" I said, not bothering to argue with my mother. She'd once declined an invitation to a cousin's wedding because butterflies were being released as the couple said their vows.

"I can't, sweetheart. I've got a gentleman caller coming."

Mum turned to face us, dripping water over the slate floor. "Oh?"

"Tell us more," teased Willow, leaning across the table towards Granny.

"It's not like that. I'll never love again after Norman. Rest his soul. I've got a Chinese gentleman coming to stick needles in me. I'm hoping he can unblock my spells. They say Chinese medicine is the closest thing on earth to real magic."

"You'd better keep that magic of yours under control," said Mum. "No spells at all while he's at your cottage, do you hear me? Who knows what could happen."

"I hear you loud and clear," smirked Granny, doing absolutely nothing to convince me.

"Anyway," said Mum. "What do you mean — you'll never love again after Dad? Have you forgotten about Bill?"

"I do not like that terrible man!" said Granny, her glasses sliding the full length of her nose. "I've said it a hundred times, but I'll say it once more in the hope it will stick in those empty heads of yours." She leaned over the table and looked at each of us in turn as she spoke. "Farmer Bill dropped a mouthful of food into his lap and I was just trying to pick it up for him. His reaction in front of everybody in the cafe was over the top, and I certainly did nothing to his cows. That's the last I'll say on the matter!"

The three of us rolled our eyes at each other. "Okay, Granny," I said. "We believe you."

"Speak for yourself," mumbled Willow. "I know what I saw."

"Right! That's enough of that backchat, Willow!" Granny's face clouded over and she scrunched her features into a porcine scowl.

"No Granny! You've got dementia!" I shouted.

It was too late. Granny clicked her fingers and the audible sizzle that accompanied spells cast in anger vibrated through the air.

Willow shuddered and looked down at her body. "No!" she shouted. "Why would you do that Granny?"

Granny's face transformed from angry to worried in less than a second. "I'm so sorry, my darling," she panicked. "I just wanted to shrink those wonderful boobies of yours for an hour or two. I must have got my spells muddled up."

Mum stood behind Willow and put her hand on her head, testing the strength of the spell. "Don't worry, dear," she soothed. "It's not too powerful. It'll only last for a day, and I'm sure you'll be able to hide them."

CHAPTER FOUR

It had been an eventful day at Mum's house, but finally It was time to leave. Veronica was due at my boat in an hour, and I needed to stop off in town to pick up supplies for the barbecue.

"I'd better drive," I said, putting my bike in the back of Mum's car.

Willow nodded, looking down at her feet. "I can't believe she did it."

"You girls look after my car!" shouted Mum from the cottage doorway. "And don't let Willow drive, Penelope. She can hardly walk properly, let alone use the brake pedal."

Willow made a strangled sound which was almost a sob. "I'm not going to drive, Mum," she shouted. "That's the least of my worries — it's summer and I can't even wear my flip-flops, thanks to Granny!"

Mum gave us a wave and began closing the cottage door. She shouted some final encouragement. "Maybe it's a good thing, darling. It will stop you obsessing about those flesh jellies of yours for a day or two."

The door had already closed, so Mum didn't hear

Willow's shouted reply. The birds did though, and several flew from the tall trees surrounding the cottage, squawking in offence at Willow's choice of language.

"You'll get the hang of walking," I said as we got in the car. "Are they comfortable?"

Wracked with guilt, Granny had carved two thin pieces of wood into the shape and size Willow's feet had once been, and taped them to her new baby sized feet. With kitchen sponges glued to the toe end of the wood, Willow could wear a pair of trainers, although balancing was a problem.

"I suppose," grunted Willow. "Come on let's get to your boat. I need wine."

The trip into town only took a few minutes, but negotiating the streets of Wickford took longer. With vintage cars everywhere, and the pavements packed with people admiring the old vehicles, it took over half an hour to find a parking space and get the supplies I needed from the parade of shops on High Street.

Susie had been right — the old cars *were* beautiful, and with the drivers dressed in clothing from the same era as their machines, it was like stepping back in time.

With ten minutes left before Veronica was due at my boat, I parked in the Poacher's Pocket Hotel car park, and helped Willow out of the car before grabbing the bags of shopping from the back seat, leaving the bike where it was. Willow and Susie were staying on my boat for the night, and I'd need my bike to get back from Mum's when I took my sister home the next day.

Michelle, one half of the married couple that owned the hotel, appeared in the rear doorway of the old building, waving at us as we made our way through the beer garden to the footpath that led down to my boat. "Hi girls!" she shouted. "It's good to see you back, Penelope! Me and Tony came down to say hello earlier but you weren't there."

"Hi Michelle!" I answered. "It's good to be back. I've been at Mums all day."

"We'll come down and see you when it's not so busy," she said, waving her arm to indicate the crowds of people that sat in the garden drinking beer and wine.

"Okay, and thank whoever it was that mowed the grass for me. It was nice to come back to a neat and tidy mooring."

"Oh, that wasn't us, sweetheart. We've been far too busy with the hotel. It was Barney. He did it yesterday, he said your Granny told him you were due home any day."

Willow tittered under her breath. "Told you he likes you."

"You just concentrate on balancing," I said. "You look like you're drunk."

Willow planted her feet a little further apart, but still swayed from side to side as I said goodbye to Michelle. I held both bags in one hand and tucked my other arm through Willow's, helping her through the beer garden and down the shaded woodland footpath towards the boat.

"What was that noise?" said Willow as we neared the bottom of the path.

"Oh no!" I said. "It's Mabel, and it sounds like Veronica's here too. She's early."

I left Willow to negotiate the last of the footpath alone, and hurried ahead, the sound of barking getting louder as I neared the mooring.

"Get away from me, you monster!" came Veronica's shrill cry.

The trees gave way to freshly mown grass, and I clamped my hand over my mouth as one of the funniest sights I'd ever seen unfolded before my eyes. Veronica was standing on top of one of the picnic benches, swinging her bag at the goose who was attempting to leap up at her. Mabel had never been able to fly due to a condition the vet had called angel wing, but it didn't stop her trying. She jumped up at Veronica again, but Veronica's swinging bag prevented her from getting onto the bench top.

"Get away you beast!" shouted Veronica, much to the annoyance of Mabel, who barked and growled even louder.

Willow giggled as she entered the clearing and stood by my side. "You'd better help her," she said. "We don't want her getting hurt."

I dropped the bags at Willow's feet, and ran across the clearing. "No, Mabel," I shouted. "Leave her alone!"

Mabel looked at me and gave an excited yap, before turning her attention back to her captive victim.

"Help me, Penelope," begged Veronica, teetering on the edge of the table. "I'm too young to die."

Swallowing my laughter, I put myself between Veronica and the goose. "Sit, Mabel!" I shouted. "Sit!"

Mabel whined and tried to look past me at Veronica, who crouched behind my back with her hands on my shoulders. "Sit!" I repeated. "Do you want a treat?"

The white goose immediately sat down on her tail, with her bright orange feet sticking out in front of her.

"Good girl, Mabel," said Willow, arriving at the bench, a bag in each hand acting as counter weights which helped her balance.

"Give her a piece of ham," I said.

Willow retrieved the packet of ham from one of the bags and ripped it open. "Here, Veronica," she said, handing a slice to the shaking woman. "You give it to her, she'll be your friend forever."

"Oh my," said Veronica, leaning over the side of the table, swinging the ham in front of Mabel. "Here you are, you vicious little creature."

Mabel stood up and snatched the ham from Veronicas fingers, swallowing it whole. She gave a contented yap and lay on her back. "You can get down," I said, bending over to tickle the goose's belly. "She's your friend now."

Veronica climbed off the table with Willow's help, adjusting her bright red skirt as she stepped onto the grass. "I've never been so scared," she said. "Are you sure the vet was right, Penelope? It seems more than a voice box problem to me. She thinks she's a dog."

When a family out for a picnic had stumbled on Mabel worrying sheep in a field, they'd caught her and taken her to the vet, with the videos they'd recorded going viral on the internet. The vet, after much head scratching and research, had proclaimed that Mabel had an elongated voice box, and was probably a little simple. The newspapers had lost interest after a week or so, and Mabel had lived in relative peace ever since.

"Yes, the vet was right. It's quite common, apparently," I lied. "In some countries."

"But, look," said Veronica. "She's doing a poo with her leg cocked."

"Not there, Mabel," scolded Willow. "Not next to Penny's boat."

Mabel finished what she was doing, sniffed her deposit, and ran in a circle chasing her tail. Veronica jumped in fright as the goose barked and sprinted across the clearing towards the canal, where two unlucky swans had glided into view. "It doesn't seem right to me, Penelope," Veronica said. "Perhaps you should have another vet look at her. Geese don't eat ham for a start."

"Geese eat anything," I said. "They're greedy. Come on, let's get you into the boat, make you a nice cup of tea, and brew up this mystery potion for Ron. Mabel won't be back for a few hours, she'll chase those swans all the way to Covenhill, or until they fly away."

"Oh, you've painted your boat," said Veronica, cheering up

UNDER LOCK AND KEY

as I led her aboard. "I didn't notice when I got here, I was too preoccupied with that... goose."

"And you've had the name repainted," observed Willow.

"I had it done last month," I said proudly. "It's all hand painted."

The boat's paintwork had been fading when I'd gone off on my four-month trip, but now it was a bright and cheerful red, with a green stripe along the centre. The hand painted name shone gold in the sun, and I smiled as I remembered the man who'd done it ask me jokingly if I'd curse him if he spelt it incorrectly. How little he knew.

Water Witch was written in large letters in a scrolling font, and beneath it in a plainer font — *Floating emporium of magick.*

"It looks lovely, dear," said Veronica, as I opened the door and led her down into the shop section.

"Willow, would you get Veronica a seat, please. I'll make her a cup of tea and check on Rosie, she's probably cowering in a corner somewhere. She's terrified of Mabel," I said.

Leaving Willow to make Veronica comfortable, I found Rosie hiding behind a wicker chair and cheered her up with a bowl of food. "You should stick up for yourself, Rosie," I said. "Granny may have made Mabel act like a dog, but she can't hurt you. She's all bark and no bite. Literally."

Rosie ignored me and got on with the important job of emptying her food bowl as I made Veronica some tea. A knock on the window behind me made me jump, and I turned around to see Susie staring down at me, a big smile on her face, and her blond hair swept back in a ponytail. She held up two bottles of wine and grinned. Never mind. I liked my elderberry wine, and if she wasn't drinking it there was more for me, and Willow — now she was old enough to drink.

"Come in," I shouted, "Veronica and Willow are in the shop."

With a cup of tea for Veronica, I made my way along the boat. Willow had set up my consulting table in the narrow space between the shelves on both hull walls, and Veronica was seated on one side of the small round table, with an empty seat ready for me on the other side. My smallest cast iron cauldron was in the middle of the table, on top of the small gas camping stove that I'd painted black with silver stars. People expected a show when they came to my shop for a potion, and painting the stove was the first thing I'd done.

Willow and Susie were behind Veronica, sitting tightly squeezed together on the steps that led onto the bow deck, and both had smiles on their faces. They enjoyed watching me make fake magic, and I was sure they were just as inquisitive as I was about what sort of potion Veronica wanted for Ron.

"Here's your tea," I said, handing Veronica the cup and saucer. "It's nice and sweet. Now... what can I help you with?"

Veronica looked over her shoulder at Willow and Susie, and then back at me. "Nothing I say will leave this boat?"

"You have my word," I said, as Willow and Susie made their promises too.

Veronica took a sip of tea and placed the cup back on the saucer. "Well, it's Ron," she said. "You know I told you he was doing all that exercise?"

I nodded.

"It's taking it out of him, Penelope... in other ways."

"Go on," I said.

Veronica bit her bottom lip, leaving a smudge of bright red lipstick on her teeth. "How do I put this?" she said. "He's having problems with... he's struggling to..."

"Yes?" I urged.

She sighed. "Snoopy won't sit up and beg."

I swallowed hard and took a deep breath. "Snoopy won't what?"

She clasped her hands together and looked me in the eyes. "Ron's little guardsman won't stand to attention, Penelope."

Willow and Susie shook with suppressed laughter, and I struggled to breathe. "So, you need a passion potion?"

"Will that put lead in his pencil?"

"I can't promise anything, Veronica," I said. "All I can do is try. Passion is a very tricky thing. Maybe I can add something that will help him get more rest too, maybe he's tired out after all his weight lifting? That won't help matters."

"Yes!" said Veronica, her eyes lighting up. "Then if it works, he can do his duty and go straight to sleep. I won't have to listen to his boring war stories!"

Willow dug her face into Susie's shoulder, but I could still hear her muffled laughter.

"Oooh," teased Susie. "You like the soldiers do you, Veronica?"

Veronica turned to look at her. "He was a tank driver in the Royal Armoured Corps. You should see his photos. If you think he's hunky now, you should see how he looked back then!"

"I bet he was a dreamboat," I said, moving things along. "One passion and sleeping potion it is."

I took the wand I used to impress customers from behind the sales counter. "I just need to cast my circle and we can begin."

"Of course," said Veronica, facing me again.

Spinning in a circle, with the wand extended as far as I could manage in the confined space, I said a few words that people expected from witches, and invited the four earthly elements into the circle. "Okay, now we can brew the potion," I said. "The circle is cast."

Veronica watched me intently as I gathered a few herbs from the shelves and dropped them in the cauldron. "What's that?" she said, as I sprinkled a powder onto the concoction.

I added some spring water to the mix and fired up the gas stove. "Oriental pine pollen," I said. "It's very potent. It's sure to help."

Veronica looked impressed. "This is exciting," she said.

I sat down again and stirred the potion with a copper spoon, moving my face closer to the cauldron as I spoke in hushed tones. "Strong as a lion, hard as a rock, Goddess give Ron a rigid — "

Veronica gulped, and Willow and Susie shook in each other's arms, their faces bright red and tears on their cheeks.

" — libido and sleep schedule," I continued, aware of Veronica's obvious disappointment.

Veronica licked her lips. "Oh my," she said. "I can't wait to test it out."

"You be sure to tell Ron," I said. "It won't work if the person it's meant for doesn't know he's taking it. Witchcraft isn't about tricking people. Don't go slipping it into his drink without warning him."

Willow rolled her eyes at me, but I didn't take any notice, most of my customers thought witchcraft was just about spirituality — they didn't *really* expect magic to happen. I wasn't tricking anyone. Anyway, the herbs I'd used had scientifically proven effects on the human body, and I'd had some great feedback from happy customers in the past.

"I promise. Ron will be just as happy as I'll be if it works, believe me," said Veronica, with a knowing wink.

I took a small glass bottle from a shelf and pulled out the cork stopper. "Just a teaspoon or two at a time," I warned, ladling the potion into the bottle.

"You have my word," said Veronica, pulling her purse from her bag. "How much do I owe you?"

I shook my head. "Not a penny," I said, handing her the bottle. "I wouldn't dream of charging you after what Mabel put you through."

"Well, you know what they say, don't look in a horse's mouth."

"Don't look a gift horse in the mouth," I corrected.

Veronica put the potion in her bag. "Yes, that's it. Thank you, Penelope. I'm going straight back to the home now. There's a little party on tonight for the residents and their families. This potion's sure to work when Ron's had a few brandies."

Susie led Veronica off the boat as I tidied up the shop. "Take care, Veronica," I called, as she shouted goodbye. "Enjoy the party!"

"And the after party," giggled Willow.

I raised my eyebrows. "At least their having fun. It could be worse."

"True," said Willow. She looked around the shop. "I am jealous of you, Penny. I'd love to live on a boat."

"You wouldn't be saying that if you'd been frozen in place for a week, waiting for the canal to thaw out so you could go and buy some more coal for the fire." I said, shuddering at the memory.

"I'm sure the good times outweigh the bad."

She was right of course. "Yes, I've had some wonderful experiences. Speaking of which, let's set the barbecue up on the bank, and drink wine with our feet dipped in the water." Willow's face dropped. "I'm sorry, I forgot," I said. "You can still dip them in the water though. You don't need to hide them from Susie, she's seen far worse than that since she's known our family secret."

"Far worse than what?" said Susie, stepping down into the shop.

"Granny shrank my feet," said Willow. "It was an accident, sort of. She was trying to shrink my boobs."

Susie laughed. "I'd keep them hidden for the moment," she said. "I've just seen a mop of ginger hair on a very tall man coming through the woods."

"Told you he likes you," said Willow, grinning.

"Barney likes you?" said Susie. "That's news to me."

"Me too," I said. "It's a fantasy that Willow and Granny have cooked up. Come on, let's see what he wants."

CHAPTER FIVE

Barney took long swaggering strides across the grass with a big smile on his face. He was still in his uniform, but I doubted it was a police related matter he was there to see me about.

His hair was quite fabulous I supposed — very ginger, and a lot of it, matching the freckles that spattered his face. His uniform was as ill-fitting as ever, with his trousers riding high on his boots, and his short shirt sleeves far too big for his thin arms. The stab proof jacket he wore looked four sizes too big, and I hid a smile as he stopped in front of me. "I hope you don't mind me popping down to see you, I just wanted to make sure that you're okay. It must be scary down here on your own."

"I'm not on my own tonight, obviously," I said, looking at Willow and Susie. "But even if I was, I'm used to it. I've been moored up in the middle of nowhere on my own, and I did just fine without a policeman to look after me, thank you very much."

Barney blushed, and guilt sucker punched me. It wasn't that I didn't like Barney, it was just that I didn't want more fuel to be added to Granny and Willow's gossip fire. "Thanks for looking in on me though, and thanks for mowing the grass. I really appreciate it."

"Just trying to be helpful to the resident witch. I want to keep on your good side, I don't want to be turned into a frog or something," he joked.

"It was really kind of you, Barney," I said.

Barney looked at Susie and Willow who were in the process of lighting the barbecue, whilst obviously listening to our conversation. "Having a barbecue, huh?"

"Yes," I said. Barney's deductive police skills were on top form as always.

"Food tastes so much better when it's cooked outdoors, doesn't it?" he said, licking his lips.

"Would you like to stay for some, Barney?" said Willow, much to my annoyance. "We've got steak, burgers, and sausages."

"And salad," said Susie.

"And salad," confirmed Willow, placing some plates and cutlery on one of the tables. "If you like that sort of thing."

"I don't suppose he can," I said, turning away from Barney so he couldn't see me scowling at my sister. "He's on duty."

"I've finished actually," he said. "I'm on standby tonight, so I can't have any of that wine," he said, as Susie opened a bottle. "But I could really tackle a steak. And maybe a sausage. Or two. And a handful of salad. Maybe a bread roll too."

"Well that settles it," said Willow. "You're staying for dinner, Barney. Would you like to cook it? I know men are better at barbecues than women, and you can't get more manly than a policeman."

Maybe Mum had been right about Willow. She did seem to be pushing her devil's dumplings out a little too far. Or maybe it was just the way she was standing — her feet were at very odd angles, and she seemed to be having trouble balancing again.

Barney slipped his stab jacket off and removed his clip-on tie, laying them on the table with his police radio next to them. I hoped that clip on ties were standard police uniform and not a reflection on Barney's dressing skills. "I'd love to cook for you ladies," he gushed, puffing his chest out.

I shrugged. "Right, well I suppose I'll have a drink. Willow would you come into the boat and help me get some of my homemade wine, please?" I said, narrowing my eyes at her.

"Of course," said Willow, smirking.

"Are you okay, Willow?" said Barney, as my sister followed me to the boat. "You're limping."

"Athlete's foot," I said. "She sweats a lot."

Barney raised his eyebrows and blushed again. "Oh, sorry to hear that, Willow. I wasn't trying to be nosy."

"Don't listen to my sister, Police Constable Dobkins," said Willow. "She's pulling your leg. I hurt myself doing gymnastics. I can get my leg right around the back of my head, and I pulled a few muscles practising last night, that's all. Shall I show you how I do it? I'll have to put some smaller shorts on, but I'm sure Penny's got some I can borrow."

Barney blushed yet again. "No, it's okay," he mumbled. "How does everyone like their steaks? Well done or rare?"

"As they come," I said. "Come on, Willow. Let's go and get that wine."

"What are you playing at?" I said, as soon as we were in the boat and out of earshot. "*Men are better at barbecues. I can get my leg behind my head.*"

Willow giggled as I followed her to the galley kitchen. "I'm just teasing him," she said. "It's obvious he likes you and you're just being a bit... bitchy to him. I was lightening the mood, and I'd stopped until you told him I had athlete's foot!"

"I was not bitchy!"

"You were."

I sighed. "I suppose I was, wasn't I?" I grabbed two bottles of wine from the rack on the counter. "You know I don't deal well with male attention, Willow. I'm not as confident as you are."

"You should be. You're beautiful, clever, and look what you've done for yourself. Not many people could make an inheritance the size Grandad left for you go this far. I'll probably waste mine when I reach twenty-one, but you own a floating shop which you live in for heaven's sake! How cool is that?"

"It is pretty cool, isn't it?" I said, looking around at the cramped but cosy surroundings. "It's not like everybody can have a different view from their kitchen window whenever they fancy a change."

"Precisely, and as for me telling Barney that men are better at barbecues... what would you prefer? Slaving over hot charcoal, or sipping wine while somebody cooks for you?"

"The latter," I smiled.

"There we are then. I just massaged his ego a little, come on, let's get back out there and see how many more times he blushes tonight!"

We giggled as I opened the double shutters that were half way along the hull on the bank-side of the boat. They doubled as a third doorway onto the *Water Witch*, and a folding set of steps allowed us to climb out of the boat. I switched the radio on, giving us some background music, and helped Willow up the steps. She'd almost perfected the wooden insoles, and negotiated the journey from the belly of the boat onto dry land almost flawlessly.

"What's so funny?" said Susie, laying on her back on the grass with a glass of wine in her hand. "I heard you laughing."

Willow sat next to her. "We were just saying how nice it was to have a man cook for us."

Barney flipped a steak, his face made even redder than normal by the heat of the coals. "Pass me some plates. You're about to find out if your trust in me was warranted."

"Everything looks lovely, Barney," I said. "Thank you."

Willow gave me an approving nod. "No salad for me, Barney. Just meat and a bread roll, please."

We sat in a semi-circle on the grass as we ate and drank. Barney had cooked the meat to perfection, and we hardly spoke as we devoured our meals, watching the colours reflecting on the water as the sun began to set.

A shy otter made an appearance on the opposite bank, but vanished as Mabel returned to the mooring and joined us on the grass, pecking at the pieces of food we'd dropped. Mabel had been quite the celebrity when the newspapers had dug their teeth into the story of the barking goose, and local people had become accustomed to spotting her on the canals and towpaths. People still found her fascinating though, and Barney spent ten minutes training her to roll over in return for a small piece of sausage.

Rosie had dared to make an appearance at one point, and sat on the roof of the boat, staring at Mabel with hatred as she ate the treats Barney offered her. I'd grabbed the last of my burger and passed it to her, stroking her as she mewled her thanks, promising her that Mabel couldn't hurt her.

Time passed quickly, and with two empty bottles of wine on the grass, and a coffee cup next to Barney, we chatted and listened to the radio in the glow of the lights from the boat. Sitting next to the *Water Witch* with the warm breeze in the trees behind me, the water lapping against the boat, and my bed a few meters away, was the reason I'd decided to live on the water, and I lay back contentedly as I listened to Barney telling us about his days' work.

"I've been trusted with a big case," he said, "Sam Hedgewick has been receiving threats. The Sergeant put me in charge. I've got to interview a few suspects tomorrow, although that's going to take some time — he seems to have rubbed a lot of people up the wrong way. He's had emails from over fifteen people."

"We heard about it," said Susie. "I was going to see if there was a story in it, but I got side-tracked taking photos of all those old cars. I only put them on my website today, and I've already got a classic car magazine asking to buy a few. They want me to cover the show too," she beamed. "I'm spending the day there tomorrow."

"He's within his rights to sell whatever properties he wants," continued Barney, acknowledging Susie's good news with a smile and a nod. "People can't just threaten him. I'll see to it that he's safe, don't you worry about that."

I smiled to myself as I imagined Sam's reaction when he found out that Barney was charged with ensuring his safety. Barney tried his best at policing, but was famous for being overpowered by one of the towns hardened criminals — Mavis Henshaw. The eighty-year-old had almost broken Barney's finger with her walking stick when he'd been called to the greengrocers to investigate reports that Mavis had been stealing lychees. Barney had been forced to call for back up, and had never fully lived the incident down.

"This is Wickford," said Willow. "I'm sure Sam Hedgewick is perfectly safe."

"Well, he's got me on his six now," boasted Barney, oblivious to our silent giggles.

"I'm sure he'll sleep well tonight," I said.

Barney's radio crackled on the table behind us. "P.C Dobkins. Come in."

Barney leapt to his feet, scaring Mabel, who gave a little

whine. "Duty calls," he said grabbing his radio. He spoke into it in a monotone voice. "PC Dobkins here."

The radio crackled again. "A body's been found. In the canal below the Lock and Key pub. We're treating it as murder."

Barney's eyes widened, and I glanced at Willow and Susie. They'd turned white.

"Do we have an ID?" said Barney, his voice cracking.

"It's Sam Hedgewick. He's been hit on the head. Get there immediately. Sergeant Cooper is waiting for you."

Barney looked at us as he put his stab jacket and tie on and clipped his radio to his belt. "Oh God," he said. "Now I'm for it. Poor Sam. I was supposed to be looking after him." His panicked face whitened and he gazed at the floor.

"Calm down," I said. "You weren't due to interview anyone until tomorrow, there's nothing you could have done tonight. You weren't his bodyguard."

"Granny said you stopped him arguing with a rough looking guy today. She actually called him a *badboy*," said Willow. "Maybe he's got something to do with it?"

"I didn't take much notice," said Barney, adjusting his stab jacket. "That was before I knew Sam was getting threats, and I was preoccupied with making sure those old cars didn't block up the roads. I can't even remember what colour hair he had!"

"Barney," I soothed. "You go now. I'll speak to Granny first thing in the morning while the memory is still fresh in her head. Go and collect evidence or whatever it is you need to do."

"I've never dealt with a murder before," said Barney. "This is new to me, and there's so many people who were angry with him."

"Go," I said. "You'll be fine."

Barney looked at us one last time, turned on the spot, and sprinted towards the footpath with Mabel hot on his heels.

"Good luck!" Susie shouted.

"Poor Barney," said Willow, as Barney vanished into the darkness and Mabel came sauntering back to us.

"Poor Sam," I said. "Barney will be fine. Sam's dead."

"Come on," said Susie. "Let's get inside the boat. I don't feel like anymore wine. We'll clear the mess up in the morning."

We trudged into the boat and made some tea, sitting at the L-shaped dinette area to drink it as we came up with theories about who could have killed Sam Hedgewick.

"Emily the florist?" said Susie. "The note in the window seemed pretty nasty."

She passed her phone to Willow so she could have a look at the photo of the note.

"Not Emily," said my sister when she'd read it. "She's too timid. And too lovely. She was just lashing out."

I brought my sister up to speed with what had happened in the allotments, and came up with my own appraisal of the situation. "Hilda Cox," I said, "most of the other allotment owners too, the badboy, and anyone else who rents a property Sam's selling. Veronica told me that Sam was a gambling man too — maybe the badboy is someone he owes money to? The police are going to have to work hard. There's so many suspects."

Susie yawned and stretched her arms above her head. "I agree," she said, "but I'm too tired to think about it now. I should be at the murder scene but I've had too much wine to drive. I'll get up early in the morning and get down there. The car show will have to wait, this is far more important. We haven't had a murder in Wickford for a long time. This is a real story."

Willow stood up. "I'm tired too. Help me make this bed,

and we'll get some sleep. Susie can share your bed with you. I'd be embarrassed if my baby feet dug into you during the night."

We laughed as we collapsed the dinette table and placed the cushions on top of it to form a perfectly good double bed. "There's bedding in the storage underneath it," I said, hugging my sister. "Sleep tight."

Susie and I top and tailed in my bed, with Rosie snuggled up in the small gap between us. I'd opened the stern doors, and a warm breeze blew over us. We lay in silence listening to the night sounds until Susie tapped me on my leg. "Tell me the story of how the haven was made," she said.

"Again? Do you never get bored of the same story?"

"I like it, and anyway, you get to go there someday, I only get to hear about it. Tell it the way your mum used to tell us when we were little."

I closed my eyes. "Okay," I said. "Once upon a time, a long time ago, when people were afraid of witches, there was a very powerful witch called Maeve. She was a good witch, but one day she caught a man trying to steal the eggs from her chickens, and turned him into a toad for a day."

"Remember the face your mum used to make when she pretended to turn us into toads?" Susie said from the darkness. "It terrified us."

"Not as much as it scared Willow," I giggled. "She was only six when we were eleven."

"Go on," said Susie. "I won't interrupt again."

"Unluckily for Maeve," I continued, "somebody saw her cast the spell and reported her to the village elders. A week later the Witchfinder General arrived with his soldiers and set about building a bonfire to burn Maeve to death on. Maeve was a brave witch, and refused to use magic to stop the soldiers from burning her. She didn't want to hurt anyone, and she knew that if she did, things would become far worse for other witches, so she accepted her fate."

I laid my hand on Rosie to settle her as an owl hooted outside. "As the flames licked at the base of her robes and burned her legs, Maeve closed her eyes tight and imagined being somewhere nicer, somewhere more peaceful, a place where she wasn't in pain. Witnesses who were watching the burning said the clouds opened and a flash of lightning burst from the sky, turning Maeve into dust. They believed it was God's doing, and it gave them the encouragement they needed to carry on burning witches... except they never found another witch. Not a real one anyway."

"Because of the haven," whispered Susie.

"Yes. Maeve had accidentally managed to cast a spell so powerful it sucked most of the magic from the world and conjured up a magical dimension, a place where witches could be free from persecution. A safe haven. Back then of course, a witch could enter at any time, but when witches stopped being hunted and killed, Maeve changed the rules of entry so witches would enjoy this world before going to the haven. Now we need to prove ourselves before Maeve grants us our entry spell."

"You'll meet Maeve one day, Penny," slurred Susie as she drifted off to sleep. "How amazing is that?"

"Very," I said, and joined my friend in sleep as I listened to the water gently lapping against the hull.

CHAPTER SIX

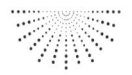

Susie shook me awake. "It's seven o'clock," she said. "I'm going to the murder scene. I want to be the first journalist there. I doubt any reporters got there last night." She applied a little lipstick and put the tube in her bag. "I've fed Rosie, cleaned up the mess outside, and Willow is going to walk me up the hill to my car. Her feet have grown back and she wants to use them. She says you don't know what you've lost till they're gone."

I rubbed my eyes and yawned. "Do you want breakfast first? I bought bacon and eggs."

"No thanks. I'm kicking myself because I drank too much last night to drive. I need to go."

"Drive safe," I said, as Willow climbed the steps from the bedroom onto the stern decking.

"I will, and remember to ask Granny about that badboy. I have a feeling Barney will need some help."

I swung my feet out of bed and rubbed more sleep from my eyes. "Me and Willow will go straight to her house when we've had breakfast. I'll let you know what we find out."

I watched Willow and Susie through the window as they

disappeared up the path with Mabel running ahead, scaring birds from the undergrowth.

As I waited for Willow to return, I cooked bacon and eggs, and poured us both a coffee when I heard her footsteps echoing through the boat. We ate our breakfast quickly, admired Willow's feet, and both took a shower, with Willow going first as it would take her far longer to fix her hair afterwards than it would me.

"Mum just phoned," said Willow, when I stepped out of the bathroom. "She's worried about Granny. She's not answering her phone, and she can't see her through the telescope."

Hazelwood cottage was on the top of a hill to the east of Wickford, and Granny's home, Ashwood Cottage, was on a hill to the west. With a perfect line of sight between the two highest points in the town, Mum had a telescope in her bedroom through which she spied on Granny, and Granny had a set of binoculars through which she returned the favour. Many a lie had been exposed in the past, and many an argument caused, thanks to the high-powered lenses.

"Granny will be fine," I said. "She's probably recovering from whatever that *gentleman caller* did to her with his needles. We'll go and see her as soon as I've got dressed, and find out about this badboy for Barney."

WICKFORD WAS BUSIER THAN NORMAL, and policemen and women were knocking on the doors of houses in the town centre. The Lock and Key pub, which sat on top of a small cliff directly over the canal and towpath, was cordoned off with tape, and Barney was standing next to the makeshift barrier, keeping people away. He looked tired, and gave me a small smile as I stopped the car alongside him.

"Where's Susie?" I said. As I lowered the window, her car was parked less than fifty metres away, but she was nowhere to be seen.

"They've let her down there with the other reporters," Barney said glumly, pointing at the narrow set of stone steps next to the pub which ran down to the canal. "She's at the murder scene, while I'm up here stopping nosy people from getting too close. It's not my fault Sam got murdered. I should be down there with them."

"Who says it's your fault?" said Willow, leaning over my lap to speak through the window.

"Sergeant Cooper," said Barney. "Well, he didn't actually *say* it was my fault, but considering I was given the job of investigating the threats to Sam, you'd think I'd be down there with the rest of them."

"He'll come around," I said, "anyway, we're on our way to Granny's. Maybe what she tells us about the man she saw arguing with Sam will help you. She's got a vicious eye for details."

"I remember he had tattoos," said Barney, leaning closer to the window, and lowering his voice as the onlookers watched him. "But I can't remember what they were. I can't remember how tall he was either — everyone looks short next to me. The sergeant hasn't even asked me if I know anything yet, he's too busy trying to impress the detectives from the CID."

"Don't worry," I said. "As soon as we've spoken to Granny I'll let you know what she said. I'll text you."

"Thank you," said Barney. "Hopefully the Sergeant won't ask me any questions before then. Don't go telling your Granny that I can't remember, though. If she does need to be interviewed as a witness, it will make me look silly if people find out that I couldn't even remember what a potential suspect looks like."

"Don't worry," said Willow. "We want to help you."

"Thank you," said Barney. "Both of you. I don't want to lose my job over this. I like being a policeman. I know I'm not Sherlock Holmes, but I like trying to help people."

Poor Barney. I put the car in gear and began edging away from the pavement. "I'll text you as soon as I know anything."

Barney put a hand up and waved as I watched him in the rear-view mirror.

"So, we're helping to solve a murder," said Willow, rubbing her hands together. "How exciting!"

I took the left turn that led us to the hill which Granny lived on. "I wouldn't go that far," I said. "We're just helping a friend keep his job. Anyway, the man Granny saw isn't the only suspect."

"The game is afoot!"

"The what is a what?"

"Don't you watch Sherlock?" said Willow. "Oh, of course you don't. You don't even own a television."

The narrow lane flattened out as we reached the top of the hill, and I turned right through the open wooden gates of Granny's property. The little cottage was as colourful as my mother's, with flowers blooming in the garden and a fresh coat of yellow paint on the old walls. A tall stack of fresh firewood filled the lean-to shed which was attached to one wall, and I parked the car next to it, happy that Granny was still fit enough to chop her own wood.

Granny appeared at the kitchen window, and I waved and smiled at her. She ducked quickly out of sight, her face looking panicked. Willow frowned. "What's her problem?" she said.

I opened the car door and stepped out. "I hope she hasn't had another dementia accident. That's probably why she's not answering the phone to Mum. Come on, let's see if she's okay."

The thick wooden front door was locked, which was unusual. Granny feared few things, and burglars were at the bottom of that very short list. Willow swung the heavy brass knocker into the metal mounting plate, the sound echoing over the hilltop and into the woods. "Granny," she shouted. "It's Willow and Penny! We know you're in, we saw you at the window!"

"Granny!" I echoed. "Mum's worried about you, and we've got some gossip! There's been a murder!"

"My feet are better too!" added Willow.

The window above us creaked open, and we stepped back to look up. Granny poked her head out and gazed down at us with narrowed eyes. "Good news on the feet, Willow, but a *murder*? Are you making that up just to get into my home? I'm trying to have a restful day. I don't need intrusions."

"No, honestly," I said. "Sam Hedgewick was murdered last night! Let us in and we'll tell you about it. You might be able to help, too. The man you saw arguing with Sam might be a suspect, maybe you can tell us something about him that will help solve the crime."

"Me, solve a crime? Like Mrs Doubtfire? Wait there, I'll let you in, but you're not to go in the kitchen. I'm... erm, baking a cake... using a... secret recipe. You can't go in there."

"She means Miss Marple," said Willow, as Granny slammed the window. "And I can't smell any baking."

The door creaked open an inch, and granny peered through the small gap. "It's just the two of you?" she said.

"Yes, just me and Willow," I promised. "What's wrong, Granny? You seem nervous."

"Nothing happened last night!" said Granny. "I mean, nothing's wrong, dear. Everything's just fine, and I'd stand up in a court of law and say exactly that if I was made to."

"Okay, that all sounds normal... are you going to let us in?" said Willow, glancing sideways at me.

Granny opened the door wide and stood aside to let us pass her.

"I can't smell a cake baking," I said.

"It's a secret recipe," said Granny. "If you could smell the ingredients, it wouldn't be a secret for long, would it? Now, go straight through to the lounge and tell me all about this murder."

With her back to the closed kitchen door, Granny stood and watched as we traipsed through the cottage and into the lounge. A familiar shudder ran through me as I looked at the spooky old oil paintings of our family's ancestors. They covered two walls, and the other walls were dotted with colourful modern canvases, giving the lounge the appearance of a room straggled across more than one time period.

Granny followed us in and sat in her comfy chair in front of the unlit fire, while Willow and I perched on the old sofa. "So," she said, staring at us over the rims of her glasses. "What's the gossip?"

We told her what we knew about the death of Sam Hedgewick, leaving out any mention of Barney's concerns. Granny ummed and aahed as the story unfolded, and her face lit up when we asked her to describe the so called badboy she'd seen.

"I knew my memory would come in handy one day," she said, settling further into her seat. "Now, let me think."

She closed her eyes and scrunched up her face, deep in thought. After what seemed like an eternity she snapped her eyes open. "Do you need to write it down?" she asked.

"No, we'll remember," I said.

"Okay. Six foot tall. Close cropped sand coloured hair. Wet sand mind, not dry sand. White t-shirt with a small black logo on the left side of the chest. White trainers with three red stripes, slightly dirty but certainly not old — this cat cared about how he looked — he wouldn't be seen dead in old shoes."

I bit my lip, and Willow shook against my thigh as she tried not to laugh. "Cat?" I said.

"You're too young to appreciate a cat," said Granny. "Your grandad was one though — he was the coolest cat in Wickford. Anyway, I digress. Faded denim jeans — blue. Tattoos on both arms. A dragon on the left forearm and a phoenix on the right. Both in black ink and leading beneath his t-shirt sleeves. Come to bed blue eyes, and muscles like a US Navy Seal."

"Navy Seal?" said Willow.

"American special forces, dear. Very well built gentlemen. No wedding ring — I noticed that first. In fact, no jewellery whatsoever, he's not the type to adorn himself with bling." She closed her eyes again for a second or two. "That's all I can tell you. I'm sorry I can't remember more."

Willow gulped. "That should be enough to go on," she said.

"Anyway, why do you girls want to know about him? Don't you go trying to capture him, like I said yesterday, he's a badboy."

"It's just in case we see him around," I said. "We could tell the police."

"You can tell the police that Sam was coming out of the lawyer's office too. That's suspicious. A man visits a lawyer in the day, and he's dead that very night."

"A lawyer's office?" said Willow.

Granny sighed. "You girls need to clean your ears out. I told you yesterday, Sam was coming out of the lawyer's office when he was accosted, then that police friend of yours came along, Penelope. I don't know why you're asking me for a description anyway. Ask Barney, with his keen police mind he'll have noticed plenty of things I missed."

"Yes," I said, ignoring Willow's chuckles. "I'm sure he's already hunting him down. There's nothing suspicious about Sam going to a lawyer though. He was selling all his properties. That's the sort of thing lawyers help people with."

"Just something to bear in mind," said Granny. "Leave no stone unturned."

"I'll mention it to Barney," I said. "Anyway, Granny, how did your acupuncture go last night? Do you feel any better?"

Granny's face whitened. "It was a load of rubbish," she said. "Not worth the money I paid for it. Nothing happened here last night though! I can assure you both of that!"

"Granny," I said. "What happened here last night?"

"As I've made abundantly clear — nothing happened here last night!"

"Granny, are you crying?" said Willow.

"Curse the thought!" spat Granny, wiping her eyes with the hem of her apron. "I haven't cried since Norman died. Rest his soul. And I only cried then because your mother did the catering for the wake. I don't know what she was thinking, but everyone knows you don't trick a vegetarian into eating a ham sandwich. Those people are vicious if they find out they've ingested meat. The vicar is adamant he won't let our family ever use the hall again."

"You'd tell us if something was wrong, wouldn't you?" I said.

Granny leaned forward in her seat. "Penelope, you've known me for twenty-three years. When have I ever lied to —"

A huge crashing sound from the kitchen made Granny jump, cutting off her sentence.

"What on earth was that?" said Willow. "Is someone here?"

"Nothing happened here last night!" sobbed Granny, rocking in her seat with her arms wrapped tightly around herself. "Nothing happened here last night!"

"I'm having a look in the kitchen, Granny," I said. "I don't care what you say."

"She can't hear you," Willow said. "She looks like one of those Vietnam veterans. You know, with the thousand-yard stare?"

I waved a hand in front of Granny's glazed eyes, but she didn't blink. "Nothing happened here last night," she mumbled, squeezing herself tighter.

"She's okay," I said. "She's just shut down for a while, like the time she discovered that the wrestling on TV was staged. She'll be fine in a few minutes."

Another loud bang from the kitchen drew our attention, and I followed Willow as she made her way down the hallway. She paused as she reached the kitchen door. "Do you think it's safe to go in?"

"It's not an intruder, otherwise Granny wouldn't have been trying to hide something. Go on, open the door."

Willow opened the door slowly, and we stared at the sight before us in disbelief. "Oh heavens," whispered Willow. "What's she done now?"

CHAPTER SEVEN

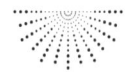

Boris the goat turned towards us as we entered the kitchen. He lowered his front hooves from the kitchen counter on which he'd been trying to tear open a packet of biscuits, and tilted his head. Pots and pans surrounded him, and another one fell from one of the open cupboards behind him. "Baa?" he said.

"Pardon?" I said, squeezing Willow's hand which she'd placed in mine.

"Maa?" he said.

"He sounds like a man." whispered Willow.

"Hello, Boris," I said, releasing Willow's hand, and taking a step towards the goat. "What are you doing in Granny's kitchen?"

Boris looked around at the mess he'd made. "Bleat?"

"Oh my goddess!" shrieked Willow. "Look at the pantry!"

The pantry door was ajar, and I took a step back as I followed Willow's frightened gaze. A man's hand hung from the gap, and the toe of a shoe prevented the door from closing fully. "Get a knife!" I said. "I'll phone the police!"

I fumbled for my phone as Willow opened a drawer and grabbed a large carving knife, which she held in front of her with both hands. "Quick," she said. "Phone someone!"

Boris took a step towards us and coughed. "There's no need for police involvement, young ladies," he said in a well-spoken upper class English accent. "Allow me to introduce myself. I'm Charleston Huang, certified member of The British Acupuncture Accreditation Board. You're perfectly safe. The man in the cupboard is me... well, to be more precise, it's the mind of this perfectly lovely creature, in my body."

"What is going on?" whispered Willow, dropping the knife a fraction. "Boris is talking to us."

Boris cleared his throat. "I could attempt to explain the not unwelcome predicament I find myself in, but I feel that Gladys would be best placed to enlighten you."

"Gladys? Granny lets you call her Gladys?" said Willow. "Only her enemies call her Gladys, and her very good friends."

"I'm certainly not the former," said Boris. "It would be a privilege, however, to be considered the latter." Boris gazed between his front legs, attempting to look beneath his body. A bald patch above his tail was the only evidence that he'd recently been attacked by an enchanted lawnmower. "Tell me, young ladies," he said, attempting to crane his neck further under his belly. "Do I need milking?"

"No," said Willow. "You're male."

The goat lowered his voice. "Splendid. Although Gladys is a remarkable woman, I really wouldn't have felt comfortable with her interfering with me in that way."

Footsteps sounded behind us. "So, you've discovered my awful secret," said Granny. "I knew it would only be a matter of time before you pesky kids found me out."

"In all fairness, Gladys," said Boris. "The incident only happened last night. It can hardly be referred to as a matter of time. It's barely been twelve hours."

"True dat," said Granny, raising a smile from Willow even as she held a knife defensively in front of her. Granny really had to stop reading Willow's books.

"Drop the weapon, Willow," said Granny. "I'll make us all a nice cup of tea and –"

"I'm not a big fan of tea, Gladys," said Boris. "Maybe a saucer full of that delightful brandy you gave me last night."

"You gave brandy to a goat?" I said.

"He was still in his human body," said Granny. "Anyway, brandy won't harm him now. He's protected by magic. He can drink brandy all day long if he likes."

"That makes my situation sound all the more acceptable," said Boris.

"You like being a goat, Charleston?" said Willow, placing the knife back in the drawer and filling the kettle.

"It's the calmest I've felt for a long time, and please, call me Boris. If I'm to occupy this grand old beast's body, the least I can do is honour his name."

"What about *actual* Boris though?" I said. "Is he happy in your body? And why on earth is he just standing in the cupboard, is he traumatised?"

Granny opened the brandy and poured a generous glug into a saucer, laying it on the floor in front of Boris. "He's in a form of stasis. He's oblivious to what's going on and he can't move. No harm will come to him, and neither he or the goat will age until I can sort this terrible mess out."

"For the record," said Boris. "I don't consider this a mess. Life has been getting to me recently. I have no loved ones to go home to, and the relief I felt when Gladys texted all my customers to cancel their acupuncture appointments was wholly liberating. I'm perfectly content with the surprising direction my life has taken."

Willow took a few tentative steps towards the pantry. "Can I have a look?" she said.

"I have no objections," said Boris, "but please excuse the look on my body's face. It was quite the shock to be on the receiving end of magic, although I've long believed that witches were real. Tell me, are you two young ladies witches too?"

"They try to be," said Granny.

"We are," said Willow, opening the pantry door.

I joined Willow and studied the man in the cupboard. He was thin and nearing sixty, I guessed, and obviously of Chinese heritage. His eyes were wide open, and his mouth formed a perfect o shape. He certainly seemed shocked.

"He can't stay in there until your dementia gets better, Granny," I said. "For a start, I can't reach the cakes, he's blocking the shelves."

"And he'll smell of spices," said Willow.

"You two can help me drag him upstairs before you leave. We'll put him in the guest bed." She looked at Boris who was happily lapping up brandy. "If you have no objections, Boris?"

Boris licked his lips. "I'm sure the guest bed will be the perfect place for my body to rest. I have no objections. I only wish I could help you carry me up the stairs."

I took a step out of the kitchen to gather my thoughts and send a text to Barney, listing as much of Granny's information as I could recall, remembering to tell him about the lawyer. When I re-entered the room, Willow was sitting at the table with Granny, and a cup of tea was waiting for me. They'd cleared away most of the mess Boris had made, and Granny was beginning to explain the previous night's occurrences.

"But how exactly did it happen?" asked Willow.

"Charleston, sorry *Boris,*" Granny said, smiling at the goat, "did wonders for my back. The needles didn't help my magic, but I feel twenty years younger."

Boris agreed. "She's been chopping wood since two o'clock in the morning."

"Why?" I said, sitting down.

"To hide his car under," Granny beamed. "It's in the lean to. You two didn't see it, did you? So, all that chopping was worth it."

"Don't blame your grandmother for what happened," said Boris. "I offered to relieve the goat's suffering."

"What?" said Willow.

"Boris was limping a little... after the lawnmower incident," said Granny. "Charlest — Boris, offered to help him with acupuncture. I didn't know there was residual magic from the mower left in the goat. It arced with the needles, and they swapped places."

Boris nodded, brandy dripping from the long white hairs beneath his chin. "And when Gladys tried to return us to our rightful bodies, which was quite the task — I've never seem my body move so fast, or eat grass — something happened which froze my body."

"Dementia," mumbled Granny, wiping her eyes. "And now they're stuck until I get better."

Boris laid a hoof on Granny's back, patting her gently. "There, there, Gladys. There's an old Chinese proverb — *coming events cast their shadow before them* — I knew there was something magical about you, I've always been very spiritual, you see, but I insisted on treating you and this goat. It's my fault as much as yours."

"Thank you, Boris," said Granny, patting the goats head. "That means a lot to me."

"Excuse me for saying, Boris," said Willow, "but you don't sound very Chinese."

"Willow!" snapped Granny, "you can't say things like that — it's racist!"

Boris chuckled. "Nonsense," he said. "It's a perfectly acceptable question, Gladys, and one I'd be happy to answer. My parents never left Britain, and I've only stepped foot in China once. I went to see the great wall, to please my grandfather. It was an underwhelming experience, and the *Chinese* Chinese food was very disappointing. I'm from a wealthy family, and benefitted from an Oxford education. I've led a privileged life, and it seems that life has still more surprises planned for me."

"A wise old goat," said Granny. She slammed her hand down on the table. "And don't you two go saying anything about this to that daughter of mine," she warned. "Or my wrath will be swift and fearsome."

"I agree with Gladys," said Boris, "although watching her sobbing in the garden last night casts some doubt on her claims of fearsomeness. I'm happy as I am, young ladies. Let's keep it between the four of us and my body. I'm more than happy to live as I am and play the part of a garden goat whenever you have visitors, Gladys. It will be quite invigorating."

My phone beeped. It was a message from Susie.

Poor Sam. Meet me when you can. I'll tell you what's happened x

I replied.

Meet us at Mum's cottage. We're on our way x

"We need to go, Granny." I said, showing Willow the message. "Come on, let's get Charleston up the stairs."

Boris tapped the floor with his hoof. "Would somebody be so kind as to top my saucer up with brandy, and pass me one or two biscuits before you begin the job of hiding my body?"

CHAPTER EIGHT

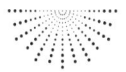

Willow picked at her torn fingernail. "He didn't look like he'd be that heavy."

"At least he's safe, and tucked up under that duvet he'll be fine until Granny can switch them back," I said.

Susie's car was already outside Mum's house when we arrived. Nobody was downstairs, but Susie's and Mum's voices were coming from upstairs.

"Hello!" I shouted. "We're here." Susie came running down the stairs. "What were you doing up there?" I said.

"I was telling her about Sam, and looking through the telescope with her. She's worried about Granny, and I don't blame her. We just saw her going for a walk into the woods with Boris, and the goat looked wobbly on his feet — almost like he was drunk. Is everything okay over there?"

We sat at the kitchen table and quickly told Susie what had happened.

"Don't tell Mum," warned Willow, as Susie rocked with laughter. "Boris and Granny are happy, and Mum already thinks Granny's got a problem with animal cruelty. There's the thing with Mabel, the chicken laying ostrich eggs, Boris and the lawnmower, and now this."

Susie closed an imaginary zipper over her mouth. "My lips are sealed, a bit like that lawyer you told Barney to go and see."

"Barney's been there already?" said Willow.

"I was with him when he got Penny's text. He went straight to the lawyer's office but was only in there for five minutes. The lawyer said he had information that may be relevant to the investigation, but he had to honour his client's confidentiality. The police need to get a court order to make him hand over the information. Barney does seem a bit more relaxed since he got the text, though. He's still worried about getting in trouble of course. He just needs a break in the case to get on his Sergeant's good side again."

"Maybe we can help him," I said. "What's been happening? What do the police know about what happened to Sam?"

Susie took her camera from her bag and turned the screen towards me and Willow. "You're not squeamish, are you?"

We both shook our heads, having a family like ours had knocked any squeamishness out of us years ago.

"They pulled Sam out of the canal in the early hours of the morning, but left him on the towpath until forensics could have a look at him," said Susie.

The photo Susie showed us was of Sam laying on the towpath, wearing a suit. His visible skin was white and wrinkled but there was no blood to be seen.

"He looks like he drowned," Willow said. "He almost looks peaceful."

Susie showed us another picture. This one displayed the rear of Sam's head as a man in protective clothing and a mask examined him. "I wasn't supposed to take these photos," she said, "But they hadn't put a tent around his body when I arrived, and I managed to snap a few from half way up the steps that lead down to the towpath."

We looked at the next picture. Susie had zoomed in on Sam's head, and it didn't take a pathologist to work out the cause of death. A long wound ran along the back of his skull, and his wet hair stuck to the shape of the gash, making it simple to deduce that the murder weapon had been cylindrical.

"They found one of those things on the towpath," said Susie. "What do you call them, the metal tools boat owners use to open lock gates?"

"A windlass," I said.

The Wickford lock was only a few hundred metres from where Sam's body had been found, and it wasn't uncommon for boat owners to forget to stow their windlasses after passing through the gates. The canal was only wide enough for one boat for almost half a mile from where Sam had been found. Maybe it had fallen off a boat, and the murderer had found it and used it as an impromptu weapon.

"They've sent it off for forensic tests," Susie said. "And they're sending Sam for a post-mortem. The police say it will take a week for the results to come back."

"Any witnesses?" said Willow. "The Lock and Key pub balcony is right above the towpath."

"No. the police think he was murdered further along the path, near where they found the windlass, and the wind blew his body as far as the pub. There were a few boats moored up where the canal widens, but the residents were all asleep."

"How was he found?" I said. "Nobody walks along the towpath at that time of night. It was almost midnight when Barney got the radio message."

Susie put her camera away. "The Lock and Key closed at half eleven, but one guy needed to relieve himself. He went down the steps at the side of the pub to use the towpath, and saw Sam. He was still floating slowly towards the lock, so he used a tree branch to snag him, and phoned the police."

"What was Sam doing down there?" Willow said. "He doesn't strike me as the type to take moonlit walks."

"He'd been to the nursing home. Remember Veronica told us they were having a party for the residents and their families?"

We nodded.

"Well, Sam's dad's a resident there," Susie said. "He drank too much to drive home, and with Wickford being so small there were no taxis running that late. He decided to walk home, and he was murdered on his way."

"Have any suspects been arrested?" said Willow.

"The police have visited nearly twenty people, including Hilda Cox from the allotment, and Emily the florist. Most of them have watertight alibis, but they're bringing in a few of them for further questioning," said Susie. "Barney seems to think it's very important to find the guy who was arguing with Sam, and to get the lawyer to talk. He wants the lawyer's information before the police get the warrant. He thinks it will save his job."

"We can keep an eye out for Granny's badboy," I said, "but we can't make the lawyer talk."

Willow tapped the table absentmindedly. "Maybe we can," she said.

"How?" said Susie, "are you going to use your feminine charms on him?"

Willow rolled her eyes. "I was thinking more of Granny's spell book, she keeps it hidden in the cellar."

"Yes, and the doors have got more locks on it than Fort Knox," I said. "Granny will never let us use it. She calls it her weapon of mutually assured destruction. She brought it back from the haven to defend herself from attacks from other witches, back when she was a survivalist. We've got no hope of getting any help from her."

Willow smirked. "We *didn't* have any hope of getting her help, but that was before we found out about Boris. I think we've got a goat shaped ace up our sleeve. She'd hate for anyone to find out what she's done."

"We won't be able to make the spells work," I said. "Especially the ones which control people. It's old magic. We've never used it before."

"We can try," said Willow. "Otherwise that lawyer's never going to talk before Barney can redeem himself."

"Okay," I said. "We'll go back to Granny's. You can come too if you want, Susie. You can meet Charleston."

"Boris," corrected Willow.

"I'd love to come," said Susie, "but I need to edit a story I wrote about the murder. Say hello to Granny for me, though."

"What are you saying about your grandmother?" said Mum, hurrying into the kitchen, an imprint from the telescope around her eye. "She's up to something. I know it. I just saw her taking Boris into her house. I'm going straight over there to find out why she's been ignoring my calls. Was she acting strangely when you two were there?"

"Boris is recovering," Willow said quickly. "That's why Granny's taken him indoors."

Mum narrowed her eyes. "Recovering?"

Willow nodded. "That man who came last night to do acupuncture really helped Granny with her back pain."

"Not her spells though," I added.

"No, not her dementia," continued Willow. "He offered to do some acupuncture on Boris – he was limping after the lawnmower incident."

"Acupuncture on a goat?" said Mum, frowning. "Are you sure?"

"Absolutely," said Willow. "Granny just wants him to be comfortable after his ordeal. She feels guilty, so she brought him indoors."

Mum sat down at the table with us. "She should feel guilty. That poor goat. It does explain why Susie and I saw him wobbling through the woods though. Poor thing. I still think I should drive over there and check on her."

"I was going to ask if I could borrow your car for the rest of the day," I said. "We need to go back to Granny's... Willow left her..."

"I left my phone there," said Willow, pushing her phone deeper into her pocket. "We'll make sure she's okay."

Mum shook her head slowly and sucked her bottom lip into her mouth. Her disappointed face. "I knew you'd regret buying that boat with your inheritance. Don't you feel silly now? Having to borrow my car when you could have bought two of your own?"

"I don't regret it," I said. "I don't want a car."

"You could have fooled me," said Mum. She turned to look at Willow. "Treat this as a lesson, Willow. When you reach twenty-one and get your money, don't go spending it on something as ridiculous as your sister did. Use it wisely."

Willow's face reddened. "I don't think she wasted it, and neither does Granny — and it was *her* husband's money. Penelope owns a business, and she's happy. How can that be a waste?"

Mum sighed, ignoring Willow's spirited interjection. "I just think you could have got a real job Penelope." She gazed across the table at Susie with a big smile on her face. "Like Susie has. She makes a difference to people's lives when they read her stories. Did she tell you she's sold a story about the murder to The Herald? That's something to be proud of."

"No I haven't told them yet, Maggie," said Susie. "I was just about to when you came in."

"Susie couldn't wait to tell me when she got here," said Mum, "and I don't blame her. What a stroke of genius she had for the title of the story." She patted Susie on the hand. "Tell them, sweetheart."

Susie gave me a pained expression. I gave her a smile. "Go on," I said. "I'd love to know."

"It's not as brilliant as your mum is making out," said Susie. "I've called it *Murder under Lock and Key.*"

Mum let out a low whistle of admiration. "Because Sam was murdered and his body was found below the Lock and Key pub, the term lock and key can also mean somethi — "

"We get it, Mum," said Willow. "Well done, Susie!"

"It's a shame that a man being murdered was the break I needed to sell a big story," said Susie.

"That's life," said Mum. "Anyway, you can use my car again, girls. I'll go to the haven to visit Aunt Eva and pick up some ingredients for a lasagne. Tell my mother I'll pop over and see her tomorrow."

"We will," I said, "and tell Aunt Eva we said hello."

CHAPTER NINE

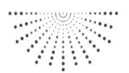

"Not you two again," said Granny as we walked into her kitchen. She'd reverted to leaving the front door unlocked again, and everything seemed normal, apart from the fact that somewhere on her property was a talking goat. Granny was studying a recipe book, and closed it as we sat at the table next to her. "Two visits in one day, to what do I owe the pleasure?"

"Where's Boris?" said Willow.

"He's in the lounge watching TV. *Antiques Roadshow* was on when I left him, he's relaxing a little before his bath."

"You're bathing him?" said Willow.

"It's either that or he lives in the garden. He's very cultured, but he does stink a little."

"That's nice," said Willow sarcastically. "Magic his mind into the body of a goat, and then threaten him with living in the garden. How very *tolerant* of you."

Granny shrugged. "He knows he smells. I've seen him sniffing his leg pits. He'll be happier when he smells of lavender bubble bath." Granny wrinkled her forehead into a frown. "Anyway, what are you two doing back here? Something tells me you haven't come to check on me and Boris."

I looked at Willow, and she gave me an almost imperceptible nod. She wanted me to ask Granny. I licked my lips. "It's simple," I said, "we haven't told Mum about what you did to Boris, and it will remain that way if you agree to help us."

Granny's frown deepened. "I don't like where this is going," she said. "This is the sort of thing people say in films before they blackmail somebody. You'd better not try and blackmail me, because if you do, my wrath will be swift and — "

"Fearsome," interrupted Willow. "Yes. We know. But not as fearsome as Mum's wrath will be if she finds out what you did to Charleston Huang, and imagine what your friends in the haven would say when the word got around. You'll be a laughing stock when you finally remember your entry spell."

Granny scrunched up her face and prepared to click her fingers. "Think about it before you cast it," I warned. "You're already hiding a talking goat, and you don't want to be responsible for something bad happening to me and Willow, do you? Mum would never forgive you."

Granny sighed and lowered her hand, sparks still arcing between her fingertips. "What help do you need that requires these levels of manipulation?"

"We need your spell book," I said.

"You can kiss my wrinkly old a — "

"Or we'll tell Mum about Boris," threatened Willow.

Granny nibbled her bottom lip. "Why do you want my spell book?"

"We want to help find out who killed Sam Hedgewick," I said.

"And help Barney," Willow said. "He was in charge of finding out who was threatening Sam."

"And Sam died on his watch," pondered Granny, "add that

to the fact that you've got a thing for him, Penelope, and I can begin to see why you think my magic can help you."

"I don't have a thing for Barn — "

Granny waved me quiet. "How exactly do you think my spell book can help?"

"We need to get information out of somebody," I said. "The lawyer you said Sam had been in to see. He's got information that could help Barney, but he's not talking — client confidentiality, apparently."

Granny nodded. "And you want to make him sing like a canary."

"Something like that," said Willow.

Granny closed her eyes and took a deep breath. "I can't give you that book," she said, snapping her eyes open. "You two don't have the experience to use the spells."

Willow spoke slowly and clearly, moving her face closer to Granny's. "Imagine if Mum ever did find out about Boris... but then you told her *you'd* been helping us learn more magic. Just picture how happy she'd be that you were helping us to ascend to the haven. She'd forget about Boris in an instant."

Granny closed her eyes again briefly. "I'll do it, but I'll only show you how to use one spell. You girls will have to work out the rest of them yourselves, and you must promise that no one will be turned into a toad."

"That spell's in the book?" said Willow.

"There's better than that in there," she said. "I compiled that book using old spells from the haven when I had that... funny few months."

"When you became a survivalist?" I said.

"I prefer the term prepper," said Granny. "There was a lot of friction in the haven at the time, the voodoo witches from Haiti were fighting with the Scottish witches, and I was afraid it would spill into this world. I wanted to protect my family. You two included. It went to my head a little, that's all."

"It took a long time to eat all those tins of food in your cellar afterwards, didn't it Granny?" said Willow.

Granny stood up. "Yes. I'll never look at another tin of corned beef again. Or peaches." She shook her head. "I don't like to talk about those days. I'll go to the cellar and get that book for you on one condition."

"Yes?" said Willow.

"The old tin bath I used to use for your mother and uncle is tucked away in the back of the pantry. Get it out and fill it with hot water and bubble bath. You can help me bath Boris, and then I'll teach you how to cast one of my spells."

BORIS STEPPED CALMLY into the bath. "It's not as if I'm undressed, is it?" he said, "because I don't want any of you to get the idea that I'd normally allow myself to be bathed by three members of the opposite sex. My days in Oxford were heady, but even then, I never came close to doing anything like that."

"Just enjoy it" said Granny. "I've used lavender bubble bath. It's calming."

"I've never felt calmer," said Boris. He lowered himself to his knees in the suds. "Help me onto my back, would you?"

Willow and Granny helped flip him over, and I placed a rolled-up towel under the back of his head to protect him from the thin rim of the bath. Only his four outstretched legs and his horned head were visible above the bubbles as he settled down, and he closed his eyes as we began massaging his matted white hair.

"You seem very natural as a goat," said Willow. "You're taking it all very well."

"Willow," said Granny. "We treat Boris as if he has always been a goat. He's trans-species. It's transphobic and intolerant of you to allude to his time as a human. Boris wants to be a goat, and we will afford him that courtesy."

"Calm down, Gladys," said Boris. "I'm really not offended. Why don't you go and sit in the lounge and let me get to know your grandchildren? You deserve a rest. You must be aching after chopping all that wood."

"I do deserve a rest, don't I?" said Granny, her knees clicking as she stood up. "Make sure his head doesn't slip under the water, girls, and just shout if you need anything, Boris. I found another bottle of brandy in the cellar alongside the spell book and an old tin of corned beef, just let me know when you're ready for a dram or two."

"She's a wonderful woman," said Boris, when Granny had left the kitchen. "But she seems very preoccupied with race and suchlike. I've heard her call three people on the TV racist today, and she refused to join me in watching *Antiques Roadshow* because somebody brought in an old Aboriginal boomerang to be valued. She began ranting about colonialism and cultural appropriation. It was quite unnerving."

I lowered my voice — Granny still had very good hearing. "She used to be an SJW," I said. "She's still holding on to some of the values."

"A social justice warrior?" said Boris. "How interesting."

"No," said Willow. "Not a social justice warrior. It was far worse than that. She was a social justice witch."

"My interest is piqued," said Boris, sighing as Willow applied shampoo to his head. "Tell me more."

"Has she told you about the haven?" I said.

"Oh yes, and it sounds such a magical and lovely place."

I passed Willow a loofah which she used to scrub behind the goat's ears. "It's not always lovely there," I said, "there's witches and warlocks in the haven from all parts of this world, and they don't always see eye-to-eye."

"Especially the Copper Haired Wizard of the west," said Willow. "Mum and Granny say he's always stirring up unrest."

"He sounds fabulous," said Boris.

"He is to his followers," I said, "but a few years ago, he decided he wanted to deport all the Haitian voodoo witches from his lands."

"And then conjure up a wall of spells around their lands to keep them inside," added Willow.

"Fascinating," murmured Boris, his rear left leg twitching as I scrubbed it.

I continued. "A few of the witches, including Granny, wanted to help the Haitians. They decided that the Copper Haired Wizard was evil, and set about defending the rights of the voodoo witches. Granny picked up a few tips from the protestors she saw on the news in this world, and before Mum and my Aunt Eva could stop her, she was the leader of a group called the Social Justice Witches."

"The group got carried away," said Willow. "When the Copper Haired Wizard capitulated to the SJW's and agreed to tear down the wall, they turned their attention to gay and lesbian witch rights, and it spiralled out of control from there."

"Your grandmother sounds like a real firebrand," said Boris.

"Oh, she is," I said. "Too much for the haven though. When she burnt down a centuries old magical rose bush, claiming that women who made love potions from the petals were demeaning themselves by needing the forced affection of a man, Maeve banished her from the haven for a year. Her blue hair is the only physical reminder of the time, but if you look closely at her nose, you can still see where her piercings went."

"I knew she was a vibrant woman when I arrived yesterday," said Boris. "Although I had no idea just how vibrant." Boris went suddenly rigid, and spun his head towards the kitchen widow, his ears splashing water across the floor, and his curled horns barely missing my fingers. "There's a car coming through the gates. Are we expecting company?"

"No," said Willow, standing up to look through the window. "It's a police car," she said, craning her neck. "It's Barney and Sergeant Cooper."

Granny came running into the kitchen, flapping her arms around her head and making loud panting sounds. "It's the feds! They must know Charleston's gone missing! I can't spend one more night in the big house – I'll be someone's bitch within the hour! If they find his car, or him in the guest bed, it's all over for me!"

"Granny," I said grabbing her wrist. "Calm down, they're probably here because Barney admitted to Sergeant Cooper that you have a better description of that badboy."

"Boris," said Granny, snatching her wrist from my grip. "You won't give the game away, will you? You'll stay in character as a goat?"

"Gladys," said Boris, blowing bubbles from his nostrils. "You have my word. Although I can assure you that no one knew I was coming here, and I have nobody in my life who would have even noticed I'd vanished."

Granny breathed more easily. "Well, I'm torching your car as soon as I get the chance! I can't have that sort of evidence right next to my cottage!"

"We can't let them see Boris in the bath," said Willow. "It's not normal!"

"Of course it's normal," said Granny. "He's just a goat and we're bathing him. I'm sure they've seen far more interesting

UNDER LOCK AND KEY

things in their line of work. Anyway, I'm not inviting them in unless they show me a warrant. They can conduct their business on my doorstep."

"Penelope," said Boris, as Granny scampered off to open the door. "Gladys just hinted that she'd been to prison. For what crime, may I enquire?"

"She spent three hours in a cell in Wickford police station," laughed Willow. "With the door open and as much tea as she could drink."

"She was arrested while she was still in social justice witch mode, after being banished from the haven." I said. "She threw eggs at the Police Superintendent and told him he was part of the patriarchy which was oppressing her. Using less pleasant language than that, though."

I joined Willow at the window and watched Granny talking to Barney and the Sergeant as she guided them back down her pathway and towards their car. Barney dwarfed Sergeant Cooper — although that wasn't hard — the sweating red-faced law keeper was almost as short as Granny, and he would have looked far more at home in a pudding baker's apron than a policeman's uniform. He scratched notes in his book as Granny spoke to him, and shook his head periodically at Barney, who gazed at his feet, looking embarrassed.

"What's happening?" said Boris.

"I think Sergeant Cooper found out that Barney needed Granny's help," murmured Willow. "Barney looks very ashamed."

Finally, Sergeant Cooper slammed his notebook closed and he and Barney got back into the car and drove away as Granny made her way back into the cottage. "Right," she said, scowling as she walked into the kitchen. "Let's teach you how to use my spell book. That horrible little man was awful to Barney. That ginger simpleton needs our help."

I took a sharp intake of breath. "Granny!" I scolded. "That's an awful thing to say!"

"Not my words, dear," she said. "That's what his Sergeant called him. You need to get that lawyer to talk, and you need to make him tell Barney what he knows. I'd like to see that smug look wiped off that Sergeant's face. Barney needs to help solve Sam's murder."

CHAPTER TEN

After helping Granny dry Boris off, and learning how to cast one of the spells in the book, Willow and I headed back to my boat with the tome of spells.

Mabel was nowhere to be seen, and Rosie was sunbathing on the roof. She leapt off when she saw us coming and scampered inside — no doubt attempting to trick me into filing her bowls again. A colourful narrowboat chugged past on the canal, and Willow and I both waved back at the elderly couple who shared the steering duties at the rear.

I handed Rosie a fish shaped treat, explaining to the overweight cat that I knew Susie had already fed her. Willow placed the big book of spells on the dinette table and opened it at the index. The musty smell of the old paper reminded me of the books Mum used to read to me when I was little, and I joined Willow in searching for the best spell to help make the lawyer give us the information Barney needed.

Granny had spent twenty minutes teaching me how to cast one of the simplest spells in the book, and my head still hurt from the effort. I'd finally managed to make the chair float half an inch above the floor, and Boris had slammed his hooves together in an excited and dangerous attempt at applause.

"What sort of spell are we looking for?" said Willow, running her long fingernail down the eclectic list of spells which were neatly written in black ink.

"I'm not sure," I said. "A truthfulness spell?"

"I don't think so," said Willow. "A truthfulness spell would probably be best for somebody who was lying. The lawyer's not lying — he's just refusing to talk."

"A spell of persuasion?" I suggested.

Willow flipped the page and ran her finger down the spells beginning with the letter P. "Here we are," she said. "Page two hundred and ten."

Willow leafed through the pages until she found the spell we were looking for. "It looks complicated," I said.

"Remember what Granny said," urged Willow. "Think the spell, and then sip the magic from the air like a fine wine."

The symbols and letters that were the spell, made little sense. A triangle here, a cross there, the number nine next to the letter W — but as I silently read the two lines of symbols over and over again, the same swelling feeling in my head occurred as it had when granny had taught me to cast the levitation spell. "Something's happening," I said. "My head hurts."

"Granny said that will pass as you get better at them," said Willow. "Have you got milk in the fridge?"

"Yes," I said. "Why? Have you suddenly developed a liking for it?"

Willow hated milk. She'd hated it since she'd been a baby, and Mum had been forced to feed her sweetened condensed milk — the type that came in a tin. Willow blamed those early days on the sweet tooth that she still needed to placate on a regular basis.

"No. I still hate it, but why don't you try and persuade me to drink some?"

I smiled, and studied the spell again. If I could get Willow to drink milk, I could persuade anybody to do anything. I skim read the symbols over and over, my eyes crisscrossing the page, and my head pounding the same way it did when I drank too much elderberry wine. Granny had assured me that the pain in my head was the spell imprinting itself on me, and when it had seared itself permanently in my mind, I'd be able to access it just by thinking about it. As she'd explained, her dementia problems were due to her thinking about one spell, but another being taken from her mind's muddled filing cabinet.

Willow put a hand on mine. "Remember what she said — when you're ready to cast it, taste the magic in the air and think hard about what you want to happen. Then click your fingers."

I closed my eyes and sucked a small amount of air between my teeth. Granny had said you could taste the magic, but all I could taste was the overpowering flavour of Rosie's tuna flavoured breakfast which permeated the living area. I licked my lips, concentrating on what I wanted Willow to do, and sucked in a little more air. The distinct flavour of metal filled my mouth — reminding me of the taste of a penny piece. Not that I often sucked on copper currency, but it was the flavour that came to mind nonetheless. I clicked my fingers, and the tips tingled with static electricity.

The cushion I was sharing with Willow settled a little as she stood up, and I opened my eyes to watch.

She looked at me with shock on her face, and began walking slowly towards the fridge. "This is weird," she said, opening the fridge door. "I know I don't want to be doing this, but I have to."

I concentrated harder. Willing my sister to drink some milk. She reached into the fridge and retrieved the carton, unfolding the spout, and lifting it to her face. She took a long swallow and looked at me in horror as she began gagging. I immediately stopped the persuasive thoughts, and Willow hurried to the sink, coughing and spluttering as she spat milk down the plug hole. She turned the tap on and shovelled handfuls of water into her mouth. "That was disgusting. I'll never understand why people willingly drink milk," she gasped. "Apart from in tea. With sugar."

"How did it feel?" I said.

Willow scooped more water into her mouth and wiped her lips on a tea towel as Rosie watched her curiously. "It was strange," she said. "It was like the feeling I get when I know I've eaten too much chocolate, but there's still some left in the box. I know I shouldn't, but I have to eat it. The lawyers got no chance if you can pull that off again!"

I smiled, buoyed by my success. "Let's go and find out," I said.

Willow looked at her phone. "It's almost four o'clock," she said. "Let's wait until tomorrow morning, and in the meantime — how about I take your sign to the top of the footpath into town? You are supposed to be running a shop after all."

"I only got back two days ago," I laughed. "I'm *supposed* to be having some time off, but go on — put the sign out. Let's earn some money."

As Willow carried the A-frame sign up the short footpath into town, I tidied the shop area up a little and went outside with a cup of tea to sit at the picnic bench and wait for her.

Less than five minutes after she'd returned, the first customer appeared at the bottom of the footpath and made her way across the grass towards the boat.

"You put the sign the right way around them," I laughed.

"My name is not Susie Huggins!" Said Willow. "Of course I did."

When I'd first had the sign made, Susie had put it at the top of the footpath on the day I opened for business. Susie being Susie, though, she'd placed it on the wrong side of the path with the arrow pointing into town instead of towards the canal. Luckily, it didn't take too long for people to realise that a floating witchcraft shop on a narrowboat would more than likely be on the canal, rather than in the town centre. Mr Jarvis from the greengrocers had kindly turned the sign around for me when two people had come into his shop asking for directions to my boat.

"How quaint!" said the customer, looking at the *Water Witch*. "What a wonderful idea — a shop on a boat."

"Oh, there's plenty of them," I said. "There's even floating marketplaces on weekends in some towns along the canal. There's floating hairdressers, floating cafes, floating sweet shops. You name a type of shop, and there's probably a floating version."

"Well, this is just the sort of thing I've been looking for. I've always wanted to try my hand at witchcraft. Perhaps you could give me some advice on where to begin."

Willow and I led her into the small shop, and she gazed around at the shelves. "I don't know what I'm looking for," she admitted.

Ten minutes later, she left the shop with a smile on her face, a beginner's book on witchcraft, a small cauldron, a chalice, and an athame.

Willow helped me as more people found their way to the shop, and we made a good team, with Willow taking money and giving change, and me offering advice to customers.

As six o'clock approached, and the shops in town began closing, the trickle of customers slowed and I left Willow to count the takings as I made my way up the path to collect my sign.

With the sign under my arm, I'd got no further than a few feet back down the path, when I heard a softly spoken male voice from behind me. "Are you closing?"

I turned to look at him, and swallowed the smile on my face. Short sandy coloured hair, muscles, and tattoos. It was undoubtedly Granny's badboy, but he looked far from bad. His red eyes told the story of a man who'd been crying a lot, and Granny would have been disappointed at the state of his clothing. His t-shirt was crumpled and needed ironing, and his jeans had muddy marks on the knees.

"Y — yes," I stuttered, looking around for somebody to help me if he did turn out to be a crazed murderer. "I'm closing."

His face crumpled. "I was hoping you could help me. I read your sign, it says you can make potions to heal all ills."

I had to get that sign reprinted. The *heal all ills* line had come back to bite me in the backside on more than one occasion, and it seemed like this time it had attracted a suspect in a murder case. Maybe *potions for a wide range of troubles,* would be more advisable. Anyway, I certainly didn't have a potion that relieved people from the guilt of murder.

I glanced around again, but the street was quiet. No one was going to help me, and my magic was certainly not at the standard needed to prevent a thug attacking me.

"I'm sorry," I said, desperately searching for a lie. "I need to get back to my boat... I've got to get ready for my self-defence course. It starts in half an hour — I'm trying out for my black belt tonight."

He rubbed his eyes with his fingers. "Maybe a bottle of whisky would be a better potion," he said, looking at me one last time and turning away.

I ran the full length of the path, ignoring Mabel who

yapped at my heels as I sprinted across the grass, and threw the sign on the ground. "Willow!" I shouted, as I leapt aboard the boat, almost losing my footing as I slipped on the decking. "Phone Barney!"

BARNEY ARRIVED QUICKLY, and after listening to my story and radioing the information in to the police station, he came aboard the boat. "Are you okay?" he said, putting a hand on my shoulder.

"Yes, I'm fine. He didn't do anything, it was just a bit of a shock seeing him and wondering if he was the man who'd killed Sam. I've never met a murderer. As far as I know, anyway."

"We don't know that he is. But it does seem odd that he was waiting outside the lawyer's office for Sam," said Barney, "and several people have alluded to the fact that Sam had a gambling problem. Maybe he was being forced to sell his properties to pay off his debts. Sometimes you've just got to put two and two together, but it would make my job far easier if that uptight lawyer would just tell me what he knows."

Barney cursed as he banged his head on a ceiling light. "Sit down, Barney," I said. "Narrowboats aren't made with people like you in mind."

He sat down next to me on the sofa, rubbing his head as Willow brought me a glass of wine. She sat opposite us, on my wicker chair, and leaned forward. "Will they find him?" she said.

"Every available police officer is out looking for him. It's harder in a small town like this without cameras everywhere, but hopefully they'll find him soon. I don't want you staying here tonight alone though, Penny," said Barney. "It's too secluded. Can you go to your mother's? Either that, or I'll stay here with you. They don't need me for the search, apparently."

"Willow's offered to stay with me," I said.

"Even though Mum's making lasagne tonight," sighed Willow. "That's sisterly love right there. Mum's lasagne is the best, especially when she's got the ingredients from the hav — "

My warning scowl stopped her before she said something that might have given our secret away. It was a silly mistake to make, but she quickly recovered. "From the half decent deli in Covenhill."

I changed the subject quickly. "Are you offering every boat owner on the canal in Wickford your company for the night, Barney?" I teased.

I knew he was going to blush even before he did, but it still made me smile. "No," he said. "Just you."

"I think it's very kind of you, Barney," said Willow, "and I think it's a good idea. Even though we don't know if he did kill Sam – you did say the guy was well built, Penny, and you said he was going to get drunk on whisky. What if he decides he wants a potion after all and comes banging on the door at two in the morning? We couldn't fight him off if he decided to turn nasty."

I doubted Barney could either, but I kept my mouth tightly fastened. "Okay," I said. "It's very kind of you, Barney, but if you think the ceiling's low, wait till you find out how short the dinette bed is. I have a feeling your feet will be getting cold tonight."

Willow and Barney went ashore and threw sticks for Mabel as I prepared a simple meal of chicken wrapped in bacon, and a fresh salad. We ate it on one of the picnic benches and watched as a line of three colourful narrowboats passed by on the canal, their bow waves washing into my cutaway and gently rocking the *Water Witch*.

"They're probably on their way to the car show," said Willow. "Susie said there's over fifty visitor's boats moored up alongside the field, and hundreds of car owners camping there."

Boat owners moved around the canals continuously, most of them using a continuous cruising licence, which allowed them to moor up in one spot for up to fourteen days at a time before having to move on again. When a gathering like the car show occurred next to the canal, boat owners would come from all over to enjoy the community spirit, helping each other out with odd jobs that needed doing and enjoying the liberated lifestyle that only liveaboards understood.

"Are the police asking questions at the show?" I said, passing Barney some buttered bread.

Barney put together a chicken and tomato sandwich, and took a small bite. "Of course," he said, chewing. "It could have been someone Sam knew who killed him, or it could have been a complete stranger who wandered into town, got drunk, and picked a fight with him for no reason. We're questioning everybody who was camping out there when Sam was murdered, but that's a lot of people. It will take time, and without a witness we're practically blind."

I dropped a piece of cucumber for Mabel, but she sniffed disappointedly at it and looked at me with pleading eyes. I relented, and handed her a piece of bacon fat which she swallowed happily. I threw another piece onto the stern deck of the boat where Rosie was watching us suspiciously. She gobbled it up and jumped onto the roof, licking her lips, and curling up next to a potted plant.

"Our best bet is the man we're looking for," said Barney. "Maybe he's new in town and nobody knows him, or maybe he's from the car show. Somebody will recognise him from his description."

We finished our meals in relative silence, watching the sunset, and listening to the jackdaws chattering in the distance as they prepared to roost. As darkness fell, the three of us stepped aboard the boat carrying our empty plates. Mabel curled up under the picnic bench after thoroughly searching the area for dropped titbits, and Rosie followed us into the middle section of the boat, slumping onto her favourite seat and falling asleep.

I made sure all three doors were securely locked and made Barney's bed up for him. "If you hear anything during the night, wake me up," he said, as Willow and I made our way to my bedroom.

It did feel safer having Barney aboard, and within fifteen minutes of getting into bed, Willow was snoring softly, and I was close behind her.

CHAPTER ELEVEN

Barney left early in the morning after receiving a phone call telling him that a witness had come forward – a boat owner who'd seen someone walking along the towpath on the night Sam was murdered. He'd told the police that it had been too dark to see much, and he'd been drinking, but Barney rushed off to interview him in the hope he could jog his memory.

I'd prepared him a quick breakfast of boiled eggs and toast, and when I'd handed him a whole piece of toast, he'd quickly cut it into soldiers and proceeded to dip them in the runny yolks, licking his fingers clean when he was finished.

When he'd gone, Willow and I got ready for a visit to the lawyers. As Granny had said — leave no stone unturned, and I had a hunch that the information the lawyer was withholding could be important to the case. I dressed in a simple white t-shirt and shorts, and Willow borrowed a short flower print summer dress from me, which did far more for her figure than it ever had for mine.

"Do you need to look at the spell book again?" said Willow, opening the book at the persuasion spell.

I shook my head. "No, it's like Granny said. I know the spell is imprinted on my mind, and I just have to think about it. It's a strange feeling — not like the simple spells we're used to casting."

Willow slammed the book shut, and I sucked a little air into my mouth, tasting copper. I accessed the spell in my mind, and Willow looked at me with wide eyes as I clicked my fingers and she began moonwalking towards the bathroom singing *Thriller*.

"What are you doing?" I joked. "I thought you didn't like Michael Jackson?"

She hit a high note and span on the spot, scaring Rosie, before moonwalking back towards me. I let my mind go blank and Willow fell laughing onto the dinette seat. "Okay!" she said. "You've got the hang of it, but my wrath will be swift and fearsome when I learn that spell myself — I'll make you do the YMCA dance in the middle of town!"

We continued laughing as we locked up the boat and headed up the footpath into town. It would only take a few minutes to walk to the town centre, and we both needed some exercise. We admired the vintage cars we saw passing through town, although with most of them already at the show, there were only a few on the roads.

Police cars patrolled the area, no doubt looking for the mystery man, and Willow stopped to look at a poster in a shop window asking for information concerning the murder of Sam Hedgewick.

"It's a terrible thing, isn't it?" said a voice from behind us.

"Hello, Veronica," I said, her voice and the scent of her rose water perfume giving away her identity before I'd even turned to face her.

She pointed at the poster. "It's awful. Sam's father is beside himself, the nurses in the home have had to sedate him three times."

"Poor man," said Willow. "A parent should never have to bury their child."

"There's a terrible doom and gloom in the home," said Veronica. "I've popped out for a while to get some sun, and to pick some herbal medicine up for Ron." She held up a paper bag to show us.

"Is he okay?" I said.

"He just needs a little pick-me-up," she explained. "That potion you made him didn't help with Snoopy, but it certainly helped him sleep. He needed the rest, mind you — he was always in that gym. He's hurt his hand too, he strained it lifting a weight that was too heavy for him."

"Even Olympic athletes need a break now and again," said Willow. "It will do him good."

"I think he's having withdrawal symptoms from the exercise," said Veronica. "He's very agitated. I hope he doesn't have that thing that body builders suffer from. Now, what was it called again?" She tilted her head as she considered. "Road rage, that's it."

"Roid rage," I smiled. "You're not telling me Ron was taking steroids, are you? I'd have never made him a potion if I'd known that."

"Oh gosh, no! Ron always says his body's a temple. He wouldn't sully it with nasty drugs."

Willow put her hand on Veronica's. "It's not roid rage then, Veronica. He'll be fine."

Veronica nodded. "I know," she said. "It's just a very stressful time at the home. Everybody's concerned about Sam's father, and I overheard a nurse suggesting the murderer might strike again! The nursing home would be a very easy target for him to find his next victim in. Especially on a Wednesday night."

"A Wednesday?" asked Willow, furrowing her brow.

"Spotted dick night," explained Veronica. "The chefs make

it for pudding every Wednesday after dinner. It's very rich, and most folk go to bed early after eating it, especially Sylvia. She thinks people don't see her, but she always sneaks a second helping." Veronica's face whitened. "The killer could easily sneak in and knock one of us off!"

"I very much doubt it's a serial killer," I reassured her. "The police are looking for a suspect, and Barney's gone to interview a witness. It won't be long before they catch whoever did it."

Veronica looked at the floor. "And to think my last words to Sam were nasty ones. I'm ashamed."

"Why? What happened?" said Willow.

"He drank too much at the party," said Veronica. "And then he wanted to drive home! I told him in no uncertain terms that he would do no such thing! We parted ways on harsh words, and then he couldn't get a taxi so he had to walk home." Veronica shook her head. "To think he was killed on the way. Maybe I should have just minded my own business and let him drive. He'd still be with us."

"He could have killed an innocent person, or himself in a crash. You did the right thing, Veronica," I said, placing my hand on her shoulder. "Come, on. Willow and I will walk you home."

The nursing home was a grand old building set in acres of manicured gardens. Once a mansion that had housed a local wealthy landlord and his family, with an army of servants, it had been an easy job to transform it into an upmarket residential home.

As we neared the steps, guarded by stone lions on pillars, which led to the large doors, a voice came from our left. "This door's open."

A short overweight woman peeped through an open doorway surrounded by climbing ivy, and Veronica waved her away. "Sylvia, get back inside. Don't use that door during the day — you'll give the game away!"

Sylvia hurried back inside, muttering to herself, and closed the door behind her.

"Give the game away?" I said. "What game's that?"

Veronica looked around, making sure nobody could hear her. "People use that door to sneak their lovers in at night," she smiled, oblivious to our shock. "The alarm's broken, so the nurses don't know when it's been opened."

"Naughty, naughty," I teased.

"Not me of course," said Veronica. "But I might need that door in the future, me and Ron are going through a rocky patch, you see. He's such a jealous man, but you can't blame him — look at me, I still turn the heads of men under sixty!"

"I'm sure you'll work things out," I said, helping Veronica up the steps.

"I hope so," said Veronica, "but I won't be told what men I can and can't talk to. My ex-husband tried that little trick on me, and we were divorced before he knew what had hit him! I'll give Ron a month or two to sort himself out, but you know what they say, a leopard never spots a change."

"A leopard never changes its spots," said Willow.

"Yes, that's it. Come on girls, now you're here you can come and say hello to him. He's sitting in his room moping, two pretty girls like you will soon cheer him up."

We followed Veronica into the home, saying hello to the receptionist that sat behind the huge dark wood desk, and waving at the residents who sat in the large communal lounge watching TV. Ron's room was at the end of a corridor lined with potted plants and oil paintings, and Veronica tapped lightly on the door before letting herself in.

"Visitors, Ronald!" she said.

Ron looked up from a seat in the corner. Veronica hadn't been exaggerating when she said he'd been in the gym a lot.

His muscles bulged at the striped pyjamas he was wearing, and he'd added inches to his shoulders.

"Oh, hello girls," he said in a flat voice. "Veronica told me you were back in town, Penelope."

"Cheer up, Ron," said Veronica. "Penelope and Willow don't want you bringing them down. Turn that frown upside down and get dressed."

"I don't feel well," said Ron. "I'm not trying to be miserable."

"You're not being miserable," I assured him. "You look very tired though."

"I'll be okay soon enough," said Ron. "Another good night's sleep should see me right."

"Come on, Ron," urged Veronica, "get up out of that chair and take a shower. What is it you always say? The devil's hands are lazy."

"The devil makes work for idle hands," muttered Ron.

Veronica nodded. "Yes, that's it. You wouldn't have lounged around all day when you were in the army, would you? They'd have kicked you out of that seat soon enough!"

"I'm not in the army anymore," said Ron. "I can sit here for as long as I like."

Veronica tutted. "Look at his pictures, girls," she said, pointing to the framed photographs that were perched on a set of wall shelves. "You wouldn't think it was the same man, would you?"

The fact that most of the photographs were black and white told me that Ron probably didn't feel like the same man these days. A lot of years had passed since Ron had posed for the photographs, some of them of him standing with other soldiers, and some of them portraits of him alone on top of a tank.

I ran my finger along the printed names of the soldiers

below a group photograph until I found Ron's name. "A sergeant. You did well, Ron." I said.

"I did okay," said Ron.

"Cup of tea, girls?" said Veronica. "I'm going to make one for Ron with extra sugar. Let's see if we can't get his energy up a little."

"No thanks," said Willow, placing a photograph back on the shelf. "We have to be somewhere."

"Well, be sure to pop in whenever you feel like it. Don't let Mr Grumpy put you off visiting us, he'll be right as rain in no time."

We promised to visit again, and made our way back into town, pausing outside the lawyer's office before we went in. "Do you think we need an appointment?" said Willow.

"Let's find out," I said, pushing the door open and striding inside.

The waiting area was sparse, with three plastic seats for clients, a fake rubber plant in a corner, and a middle-aged woman sitting at the tiny reception desk in the corner. Her face lit up when she saw us. "Are you here to see Mr. Sandler? He'll see you right away."

We didn't need an appointment, it seemed. I doubted that Mr. Sandler was inundated with clients in a town as small as Wickford, but he must have been doing something right to afford the BMW that gleamed in the sun, alongside the office.

"Thank you," I nodded. "We'd love to see him."

She hurried from behind her desk and knocked on the panelled wood door to the right of her work space. She pushed it open and led us in. "Two clients to see you, Mr. Sandler," she said.

The lawyer spun his seat around to face us, smiling at us over the vast expanse of wooden desk. "Thank you, Louise," he said.

Louise left the room and Mr. Sandler indicated the two seats reserved for clients. "Please sit down, ladies," he said, his tongue tracing his top lip, and his eyes on Willow's chest for far longer than was polite. I'd feel absolutely no guilt about casting a spell on a man who openly ogled my sister in that way.

Willow seemed unfazed. She even leaned across the desk to shake the lawyer's hand, bending far too low for my thin summer dress to keep her assets captive. Maybe I wouldn't need a persuasion spell after all. Mr. Sandler held onto Willow's hand for a few seconds too long, and smiled at us in turn as we sat down. He crossed his legs, picked up a pen which he rolled between his fingers, and flashed a bright white set of teeth at us.

"How can I help you, ladies?" he drawled.

Willow looked at me and smiled. "Why don't you ask him, Penelope?"

I returned her smile, and accessed the persuasion spell, sucking in a small amount of air and immediately tasting copper. It seemed I was a faster learner than Granny had given me credit for. I clicked my fingers beneath the desk.

"Mr. Sandler," I said, my head gently throbbing.

"Derek, please," he replied.

He didn't look like a Derek. More like a Brad, or a Pierre. Looks could be deceiving though.

"Derek," I smiled, already imagining what I wanted him to do. I took my phone out, brought Barney's number up, and slid it across the desk. "That's PC Dobkin's phone number. The police man who came in to ask you why Sam Hedgewick had been to see you on the day he was murdered. I'd like you to ring it from your phone and tell him what he wanted to know."

Derek picked up his phone from the desk and gave me a

wry smile. "I'm afraid I can't do that," He said with a wink. "Client confidentiality, you see."

He turned my phone around and glanced at the number as he keyed it into his own phone. Confusion crossed his face, and I smiled sweetly at him as his eyes narrowed. "I really can't do that," he said, bringing the phone to his ear. "I could lose my licence."

He stared at me and Willow in turn. "I'm sorry," he said, "the police will just have to wait until they get their warrant."

"Ah, hello, PC Dobkins," he said. Barney must have answered. "I've reconsidered. I will tell you why Mr. Hedgewick came to see me." His eyes opened wide as he spoke, and his hand trembled as he attempted to move the phone from his ear.

I concentrated hard, and Derek visibly shuddered.

"I asked Sam to come and see me," he continued, his face becoming whiter by the second. "His soon to be ex-wife had been in to see me the day before. She seemed quite desperate. She wanted to know all about the properties Sam was selling. She said Sam was leaving her for someone else and intended to move abroad. She seemed quite panicked about what would happen to her financially. I felt it was my duty to inform Sam."

He listened as Barney spoke. "No," he said, "I wasn't breaking client confidentiality in that instance. Mrs. Hedgewick was not a client, you see." He nodded as Barney spoke. "I'm sure you will get straight on it, PC Dobkins," he said. "Good luck with your investigation."

He put the phone down slowly and stared at me. He rubbed his head with his hands and pressed the intercom button on his desk. "Please cancel the rest of my appointments for the day," he said when Louise answered. "I don't feel myself. I need to go home and have a lie down."

"You have no more appointments today, Mr. Sandler," said Louise.

"That makes your job easier then, doesn't it?" he snapped. He pointed to the door. "You two should leave," he said. "I don't know what just happened, but I don't feel right."

With the spell still fizzing in my mind, I stared at Derek. "I suggest you don't tell PC Dobkins that we were here. You decided to phone him out of a sense of moral obligation, not because I asked you to."

He stared at me open mouthed and nodded.

"Thanks for your help, Derek," said Willow, offering him her hand again, which he refused with a quick shake of his head. "I hope you feel better soon."

CHAPTER TWELVE

"I think it was a drunk stranger, on the towpath, with the windlass," said Susie.

I didn't put my theory forward that it was Sam's wife. We hadn't told Susie and Granny about our trip to the lawyer's office yet. Mum didn't know we'd blackmailed Granny for her spell book, and she'd have never believed that Granny would simply have handed it over to us. She'd have found out about Granny's accident with Boris and Charleston within minutes.

"I bet it was my badboy. I bet Sam owed him a gambling debt and he called it in, using the only method an alpha male like him knows... violence, intimidation, and ultimately, sad as it may be — murder," said Granny, spooning a second helping of lasagne onto her plate. "This isn't half bad for reheated food, Maggie," she said.

"It was far tastier last night," said Mum, choosing to keep her suspicions as to the identity of the murderer to herself. "Willow would have known that if she'd spent the night here, where she lives, instead of staying on Penelope's floating emporium of loneliness, in fear for her life."

Willow scowled. "There's nothing lonely about Penny's boat," she said, wincing as she snapped a piece of garlic bread off the steaming hot baguette in the centre of the table. "And no one was in fear for their life."

"Thanks to Barney," said Mum. "I'd have been far less happy about you two staying there last night with a potential murderer casing the joint, if that strapping young man hadn't been there to look after you both." Mum looked at the wall clock. "He's beginning to go down in my estimation though. I invited him for a family evening dinner as a thank you for saving my daughter's lives, and he decides he's going to be late."

"He'll be here soon, Mum," I said. "He's involved in a murder investigation, remember? And that's a *little* more important than lasagne and roasted vegetables."

"And he didn't save our lives," said Willow, stabbing a piece of courgette with her fork.

"I read your story in the newspaper, Susie," said Mum, refusing to acknowledge Willow. "It was very informative and very well written."

"Thank you, Maggie," beamed Susie. "The police have asked me not to write about their ongoing investigations, so I'll have to wait until they catch the murderer before I write a follow up piece."

Mum nodded as Susie spoke, her hands clasped beneath her chin. "Well, I'm sure it will be just as gripping as the one I read today, dear."

"I'm going to the car show tomorrow," said Susie. "The classical car magazine still wants a story, it's Saturday tomorrow, and I could do with a day out. Maybe I'll have a wine or two while I'm there."

Mum smiled her approval, before standing up. "I think Barney's here," she said, as the sound of a car engine floated through the open window. "I'll let him in."

As soon as Mum had left the room, Granny looked at Susie. "I'm assuming these two tattle-tales have told you about my accident with Boris?"

Susie looked at me, and I nodded my permission. "Yes," she said. "It wasn't your fault though."

Granny waved her hand in the air. "Who's to blame is a ship long sailed," she said. "Speaking of ships, you girls are going to do me a favour. And if you refuse, you'll see exactly what blackmail is — and I don't mean that amateur stuff you pulled on me yesterday — I'll take you to hell and back! You mark my words!"

"Okay, Granny," I said, leaning back in my seat to put as much space between us as possible. "Calm down. What do you want?"

"Two birds with one stone," she said, speaking quickly as Barney's car door slammed shut and Mum shouted hello to him. "Boris heard about the car show on the radio, and wants to visit it. He's also a big fan of boats. I want you to take him to the car show on your boat. The show finishes on Sunday morning, so tomorrow's his last chance."

"We can't," I protested. "He's a goat, Granny. Goats don't admire old cars."

"Or go for boat trips," offered Willow.

Granny smiled. "Of course he can go on a boat, and on the radio it said there's a mixed livestock competition being held at the car show tomorrow. Enter him in that if you must. I'll even plait his beard. He'd like that."

"A livestock competition at a car show?" I interrupted.

"Yes," said Granny. "Along with a tent for bands to play in, with a bar. They've got rides for the kids too, and stalls selling all the usual tat. Boris will have a wonderful day out."

The front door slammed shut and two sets of footsteps echoed down the hallway. "I'm not doing that," I hissed. "It's ridiculous!"

Granny gave me the smile she reserved for people who were about to regret crossing her. "I will come down on you so hard you won't know if you're a witch or a warlock."

"I think it's a wonderful idea," said Susie, her face white. She'd seen Granny angry before and her expression told me she didn't want to see it again if she could avoid it. "I'll come on the boat with you, it'll be fun."

"What will be fun?" said Mum, breezing into the kitchen with Barney hot on her heels, ducking to avoid banging his head on the doorway.

"The girls have decided to take Penelope's boat out for the day tomorrow," smiled Granny, raising her eyebrows at me, her glasses sliding dangerously close to the tip of her nose. "They're going to the car show. I'm sure they'll have a wonderful time."

Mum rolled her eyes. "Each to their own," she said. She looked at Barney. "Do you see what all the fascination is with boats?"

"Leave Barney out of your campaign to get Penelope off that boat," snapped Granny. "He's an officer of the law."

Barney looked at his feet, but he couldn't hide the redness that rose in his cheeks. He really was too easy to embarrass.

"Scoot up, Willow," said Granny. "Let Barney have your seat, he and Penelope probably want to sit together."

It was my turn to blush, but Barney seemed happy with the idea, and sat down next to me as Willow made her seat available. I ignored Granny's cringingly overt matchmaking attempt, and poured my new neighbour a glass of iced lemon water.

Mum slid a plate heaped with food in front of him. "Tuck in," she said, "you'll need your energy if you're going to catch the killer."

Granny offered Barney some garlic bread. "Are you any closer to finding out who murdered that poor man?" she said.

Barney looked around the table. "I'm not really supposed to say anything," he said, picking up his cutlery. He glanced nervously at Susie. "Especially with a journalist in the room."

Susie swiped a finger over her chest in the shape of a cross. "You have my word, as a responsible freelance journalist, that anything you say will not make it into print."

"Or on the internet?" said Barney suspiciously.

"Or on the internet," confirmed Susie with a smile of encouragement. "Anything you say will stay at this table."

Barney took a bite of lasagne, made an exaggerated sound of appreciation, and nodded his approval at Mum, who shrugged. Everything she cooked tasted good, and annoyingly, she knew it.

"There's not much to tell, really," said Barney. "We're waiting for the test results on the windlass and the results of Sam's post-mortem. We're no closer to finding the man who was seen arguing with Sam, and the boat owner witness I interviewed this morning can only confirm it was a male he saw on the towpath near the Flirting Kingfisher."

"The Flirting Kingfisher?" said Willow.

Barney sipped his water and reloaded his fork with food. "Sorry, that's the name of his boat — *The Flirting Kingfisher*. He says the man was wearing a blazer or jacket with some sort of logo on it, but he can't recall what. It was dark, and he'd drank a few whiskies."

"It's something to go on at least," said Susie.

"That's not all that happened today," said Barney, puffing out his chest. "You know that lawyer I questioned?"

"Yes," I said, shifting in my seat and ignoring Willow's smile.

"My hard-line questioning paid off," said Barney. "He obviously realised I wasn't to be messed with, and today he crumbled — he couldn't take the heat I'd brought down on him. He phoned me and told me exactly what I needed to know. Sergeant Cooper's very impressed. He even gave me a coffee break."

"And what was it that the lawyer told you?" said Granny, giving me a proud look of approval.

Barney told everyone what Willow and I already knew, and then blew out a frustrated blast of air between his teeth. "That was a waste of time too," he said. "We'd already questioned her when Sam's body had been found, but she'd failed to mention they were getting a divorce, or that she'd been to see the lawyer."

Granny slammed her fist down on the table, making everybody jump. "Guilty!" she declared.

Barney shook his head. "No, she's got a watertight alibi. It transpires that Sam was leaving her for somebody else because she'd been cheating on him for years. She was with the other man on the night Sam was killed, and they've got witnesses. They went out for a meal in Covenhill, and the restaurant staff say they left at half eleven. The taxi driver told us he took them back to the man's house in Covenhill. Sam's wife spent the night there."

"That smells fishy," said Willow. "Why didn't she tell the police they were getting divorced when you first spoke to her?"

"Money and shame," said Granny, adjusting her glasses. "She wanted to make sure she kept up the pretence of being his loving wife to ensure she gets all his assets, and she was ashamed that she'd been to the lawyer on the very day he died — to try and keep her dirty cheating hands on his properties and cash."

"I couldn't have put it better myself," said Barney, making Granny swell with pride.

"What about the woman Sam was leaving his wife for?" said Mum. "Maybe she killed him."

"Sam's wife doesn't know who she was, and we can't find

any evidence pointing to her," explained Barney. "We're working on the theory that she never even existed. We think it was a smoke screen so Sam could finally leave his wife. She refused to leave him because she'd lose out on his money, so maybe Sam was stuck in an unbearable situation and needed a way out."

"What about gambling?" I said. "Did you find out if he's in debt?"

"There's no evidence of it," said Barney. "But serial gamblers don't tend to leave paper trails. It's all hearsay at the moment, but we really want to speak to the man we're looking for. Maybe Sam owed him money."

"What a wicked web we weave," murmured Granny. "Anyway. Enough of this doom and gloom. Maggie, didn't you say you had a bread and butter pudding in the oven? I'm still peckish."

With the bread and butter pudding demolished, and everyone beginning to get tired, I decided to cycle back to my boat and see to Rosie's needs. I refused the offer of a lift from Barney, and reassured everyone that I'd be all right on my own for the night.

Granny followed me out of the cottage as I was leaving and watched me getting my bike out of mum's car. "So, you made a spell work. You got that lawyer's tongue to wag."

"It wasn't so hard," I said. "Not as hard as you said it would be, anyway."

Granny shook her head. "Those spells *are* difficult, give yourself some credit. Some of them even I've never mastered. You did well. You're going to be a powerful witch someday, Penelope. It won't be long before Maeve gives you your entry spell if you carry on as you are. Just keep practicing, and remember that once a spell is imprinted in your mind, you'll never need to learn it again."

"Unless I get witch dementia," I smiled, freeing a pedal from the lip of the car boot.

"My spells are still up here," said Granny, tapping the side of her head with a finger. "They're just more muddled up than your relationship with Barney is."

"There is no relationship with Barney," I said, looking away. "Just a friendly one."

"You'd better tell him that," said Granny. "Didn't you see the way that cute little freckly face of his lit up when he knew he could sit next to you?"

I sighed and swung my leg over the bike. "I'm going now, Granny."

"I'll bring Boris to your boat first thing in the morning, and don't you dare leave without him."

"You have my word," I said.

"Good. It will give me chance to drive into Covenhill without worrying about him. I need to buy one of those computer things."

I took my foot off the pedal and stared at her. "What in the name of the goddess do you need with a computer? You said the manufacturers rape the land for the rare elements they need to make them."

"It's not a crime to have a change of opinion," said Granny, pushing her glasses up her nose. "Anyway, it's not for me. It's for Boris."

"Two questions. Why are you paying for a computer for Boris, and why does a goat even need a computer?"

"I'm not paying for it," said Granny. "Boris is letting me take Charleston's credit card. He's a very wealthy man — the acupuncture was more of a hobby than a job. He didn't need the money if his bank balance is anything to go by. He wants to start one of those blog thingy's, I'm not really sure what they are, but Boris is very excited at the prospect."

"But he can't use a computer. He's got hooves!"

"Precisely what I said," agreed Granny. "Boris came up with a solution though — voice recognition software. He just needs to speak to the computer, it all sounds very clever."

"It all sounds like madness," I countered.

"You let me and Boris do what we like, young lady. Anyway, a new hobby will do him good. He's far too fond of the brandy, he needs something to keep him occupied."

"You said brandy couldn't harm his body, what's the problem?"

"He can still get drunk, and he gets a little ... problematic, when he's three sheets to the wind."

The conversation was becoming too surreal. "I'm going, Granny," I said. "As much as I'd like to stand here all evening talking about an alcoholic tech savvy goat, I want to be back at my boat before it gets dark."

Granny waved me off, reminding me with a scowl that I wasn't to leave without Boris in the morning. I pedalled quickly, and within fifteen minutes I was leaning my bike up against a picnic bench and patting Mabel on the head as she sniffed at my boots.

I stepped aboard the *Water Witch* and grabbed some incense from one of the shop shelves as I passed, lighting it on top of the wood burner, and giving Rosie a belly rub before feeding her and settling down at the dinette table with the spell book.

I chose a spell that sounded like it could be useful, and silently read the symbols and letters until my head throbbed. Sucking a small amount of air into my mouth, I tasted copper and concentrated on making the wilting plant in a pot on the kitchen counter come back to life.

A searing pain made me gasp, and I slammed the book

shut, making Rosie jump. Granny had been right – some spells were much harder than others.

When the pain in my head had subsided, I opened the book again and read a few random spells, my head throbbing, but not hurting, as the symbols imprinted themselves on me. Any spells that began making my head hurt I ignored, and went onto the next one. After twenty minutes of study I closed the book, placed it in the storage area beneath the dinette seat, and prepared myself for bed. Maybe I would get to visit the haven sooner than I'd imagined, I certainly felt more magical, and I was beginning to understand how exciting it must be to finally be granted the entry spell.

CHAPTER THIRTEEN

*G*ranny and Boris arrived at the boat ten minutes after Susie and Willow had arrived together. I knew better than to ask Granny how she'd managed to get Boris into her car — it would probably have been very intolerant of me to assume a man in goat's body couldn't mange the simple task of sitting in a car. Boris had a collar around his neck, and Granny held onto the end of a dog leash as she guided him across the clearing. Boris's beard was just as Granny had promised, and a small piece of red ribbon was tied around the tightly woven plait. The goat — or man. I still hadn't quite made my mind up — looked happy enough to be led by Granny, but I still confronted her about the new development in her treatment of Boris.

"What are you doing?" I said. "Surely Boris doesn't like being led around like your pet?"

Boris spoke for them both as Granny removed the backpack she was carrying and placed it on one of the picnic benches. "It was my idea, Penelope," he said. "To avoid arousing suspicion from any quarter today, I suggested the dog leash. If you're going to be taking me to a public place it seems sensible to treat me like this. You might receive unwanted attention otherwise. I mean, it's not many goats that walk side by side with their owners around a field full of vintage cars, now, is it?"

He had a point. "Okay," I relented, "but you just let me know if that collar starts hurting you."

"That collar won't hurt!" spat Granny. "It was the most expensive one in the pet shop. It's a comfort fit."

"And very nice it is too," said Boris. "I think the red breaks up the white of my hair, and it matches the ribbon in my beard."

Granny placed an affectionate hand on the goat's head. "You're sure to win the competition, Boris. You look like a million dollars."

"Gladys has cleared a space on the mantelpiece for the trophy, just in case I win," said Boris. "The last trophy I won was for being in the winning crew in the boat race against Cambridge university. I love boats, and I can hardly wait to get aboard yours, Penelope."

"Come on then," said Susie, arriving at my side. "I'll show you aboard, Boris."

As Susie led Boris to the bow of the boat and helped him negotiate himself aboard, Granny passed me the little backpack. "There's a little bottle of brandy in there," she said. "Give him a sip before the competition – it will give him confidence. There's some chocolate biscuits in there too, and a brush for his hair. You make sure he wins that competition, Penelope. He may not show it, but he's got his heart set on coming first."

I took the bag and smiled as Granny looked over my shoulder, watching Boris as he disappeared down the steps into the shop. "You really like him, don't you?" I said.

Granny sighed. "It's lovely having an educated man, I mean goat, around the house. I hadn't realised how lonely I was until Boris moved in with me. You be sure to look after him today, Penelope. I'm holding you accountable for his safety."

"He'll be fine," I promised. "Now you go and buy his computer for him. I'll bring him back to you tonight."

Granny waved at Boris as he peered through one of the boat's windows. "Have fun, Boris!" she called.

"I will!" came the muffled reply.

Granny turned her back and hurried toward the footpath to the hotel and car park. "Don't bring him back too late," she shouted. 'I'm cooking for him!"

When Granny had vanished into the trees, I stepped aboard the boat, lifted the engine hatch in the stern deck and checked the oil levels. Willow untied the mooring ropes and joined me next to the steering tiller as I prepared to start the engine.

Susie appeared at the bottom of the steps that led from my bedroom, with Boris behind her. "Don't you dare start her up without us," she said. "Boris really wants to watch."

With all four of us standing on the stern decking, it was crowded, but we had enough to room to move about. Boris watched as I turned the key in the ignition and pressed the engine start button.

"What a beautiful sound," he shouted over the noise as the old diesel engine burst into life, vibrating beneath our feet. "They don't make them like that anymore!"

He was right. The engine in my boat was from the nineteen sixties, and it chugged away at a far slower pace than modern diesel engines.

Willow had given the boat a small push as she'd jumped aboard, and we were already floating slowly away from the bank.

I pulled the control lever backwards, putting the gearbox in reverse, and the propeller churned the water behind us as

I grabbed the long steering tiller and began reversing the boat onto the main body of the canal.

"Well done!" shouted Boris, as I manoeuvred the long boat. "You're quite the expert!"

As the bow cleared the turning to my mooring, I put the boat in neutral and straightened up as the boat continued to float backwards.

"Can I have a go of driving?" asked Susie, stroking Rosie, who sat on the roof in front of us.

"Of course," I promised, "just let me get us going."

Looking down the long roof, past the potted plants and the chimney, I aimed the bow of the boat and selected forward gear. The engine throbbed beneath us, and the boat began slowly gaining speed as water churned white behind us. With a speed limit of four miles an hour imposed on the canal system, we were never going to break any speed records, but we chugged along at a pleasant pace, and I stood aside to let Susie take the controls.

"Push the tiller in the opposite direction than you want to go," I explained, as Susie steered us towards an overhanging branch.

She straightened the boat up, and Boris gazed around happily at the fields that took the place of trees on the opposite bank. The bank on our side of the canal was lined with walls and cliffs which homes and shops sat on top of, with people in some of the gardens who waved cheerily at us as we passed.

Steam rose from the Wickford brewery chimney, and the smell of yeast in the air made Willow scrunch up her face in disgust. "That's why I don't drink beer," she said. "It's horrible."

"There's nothing like a real ale on a Sunday afternoon," countered Boris, sniffing the aroma. "It's an acquired taste, but when you acquire it, it will be with you for life."

Susie kept the boat in a straight line, and slowed down as we passed moored boats, preventing our bow wave from disturbing them. It would take an hour to get to the car show, and we had one lock to negotiate on the way. We passed under one of the bridges that attached one side of Wickord to the other, and Willow dragged her hand down the stone walls as we chugged beneath it, the engine echoing in the confined space. The canal beneath the bridges was barely wide enough for my boat, and any boats coming in the opposite direction would have had to give way and wait for us to pass under the bridge before continuing their journey.

"Would you mind if I went to the bow deck?" said Boris. "I can't drive with these hooves, so I'm just taking up space back here."

Willow laughed. "Come on, I'll go with you," she said, leading Boris down the steps into my bedroom.

They walked the length of the boat before emerging on the bow deck, sixty feet in front of us. I leaned out and looked down the side of the boat, smiling as Boris planted both hooves on the tip of the bow and held his head high in the air. "Are you having fun?" I yelled.

"I'm on top of the world!" he shouted, eliciting giggles from me and Susie.

Ducks and swans swam alongside us, and soon we approached the area of canal where Sam had met his untimely end.

A small cliff rose from the towpath on our left, and we passed beneath the Lock and Key pub, saying a few words for Sam as we spotted the police tape still wrapped around a tree trunk, the other end floating in the margins of the canal.

"The lock's just past the next bridge," I said to Susie, trying to take my thoughts off the murder. "Do you want to go ashore and operate it, or shall I ask Willow?"

"I'll do it!" said Susie.

We passed beneath the final bridge in Wickford, and the lock came into sight a hundred metres to our front. I slowed the boat as we approached it, and Susie grabbed the windlass she'd need to open the gates. The windlass was an L-shaped metal tool that was used as a winding lever to operate the heavy lock gates, and I winced as I imagined how it had felt for Sam, if he had indeed been murdered with one.

As the boat neared the bank, Susie prepared to leap ashore, and when the gap was only a few inches she made the jump and hurried to the first set of gates. Boris and Willow joined me on the stern deck as I steered the boat towards the entrance to the lock, and stood either side of me as I moved the boat forward. The lock was set in our favour, with the first set of gates open and the second set holding back the water in the canal above us.

The walls of the lock loomed fifteen feet above us on either side of the boat, with barely three inches between the hull and the stonework. Soon, Susie would close the gates behind us and open the gates in front of us, flooding the lock with water and turning the high walls into the low banks of the canal.

When the boat was safely clear of the gates behind us, Susie used the windlass to operate the gate mechanism, trapping us between the two sets of thick nineteenth century wooden gates. She waved as she climbed the grassy hill and shouted down to us. "Ready?" she asked.

"Go on," I shouted, "open them!"

As the gates to our front opened, the boat floated upwards like a cork in a glass being filled with water. I kept the engine engaged in forward gear, applying just enough power to prevent the wash of incoming water pushing us backwards, and soon we were floating fifteen feet above the stretch of the canal behind us, with the rest of the canal stretching ahead of us.

I pulled the boat ashore a few metres past the gates, and waited for Susie to get back aboard, a big smile on her face and the windlass safely in her hand. With everyone aboard, I pulled away from the bank and we continued our journey, admiring the beautiful countryside that had opened up on both banks.

CHAPTER FOURTEEN

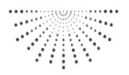

*B*oris gasped as we rounded the bend in the canal and the festival fields opened up on our left. "Wow," he said. "That's quite a sight."

It was quite a sight, and quite a smell. Chrome shone and twinkled for hundreds of metres as the sun bounced off the rows and rows of cars, and the scent of frying onions and bacon wafted through the air from the assorted vans and stalls selling hot food of all kinds.

More delicious cooking aromas drifted from the line of colourful boats that were moored up alongside the canal bank, and the sound of children's laughter, and music coming from the big tent in the middle of the field lifted my spirits. I was going to enjoy myself, I realised with a smile.

In the field adjacent to the one the cars were on show in, lines of tents, caravans, and camper vans dotted the landscape.

It was the last day and night of the show, and people seemed to be making the most of it. Groups of men and women sat in huddles on the grass near the canal, drinking beer and wine from plastic cups or cans, and other people wandered along the rows of vintage cars, admiring the old machinery.

It was a real festival atmosphere, and we began to make plans as we cruised past the lines of boats, searching for a mooring spot for the *Water Witch*.

"How about we look at some of those magnificent cars," suggested Boris, the ribbon in his beard fluttering in the gentle breeze, "then get a hotdog and a beer. It's been too many years since I savoured food bought from the back of a greasy van."

"That's a great idea, Boris" said Willow, "I'm starving!"

All the best mooring spots had been taken, but finally we found one, at the end of the long line of boats, beneath an old gnarled oak tree surrounded by bushes. I manoeuvred the boat into the space and Willow jumped ashore to tie the *Water Witch* up. With the engine switched off, the sounds of the show were even more vibrant, and I picked Rosie up from off the roof and ushered her inside the boat. "You stay in there," I said. "It's far too busy and loud for you out here."

She gave me a look that I interpreted as a thank you, and sauntered off to relax on her favourite seat.

"Let's go," said Susie, hooking her camera bag over her shoulder and stepping onto the grassy bank. "My camera finger's itching to get some photos of those cars."

Boris leapt gracefully ashore and waited as I attached the dog leash to his collar. "Don't worry, Penelope," he said quietly as I apologised. "I really don't mind, and I couldn't ask for a nicer person to be on the other end of my leash."

I was beginning to realise why Granny had such a soft spot for him. He really was a charming goat.

"Come on," I said, "let's go and have a nice day."

We walked alongside the line of boats, saying hello to the boat owners that sat on their roofs, drinking and eating, and telling us what a lovely looking goat Boris was. Boris made low sounds of appreciation at every compliment he received, and even allowed a friendly old lady to tickle him behind his horns.

We were just about to veer off to the right, and away from the canal, when Willow grabbed my arm. "Look," she said, pointing at a beautiful yellow and purple narrowboat. "It's the *Flirting Kingfisher*. The boat that Barney's witness lives on."

The boat had a fresh paint of coat and the windows gleamed like they had been very recently cleaned. A man wearing just shorts sat on a deckchair on the bow of his boat, sipping a drink and reading a book. His chest and shoulders were bright red, and I guessed he'd be applying an aftersun soothing cream by the end of the day.

"Do you feel like trying some magic?" said Willow with a suggestive grin. "To see if we can get more information out of him than Barney could?"

Without warning, a spell popped into my mind, almost begging me to cast it. "A spell of enhanced memory," I said. "It's just made itself known to me. It must have imprinted on me last night when I was flicking through Granny's book."

"Do it," urged Susie, "you might make him remember something that solves the murder."

Boris agreed. "I'm not privy to the story about this witness, but I'd love to see some magic in action."

"He saw someone on the towpath," I explained to Boris. "He said there was a logo or something on his jacket, but he can't remember what."

"Then help him remember," said Boris in a low voice, being careful not to let anyone hear him speaking. "There's still a murderer at large."

The man looked up from his book. With three girls and a goat staring at him, I felt it was necessary to explain our interest in him.

"I'm sorry to bother you," I said, approaching the boat. "I'm a friend of the policeman who interviewed you about the man you saw on the towpath on the night Mr Hedgewick was killed."

He looked at me with confusion on his face. "How on earth do you know it's me?" he asked.

"The boat name," explained Willow. "We're on a boat too, my sister lives on the canal, like you. We just want the murderer caught. It scares me to think of my sister alone on her boat at night with a killer on the loose. A killer who's already killed someone on the canal towpath."

His guard visibly dropped when he knew I was a live-aboard. Boat owners always helped each other whenever they could, and Willow's fear-mongering seemed to have made him even more willing to talk to us. "It is unnerving," said the man. "But I told the police everything I remember."

"Can I ask you a question or two?" I said.

"Of course, but as I've said. I can't remember much. It was dark and I was drunk." He winked at me. "Whiskey's my weakness," he added with a smile. He gestured at us with a wave of his hand. "Come aboard," he offered. "Would anybody like a drink? I'm getting myself a top up."

We refused the offer of a beverage as we stepped aboard the *Flirting Kingfisher* and sat together on one of the hulls curved built in benches. The boat owner stepped down into his boat, and Boris remained on the bank with his leash tied off on the bow of the boat. "I would have liked one of what he was drinking," he complained. "I was surprised to find out what good noses goats have, and this excellent nose tells me that the golden liquid in that gentleman's glass is not a whisky bought from the supermarket."

"You can have a brandy when we finish speaking to him," I whispered, tapping the backpack Granny had given me.

The boat owner emerged from the belly of his boat with a

full glass, and reclaimed his seat. He took a sip of whisky and looked at us in turn. "Okay," he said. "How can I help you?"

"I want you to try and remember what you saw that night on the towpath," I said. "What was the man you saw wearing? What was the logo you said you saw on his jacket?"

He looked up and to the right as he thought. "Like I told your policeman friend," he said after a moment. "I can't remember. He was quite far away, and he was only lit up by the moon for a second or two."

I accessed the spell and tasted copper. "Try again," I urged, my head gently throbbing. I clicked my fingers behind my back. "What was the logo or badge on the man's jacket?"

He sucked his bottom lip into his mouth. "I'm sorry," he said. "I really can't — "

He paused, and excitement flashed in his eyes. I concentrated harder. "Do you remember something?" I said.

"Wow," he murmured. "I do." He looked at the drink in his hand. "It must be this stuff," he marvelled. "It's as if I can zoom in on my memory. It's all becoming clearer!"

I took a deep breath. "What did you see?"

He scrunched his eyes up as he concentrated. "He was wearing a blazer or jacket," he said softly, his eyes still screwed tightly closed.

"What did he look like?" I whispered, as Willow and Susie both leaned forward, watching the man.

"I can't remember his features," he said. "I can just see the badge on his clothing, but it's not clear."

I sucked more air through my teeth, and the taste of copper filled my mouth and throat. "What was the badge on his blazer?" I said slowly.

He straightened in his seat. "Wait," he said. "I can see something. A crown and letters. There was a crown on the badge with letters below it!"

My head pulsed as I concentrated. "What were the letters?" I said.

He took a long breath. "The letter B," he said. He shook his head. "No, it was an R. Then an A, and the last letter was a C!" He opened his eyes. "RAC!"

"Can you see anything else?" I urged.

"No," he said, with a perplexed expression on his face, "but my head hurts. It must be this whisky. It' a special blend I got from a distillery in Scotland. It's very strong."

Boris leaned over the hull wall and put his mouth next to my ear. "Told you," he murmured.

Susie tapped me on my leg. "Look," she said, pointing at one of the old cars near to the canal bank. "Look at the badge on the front."

The old car's polished paintwork shone in the sun, and heat waves rose from the warm metal. The badge Susie was pointing at was attached to the grill at the front of the car, and I smiled as I studied it. RAC was written in large letters with a crown above them. I stopped the spell, and the man's face went blank. "It's gone!" he said. "I can't picture it anymore."

"I think you've given us everything we need," said Susie.

"RAC," said the man. "That's the Royal Automobile Club. Most of the owners of these cars will be members of the RAC," he said. "It's a huge club. Do you think the murderer is here? At the car show?"

"I don't know," I said. "But I need to let the police know what you told us."

He drained the last of his whisky and massaged his forehead. "Be sure to tell your police friend that I gave you the information. I was very disappointed that I couldn't help him when he came to my boat asking questions."

"I will," I promised. I took my phone from my pocket. 'I'll tell him right now."

Barney didn't answer his phone, so I sent him a text message instead, telling him where I was and what I knew. "I've told him the information came from you," I said to the man as I climbed off the *Flirting Kingfisher* and joined Boris on the bank. "He'll be very happy."

Susie and Willow followed me off the boat, and we left the man looking pleased with himself as he headed back into his boat to top his glass up again.

"What do we do now?" said Susie, snapping a photograph of a man dressed in old fashioned clothes changing a wheel on his car. He pumped the jack handle up and down, and cursed as it slipped and hit his finger.

Even I recognised the car as an old Rolls Royce, and joined Boris in admiring it. "There's not much we can do," I said. "If the murderer did come from the car show, he could be long gone, or he could be anybody here." I looked around the huge field and estimated there to be well over two hundred cars. "Lets just enjoy our day, and if we see anything suspicious, we can let the police know. It's up to them now. They're still looking for Granny's bad boy, so we can keep an eye out for him too, but right now I'm hungry. Who fancies a burger?"

CHAPTER FIFTEEN

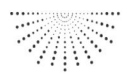

We chose a burger van with a relatively short queue of people waiting to be served. Two children fussed and patted Boris as we waited. He did his best to act like a goat in a petting zoo; nuzzling the children's hands and accepting the blades of grass they fed him, spitting them out in disgust when the children's parents had been served and the family had left with their meals.

"I will do most things expected of a goat," said Boris under his breath, ejecting the last of the grass from his mouth. "But I won't do that."

It was our turn to be served, and I left Boris standing next to Willow as I approached the food van. The white van was emblazoned with large red letters which read *Mr. Meaty*. The vendor was far from meaty though, and I doubted he ate any of the greasy products he sold. I ordered our food and passed it around as it was served. A hotdog with onions for Susie, a cheeseburger for Willow, and a chicken burger for me. Boris chose a triple burger with bacon and cheese with a side of fries, and I scowled as I refused Mr Meaty's offer of a spork.

We found a secluded area away from the crowds, where

Boris could speak freely, and sat beneath the shade of a horse chestnut tree, watching people go by and enjoying the scent of the wild flowers that flourished in the the hedgerow behind us.

Boris ate his meal with less decorum than I would have expected from such a cultured individual, but I supposed eating without cutlery or fingers *could* only finish in a mess of sauces and food scraps. No sooner had he licked the last of the mustard from the cardboard tray, he looked up at us. "I'd like a dram of brandy now please, young ladies. I need a boost of confidence for the show."

We'd checked what time the mixed livestock competition was starting, and had watched as people had begun arriving at the makeshift circle of hay bales, some leading pigs and sheep, and a few with goats, which Boris had eyed with envious suspicion. There was still half an hour to go until the show started, so I opened Granny's backpack and took out the bottle of brandy and the saucer she'd provided.

Willow and Susie styled Boris's hair with the brush Granny had provided as he slurped brandy from the saucer. When he'd had six saucerfuls, I wiped the remains of his meal from the hair around his mouth, and tightened the plait in his beard.

"How do I look?" he said, wobbling slightly as he walked back and forth in front of us. "I'd better look good. I'll blame you three if I don't win the competition. You see if I don't! I'll tell Gladys that you messed up my chances by feeding me that fast food rubbish!"

"You look drunk, Boris," said Susie, taking a photograph of him.

"And you sound drunk," said Willow. "That wasn't a very nice thing to say to us."

Boris looked at Willow and gave what I assumed he thought was a smile. In reality it was a grimace which showed off his yellowed grass worn teeth. "You know I love you, don't you? I love all of you. I bloody love — "

"That's enough, Boris," I snapped. "I'll put a spell on you if you don't stop swearing and start behaving. I'm sure I've seen a sleeping spell in Granny's book."

Boris tilted his head from side to side and mimicked me in a high-pitched voice. "*I'm sure I've seen a sleeping spell in Granny's book!*" he teased. He stamped his hoof. "Get over yourself, Penelope Pitstop. You couldn't *spell* spell! Let alone cast one on me!"

Willow burst into laughter, and Susie continued snapping photographs of the drunk goat.

"Granny said he gets problematic when he's had a few brandies," I whispered to Willow and Susie. "I didn't think she meant she meant this problematic though."

"What are you saying about Granny?" demanded Boris, lowering his head and waving his horns at me. "I'll ram you if you say one bad word about her. Just try me. Go on, I dare you. Say one bad thing about that wonderful woman and see what I do! Go on, I dare you. I double dare — "

"Right, that's it!" said Willow. "Now you're just being rude!" she scrunched her face up and clicked her fingers. Boris's shouting stopped immediately, but his mouth continued opening and closing as he tried to speak.

"Where did you learn that?" I said, impressed.

"You're not the only one who learnt a few spells from Granny's book," she said with a wink. "A spell of silence. I learnt it for the next time mum teased me about my..." she looked down at her chest, " ...boobs."

"Look at him," laughed Susie. "He's writing something in the dirt."

Boris dragged his hoof through the dry dirt at the base of the tree we sat beneath, and Willow stood up to read his message. "Give me my voice back," she read. "You can't silence me, you bunch of — " Willow wagged her finger at the goat. "No, Boris! that's rude! I won't read that, and you can't have your voice back yet, that spell lasts for three hours."

Boris rammed the tree in frustration, the thwack of horn on wood gaining the attention of a young couple walking past. Willow grabbed him by the horns. "Calm down, Boris," she demanded. "Or we won't enter you in the show. I'll put you in that field behind us with the cows, and pick you up when we're ready to go if you can't behave."

Boris struggled to release his horns from Willow's grasp, stamping his hooves into the ground.

"Right, I'm phoning Granny," I said, retrieving my phone from my pocket. "She'll sort him out."

Boris looked at me with alarm and stopped struggling, he scratched his hoof through the dirt again. "I'll be good," read Willow. "Don't phone Gladys. It's not me talking. It's the brandy. It's a weakness."

I slipped my phone back into my pocket and looked at Boris with my sternest of stares. "You're going to behave?" I asked.

He nodded and stumbled as Willow released his horns, almost falling over completely.

"Are you sober enough to enter the contest?" I said.

Boris nodded again, opening his mouth as he tried to speak. He nodded once more and I smiled at him. "We've all had too much to drink at one time or another, Boris. Maybe you should stay off the brandy though? It doesn't seem to agree with you."

Boris dropped his head in shame and staggered over to Susie, dropping to his knees beside her. He nudged her camera with his nose, and Susie laughed. "You want to see the pictures I took of you?"

Boris nodded, so Susie turned her camera on and showed

him the large screen on the rear. He shook his head shamefully as Susie flicked through the pictures of him hurling abuse at us.

"Don't worry," said Susie. "I'll delete them."

Willow glanced across the crowd of people to our front. "It looks like Boris's competition is starting soon. We'd better get over there and sign him up before it's too late," she said.

Susie held onto Boris's leash as we made our way through the cars and people, pausing now and again to admire any particularly beautiful vehicles. When we got to the circle of hay bales surrounded by onlookers, and full of people with their animals on ropes next to them, Susie went to the judges table to sign Boris up for the competition, and Willow and I took a seat on a scratchy bale of hay.

"Who's going to lead him round the ring for the judges?" said Willow.

I took a coin from my pocket. "Heads or tails?"

"Tails as always," said Willow. "If it's tails, I win, and you parade him around the ring."

I flicked the coin and caught it in one hand, slapping it onto the rear of the other. "Heads it is. Make sure he behaves."

CHAPTER SIXTEEN

Willow led Boris into the ring and stood between a woman with a very grumpy looking pig, and a man with a particularly woolly sheep — far too woolly for the warm weather in my opinion. The sheep looked happy enough though, and tried to sniff Boris's face, who reacted by turning his nose in the air and looking the other way.

Willow gave us a nervous smile as a man's voice burst out over the tannoy system. "Ladies and gentlemen! It's the show you've all been waiting for — the Wickford and Covenhill beautiful farmyard animal of the year competition!"

I glanced around at the crowd. There were no more than twenty spectators, and most of them looked like they were only there to use the hay bales as make shift seats to enjoy their beer on.

The man continued. "This year, I'm proud to announce the return of the 2014 winner — Harry the pygmy goat! Give him a big round of applause!"

A mild smattering of clapping caused a nervous Shetland

pony to buck his rear legs, and the owner, an equally nervous looking woman, calmed it with a hand on its head.

The tannoy crackled again. "Without further ado, let's get the show on the road! The rules are simple. The animals are to be walked around the ring three times, and after the last lap, each animal is to be halted in front of the judge's table so they can admire them and make their final decision! Competitors... begin your walk!"

A competition official, who stood in the middle of the circle of animals and owners, waved her arm and directed the competitors in a clockwise direction around the ring. Some animals tried to resist their owners, particularly the pig who led the way in front of Willow and Boris. He grunted and pulled at the leash around his neck, causing his owner to almost drag him along behind her. Boris displayed no such reluctance to show off. He lifted his head high, and still a little unsteady on his feet, began to trot. Ripples of applause spurred him on, and Willow glanced at us nervously as the goat bounced over the sun dried earth beside her.

"Unbelievable!" came the excited voice over the tannoy. "A goat doing dressage! Will you look at that ladies and gentlemen — that's the best trained goat I've ever seen!"

Boris lifted his legs higher with each stride he took, and danced along next to Willow, his snout pointing at the blue sky and his chest puffed out before him.

The owner of Harry the tiny pygmy goat, stared at Boris in disbelief, and tugged firmly on her animal's leash. The little goat didn't take favourably to her bullying tactics, and dug his hooves into the dirt, dropping his head in protest and refusing to move.

Boris continued showboating beside Willow, and as they passed the dissident pygmy goat, he sneaked a sly hoof beneath the little goat's rear leg and tripped him up. Harry sprawled on the floor bow legged and gave a little bleat of shock, which Boris ignored.

A man behind me laughed and broke into loud applause. "That goat's amazing!" he shouted.

Susie turned to look at him. "His name's Boris," she smiled. "And yes, he is rather amazing."

He clapped even louder. "Go, Boris!" he yelled. "You've got this!"

Willow and Boris had drawn the stunned attention of the other competitors, who stared in disbelief as Boris trotted around the ring, occasionally glancing at the three judges behind the trestle table and offering them hideously toothy smiles.

The nervous Shetland pony dragged its owner towards a spectator eating a hotdog, and an angry looking ram butted the pig in front of it. The official in the ring pointed at the space in the hay bales that acted as an entrance. "That ram is disqualified!" she shouted. "No aggressive animals allowed!"

"But that weird goat tripped the pygmy goat!" the owner protested. "Why is he still in the competition?"

"I didn't see any such incident," said the official, watching Boris as he drew more attention from the crowd. "Get that ram out of my ring!"

The ram's owner begrudgingly led his animal out of the ring, and Boris celebrated by wriggling his rear end at him.

The man behind me shouted again. "Go, Boris!"

Other spectators joined his supportive shouts, whistling, yelling and clapping. The sound of the crowd's excitement attracted more people to the ring, and as the crowd swelled in size, so did Boris's ego. Some of the other animal owners had given up trying to win, and stood still next to their animals as Boris raised himself onto his rear legs and stepped in time with Willow. He looked to the left and right and smiled at the people who cheered him on.

"Boris! Boris! Boris!" chanted the crowd.

Even the judges joined in, banging their fists on the wooden table in time with the chants of Boris's newfound groupies.

"This is going to make an amazing story," said Susie, snapping photographs of Boris and Willow. "He really knows how to work a crowd!"

"The brandy may have turned him into an angry drunk," I said, "but it's certainly given him confidence!"

The official in the ring waved her arm. "The third lap is complete. Bring your animals to the judges table one at a time!" she yelled over the noise of the ever growing crowd.

Willow and Boris joined the line of competitors as they took their turns standing in front of the judges. Boris gave gentle nods of his head to the spectators as they continued to shout their support for him. People erupted into louder cheers as Boris lowered himself to the knees of his front legs and took a low bow.

"I think it's safe to say he's won," said Susie as the judges called Willow forward, all three of them standing up and clapping as Boris stood before them.

Boris raised himself onto his rear legs, and I put my hand over my eyes, watching him through my fingers. Boris was taking it too far. "What's he doing?" I said.

The tannoy crackled. "I'm lost for words!" the excited man shouted. "A pirouetting goat!"

Boris span furiously on the spot, his front legs tight against his sides and his nose pointing high above him. Willow had dropped the leash, and it span in the air around Boris as he gained momentum.

"Look at him go..." murmured the man behind me, "...beautiful."

It was quite beautiful. The plait in Boris's beard whizzed through the air, and dust swirled at his feet as he span faster and faster. A blurry white whirling dervish, Boris transfixed the crowd as he wowed the judges and drew envious looks from the other animal owners.

"We have a winner!" shouted one of the judges — an elderly female with snow white permed hair. "Ladies and gentlemen, I give you the winner of the Wickford and Covenhill beautiful farmyard animal competition — Boris the dancing goat!"

The crowd cheered, and a lady beside me held her phone up as she filmed the show. "This is going on the internet," she said excitedly. "It'll go viral!"

Boris slowed his spinning and lowered himself onto all four legs. He wobbled a little as he tried to regain his balance, and fell in a heap at Willow's feet. He sprawled on his back with his legs straightened out above him like a dying fly, and his chest heaved as he panted.

"Get that goat some water!" shouted the official.

"He'd prefer brandy," said Susie, with a giggle.

A man ran into the ring with a bucket of water and splashed some on Boris's face. Willow helped Boris onto his front, and he slurped greedily at the water, occasionally lifting his head to nod his thanks at the chattering crowd.

"When he's recovered, bring him forward for his rosette and trophy!" shouted a male judge. "He truly deserves them, and so do you, young lady," she said to Willow. "That is the most well trained animal I have ever seen."

My phone vibrated in my pocket. I took it out and looked at the screen. It was Barney.

Susie was already on her way to join Willow and Boris in the ring, her camera ready to catch the prize giving action, so I backed through the crowd to a quieter area and answered Barney's call.

"Did you get my text?" I asked as I answered.

"Yes, and it ties in with with new information we've

acquired. We know who the mystery man is," said Barney. "We've got his name, his photo, everything. He's bad news, Penelope. I shouldn't be telling you this, but I wanted to warn you incase he comes near your boat again. He's our prime suspect now."

"Tell me what you know, Barney," I said, clutching the phone tight to my ear.

Barney continued, speaking urgently. "His name's Jason Danvers. We got in touch with all the tattoo parlours within a fifty mile radius, and one of them remembers him from our description. He did the phoenix tattoo on his arm." Barney paused for a moment. "Jason owns a casino, but get this — Sam owed him a lot of money, and Jason has got a police record for violence in the past. He's also got a warrant out for his arrest — he beat up somebody else who owed him cash and put him in hospital. I think it's safe to say that he's our guy."

"So where is he? Are you any closer to finding him?"

"We've got a photograph of him. It won't take long, but if you see him again, please stay away from him and phone me straight away. He's a dangerous man. I don't like the thought of you at the car show. We've found out he has a small collection of classic cars, and that matches neatly with the information the witness gave you about the badge on his blazer. We're checking with the Royal Automobile Club to see if he's a member." He paused momentarily. "How did you get that information, Penny? That witness was adamant he couldn't remember anything."

"He was drinking whisky again," I said, thinking quickly. "He thinks it jogged his memory."

"That makes sense," said Barney. "There's more too. The results have come back from the suspected murder weapon and Sam's post-mortem."

"And?" I urged.

"The coroner found a lot of alcohol in his stomach, and what he thinks are drugs. He's sent a sample off to the toxicology department to be analysed."

"Sam Hedgewick on drugs?" I said. "Really?"

"If he was mixing with violent gambling men, who knows what else he was into," said Barney. "Anyway, the windlass wasn't the murder weapon, but the wound on Sam's head was definitely made with a cylindrical metal object. There's small imprints on Sam's skull — the pathologist says they could have been made by some sort of hand grip on the weapon. We're thinking the handle of a car jack, based on the information my witness gave you, and the fact that Jason is involved with cars. It's an assumption, but the best one we have."

I remembered the man I'd watched changing the Rolls Royce wheel. A jack handle certainly had the potential to be used as a murder weapon.

Barney continued. "I'd prefer it if you took your boat back to the hotel," he said. "Just until we've caught him, and make sure you're not alone tonight. We've put road blocks around Covenhill and Wickford, so if he is still in the area, he might try and walk out following the canal towpath."

Cheering erupted from the circle of hay bales, and Willow, Susie, and Boris walked past a line of clapping people towards the entrance. Boris had a red rosette pinned to his collar, and Willow was carrying a small silver trophy.

"We're about ready to leave," I assured Barney. "We'll head back to the boat right away."

"Good. I've got to go, Penny," he said. "We're on our way to the car show. When we get there no-one will be able to leave until we've searched the place from top to bottom. So unless you want to stay there, I suggest you leave now."

I said goodbye to Barney and shouted to the others to join me. They made their way towards me with several people still following Boris, taking photographs and videos and patting him on his head and back. "Are you sure you won't let me interview you, Willow?' shouted a man with an open notebook. "It would make a great story!"

"No thanks," said Willow. "How I trained him is my secret, and it's staying that way."

"Plus, I'm writing the story," laughed Susie as she neared me. "There's going to be so many videos of Boris on the internet, somebody needs to lie about how he was trained to pirouette."

The distant sound of police sirens reminded me we had to hurry. I quickly explained everything that Barney had told me, and we rushed to the boat, climbing aboard and starting the engine as the police sirens grew louder and the first of the cars sped through the gate on the opposite side of the field in a cloud of dust.

Other boat owners stood on their roofs to see what was going on as I guided the *Water Witch* past them, and soon we were out of sight of the car show and heading towards the lock.

"My head hurts," complained Boris, "from alcohol, and from shame about the way I spoke to you lovely young ladies. I'm truly sorry, and highly ashamed of myself."

"Don't feel bad, Boris," I said, steering the boat around a gentle bend in the canal. "You've been through a lot recently. Anybody in your position would want to let their hair down a little."

Willow agreed. "Don't let what you said to us ruin the memories of your competition performance. You were outstanding, Boris."

"You were," nodded Susie. "I doubt any animal is ever going to beat that performance."

I laid my hand on the goat's back. "Why don't you have a lie down?" I said. "Go on, use my bed."

He looked up at me with thankful eyes. "I think I will," he said. "Thank you, Penelope. The offer of a bed to sleep in is one of the kindest gestures a person can make."

Boris climbed down the two steps from the deck into my bedroom, and jumped up onto the bed. He walked in three circles and plopped himself down, falling asleep almost immediately.

Willow followed him into the boat, placed his trophy next to him and draped a blanket over his back. Rosie mewled, and leapt up alongside him, sniffing him and curling up next to his chin, joining him in sleep.

WITH THE LOCK BEHIND US, and a crowd of ducks following the *Water Witch,* we negotiated the last of the bridges between us and my mooring, and Willow took over the steering duties for the last ten minutes of the journey. She expertly guided the boat closer to the bank on our side of the canal as another narrowboat approached from the opposite direction. We shouted hello to the frizzy haired man who drove the other boat as we glided past one another, and he gave us a friendly wave.

I left Willow in charge of the driving and stepped down into my bedroom to wake Boris. Susie had offered to drive him home, and I wanted him to look respectable for Granny. Not hungover and tired.

I shook the goat gently, and Rosie sniffed at my hand. "Boris," I said. "We're nearly home. Would you like a bowl of black coffee to help with the hangover?"

He opened his eyes and yawned. "That would be wonderful, Penelope," he said. "And one or two of those biscuits that Granny packed for me would compliment the coffee perfectly."

I helped him down off the bed, and Rosie leapt to the floor with him. "I'm going to take a stroll through the boat and onto the bow deck," Boris said. "The breeze on my face will make me feel better."

"Good idea," I said. "Can you manage the doors to the deck on your own?"

"I've learnt a lot of things since being in this body," said Boris, "and opening doors was amongst the first. This mouth is very versatile, you'd be surprised."

I followed Boris as far as the kitchen, and began making coffee as he continued along the boat and brushed past the purple curtain into the shop area.

Watching a moving vista through the windows from inside my own boat was not something I experienced often, and I leant on my kitchen counter as the kettle boiled, watching the steam from the brewery chimney rising above the elm trees.

Something nudged my leg, and I looked down to see Boris staring up at me, his eyes wide with shock. "Don't say anything," he implored in a panicked whisper. "Your safety is at risk if you utter a single word. Join the others on the back of the boat, and get your phone ready. You need to speak to the police."

CHAPTER SEVENTEEN

I stepped up onto the stern decking with Boris close behind me and Rosie in my arms, who I placed on the floor at my feet. The sound of the engine was loud enough to disguise any conversation, but I still warned Susie and Willow to keep quiet. "Something's wrong," I said, the breeze ruffling my hair. I turned to the goat. "What is it, Boris?"

"I want you to all remain calm," he said in a low voice. "I opened the bow doors and stepped outside for a moment or two, but the smell from the brewery made me rather queasy. When I went back inside the shop, I thought I'd have a look around." Boris craned his neck and looked down into the boat. "Penelope, there's a man crouching behind the counter in your shop. I'm no detective, but from the description you've given us, I think it's safe to say he's the murder suspect."

Willow gasped. "But he's seen you, Boris, and he knows you've seen him. He'll kill us! We need to jump overboard and escape!"

"Calm down, Willow!" demanded Boris. "I'm a goat,

remember. He looked a little shocked to see me, but I kept my cool and sniffed around his feet. I even licked his hand and nibbled some of those herbs in the box behind the counter. Very tasty they were too. He shooed me away and pushed himself further into the corner. We'll be fine if we carry on as we are."

I'd already dialled Barney's number, and he answered quickly. "Barney," I said, panic bulging in my throat. "The man you're looking for is on my boat. He doesn't know that we know he's onboard, but he's hiding in my shop. Jason Danvers is in my shop!"

Barney sounded more nervous than I felt. "Where are you?" he snapped, his voice cracking.

"A few minutes from my mooring," I said. "What do we do?"

"Carry on as if nothing's wrong," instructed Barney. "Moor up when you get back to the hotel, and get off the boat. We'll be there as quickly as we can. There's no police in Wickford at the moment, we're all here at the car show. It'll take us a while to get to you."

"Hurry, Barney," I said.

"I will, I promise." He paused for second or two. "Please don't do anything stupid, Penny. I'd hate for anything to happen to you."

"I won't," I said. "We'll get as far away from the boat as possible as soon as we moor up."

"Penny?" shouted Barney. "Are you there? I'm losing — "

I put my phone in my pocket. "He's lost his signal," I said. "But they're on their way. We've just got to carry on as if nothing's wrong. As long as we stay at the back of the boat until we've moored up, we should be okay, I doubt he'll do anything if he doesn't know we're aware he's onboard."

Willow closed and locked the stern doors. "That's a little safer," she said.

I pushed the boat's power lever forward and the engine throbbed, the propeller spewing water behind us. I had bigger things to worry about than a canal speed limit, and I gave the engine more revs than I'd ever given it before.

We stood together nervously, and Willow placed her hand next to mine on the steering tiller. "I'm scared," she admitted.

"It'll be over soon," I said. "Look, the entrance to my mooring is just around the next bend."

We kept quiet as I negotiated the final stretch of canal, and Boris kept his nose pressed against the pane of glass in the doors, looking out for movement inside the boat.

I slowed the boat as we approached the gap in the trees, and steered the bow slowly into the entrance, putting the gearbox in reverse to slow our momentum as we made contact with the bank. I turned the engine off and whispered to the others. "Get off the boat," I said. 'You tie the stern rope, Willow, and I'll do the bow."

The four of us climbed off the boat, Boris making a graceful leap ashore that even under the dangerous circumstances impressed me. Rosie decided the roof was a better option for her, and leapt onto it, licking her paw and watching us curiously.

Willow tied off the stern rope, and I walked to the front of the boat as casually as I could, incase Jason was watching me through a window. I had considered leaving the bow rope untied, but narrowboats had a habit of breaking away from their moorings if both ropes weren't securing them to the bank. Even though my boat couldn't have floated onto the main body of the canal, it would have made the police's job harder when they finally arrived.

A loud yapping sound echoed around the clearing, and Boris looked up in shock as Mabel sprinted over the grass towards him. "What on earth?" he said, backing away from the blur of white that approached him.

"It's okay," said Willow, 'it's only Mabel."

"Gladys told me about her," said Boris, "but seeing her in real life is vastly different than how I imagined."

Mabel ran at Boris, but Boris lowered his head and threatened her with his horns. "I've got no time for your nonsense, goose dog," he shouted. "We need to make good our escape!"

Mabel backed down as Boris charged her, and ran towards the front of the boat in panic, whining, yapping, and flapping her wings.

"No, Mabel!" I shouted, as the scared bird leapt onto the bow deck and scurried into the shop through the doors that Boris had left open.

"Get off me!" came a man's voice. "Get off!"

The boat rocked a little, and Mabel's vicious growls increased in volume.

"Get off me or I'll hurt you!"

"What do we do?" said Susie. "We can't rescue Mabel, the man in the boat is a murderer!"

Boris stamped his hooves. "Nobody's harming a fellow magical animal on my watch!" he yelled. Grass and mud flew from beneath his hooves as he sped towards the front of the boat. He leapt onto the bow deck, slipping as he attempted to take the tight turn through the open doors, and threw himself down the steps.

"Unhand that goose, you cad!" he shouted as he disappeared from view, the clacking of his hooves on wood echoing through the clearing.

"We have to help!" I shouted, sprinting alongside the boat and clambering aboard.

The man shouted again, this time with fear apparent in his voice. "Help! What are you? What are you? No! Please don't bite me there!"

He screamed, and the pain in his voice made me wince. I

jumped down the steps into the boat with Willow and Susie close behind me, and took stock of what was happening.

Jason's feet kicked and scraped along the floor as Boris dragged him from behind the small plywood counter, his teeth buried deep in the murder suspect's crotch, and Mabel sitting on his back, flapping her wings and growling. Downy feathers fluttered in the air around the goose, and she jabbed her beak in Jason's direction as Boris pulled him from his hiding place.

Stock fell from my shelves as the man struggled, and his screams of pain hurt my ears in the confined space.

"Boris! Leave him!" I shouted. I was sure I'd read that a man could die from a severe injury in the area that Boris was attacking. "You'll kill him!"

Boris relented a little, visibly relaxing his grip on the man's jeans.

"Will you stay where you are until the police get here if the goat let's go?" I said.

Willow grabbed an athame from a shelf and pointed it at the man. "I'll stab you if you try anything," she threatened.

The ritual witchcraft knife glinted in the dim light from the shelf covered windows and the doorway behind me, and Jason nodded frantically. "Yes!" he squealed, his voice far too high for such a muscle bound badboy. "Call him off!"

"Let him go, Boris," I ordered, "let's see what he's got to say for himself, starting with why he's on my boat."

Boris released the man and took a half step backwards. "I've got my eye on you," he warned. "If you make any funny moves I'll bite you so hard you'll be able to shatter glass with your voice."

"The goat's talking," the man said in horror. "The goat's talking to me."

"Nonsense," I said, winking at Boris, who acknowledged the message with a nod of his head. "You're hallucinating because of the pain you're in. Goat's can't talk, but you can, and you're going to answer some questions." The man nodded again, his thick tattooed arms between his thighs, his hands clutching his manhood. I continued. "What are you doing on my boat, and why did you murder Sam Hedgewick?"

He groaned as he held his crotch. "I'm on your boat because I heard the police arriving at the show. I've been living in a tent at the car show since the police started looking for me. Look at the state of me — I haven't had a change of clothes in days."

He certainly looked disheveled, and it explained why he'd looked so run down when I'd encountered him at the top of the footpath. His jeans were muddy, and his crumpled t-shirt hung limply from his large frame.

"Why my boat?" I said. "And how did you break in? The doors were locked."

He scrambled a few inches away from Boris. "It was the only boat that was hidden. It was at the end of the row and nobody could see me getting onto it. You should remember to lock the shutters on the side of the boat as well as the doors."

The last time I'd opened the shutters was during the barbecue. I made a mental note to check they were locked every time I left the boat.

Sirens wailed in the distance, and Boris snorted. Mabel flapped her wings and growled, and Jason squeezed his thighs together protectively.

"The goat talks and the goose is a dog," Jason mumbled. "What's going on here?"

"I'm asking the questions," I said. "Why did you kill Sam? The police know you did it. You'd better get used to small spaces like this, you'll be spending a long time in one."

Jason made a strangled sound in his throat. "I didn't kill Sam," he sobbed. "I wouldn't have harmed a hair on his head."

"You killed him because he owed you money," said Susie. "A gambling debt. We know all about you. One of our friends is a policeman, and he told us you've got a violent history and a warrant out for your arrest."

"I've done things I'm ashamed of," said Jason. "But I would never have hurt Sam. He helped me change who I was. We were moving abroad together so we could both have a new start. I loved Sam, I loved him so much."

He broke down into loud body shaking sobs, and I used a gentler voice as I spoke. "So you're the woman he was leaving his wife for, although obviously you're not a woman."

The police sirens got louder and then stopped. They'd arrived. It would take them less than a minute to run to my boat.

"She'd been cheating on him for years," Jason said, tears streaming down his cheeks. "When Sam couldn't pay his debt to me, I took pity on him and we became close. Sam wanted to sell everything he owned so we could buy a vineyard in Spain." His sobs got louder. "We were going to make wine! Sam loved Tempranillo!"

"Why did you stay in the area when you knew the police were after you?" I asked. "You could have been miles away by now."

He fixed me with an angry stare. "I wanted to stay around until the police found out who killed Sam. Whoever did it will wish they'd never been born when I get my hands on them."

I considered getting Granny's spell book and quickly learning a truthfulness spell, but it wasn't needed. I was convinced that Jason was telling the truth.

I looked at the door as a voice outside shouted my name. It was Barney. "Penny! Penny! Where are you?" he yelled.

"We're in here!" shouted Susie, poking her head through the doorway. "We're okay!"

Boris," I said, "take Mabel into my bedroom. I don't want her attacking anyone else."

Boris pushed through the purple room dividing curtain, and Mabel happily rode him, looking more content than she had for a long time. It seemed she'd found a new friend.

Heavy boots thudded on the boat's decking, and Barney appeared in the doorway with his nightstick in his hand. "You, stay still!" he shouted at Jason. Bone cracked on wood as he hit his head on the doorway, and he cursed as he came to my side. "Are you okay? Penny," he asked, grabbing me in a firm hug.

I waited until he'd released me, and gave him a reassuring smile. "I'm okay," I said. "We all are."

Sergeant Cooper stepped down into the shop and tripped on the bottom step. He hit the floor with a heavy thump and groaned.

"Are you hurt, sarge?" said Barney, going to his aid.

"I'm fine, Dobkins," he barked, getting to his knees. "Arrest that man!"

Barney handcuffed Jason, who was still crying, and read him his rights.

"I don't think he did it," I said.

Willow agreed. "I don't either."

Sergeant Cooper stood up. "And who do you two think you are, bloody Cagney and Lacey? Leave the police work to us, and you carry on selling this cheap tat." He kicked a wand and sent it skidding beneath a shelf unit.

Barney span on the spot, his face crimson with rage. "Don't you speak to them like that!" he yelled. "Say what you want to me, but if you ever speak to Penelope or her sister like that again, I'll lose my job because of what I'll do!"

I'd never seen Barney so angry, and pride swelled in my chest.

Sergeant Cooper opened his mouth to say something, but thought better of it. He turned away from us and began making his way up the steps. He paused and glanced over his shoulder. "I'm sorry," he said, looking at me and Willow. "That was highly unprofessional of me. It's been a busy day, and I've been under a lot of pressure trying to catch that man. PC Dobkins, make sure your friends are okay and then bring the suspect out."

Barney calmed down as quickly as he'd exploded. "I will, Sarge," he said, "and I'm sorry too. It's been a stressful day for us all."

Sergeant Cooper shook his head. "Sometimes people like me need reminding of a few things. I respect you for your honesty, Barney."

"He's never called me by my first name before," said Barney, as Sergeant Cooper stepped off the boat.

The handcuffs jangled as Jason got to his knees. "There was a talking goat," he said. "He bit me in the family jewels."

Barney clicked the button on his radio. "Can we get a drug testing kit ready for the prisoner, please?" he said.

"Affirmative," came the crackling reply of a woman.

Barney placed an arm under Jason's armpit and helped him to his feet. "Come on, let's get you down the station," he said. "You've got a lot to answer for."

"Barney," I said in a low voice. "I really don't think he did it."

"We'll find out soon enough, Penny," Barney said, guiding Jason to the steps. "He'll be questioned as soon as I get him back to the nick."

Susie, Willow, and I, followed Barney and Jason up the steps, and stood on the decking watching as the prisoner was escorted up the footpath with a policeman on either side of him.

"If he didn't do it," Susie said. "There's still a murderer on the loose."

"The police will find out soon enough," said Willow. "Who knows — maybe Jason's just a really good liar — there's still a chance he did it."

Boris's voice came from inside the boat. "Penelope," he said. "I'm looking at all the things that have been knocked off your shop shelves in the struggle, and there's a few items I'd like to buy for Gladys."

"Of course," I said, stepping down into the shop and joining Boris in the mess of stock that littered the floor. "Granny would appreciate a present. No charge though, Boris. Just take what you like."

"I'll hear no such thing!" protested Boris. "You don't run a business by giving things away. Of course, one of you will have to loan me some money until Gladys can go to a ATM machine for me."

WHEN THE SHOP had been tidied, and any broken stock reluctantly thrown in the bin, Susie fulfilled her promise of driving Boris back to Granny's and led him up the footpath to the car park.

He'd have quite a story to tell Granny when he got home, and in the backpack he'd put the gifts he'd chosen for her — a witch themed mug, a bumper sticker for her car, and a small metal tin that Boris said would be ideal for the mints Granny enjoyed sucking on.

Mabel watched on forlornly as her new friend left with Susie, and Rosie stood a few feet behind her, beginning to gain confidence now she'd seen that Boris trusted the goose.

Willow and I went inside and opened a bottle of wine. We deserved a drink, and Willow balanced her half full glass on her knee as she phoned Mum to explain what had happened, and to tell her she'd be staying on my boat again for the night.

"Mum wants us to have breakfast with her tomorrow," said Willow as she finished the call. She took a long sip of wine and gazed out of the window at the water and trees. "She also suggested I move onto your boat as I seem to be here more than at home." She took another sip of wine and smiled at me. "That's not such a bad idea, is it?"

CHAPTER EIGHTEEN

A pair of hands carrying a tray laden with croissants, muffins, and crumpets appeared through the shimmering sheet of blue that filled the doorway. The rest of Mum emerged through the light, and the spell fizzled out, returning the doorway to its intended function — an entrance to the lounge, and not a portal to a magical realm.

It was Mum's second trip to the haven in the space of ten minutes, and the kitchen table was laden with food prepared by Aunt Eva. "She's got the cooking bug again," explained Mum. "But this feast is to congratulate you for catching a murderer. She's very proud, she says bravery runs in our family."

"We didn't really catch him," I said. "He caught himself by stowing aboard my boat, and as we've already told you, we don't think he's guilty."

"That's not what it says in the newspaper," said Mum, laying the tray on the table. "Unless you're calling your friend a liar. It was Susie that wrote the article, and she was on the boat with you. I think she knows what happened."

"She's just reporting what the police are saying," Willow

said, her hand hovering over a plate laden with crumpets. "She has to. It's her job."

"Where is she anyway?" said Mum, sitting down. "Eva made this breakfast for her too."

"The police are holding a full press conference," I said. "Barney's making sure she gets a front row seat."

"I hope the police commend you all on your courage," said Mum. "Although the whole incident yesterday has just made me all the more nervous about you living on that boat, Penelope. I mean, if a murderer can just sneak aboard, then you're hardly safe, are you?"

"I'd rather forget about the whole thing for now, and eat," said Willow, saving me from another of Mum's lectures, although I had to agree with her about my safety. It had been quite unnerving to find out how simple it had been for someone to break into my home and business.

"Eat what you can," said Mum. "I'll put the rest in Tupperware boxes and take some to your grandmother now I've got my car back. I need an excuse to go and visit her. She's still ignoring my phone calls, and I caught her watching me through her binoculars this morning. Nosy old thing that she is."

"You caught her watching you through her binoculars, how exactly?" said Willow, buttering a hot crumpet. She reached for the pot of plum jam. "While you were spying on her through your telescope by any chance?"

"It's my job to keep an eye on her!" snapped Mum. "She's elderly, and she has witch dementia. It's a daughter's duty to look after her mother. Especially in times of illness." She pressed two slices of freshly baked buttered bread together, sandwiching three slices of crispy bacon between them. "She has no need to be watching me, though! She should respect my privacy."

I waved my hand over the muffin on my plate. "There's a

spell on this muffin," I said, impressed with how much progress I'd made with my magic over the previous few days. "But it's only one to help it rise in the oven. It's safe for me to eat."

Mum's eyes showed she was equally impressed. "Since when have you been able to do that, Penelope?" she said, staring at me. "The magic in that blueberry muffin is ancient haven magic. It should be well beyond your capability to detect it."

"Let's just say that Willow and I have been practising like you wanted us to," I said. "The days of you and Aunt Eva magically conspiring to stop me living on my boat are over."

Mum feigned shock, but not very well. "I'm glad that you've both been practicing," she said, "it makes my heart happy to hear that, but I'm hurt that you think I've been conspiring against you, Penelope. Those other spells were Eva's doing, not mine. To imagine that you think that poorly of me. Oh my!"

I bit into my muffin. "Okay, Mum. It wasn't you. I get it. I'll never mention it again."

Mum nodded. "Good. That's the ticket! Anyway, if anyone's conspiring, it's that grandmother of yours. I saw her driving that goat somewhere yesterday morning. She even put it in the front seat with a seat belt on!"

"Safety first," I said.

"Boris is a goat, Penelope! Goats shouldn't want to get into a car! Then I saw her coming home a couple of hours later without him, but she had shopping bags from that computer shop in Covenhill." Mum licked some bacon grease from her top lip and continued. "You tell me why she needs a computer! She specifically told me that computers were a way for the government to control us. That's why I've never bought one, and I really wanted one too."

"What do you want a computer for, Mum?" said Willow.

"One of the ladies at the Wickford rose and geranium fancier's club mentioned she can get all the music she wants on hers," Mum said. "When your dad left me, he took all my Lionel Richie records with him." Mum gazed upwards, with a twinkle in her eye. "I was so in love with that man at one time. He was my everything."

"Don't waste your emotions on that waste of skin," I spat. "Dad cheated on you and spent all your money. He spent no time with me and Willow, and he never looked for a job! You should be happy he left with that woman, Mum!"

"Not him, silly!" said Mum. "Good riddance to him! That's why you two carry my maiden name along with me. I want no memory of him at all. No, I was in love with Lionel Richie. Those eyes, that voice. The way he caressed his microphone. Of course, he's far too old for me now, but when I was a teenager he was my older man fantasy. I miss listening to him. That's why I wanted a computer."

I placed my hand on Mum's. "Get one then, I'll help you find all the music you want."

"Maybe in the future" she said. She slid her hand away from mine and picked up a crumpet. "Come on, let's finish breakfast, then the three of us are going to visit my mother. I want to know what she's up to."

I glanced at Willow, who shrugged her reply. She was right, we couldn't help Granny keep her secret forever, Mum was eventually going to find out what she'd done to Boris, however hard we tried to keep it from her.

I excused myself from the table and went upstairs, pulling my phone from my pocket. I could at least give Granny a heads up that Mum was calling to see her.

Granny didn't answer after thirty seconds, so I went into Mum's pristinely tidy bedroom. The colourful quilt she'd taken almost a year to make by hand was laid neatly on her bed, and photographs of family members decorated the large oak chest of drawers, with old pictures of me and Willow taking prime position at the front. I stood by the large window and gazed out over the woods and Wickford beyond them. The canal twinkled in the distance, and I could just make out the roof of the Poacher's Pocket hotel. Mum's huge telescope was pointing directly at Granny's cottage which was perched on the peak of the hill on the opposite side of the valley, and I closed my left eye as I looked through the viewfinder with my right.

I made sense of what I was seeing through the telescope, and grabbed my phone from my pocket. I rang Granny again, silently urging her to answer. Granny continued what she was doing in the garden, oblivious to her land line ringing inside her cottage. I tried once more and gave up with a sigh.

Oh well, I'd done my best. It would be up to Granny to explain to Mum why she was sharing cocktails in her garden, with a goat, at ten o'clock in the morning.

CHAPTER NINETEEN

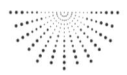

Granny obviously hadn't heard the car pulling up outside her home. Music floated over the roof of her cottage, and I winced when I heard the laughing voice of Boris.

"What in the name of all that is moral!" gasped Mum, slamming her car door shut and shoving the three Tupperware boxes at my chest. "Is she entertaining a man in her garden?"

Mum didn't wait for an answer from either me or Willow. She stomped alongside Granny's cottage, following the path past the lean-to which hid another of Granny's secrets, heading determinedly towards the back garden. Her hips swayed and her hair bounced, and Willow and I followed in her wake, casting nervous glances at each other, both resolved to the fact there was nothing we could do to keep Granny's secret any longer.

Mum rounded the corner of the cottage a few metres ahead of us, and her shriek made Willow jump.

I turned the corner just in time to see Mum holding a hand to her chest and staggering backwards, finding support

UNDER LOCK AND KEY

from the trunk of a young peach tree which groaned under her weight. "What on earth?" she gasped. "What in the name of the goddess is going on?" She clutched my arm tight as I dropped the boxes and helped her stand up straight. "Tell me I haven't gone mad, Penelope," she mumbled. "Tell me that Boris is smoking a cigar and drinking what looks like a mojito. Tell me I'm not hallucinating."

Mum hadn't gone mad, and neither Granny or Boris had spotted us, or heard Mum's shriek. They continued what they were doing, oblivious to their audience. Granny was sitting in a deck chair at the bottom of the garden with a white sun hat on, clutching a glass in her lap. At her feet was a large glass jug, the mint leaves spilling from the top giving away the nature of the cocktail it contained.

Mum's gaze of horror was firmly fixed on Boris though. He lay on a tartan picnic rug with a glass beside him, from which protruded one of the curly straws Granny had bought for me and Willow when we were younger. To the front of him was my grandfather's vice which he'd used to tie his fishing flies. In place of a fishing lure, though, was a large cigar, on which Boris took a long drag and blew a cloud of smoke into the air, creating three perfect rings which Granny broke apart with a finger.

Granny laughed, her voice barely audible over the music which pumped from the radio beside her seat. The chickens in the nearby coop stared on in fascination, with one of the more intelligent ones using the diversion to peck at the pieces of corn that Granny scattered each morning. I hoped it was the chicken who'd squeezed out an ostrich egg. She deserved extra rations.

Mum took a deep breath. "Do you two girls know anything about this... this... travesty of normality?"

I looked at my feet, and Willow squeezed her thumb between the fingers of her other hand.

"I'll take that as a yes then," glowered Mum.

Willow began to speak. "It was an accident — "

"I want to hear it from my mother's mouth," said Mum, regaining her composure, and beginning the walk over the lawn towards the partying couple.

Granny looked up and spat liquid from her mouth. She fumbled with the radio, and the music stopped. A lone crow squawked in a nearby tree, and the chickens seemed to move forward a fraction.

"Don't speak, Boris," hissed Granny, in a voice that everybody in the garden heard. "Act dumb! I've got this."

Boris blew smoke from his nostrils and stared in terror at the approaching behemoth that was my angry mother. He coughed and spluttered and looked up at Mum as she came to a halt directly before him. "Maaaa? Baaaa?" he said.

Mum studied the goat for a second or two before turning her gaze on Granny, who sucked at her straw and smiled. "Good morning, dear. Fancy a cocktail?"

With her hands on her hips, Mum bent at the waist and looked Granny directly in the eyes. "It's not even midday, Mother. Now, I'm giving you two choices. You either tell me exactly what's going on here, or I go straight to the haven and tell everybody who respects you that you're drinking alcohol before noon with a goat which you've quite obviously enchanted."

Granny sighed. "The game's up, Boris. It was good while it lasted. Take Penny and Willow indoors and show them your study. I'll talk to Maggie."

"Study?" spluttered Mum. "Your goat's got a study!"

Boris got to his feet and cleared his throat. "Allow me to introduce myself, dear lady. I'm — "

Mum's scowl scared even the chickens, and Boris took a stumbling step backwards. "I'll show the young ladies my study," he said in a low voice, with his head bowed.

UNDER LOCK AND KEY

Willow and I followed Boris across the lawn and picked up the Tupperware boxes. Mum waited until we'd opened the back door to the cottage before unloading her verbal barrage on Granny.

"Is that my father's fly tying vice with a cigar in it?" shouted Mum.

"Boris likes to smoke," said Granny. "We tried taping a cigar to his hoof, but it didn't work out so well. He fell asleep after a few drinks with the cigar still lit. It's a good job the fire brigade gave out those free smoke alarms or Boris would have had more than a few singed hairs."

Boris held up his leg and showed us the browned hairs above his hoof.

"I am about to explode!" yelled Mum.

Boris shook his head. "Poor, poor Gladys," he said. "All she's tried to do is be good to me."

I laughed. "Don't worry about her," I said. "She'll twist Mum around her little finger within ten minutes." If Granny remembered to tell Mum she'd been helping us with our magic, as Willow had suggested when we'd blackmailed her for the spell book, she'd calm Mum down within five minutes. I smiled at Boris. "Come on, let's see this study of yours."

Boris led us through the cottage, and pushed open the door to Granny's back room with his nose. Willow looked at me, and I raised my eyebrows. Neither of us had been in the back room for months, and as far as we knew, neither had anyone else.

Granny's back room overlooked the rear garden, and was her home's showpiece. It was the room reserved for revered guests, or people she wanted to impress. It was an important person who was invited into the back room of Granny's cottage. It was an exceptionally lucky individual who was granted permission to convert Granny's back room into a study — especially a study that was a cross between a barn and the office of a nineteen seventies TV private eye.

An ashtray filled with cigar butts, placed next to the laptop computer on a low coffee table, masked the usual scent of expensive beeswax and furniture polish, and most of the deep pile carpet was embedded with white goat hair. A dog cushion with a goat shaped dip in it was placed in front of the table, and drinking glasses with straws in them dotted every available surface, some with an inch of amber liquid still in the base.

Willow picked one up and held it up to the light. "This is Granny's best cut crystal," she said.

"You don't put good brandy in cheap glasses, Willow," Boris said, curling up on the cushion in front of the table. "It ruins the experience. Come here, let me show you my blog."

Boris spoke into the microphone next to the computer. "Wake up," he commanded. The computer flashed to life, and a smiling picture of Boris greeted us on the screen. "Granny took the photo," he said. "She really caught my good side. That's the picture I'm using for my blog!"

"You've got to be kidding!' I said. "You can't write a blog as a goat, Boris!"

"Don't worry, Penelope," said Boris. "I shall be pretending I'm a human writing as a goat. There's all sorts of things on the internet these days. People will be none the wiser. They'll think I'm a mad man."

Laughter from the garden caught my attention, and I looked through the window to see Mum and Granny walking towards the cottage, both of them smiling. "Told you, Boris," I said. "Granny's calmed Mum down already."

Mum walked into the study ahead of Granny and stared at the mess. She smiled at Boris, ignoring the chaos. "I'm Maggie. It's nice to meet you, Boris"

Boris stood up and bowed his head. "I'm pleased to make

your acquaintance," he said. "Gladys has told me a lot about you."

Granny stepped forward and winked at me. "I've told your mother how I've been helping you girls with your magic," she said. "I've always felt it was my duty to aid you both in furthering your skills, and as your grandmother and mentor, I'm very proud of you both. Giving you that book that meant so much to me, and showing you how to use it, was more than just an extremely generous gesture on my behalf, it was my way of letting you both know how much I love you."

Granny was really over egging the pudding, but Mum was lapping it up. "You've done a wonderful job," she said, touching Granny's arm. "Penelope even detected one of Eva's spells in a blueberry muffin this morning." She gazed at me and Willow adoringly. "These girls will get into the haven sooner than I ever expected if they carry on the way they are."

'How wonderful," said Boris. "It's lovely to see a family so close. It could bring a goat to tears."

I rolled my eyes at Willow, and she giggled.

"Boris," said Mum. "Would you mind if Gladys took me upstairs and showed me Charleston?"

"Not at all," said Boris, "but you must promise not to try and reverse Gladys's spell. I'm quite happy as I am. Happier than I've ever been in fact."

Mum crouched in front of Boris. "I promise," she said, holding the back of her hand an inch from Boris's nostrils.

"He's not a dog, Mum," I said. "He doesn't need to smell your hand!"

"I thought it would gain his trust," said Mum. "I'm sorry if I offended you, Boris. It's going to take some time to get used to you."

"No apology required," said Boris. "I'm perfectly aware of how strange this situation is."

My phone buzzed in my pocket. It was a text from Susie.

The results from toxicology have come back. The police said it isn't drugs in Sam's stomach. It's oriental pine pollen.

I showed Willow the text, and her eyes widened. She'd come to the same conclusion as me.

I sent Susie a reply.

Meet us at the nursing home.

"Mum," I said. "Can I borrow your car?"

"Take mine, girls," said Granny. "I can't drive today. I don't know how many mojitos I've had, but I feel quite giddy. Are you going anywhere nice?"

"To see a woman about a potion," I said.

CHAPTER TWENTY

"You don't think the potion had anything to do with Sam's death do you?" asked Willow as we climbed the steps to the nursing home entrance.

"Of course not," Susie said, "that's why I didn't say anything to the police. They think the pollen's from a food supplement. I thought we'd give Veronica a chance to explain why she'd given Sam a libido boosting potion before the police get involved. The least we can do is prepare her for any embarrassment coming her way."

I laughed. "Veronica and Sam? I doubt it. If you believe Jason Danvers, Sam was into men these days anyway."

"He was married to a woman," said Susie. "He obviously liked both sexes."

"Veronica's old enough to be his mother," I said, opening the door and stepping inside the home. "And she's with Ron. I very much doubt that potion was in Sam's stomach to help his little guardsman stand to attention."

The three of us laughed as we approached the reception desk, but straightened our faces as an angry man stormed from a corridor to our right. "I don't know why I pay so much to live here," he shouted, "if you can't even replace gym equipment when it goes missing!"

"We've ordered a whole new set of weights, Mr Richards," said the petite nurse rushing after him. "It's only one little bar that's been misplaced. There's plenty of other equipment you can use."

"I need both dumbbells," protested the man. "Or I'll have one arm bigger than the other."

"Can't you do one arm at a time?" asked the flustered nurse.

The man turned on the spot. "I pay more money a month to live here than you *earn* in a month, young lady. I shouldn't have to put up with this nonsense. Just make sure those weights get delivered soon!"

The nurse sighed as Mr Richards stomped off, his lycra clad belly bouncing as he flounced around the corner. "I'm sorry you had to witness that," she said. "Mr Richards has got a short fuse. How can I help you?"

"We're here to visit Veronica Potter," I said.

She smiled. "Oh good, the poor woman needs cheering up."

"Is she okay?" asked Willow.

The nurse winked. "Man trouble," she giggled. "Do you three know Veronica well?"

"Well enough," I smiled.

"So you know about her relationship with Ronald?"

Willow nodded. "Oh yes, we know *all* about that."

"It seems they're having a few problems," said the nurse. "They've been arguing a lot and Veronica's quite upset. She's probably in her room, go on through, she'll be happy to see you." She walked back the way she'd come, muttering to herself about selfish old rich people.

Willow, susie, and I made our way through the lounge and along the corridor which led to Veronica's room. Her door was closed, and the sound of loud sobbing came from the other side. Willow knocked, and Veronica stopped crying and cleared her throat. "Come in!" she called.

Willow opened the door and the three of us entered together. Veronica was on her bed with an open book on her chest and scrunched up tissues surrounding her. Her face was devoid of make-up and she looked twenty years older. "Oh, it's you three," she said. "I thought it might be nurse with a sedative."

"Are you alright, Veronica?" I said, sitting on the bed and taking her trembling hand in mine. "What's happened?"

"Oh, Penelope," she said. "It was awful. Ron lost his temper because I went for a walk around the grounds with Wally. Wally picked a flower and Ron saw him giving it to me. He called me terrible names and said I was a cheat."

Willow sat on the other side of the bed, and Susie perched near Veronica's feet.

"That's horrible," said Willow. "I hope you gave as good as you got."

"I tried," sobbed Veronica, "but he teased me about my make-up. He said I looked like a painted sex clown!" She took a fresh tissue from the box beside her and blew her nose. "It's over now. I'm a free woman again." She managed a small smile. "Don't you girls worry about me. It won't take me long to find a new breakfast companion. I'll soon bounce back with lovely young ladies like you visiting me."

"What a nasty man," I said. "I've got a good mind to go and tell him what I think of him."

Veronica squeezed my hand. "He's in no mood for visitors, dear. He's hardly left his room in a week. As far as I'm concerned he can rot in there!" Veronica released my hand and dragged herself into a seated position. "Enough about my woes," she said. "You know what they say, misery loves company."

I smiled at her. "That's exactly what they say."

Veronica managed another smile. "So, girls, to what do I owe the pleasure of this visit? No one knew about mine and Ron's problems outside of the home, so you didn't come here to console me."

I glanced at Susie and Willow. Susie looked away, and Willow gave me a gentle nod of encouragement.

"It's a sensitive matter, Veronica," I said. "It's about that potion I made for you."

Veronica's face whitened. "What about it?" she said, clutching a tissue to her chin.

"Is it possible that Sam Hedgewick could have drank any of it, Veronica?" I asked with care.

Veronica's body shook, and she broke into gasping sobs that rocked the bed. "I knew it would come back to haunt me," she wailed. "I don't know why I thought I could get away with it! I should have told the police when I had the chance. They were sure to find out with all their fancy modern equipment. It's not like in the old days! I don't know why I thought I'd get away with it! I'm in a lot of trouble, aren't I?"

Willow stared at Veronica slack jawed, and Susie sat upright.

"What are you saying, Veronica?" I said. "Did you hurt Sam?"

Veronica gasped. "No! Of course not, but I'm guilty as charged of administering a substance to an unwitting recipient! I only wanted to stop him driving under the influence of alcohol! Are the police coming for me? Will I go to jail? I don't think I could take jail. Your grandmother only spent three hours in a police cell, and it broke her, Penelope."

I rolled my eyes at Willow. The only thing broken by Granny's stay in a cell was the police station kettle, and the teabag fund.

Veronica sighed as I helped her sit fully upright and plumped up her pillow. "Tell us what happened," I said.

"It was during the argument I had with Sam," said Veronica, "about him driving under the influence."

I nodded my encouragement. "Go on, what happened?"

"Earlier in the night I'd given Ron some of the potion, you know, to try and get a little warm blood in his veins, but it didn't work." Veronica paused and gazed at her feet. "Well, that's not entirely true. The part of the potion that you made to help Ron sleep worked just fine — he went out like a light. He snored like a pig too."

"Why did you give Sam some of it?" asked Susie.

"I didn't want him to drive! He'd had far too many beers, and not that horrible stuff from Belgium. He was drinking that strong local beer from Wickford brewery. You know, the one with the picture of the rock music guitar player on the tin?"

"Wickford headbanger," said Willow. "That is strong stuff."

"He'd had one and a half!" said Veronica. "I'm sure he'd have struggled to open his car door, let alone drive the thing."

Susie coughed. "That *is* a lot," she said tactfully.

It was too much to consider driving after, but nowhere near the amount Susie and I had drank on a regular basis when we'd been teenagers — usually behind the youth club, but often in my grandfather's potting shed. Granny had caught us once and threatened to tell Mum, but had soon calmed down when she'd tasted the beer and pulled up an old crate to sit on and join us. Granny had managed to drink three before finally succumbing and falling asleep with her head on an open bag of compost.

Veronica took a deep breath. "I'm glad you agree," she said. "I thought maybe I'd overreacted. I just didn't want Sam hurting himself or somebody else, so I poured the rest of the potion into his beer, hoping it would make him fall asleep.

There are plenty of spare rooms here, he could have stayed the night." Veronica shook her head. "It didn't work though, he didn't get sleepy, and eventually he agreed to take a taxi home. He couldn't get one of course, so he walked home, and you three know how that worked out for him."

Veronica broke into sobs again. "It feels so good to finally get that off my chest! I know I didn't kill Sam, but I do wonder whether he'd have been able to fight off his attacker if I hadn't slipped that potion in his drink."

"He was attacked from behind," Susie said. "I doubt he even heard his attacker coming. There were no signs of a struggle, Veronica. You weren't to blame in any way at all."

"I heard on the news that they'd caught a man," said Veronica. "I hope they lock him in and throw the key at a book!"

There were far too many things wrong with Veronica's sentence, so we all let it go.

"We'll see," I said. "The police are still investigating."

"The man on the radio said the killer was hiding at the car show," Veronica said. "The organisers said the police ruined the last day, running around and looking in everybody's tents and cars!"

"In all fairness to the police, they were looking for a murderer," said Willow.

"The whole things shocking," continued Veronica. "And to think the suspect was a soldier too! He's brought shame on Her Majesty's Armed Forces. That's what he's done!"

Susie looked blank. "The police didn't tell me that at the press conference," she said. "Who told you that, Veronica?"

Veronica dabbed the last of the tears from beneath her eyes. "The man on the radio. He said they were trying to find out if the suspect was connected with the RAC. He was wearing a badge on his clothing apparently. You girls really should pay attention."

"We know that, Veronica," said Willow. "That's the reason the police thought he was at the car show. Most of those vintage car owners are members of the Royal Automobile Club. The suspect owns a few old cars himself. Nobody said he was a soldier though."

Veronica gave a sigh of relief. "That's good to know. I hate the armed forces being brought into disrepute. I thought the radio presenter had meant the Royal Armoured Corps. Ron would have been livid to know one of his own was the killer!"

CHAPTER TWENTY-ONE

"Veronica," I said. "Has Ron ever been violent?"

Willow and Susie fidgeted, casting me nervous glances. We'd all come to the same conclusion, and the atmosphere in the room had electrified.

Veronica furrowed her brow and narrowed her eyes. "That's an odd question, Penelope," she said. "I may be old, and I know I get my proverbs muddled up from time to time, but stupid I am not. I saw all your faces drop when I mentioned the Royal Armoured Corps." Veronica looked at each of us, her cheeks reddening. "You think Ron killed Sam! Admit it!"

I stood up just in time to avoid being hit by Veronica's legs as she swung them off the bed and stood up. She pointed at the door. "Go!" she said.

"You're throwing us out?" said Willow. "Veronica, just think things through for a moment. Is there any chance at all that Ron could have — "

"I'm not throwing you out," said Veronica, marching towards the door. "I'm coming with you to confront that old sod! I think there's every chance he killed Sam. So many things are making sense now."

"Like what?" I said.

"I'm saving those questions for Ronald! Let me at him!"

Susie beat Veronica to the door and put her back against it. "Calm down for a moment, Veronica," she said. She took her phone from her bag. "We need to phone the police first."

"Wait," I said, as Susie dialled. "Let me ring Barney on his personal phone. We don't want cars full of police turning up here and scaring all the residents, and I'd like Barney to be the one who makes the arrest if it was Ron who killed Sam. He deserves it."

Veronica reached past Susie and grabbed the door handle. "You telephone Barney, Penelope, but we're going to get the confession from Ron before he gets here. Ron will clam up in front of authority, the army did that to him, but I'll get what you want to know out of him! Oh, I'll get it out of him all right!"

I dialled Barney as Veronica pulled the door open with an angry tug, making Susie stumble. Barney answered the phone, and I spoke quickly as I followed Veronica along the corridor towards Ron's room, with Willow and Susie on either side of me. "Come to the nursing home," I said. "Quickly. I'll explain when you get here. We'll be in Ron's room. I'm not sure what number it is."

"Fifty-three," snapped Veronica, glancing over her shoulder.

"Room fifty-three," I repeated. "Hurry, Barney."

I slipped the phone into my pocket and took a deep breath. I was about to see somebody being accused of murder, and I was more nervous than the first time I'd kissed a boy. Muscles cramped in my stomach, and my legs struggled to hold my weight.

Veronica stopped outside Ron's door, and I looked at

Willow for support. Her face was white and her bottom lip was crushed between her teeth. It was a relief to know I wasn't the only person who was terrified.

Veronica showed no such nervous tendencies. She paused for the briefest of moments, sucked a lungful of air into her chest, muttered something under her breath, and swung the door open with a shove so violent a painting in the hallway shifted on its mounting.

"What have you done?" she screamed as she entered the room with the rest of us close behind her. "What did you do?"

Ron stared at us from his seat. A few days worth of grey stubble cloaked his chin and cheeks, and I had to remind myself that the person I was looking at was a potential murderer, not simply an elderly man in his dressing gown and slippers. A well built elderly man, but elderly nonetheless. "What are you babbling on about, Veronica?" he spat. "If you've got a problem with me, come here on your own, not with your little army of troublemakers."

I hadn't been labeled a troublemaker since I'd left the school gates behind me for the last time, six years ago. Veronica didn't appreciate the insult either. "How dare you speak about them in that way!" she shouted. "They're here so I don't have to confront a monster like you on my own!"

Ron scratched his chin with long fingernails. "You've lost your marbles, Veronica," he scoffed. "What the heck are you talking about, woman?"

Veronica approached him and bent at the waist, placing her face inches from his. "I'm talking about you killing Sam Hedgewick. I don't know why you did it, or how you did it, but my gut says you did it, and this gut hasn't been wrong for three decades."

"Get lost," said Ron. "Get out of my room and go and find Wally. You've been flirting with him for weeks woman, you're a common wh — "

"I was wrong," said Veronica, in a tone so menacing my eye twitched. "My gut *has* been wrong in the last three decades. It was wrong on the day I said yes to your invitation to watch you play in the Wickford bowls championship final. I *should* have gone with Wally when he asked me. I doubt he needs a special potion to get his compass pointing north. He certainly knew how to handle those big balls of his, and he beat you at bowls that day, didn't he, Ron?"

Ron's smirk tightened into a scowl, and a flash of anger darkened his eyes. "Shut up, Veronica, or — "

Veronica tilted her head and moved her face even closer to Ron's, her nose almost touching his. "Or what, Ronald? You'll kill me like you did Sam?"

Ron's hands tightened into fists, and I took a step forward, sucking air into my mouth and tasting copper. I wasn't sure what spell I was about to cast, but it felt right. I pressed my fingers together, but just as I was about to click them, Ron relaxed his hands and laughed. "This is silly," he said, leaning back in his seat. "Come on, Veronica. We had a good time together, but it's over. There's no need to come here making crazy accusations."

I blew out air and flexed my hand. It had been close, and electricity still tingled in my fingertips.

"Answer some questions for me, Ron," said Veronica. "If you didn't kill Sam you'll have all the answers, won't you?"

Ron crossed his arms and smiled. "Ask away," he said.

Veronica straightened her body and stared down at Ron. "Why was your door locked on the night of the party? The night Sam was killed. I came here two or three times, but you didn't answer when I knocked."

"Because you gave me some of that bloody potion, you daft old bag. It knocked me right out, didn't it? Probably so you could have fun at the party without me."

Veronica pointed at Ron's hand. "How did you get that

injury, Ron? It doesn't look like a strain from weight lifting. It looks bruised."

"I dropped a heavy bar on it," said Ron. "Next question." He looked at me, Willow, and Susie. "Enjoying the show, girls? Do you like watching a mad woman bullying an old man?"

"It's best you just answer her questions, Ron," I said.

"And to think I gave you all those green beans last year," he growled. "You can forget about any next year, and I'll make sure everyone else at the allotment knows how cruel you are. There'll be no more free vegetables for you, Penelope."

Veronica laughed. "We don't even know if the allotments will even be there next year, you old fool. The land owner's dead. Remember? You won't be growing beans next year anyway, Ron. You'll be behind bars, where you belong."

"Have you finished, woman?" said Ron. "I want you out of this room, and out of my life."

'I've got one more question for you, Ronald."

Ron waved a hand. "Hurry then, I haven't got all day."

Veronica pointed at the wardrobe built into the wall behind Ron's seat. "What are you hiding in there?" she breathed.

Ron's whole body tensed. His striped pyjamas tightened across his chest, and the tendons in his neck bulged. "I'm not hiding anything. Now get out. I've answered your questions."

"What's in there, Ron?" pressed Veronica. "You haven't let me put your clean washing away all week, and you've moved your seat so you can sit there guarding the wardrobe."

"I moved my seat here because I fancied a change. That's all."

"You can't even see your television from there, Ron," said Veronica. "Do you think I'm stupid?"

'Why don't you just let Veronica have a look, Ron?" said

Willow. "The police are on their way. You'll be forced to open it when they get here."

Ron's whole demeanour changed. "Oh, the police are coming are they? Why didn't you say that in the first place?"

He stood up, towering over Veronica. He pushed out his chest, rolled his shoulders, and rocked his head from side to side, stretching his neck muscles. Veronica stepped backwards as Ron grabbed the seat and pulled it away from the wardrobe. He slid the door open and bent over, fumbling around in the bottom. Veronica moved forward and tried to look over Ron's shoulder. "What are you doing?" she said. "What have you got in there, Ron?"

Ron's voice echoed in the wardrobe. "You'd better phone the police," he said, "and tell them to bring an ambulance with them."

For such a large and elderly man, Ron moved quickly. He stood up, span on the spot, and raised a hand above his head. A glint of silver caught my eye, and Veronica shrieked. "No, Ron!"

Ron swung the metal bar in an arc towards Veronica's head, and either Susie or Willow screamed behind me. Copper flooded my mouth and filled my throat, and my fingers stung with the force of the electricity which coursed through them. A sizzle accompanied the click of my fingers, and the metal bar stopped moving, centimetres from Veronica's frightened face.

"Catch her!" I shouted, as Veronica's legs shook and gave way beneath her.

Willow leapt forward and caught Veronica as she fainted. Susie helped carry her to the bed, and Ron stared at me with wide frightened eyes. "What's happening," he said. "I can't move."

"Never mind what's happening," I said. I nodded at the metal bar in Ron's hand. It was red with dried blood, and a few hairs stuck to it. "I take it that's the murder weapon? The missing weights bar from the gym."

Ron nodded, his eyes dropping to the purple sparks which arced between my finger tips as I held my hand at waist height. Interesting, I thought. He could communicate and move his eyes, but the rest of his body was completely paralysed. I wasn't sure what spell I'd cast, or how I'd learnt it. I didn't remember reading a spell like it in Granny's book, but maybe my subconscious brain had stored it in my mind as I'd been flicking through the pages. I'd have to ask Granny.

"What are you?" stammered Ron.

"What do you think I am, Ron?" I said. "I'm a witch of course, and if you don't tell me exactly what you did to Sam, and why you did it, you won't be going to jail, you'll be swimming around in that pond outside, croaking and eating flies."

Ron grimaced. "Okay, I'll tell you!"

I raised my hand and turned it in the air, sparks sizzling and crackling from my fingers. "Talk."

"I was jealous. I've always been a jealous man. It's my flaw."

"Jealous of Sam?"

Ron nodded.

"Why?"

"That potion you made for Veronica. It didn't work the way she wanted on me, it only made me drowsy. I missed the party because I was asleep, and when I woke up I was hungry so I went to see if there was any food left, and then I saw it!"

"Saw what?" I said.

"Veronica spiking Sam's drink with the passion potion! She couldn't get what she wanted from me, so she found the next available man to try it out on! It didn't work on Sam either though, so when he left, I followed him. I'd lost my temper, I didn't know what I was doing! I just wanted to warn him to stay away from Veronica, but I hit him too hard."

"You're a vile pig, Ron. You got out through the door with the broken alarm, didn't you? So nobody knew you had left. You locked your door so people would think you were asleep." said Veronica. She'd woken up.

I turned to her. "I can explain," I said, looking at my sparking hand.

"There's no need, dear." she said. "You can tell me in your own time. Concentrate on getting the rest of the confession out of him. Your police friend will be here soon, and I'm not sure you want him to see you in such a compromising situation."

She was right. I'd had it drilled into me since I was old enough to speak that I should do everything I could to prevent mortals from discovering the existence of witches. In the past week alone I'd cast a spell on a lawyer, a boat owner, and now a murderer. A talking goat had attacked an intruder on my boat, and I was in the process of performing magic in front of one of the biggest gossips in town. I wasn't doing too well at the whole keeping witchcraft a secret thing, and I didn't want to add Barney to the growing list of witnesses to my magic.

Ron grunted. "It hurts," he said. "All my muscles ache."

"Think how much pain Sam felt," spat Veronica. She stood up, pushed passed Ron, and bent down to rummage in his wardrobe. She held a black piece of clothing aloft. "Exhibit B!" she said.

She turned the blazer around and showed us all the badge. The owner of the *Flirting Kingfisher* had been correct. There was a crown, and the letters RAC were below it. We'd all been too quick to assume the badge the boat owner had recalled while under my spell was the same as the badge on the front of the car next to the canal.

"I don't understand," said Willow. "Why did you bring the murder weapon and the blazer back here, Ron? There's probably evidence on the blazer, and there's *definitely* evidence on the weights bar. Why didn't you throw them in the canal?"

"He wouldn't throw his blazer away," said Veronica. "It meant too much to him."

"It's been wth me for forty years," said Ron. "Of course I wouldn't toss it in the canal. I was going to return the bar to the gym, but I panicked. I thought I'd keep it hidden until all the fuss died down."

"You call a murder investigation *fuss*," said Veronica. "You really are a piece of work, aren't you?"

Ron swivelled his eyes, attempting to look at Veronica. "I did it because I loved you, Veronica. I couldn't bear it when I saw you giving Sam that potion. The thought of his hands all over you, and the fact that you wanted him to do it sent me mad!"

"I put that potion in his drink to try and make him fall asleep," said Veronica. "So he wouldn't drive home after drinking. You're a fool, Ronald. A murdering, sadistic, jealous fool, and I hope you get what you deserve!"

Footsteps sounded in the hallway outside. "It's that room on the right, officer Dobkins," said a woman's voice.

"Quick," said Veronica. "Stop doing whatever it is you're doing, Penelope!"

My fingers stopped tingling and the spell broke. Ron's arm continued the swinging arc through the air to my front, and Barney roared a warning as he entered the room. "Drop the weapon," he shouted. "Get out of the way, Penelope!"

I moved aside as Barney ran at Ron, his nightstick above his head and anger on his face. "How dare you attack Penny," he shouted, twisting Ron's arm behind his back. The metal bar thudded on the carpet, and Barney kicked it away. "If I wasn't in uniform, I'd do more than put handcuffs on you, you piece of — "

I touched Barney's arm. "He wasn't attacking me — "

"Yes he was," said Veronica, raising her eyebrows at me. "And he killed Sam Hedgewick. That's the murder weapon on the floor. I think you'll find it matches Sam's wound perfectly. Well done, constable! You've bagged yourself a killer!"

Ron groaned. "That girl's a witch," he said, looking at me.

Veronica bristled. "And you're a bast — "

"Everybody, calm down!" demanded Barney. "Will somebody please tell me what's going on here?"

CHAPTER TWENTY-TWO

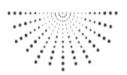

*D*aisies had started showing their heads again, and the grass around my mooring was an inch too long. Barney wiped a hand over his sweaty brow as he pushed the lawn mower. "Would you like another drink? I yelled, making myself heard over the petrol engine.

Barney shook his head, his face red, and his ginger fringe stuck to his damp forehead. His white torso glared in the sun, and the two layers of sun cream had begun running down his chest. "No thanks," he shouted, forcing the mower over a bump in the ground. "I haven't got much left to do, and then I have to go to the police station before I go home and get ready for the party."

Willow poured me another iced water from the jug on the picnic bench. "Isn't it exciting?" she said. "You and me living together on a boat!"

"We should raise the rent," said Tony from beside me. "You'll be using more electricity now."

Michelle slapped his hand. "He's joking, girls!'

I wasn't so sure.

Mabel snarled at Tony, and he shooed her away with the

hem of his striped apron. Although Tony and Michelle employed two full time chefs, Tony still insisted on working in the hotel kitchen. He'd made a deal with Michelle — when either of the chefs could make a Lancashire hotpot as legendary as his, he'd put his kitchen duties behind him and help Michelle run the rest of the hotel. I doubted it would happen soon. I'd never tasted a Lancashire hotpot like Tony's, even in Lancashire.

"You need to keep that goose under control," said Tony. "It scared all the customers in the beer garden last night, and ate half a chicken from a plate." He looked around the clearing. "She stole the basket too. It's probably around here somewhere."

"We were having a seventies themed food night," explained Michelle. She tapped her husband's hand again. "Anyway, Tony. It's not their goose. It just happens to live here."

"Are you sure you two won't come down for a drink later?" I asked, guiding the subject away from enchanted animals.

"We can't, dear," said Michelle, the scent of her expensive perfume competing with the aroma of freshly mowed grass. "The hotel's too busy to step away from for even a minute in the evening, but you two enjoy your party — it must be so exciting for you both. Two sisters living together on a boat."

It was exciting, and it was surprisingly all thanks to Mum. She'd been the person responsible for suggesting the idea to Willow, and I'd jumped at the chance of having my sister living and working with me. We'd already planned a two week trip along the canals, and were leaving the next day. The school summer holidays were starting in two days time, and the touristy villages and towns along the waterways would be brimming with holidaymakers and potential customers.

"It's hardly a party," I said. "It's just a small gathering of family and friends."

"That's the best kind of party," said Michelle with a smile. She gave Tony a playful dig in his ribs. "Come on, big boy," she said. "The hotel won't book the guests in itself."

The couple made their way back up the hill to the hotel, ignoring Mable who ran in circles around their feet. Rosie leapt up onto the picnic bench, and rubbed herself on my bare arm, ignoring the goose when it came bolting back towards us. Mabel jumped up at the picnic bench, barking and growling at Rosie, who padded to the edge of the table-top. She watched Mabel intently as she bounced up and down, and when the time was right, landed a perfectly timed paw swipe on her beak.

The goose let out a whelp of shock, and sat down, gazing up at Rosie, averting her eyes when Rosie stared back.

"There," I said, stroking Rosie's back. "I knew you could be friends. It only took Boris to prove to you that Mabel isn't so dangerous."

"I don't think they're friends exactly," said Willow. "I just think the tables have turned. Rosie's the boss now."

Mabel lay submissively on her back and presented Rosie with her fat belly and extended neck. The cat leapt down from the table and sniffed at the bird's white feathers, before turning her back and sauntering away, leaping onto the boat and disappearing inside.

The mowers engine spluttered and stopped, and the birds began singing again. "Finished," shouted Barney.

He'd done a good job, and I grabbed his t-shirt from the table and walked it over to him. "Bend down," I said, as I stood in front of him.

Barney smiled and lowered his head, his lips puckered as he leaned towards my face.

"What are you doing?" I said, guiding his t-shirt over

his head.

Barney's face turned a deep shade of crimson. "I'm sorry," he mumbled. "I thought you were going to give me a thank you kiss. Not a full kiss of course. Just a peck on the lips." The hue in his cheeks spread to his neck. "Or the cheek."

"Your hands are dirty, Barney," I said, "you'd have got fingerprints all over your white t-shirt. I was just trying to help."

Barney stood up straight again. "Thank you," he said, his face still matching the colour of my shorts.

He pushed the lawnmower towards the path. "I'll just take this back to my dad. He want's to do his own lawn tomorrow. Then I've got to go to the station and finish the paperwork for Jason Danvers's bail conditions. He's being released from custody today."

It had been six days since Ron had been arrested and charged with the murder of Sam Hedgewick. I'd convinced the police not to charge Jason with breaking into my boat, even threatening Sergeant Cooper with the promise that I'd stand up in court and say I'd invited him aboard if I had too. Barney had told me that without the additional charge of breaking and entering, it was likely that Jason would be awarded a suspended sentence for the crime he was already wanted for. The thought of him having lost Sam, and then having to languish in jail, had been too much for me, and I'd dropped the charges happily.

I caught up to Barney and tapped him on the back. "Bend down," I said, as he turned around. His constant blushing was becoming a little too much, and I smiled as I gave him a kiss on his reddened warm cheek.

He stood up straight with a wide grin on his face, and his whistling echoed through the trees as he pushed the mower up the footpath, almost tripping over his own feet once or twice.

I sat down opposite Willow on the bench, and we opened the bottle of elderberry wine that was waiting for us in the shade beneath the table. The clink of our glasses startled Mabel, and we kept our drinks touching as I made a toast. "Here's to life together on the water," I said.

Granny and Boris arrived first. Boris had wanted to be one of the first at the party so he could speak freely for a while before the rest of the guests arrived. "Here they are!" said Granny, as she placed her backpack on the table and hugged us both in turn. "My special little homicide detectives!"

Willow laughed, freeing herself from Granny's arms. "We didn't solve the crime," she said. "It was a joint effort. Veronica actually came up with the most important clue, and Penny's magic extracted the full confession."

"Well, we're extremely proud of you both, and Susie of course, aren't we Boris?"

"Profoundly," said Boris, inspecting his hooves. "Although I can't help observing that my part in all of this has been played down a little. If you remember, it was I who discovered and proceeded to entrap the man we wrongly assumed to be the villain. Of course, at the time, I had no idea he was innocent. I placed my life in the direst of danger, and not a mention of my heroism has been made in the newspaper."

"Not this again, Boris," said Granny. "Will you stop harping on about it if I pour you a drink?"

Boris lifted his head. "Naturally."

"Boris can't drink alcohol!" I said. "Barney will be here soon, and Veronica and Wally are coming. How do we explain why a goat is drinking Brandy?"

"Veronica knows you're a witch now, Penny, although I

suspect she's known about our family since her and I were teenagers."

"She doesn't know Boris is a man in a goat's body," I protested, 'but go on, what happened when you are a teenager?"

"It was a cold winter," said Granny, pushing her glasses along the bridge of her nose and sitting down next to Willow. "Wages were low and tensions were running high in the town. You have to remember that back then we didn't have computer games, we had to make our own fun, and fun was hard to come by. There was no — "

Boris snorted. "Cut to the chase, Gladys. I need that drink."

Granny fixed Boris with a fiery stare, but Boris simply nudged the backpack with his nose.

"I turned Veronica's uncle into a garden gnome," said Granny. "A gnome with a fishing rod — Harold enjoyed casting a fly."

"You turned Veronica's uncle into a garden gnome and you *suspect* she knew our family were witches?" I said. "How did you turn him into a garden gnome when you were that age anyway? That's powerful magic!"

"I practiced a lot, dear. Like I said, it was a cold winter and wages were low — "

"You turned a man into a garden gnome," said Willow. "Of course Veronica knew you were a witch! And her uncle must have known!"

"I cast a spell of forgetfulness on her," Granny explained, "and on Harold when he transformed back into himself. No damage was done, and they were both fine when they remembered how to walk and talk again, although Veronica's given me odd looks ever since, and Harold began wearing a fez everywhere he went." Granny shrugged. "I may be way wide of the mark of course. Maybe I'm overreacting. It's just a feeling I get about her."

"You're not overreacting," I said. "Good grief, Granny! I'm surprised you haven't been burnt at the stake!"

Boris nudged the backpack again. "Drink."

Granny opened the bag and took out a large glass mixing bowl. She placed it on the grass and withdrew a bottle from the backpack.

"It's mother's ruin," said Boris. "People will think it's water!"

Granny filled the bowl with gin, and Boris began lapping it up. He lifted his head as Mabel approached. "None for you, you're violent enough without alcohol in you."

"Speaking of mother's," said Granny. "Yours is on her way. She's got news for you."

"Mums's coming?" I said. "She said she'd never come anywhere near my boat."

"Boris had a talk with her," explained Granny.

"I once did three years of a five year psychology course," said Boris, "and it's enabled me to get to the source of her difficulties. It transpires that your mother is more afraid of ingesting insects than we imagined. It's not your boat she's snubbing, the boat is simply a convenient excuse. It's the insect life that thrives along the canal banks which keeps her away from you."

"But she doesn't have to eat anything while she's here," I said.

"Phobias have a nasty way of amplifying if left untreated," explained Boris. "In your dear mother's case, it's progressed to a fear of an insect flying into her mouth."

"Poor Mum," said Willow.

Boris licked his lips. "Don't worry. I'm working on it with her. I'm convinced I can cure her, but in the meantime, we've come up with a compromise."

CHAPTER TWENTY-THREE

Mum's bee keeper's hat didn't look too out of place. There *were* a lot of insects swarming around the tables laden with food, and we'd told Barney, Veronica, and Wally that Mum was allergic to bites to save her from any embarrassment about her real condition.

Wally was dressed in a tweed jacket with a silk cravat, and spoke about his career as a TV comedy writer as he tucked into sandwiches and cakes. Boris looked on with admiration, and whispered to me as Wally raised another laugh from his captive audience. "I could really get along with that chap," he said.

Nobody mentioned how remarkably quickly Veronica had moved on from Ron, and we thought it best to avoid conversations about the murder altogether.

Susie had shown me the front page of the newspaper when she'd arrived, and as requested, she'd kept mine and Willow's names out of it, but had elevated Barney to hero status. Barney had begrudgingly accepted that we wanted him to take the glory for solving the crime, and had admired the photograph of himself in the newspaper, remarking on how much he resembled Prince Harry.

Willow and I helped Mum onto the boat, and after a few initial reservations about the size and the lack of a full sized freezer, she soon warmed to it, even testing the beds out for comfort and lifting the protective screen on the front of her hat so she could rummage though the stock in my shop.

With a witch on a broomstick fridge magnet in Mum's bag, and another bottle of wine in my hand, we stepped ashore and enjoyed the rest of the evening.

Willow and I sat apart from the group for a while, finishing the bottle of wine and planning our trip. Veronica grabbed an empty glass from the table and joined us, curling her legs beneath herself as she sat on the grass.

"So, you're witches," she said."Just like your grandmother."

Willow looked down. "You know about Granny?" she said, fiddling with her bracelet.

Granny cast nervous glances from her seat and waved at Veronica, who raised her hand in return. "Of course I do," said Veronica. "She doesn't know it though. She thinks I've forgotten, but I remember what she did that day."

I feigned ignorance. "What day, Veronica? What did she do?"

"It was a long time ago. My uncle had shouted at me and Gladys for throwing stones at the barges on the canal, but we were bored you see, you know how kids can be?"

I nodded.

"Well, he really upset Gladys, and she almost cried. When I saw you at the nursing home with those sparks coming from your fingers, it all came flooding back to me again. That's exactly what Gladys did, but I seem to remember she'd screwed her face up too."

"She does that," said Willow.

"Well, that's when she cast her curse, or whatever you witches call them, and my uncle was never the same again."

'I'm so sorry, Veronica," I said. "For whatever she did."

"No!" Don't be sorry!" laughed Veronica. "I've been wanting to thank Gladys for years, but I didn't know how. I think she thought she was doing something bad to my uncle, but it turned his life around — he was lonely after my aunty died, and thanks to Gladys, he met the woman he spent the rest of his life with."

"Huh?" spluttered Willow, choking on wine.

Veronica lowered her voice. "She cast a silly curse which made him enjoy wearing ridiculous hats! He took to wearing one of those fez things everywhere he went. When he'd recovered from the plague of course."

"Plague?" I said.

"That was what me and my uncle called it. The doctors had no idea what was wrong with us. We caught it together, and we both forgot how to walk or talk for a month. It was all very odd."

"It sounds awful, but how did wearing a fez change his life?" said Willow, expertly skirting the subject of forgetfulness spells.

"There was a very famous comedian who arrived on the scene, I doubt you've heard of him, Tommy Cooper was his name."

I nodded, but Willow shook her head.

"He was famous for wearing a fez you see, and my uncle loved him! He went to every Tommy Cooper show that he could, and it was at one of his shows that he met Sarah. His life changed from that day forward, and it was all thanks to that lovely woman over there, whispering in her goat's ear."

Veronica sipped her wine. She spat it on the grass and made a face. "This wine's awful," she said. "Where on earth did you buy it?"

"I made it," I smiled. "It's elderberry."

"Anybody else would apologise and beg your forgiveness," said Veronica. "But not me, I'm honest. Penelope, this wine is vile."

"It is quite awful," said Willow, laughing.

"You'd better get used to it," I smiled, standing up and brushing grass clippings from my legs. "There's twenty-two bottles left on the boat."

As darkness approached, Wally and Veronica left. They walked side by side and linked arms as they reached the steepest part of the hill, disappearing into the gloom together.

Susie broke down into sobs until we reminded her we'd only be gone for two weeks. "We're not going far either" I said, hugging her. "You'll be able to drive out and visit us."

When it was Barney's turn to say goodbye, he lifted and dropped his arms nervously until I took charge of the situation. I wrapped my arms around him and squeezed him tight.

"Thank you for everything you did," he said. "You solved Sam's murder and let me take the credit. I'll never forget. Maybe I could take you out for a meal when you get back — as a thank you of course, nothing else!"

I smiled. "I'd like that, Barney," I said.

Barney turned and waved as he climbed the footpath. "Enjoy your trip!" he shouted.

"Thank goddess they've all gone!" said Mum, when Barney had vanished. "Now we can get down to the real business. I've got some exciting news for you, Penelope."

"I was dying to tell her when I got here!" said Granny, "but I kept my mouth closed! It was so difficult!"

"Thank you. Mother," said Mum. "That was very brave of you."

"Gladys is nothing if not brave," said Boris, staggering to the empty glass bowl and licking the base. "She's a wonderful woman," he mumbled.

"What's the news?" said Willow. "Come on, Mum."

"I went to the haven today," she said, taking a seat at the picnic bench and picking up a mini sausage roll. For a brief moment I thought she was going to eat it, but a moth flew past and she threw the pastry back onto the plate, slapping the crumbs from her hands. "Eva overheard something, Penelope," she continued.

'Tell her!" said Granny, "before I have to!"

"Eva overheard Maeve talking about you, Penelope. She found out what you did in the nursing home, you know, saving Veronica from a metal bar in the head. You remember don't you?"

I sighed. "Yes, Mum, I remember that not insignificant incident in my life from less than a week ago."

"Well Maeve is very impressed, and according to Eva, you can expect your entry spell to be made known to you in the very near future! You'll be able to visit the haven, Penelope! Isn't that exciting!"

"And all thanks to Gladys, because of her willingness to share her spell book with her granddaughters," murmured Boris, before collapsing in a heap. "She's a remarkable woman."

CHAPTER TWENTY-FOUR

Willow pushed the start button and birds flew from the trees as the engine burst into life. We'd intended to leave before eight o'clock in the morning, but it was half past nine as we pushed away from the bank, with Willow in control of the boat, and me instructing her on how to negotiate the boat out of the mooring and onto the canal.

Mabel had gone chasing swans again, and I placed the left over breakfast sausages on the bank for her. Hopefully she'd get back before a lucky water rat found them.

"Wait!" came a man's voice. "Wait!"

Willow looked up. "One of us has got a secret admirer," she said.

The man running down the path moved the huge bunch of flowers from in front of his face and shouted again.

"It's Jason Danvers," I said. "What on earth does he want?"

I tossed a mooring rope onto the canal bank. "Pull us ashore," I said.

Jason took the rope in one hand, and his muscles bulged as he pulled us the few feet back to shore. He looked far better than the last time I'd seen him, but the last time I'd seen him, he'd been cowering in the corner of my shop with a goat between his legs. It was hardly a fair comparison.

He wore clothes that were obviously expensive, but beyond my limited knowledge of designer wear. Willow would have known what they were, but she was too busy trying to work to how to turn the engine off. "Turn the key," I said. "Just like a car."

Jason pulled us close to the bank and wrapped the rope loosely through the iron hoop in the ground. "I'm glad I made it in time" he panted, still trying to catch his breath. He held the flowers out towards me. "These are for you," he said.

"What are they for?" I asked. Mum had taught me never to take flowers from a man until I knew precisely what his intentions were.

"A thank you," he said, shaking them gently in front of me. "For not sending me to jail. If you hadn't dropped the charges, I'd have been eating stodgy porridge this morning instead of the fried breakfast I just had at the Coffee Pot."

I took the flowers and smelt them. Mum had also taught me that when you finally accepted the flowers, you showed your gratitude. "Thank you," I said. "They're beautiful. You didn't get them from he convenience store though. They're far too nice."

"And they're alive," added Willow.

Jason laughed. "I got them from Emily's florist."

"Emily's is open again?" I said. "I thought Sam had already sold his properties."

Jason's face dropped at the sound of Sam's name, and my throat swelled with guilt. "I'm sorry about Sam," I said. "I didn't really have the time to offer my condolences the last time we met."

Jason smiled. "Thank you," he said. "It's hard, but I can do good things for this town in his name now. I'll keep his memory burning."

"What do you mean?" said Willow, wiping oil from her hand onto the rag that hung from the roof of the boat.

"Sam left all his assets to me. Everything; his money, his properties, his cars. Not that I needed them, I've done well in life for myself."

"Wasn't he getting rid of his properties though?" I said. "Why would he have named you in a will if he was selling everything?" I stopped talking — I realised what I was doing. "Tell me to shut up if I'm being nosy," I added.

"You're not," he said. "You helped the police find out I was innocent, you have every right to know what went on. When he received all those threats and found out his wife was sniffing around his lawyer, he went to a different lawyer in Covenhill and drafted a will with me named as the beneficiary." He paused and tugged at his t-shirt. "He didn't expect to die though, it was just a symbolic dig at his wife and father more than anything else."

"I can understand him wanting to cut his cheating wife out of the will," said Willow, "but why his father?"

"His father was old fashioned," said Jason. "I forced Sam to tell his dad that he was in love with a man. I think it was your grandmother that witnessed the argument I had with him about it? Outside the lawyer's office."

"Yes, that was Granny," Willow said.

'I threatened not to go to Spain with Sam if he didn't tell his father about us. I feel awful, but I just wanted everything to be honest, you know?" Jason dropped his eyes. "Sam had really helped me change in the months I knew him, and the honesty he taught me in my business affairs spilled over into my personal life. I should have let him do it his way."

"Sam's dad didn't take it well, and that's why he cut him out of the will?" I said.

Jason nodded. "He was really horrible to Sam, but I understand why. He's from a different generation. He's suffering now though. He's devastated about the things he said to his son, but I'll make sure he's okay. Financially anyway, I can't help with his conscience."

"Why don't you go to Spain on your own and do the things you planned with Sam?" I said.

"No," he said. "I want to do good things here with Sam's money. I want to help. I've spent most of my life hurting and conning people. I'll spend the rest of my life making amends."

"You've let Emily open the florist's again," I said.

"Along with every other business that Sam was selling," he said. "They've all got their leases back and they're all open again. Which brings me onto the other reason I'm here. I want to do something for you, for helping me, and to make up for the ordeal I put you through on the boat."

"The flowers are enough," I said, bringing them to my nose.

"Hear me out," said Jason. "Your friend Susie did."

I frowned. "Susie?"

"She was on the boat too when that whole... incident occurred. I scared all three of you. I want to make it up to you all."

"What have you done for Susie?" said Willow.

"She's just accepted the keys to a flat above a shop in town," he said. "I overheard her talking to the owner of the Coffee Pot while I was having breakfast, she was telling her the flat she lived in was too big and expensive for her to live alone in after splitting up with..."

"Robert," I filled in.

"Yes, Robert. Anyway, I offered her a flat free of rent for as long as she needs it, and she accepted."

"Free of rent!" said Willow. "I don't blame her!"

"And that's what I want to do for you two," said Jason, smiling.

"We've got a home," Willow said, tapping the roof of the *Water Witch*, "and I've only just moved aboard. I'm not going anywhere."

Jason nodded. "And a beautiful home it is too" he said. "I was quite taken with how cosy it was when I was... stowed away onboard."

"Breaking in," you mean, said Willow. She put her hand to her mouth. "I'm sorry, that was uncalled for, you've been through a lot and you're trying to do the right thing."

"It's okay," said Jason. He looked towards the bow of the boat where the shop was. "I couldn't help noticing how small your shop is, though," he said. "There's barely enough room to swing a cat in there."

"But enough room for a goat to swing a man," I grinned.

Jason winced, and put a hand to his thigh. "The less said about that the better," he said, "but that goat was odd, very odd. The police said it was the pain playing with my mind, but..."

"What about the size of Penny's shop?" said Willow.

The less said about Boris the better.

"That shop I told you about, below the flat Susie's moving into?"

"Yes?" I said.

"I own it now and it's going to be empty within a week, the couple who rent it are retiring. I want you two to have it. I thought maybe you could move your shop there, or start a whole new business, or keep a floating shop and a static shop. It's up to you, and it would be rent free of course."

Willow put her hand on mine. "It's a yes, isn't it, Penny?"

I wasn't sure. Granny had always said nothing in life was free.

"It's right at the top of that path into town," Jason said,

pointing up the hill. "Next to that greengrocers with the strange name."

"*The Firkin Gherkin,*" I said. "Mr and Mrs Potter run the shop next door. They're retiring?"

"They said the bottom's fallen out of the VHS rental market. They're quite old aren't they?"

"Bill's expecting a telegram from the Queen on his next birthday," I said. "They didn't just rent videos though. They cut keys too."

"That was the backbone of the business," agreed Willow.

"Well, they've thrown the towel in. They own a villa in Portugal apparently, so they'll need to leave the Queen a forwarding address."

"Come on, Penny," Willow said. "It'll be great! We can live on the boat, and keep the shop on it too. We'll have a shop in town and a shop to take on the canals."

"Can we think about it?" I said.

Jason smiled. "Of course you can. Take as long as you want."

"We'll be back in two weeks. We'll give you an answer then," I said, turning the key in the ignition and pressing the engine start button.

Jason tossed the mooring rope onto the boat, and pushed us away from the bank. "I'll be right here," he said. "I'm buying a house in town. You'll see me around."

Willow took the controls and guided the boat backwards as Jason watched from the bank. She successfully negotiated the corner and put the gearbox into forward gear.

"Hey!" shouted Jason. "That goat did speak didn't it? I have to know!"

My phone buzzed in my pocket. It was a message from an unknown number.

Hey, Penny. This is my new number. Check out my blog. It's live. www.goat2bekidding.com luv Boris.

I smiled. "Of course not!" I shouted at Jason. "Goats can't talk!"

The End

Four & Twenty Blackbirds

A Water Witch Cozy Mystery - Book Two

Sam Short

Copyright © 2017 by Sam Short

All rights reserved.

No part of this book may be reproduced in any form or by any electronic or mechanical means, including information storage and retrieval systems, without written permission from the author, except for the use of brief quotations in a book review.

❦ Created with Vellum

For Archie. May your life be magical.

CHAPTER ONE

My sister steered the boat through the narrow gap in the trees with the skill of somebody who'd been driving sixty-foot narrowboats for years. Nobody would have guessed it was the first time she'd attempted the tricky manoeuvre.

"Well done, Willow!" shouted Susie from the bank-side, eliciting a proud grin from my sister. "And welcome home!"

Home was a narrow dead-end channel of water which led off the canal at a tight right angle. The Poacher's Pocket Hotel, which I leased the exclusive mooring from, was hidden by trees on the hill above us, and the aroma of the guest's breakfasts being prepared made my stomach rumble. The early morning sun twinkled on the water, and an already warm breeze brushed my face as I prepared to help moor the *Water Witch — Floating emporium of magick*.

Willow put the gearbox into neutral as she steered the boat tight against the bank, and switched off the engine as I threw a rope to Susie. "Catch!" I dared.

My best friend snatched the rope from the air and threaded it through one of the iron hoops embedded in the thin strip of stonework that kept water and grass separate. "I can't wait to show you the shop!" she said, tying a knot and checking it was secure. "You're both going to love it!"

Willow giggled. "I'm sure we are," she said, offering me a meaningful glance.

I was happy, but my sister was at least three rungs higher than me on the excitement ladder. She'd only lived on my boat for two weeks, but the lack of her own bedroom had begun to take its toll. Willow was eighteen and needed her own space — especially when she'd run out of chocolate, and with a third of the boat's length taken up by my witchcraft shop, space was at a premium.

My sister and I had been on a two week business trip along the canals of South England, and while moored up in the quaint village of Bentbridge, on market day, we'd made a joint decision — we were going to convert the shop area into a bedroom for Willow, and take Jason Danvers up on his generous offer.

Jason had recently been accused of murder, and when Willow, Susie, and I, had helped clear his name, he'd insisted on showing us all his appreciation. Being the wealthy owner of several properties in Wickford, and eager to turn over a new leaf, Jason had offered Susie an apartment free of rent, and Willow and I the shop premises directly below it.

The temptation of paying no rent had been hard to resist, but we'd all insisted that we would only accept his offer if he took half of the rent from us each month — a deal which Jason had reluctantly agreed to.

"Just think," said Susie, tying the final boat rope to a hoop. "I'll be living above your shop, and your boat is only a two minute walk away! It's almost like living next door to each other."

I opened my mouth to answer, but a loud barking from the tree-line interrupted me. "Mabel!" I shouted, as the white goose sprinted across the grass towards us, wagging her tail feathers and flapping her wings.

A medical condition prevented her from flying, but the fact she thought she was a dog was down to an accidental spell being cast on her. My grandmother had developed a bad case of witch dementia, and Mabel had been the first victim of Granny's muddled up spells. She'd continue thinking she was a dog until Granny found a cure for her dementia, although it seemed the goose was perfectly happy with her canine lifestyle.

I patted and tickled the yapping goose as she leapt at my legs, and Rosie jumped off the boat to greet her with a happy mewl. The black cat had once been afraid of Mabel, but after finally sticking up for herself, she was now the dominant animal. Mabel allowed Rosie to sniff her face, and the two of them ran across the grass together, Mabel picking up a stick, and Rosie making an athletic leap in a failed attempt to swat a colourful butterfly from the sky.

"I've missed this," I said, hugging Susie. "It's good to be home."

The peaceful vibe was rudely ruined by a bang so loud it made my stomach flip. Susie went rigid in my arms, and my sister screamed. Mabel barked, and Rosie streaked over the grass and leapt aboard the boat, disappearing down the steps into my bedroom as another bang echoed around the clearing. Crows rose from the fields beyond the hedgerow on the other side of the canal, and a man shouted, his voice barely audible above the noise of the angry birds. "Get off my crops! I'll kill every last one of you if I have to!"

"He's shooting!" yelled Willow, leaping ashore and crouching behind the steel hull of the *Water Witch*.

Another bang proved my sister correct, but it seemed the shooter's aim was becoming less proficient as shot gun pellets snapped through the hedge and peppered the water next to the boat.

"Stop shooting!" yelled Susie, as more crows joined the circling mass of birds in the sky. "You're going to hurt somebody!"

Susie and I lowered ourselves behind one of the two picnic benches a few feet away from the waters edge, and Mabel joined us, shaking with anxiety. I placed a calming hand on her back, and she relaxed a little, lowering herself onto her tail, her orange feet stretched out in front of her in a position that would have been comical under any other circumstances.

The man shouted again. This time speaking to us and not the birds. "Hello?"

"Over here!" I yelled, "across the canal! You almost hit us!"

Cracking twigs and shaking leaves pinpointed his position as he fought his way through the hedge and stumbled onto the towpath on the opposite bank. He lifted his flat cap and shielded his eyes from the sun as he pointed the barrel of his gun safely at the ground. "Are you all okay?" he said, glancing nervously through the gap in the trees.

Willow stood up, wiping dirt from her knees and adjusting her shorts. "Yes, luckily for you," she said, raising her voice as the crows continued to register their annoyance. "You shouldn't be shooting so close to a public footpath, even I know that. The police will take your gun licence away if they catch you."

"It's Gerald Timkins," said Susie, tightening the ponytail in her long blond hair.

I'd recognised him too. The land he'd been shooting on was his, but that was still no excuse for nearly putting holes in one of us, or my boat.

"The crows are causing havoc this year," explained Gerald, breaking the barrel of his shotgun open and making me feel a little safer. "They've devastated one of my fields already."

"Get a scarecrow," shouted Willow. "You'll have more than failed crops to worry about if you carry on shooting that thing so close to a public footpath."

"I've got a scarecrow," said Gerald. "In fact, I've got two of the buggers — fat lot of good that they do. The crows just sit on them. They're going on the bonfire! I bought three of those electronic scarecrows last week — the ones that make bangs every few minutes, they're being delivered today, then maybe I can get some peace. I can hear those crows in my blasted dreams!"

The crows *were* loud, and I imagined a flock the size of the one that circled above us would make short work of a field of wheat, or whatever crop it was that Gerald grew.

The red faced farmer continued his rant. "I've got the bird watching brigade on me too, telling me I shouldn't shoot the crows. Bloody twitchers! I'd like to see what they'd say if it was *their* livelihood being eaten by the buggers!"

"I'm sorry you've got crow trouble, Mr Timkins," I said, "but can you try and be more careful in the future? I really don't like the thought of being shot, and I only had my boat painted a few weeks ago!"

Gerald nodded. "Of course," he said, "but do me a favour, girls? Don't go reporting me to the police, will you? I've got enough problems on my plate with these crows without the law sniffing around too."

None of us were the type of person to go running to the law because of an accident, and nobody had been harmed, although I had an awful feeling that a few crows wouldn't be seeing another sunrise. "We won't," I promised. "You have my word."

Gerald thanked us with a wave of his cap, and fought his

way back through the hedge as the crows continued to chastise him.

"Nothing like a little excitement first thing in the morning to get the blood flowing," said Susie.

Willow smiled. "I'm ready for more. Come on, Susie, show us our shop!"

CHAPTER TWO

"Where's Jason?" I asked as Susie fished a large bunch of keys from her jeans pocket. "He said he wanted to be here when we saw inside the shop for the first time."

Susie opened the door and stood aside, letting me and Willow enter before her. "He was called away to a fire," she said, "but I'll show you around, and he said he'll be back as soon as he can."

"Called away to a fire?" I asked. The last time I'd seen Jason he'd been released from police custody after being suspected of murder. Why he'd been called to a fire was anyone's guess.

"He volunteered as a part-time fireman," explained Susie. "It seems he meant it when he said he wanted to do good with his life from now on."

All thoughts of Jason fighting fires faded as I looked around the room which was soon going to be my shop. The space was perfect. It had been a VHS rental shop until recently — when the elderly couple who'd owned it had begrudgingly admitted that the bottom had fallen out of the market, and retired to a new home in Portugal. The shelves which had once housed videos would be perfect for wands, cauldrons, and spells, and the service counter still had an old fashioned metal till on top of it. It made a pleasant ringing sound as I opened it, and I promised myself I'd never change it for a modern beeping electronic model. It fitted in perfectly with the vision I had of how the shop would look when it was decorated and filled with stock.

The path down to my mooring ran alongside the right-hand side of the shop, and adjoining it on the left was the *Firkin Gherkin* greengrocers, which would be invaluable in helping persuade me to eat a healthy lunch each day. The Golden Wok Chinese restaurant and takeaway was opposite, and the smell of fried onions was already heavy in the street even though it wasn't quite nine o'clock in the morning. I'd eaten there once, and had vowed never to repeat the experience after discovering that Dennis, the chef, used microwavable rice and jars of shop bought sauces to make his underwhelming offerings.

The entrance to Susie's flat was a set of steps at the rear of our building, which led up to a balcony and a bright red door. The balcony was decorated with colourful plants in pots and overlooked the canal a few hundred metres away. If you leaned out over the stone wall and craned your neck, you could just make out the bow of the *Water Witch* in her mooring.

Willow span on the spot pointing at shelves and cubbyholes. "We'll put the goblets on that shelf, and the cauldrons below," she enthused. "The crystals can go on the shelf near the window where they'll catch the sun, and we can set up a table to make potions on! It's perfect!"

Susie gave a giggle and a wide grin. "I knew you'd love it," she said. "And I've got some good news of my own too." She opened her bag and retrieved a badge. "It's a press pass," she beamed, holding it up for us to inspect. "The Herald liked the work I sold them during the Sam Hedgewick case, and they offered me a position as a journalist! I can work from home, right above you two! No more freelancing for me — I've got a job!"

Mine and Willow's excited congratulations were cut short by the ringing of the bell above the door as it opened. The bell made a sound a lot louder than the till, but not loud enough to ever become an annoyance.

"Hello!" said a big man, filling the doorway with his bulk. "I was hoping you could tell me what time the greengrocers opens. There's no sign in the window, and I'm desperate for some celery." He rubbed his almost spherical belly with a big hand. "I'm starving!"

I didn't like to say it, and I even felt guilty for thinking it, but starving was not an adjective I'd have used for the man. His stomach reached us a full foot and a half before the rest of his body as he closed the door and shuffled into the shop, and his t-shirt cast doubt on his claim he was a fan of celery. *'I ate all the pies!'* it proudly proclaimed, beneath a cartoon image of a pie, and *'South of England pie eating champion 2015,'* was emblazoned below.

He smiled as the three of us read his t-shirt. "And twenty-fourteen, *and* sixteen," he offered, with more than a hint of pride in his voice, "but they didn't do a t-shirt at last year's competition, they found better sponsors and commissioned an oil painting of me instead. It's in my bedroom, above the bed. The wife hates it, she says it stops her from falling asleep, but it makes me feel safe. The artist captured the crumbs in my beard perfectly."

I narrowed my eyes. His full black beard was currently

crumb free, and it appeared to have been combed. It was a pretty nice beard all round, as beards went.

"Allow me to introduce myself," he continued, his voice remarkably high-pitched for such a large man, but then again, his jeans did seem to be constrictive in the groin area. "I'm Felix Round."

Willow opened her mouth to speak, but Felix interrupted her. "I know what you're going to say," he declared. "Round by name, round by nature! I hear it all the time!"

"Erm, no," said Willow. "I was going to tell you the greengrocers opens at quarter-past nine."

"Oh," said Felix, looking dejected. "I bet you want to know why I'm so desperate for celery though, don't you? Come on admit it! Look at the size of me… why would I be eating celery? One of you must want to know!"

Willow had the least tact. "I am slightly intrigued," she admitted. "Although I'm guessing it's because you're on a diet?"

Felix smiled and shook his head. "Incorrect! It's not a diet — it's my secret weapon," he boasted. "I only eat celery for two days before a pie eating contest. I've almost collapsed from hunger in the past, but it does the job — I'll be half dead from starvation by the time the pies are placed in front of me, and I will smash them! I'm aiming to eat nineteen this year!"

"But the contest isn't for *four* days," said Susie. "You can't live on celery for that long. *I* couldn't live on celery for that long."

It was the first I'd heard of a pie eating contest, but I supposed it hadn't been top of Susie's list of things to tell me about when I'd arrived back in Wickford.

Felix frowned. "I'm forced to extend two days to four days. I must be strong. Dark times are upon us," he said, lowering his voice. "Rumour has it that The Tank is coming out of retirement after a three year break. I'm going to need to be extra hungry if I want to beat that bruiser."

"The Tank?" I said.

He moved nearer to us, and I took the opportunity to take a closer look at his beard. Definitely no crumbs.

"The Tank," he confirmed with a nod. "Winner of the South England pie eating contest for three years running. He once ate twelve meat and potato pies, *and* six lamb and mint — in forty-six minutes and twelve seconds. I need to be running on empty if I'm to be in with a chance of beating him. If I win this year I'll beat his record. So celery it is… for now." He fell silent for a moment and narrowed his eyes. "Then I will dominate!" he shouted, his belly wobbling and his voice trembling as it rose in volume. "The tank will wish he'd choked on the last pie he ate. I'll send him back to whatever dark corner of the county he's crawled out of and I'll fu—"

"What's going on here?" said a loud male voice. "Are you girls okay?"

Felix's shouting had disguised the sound of the bell ringing as the door opened, and Jason Danvers stood in the doorway. His tight fire brigade t-shirt moulded itself to his bulging muscles, and the soot on his face was as black as the tattoos which covered his arms. Granny had once or twice referred to him as a badboy, and he certainly looked bad as he leapt into action, taking long strides through the shop with the obvious intent of stopping Felix committing whatever heinous act Jason imagined he was about to.

Felix whimpered, and I stepped between the two men. "It's okay!" I said, placing a hand on Jason's chest. "He was just telling us a story, he got himself over excited."

"It's hunger pangs," said Felix, shrinking under Jason's gaze. "I get a little edgy when I'm hungry. The doctor said I've developed diabetes, but you can't trust the quacks, can you? What can one little blood test really tell a doctor about the intricate workings of the human body? I was told I wouldn't see Christmas twenty-ten if I didn't cut down on yak's milk, but look at me. I'm still here, and as strong as an ox!"

The door opened again, and in hurried a short thin woman with a scowl on her face, bright green polish on her fingernails, and a hairdo so large it bounced as she walked. "Felix, what on earth are you doing?" she said, taking the big man by the hand. "You only came in to ask what time the shop next door opens. I've been sitting in the car waiting for you."

"Sorry, darling," said Felix. "The young ladies were interested in hearing about the pie eating contest. You know how I like to talk."

Felix dwarfed his wife, and she sighed as she turned her husband towards the door. "Nobody wants to hear about your wretched competition, Felix. And I wish you wouldn't wear that t-shirt everywhere. It's not clever to show off about giving yourself heart disease and diabetes."

"I don't have heart disease," protested Felix, as he followed his wife. "And as you know, sweetheart, I'm dubious about the diabetes diagnosis."

His wife sighed. "I do wish you'd listen to the doctor, Felix. I'm worried sick about you, and you don't seem to care!"

"Look," said Willow, pointing through the window and relieving the tension. "It's Mr Jarvis. He owns the greengrocers. Go and get your celery, Felix, and we wish you luck in the competition. We'll be rooting for you."

I considered relieving the tension even further by pointing out Willow's possible pun, but I wasn't quite sure if celery *was* a root vegetable or not.

"Celery?" said Jason, watching the oddly matched couple leave the shop.

"Long story," I said, as the door closed behind them.

Jason wiped his forehead with the back of his hand. "I've got a story too," he said. "A story which I think you'll want to hear."

CHAPTER THREE

Willow carried a large glass of water from the small kitchen in the rear area of the shop, and Jason drank it with long thirsty gulps. He wiped his mouth with the back of a hand and leaned against the serving counter, sweat beading on his forehead.

"That fire I just got called to," he said, "was strange."

"Strange?" I said. "In what way?"

Jason took a breath and looked at us in turn. "Some thugs rolled a burning car over a cliff in the quarry. Luckily someone was walking his dog and reported it, or the fire would have spread to the trees."

"Idiot kids," said Susie. "Probably from Covenhill. I'd hate to think we have young adults like that in Wickford."

"That's not what was strange," Jason said. "What was strange is that a goat wearing a balaclava came galloping out of the trees and attacked the firemen, me included."

"A goat?" said Willow casually.

Jason nodded. "Yes, a goat. A goat which I'm almost certain is the same goat that attacked me on your boat."

"I thought you said it was wearing a balaclava?" I said,

mentally piecing together the jigsaw of what had happened in the quarry that morning, and it wasn't a difficult puzzle to put together. "How can you be sure?"

The goat *had* to be Boris — another animal which had fallen foul of Granny's witch dementia. The goat wasn't *actually* a goat — well, the body was, but the mind was that of certified acupuncturist Charleston Huang, which had accidentally been transferred into the animal. Charleston Huang was quite happy being trapped in the goat, and his body, along with the mind of the *actual* goat, was languishing in a form of magical stasis in Granny's guest bedroom, beneath her most expensive summer duvet.

Granny had promised she was going to burn Charlestons's car when she'd thought the police were looking for him. It seemed she'd followed through on her promise, and had enlisted the help of Boris.

Jason looked at me with amusement playing on his face. "Really?" he said. "Are you trying to tell me that a balaclava wearing goat which attacked me today, isn't the same got which attacked me on your boat?"

"Maybe," said Susie. "Plenty of people keep goats, Jason. It's really not unusual, especially in rural areas of the country."

Jason narrowed his eyes and licked his lips. "Talking goats?"

Susie had no answer.

"Not this again," I said. "The police told you that was all in your imagination. When the goat bit you… down there, you hallucinated because of the pain you were in — you imagined the goat had spoken to you."

Susie and Willow nodded their agreement, though both of them knew full well that Boris had indeed hurled insults at Jason before he'd dragged him from his hiding place on my boat.

"That doesn't explain today," said Jason, shaking his head. "He spoke to me again. I know he did! He called me a 'diabolical yellow helmeted moron.' I had to take my helmet off and hit him with it to stop him biting through my water hose."

I laughed. At least I'd tried to laugh, but it came out as a snort. "Smoke inhalation," I proclaimed. "It has to be. You breathed in too much smoke and imagined the goat was talking."

Jason raised his eyebrows. "What is it with that goat?" he said, "and what is it you're hiding from me?"

"Nothing," I said. Certainly not the fact that Willow and I were Witches, along with everyone else in my family. "You've overheated, Jason. Come on, I'll sign the rental contract for the shop and then you can go home and lie down. You look like you need a long shower and a rest."

Jason nodded. "The animal welfare people are out looking for the goat anyway. They say he could suffocate if they don't find him soon and remove the balaclava."

Willow and I swapped glances as I signed the paperwork for Jason, and my sister whispered in my ear as Jason took his empty glass into the kitchen. "So, Granny and Boris are arsonists now?" she said. "Do you think we should go and find out what's going on?"

****

Willow and I locked the shop up and said goodbye to Jason and Susie — refusing the offer of a lift from both of them, and began the walk to Granny's cottage. Ashwood cottage was high on a hill to the west of Wickford, and Willow and I took deep breaths as we climbed the steep and narrow country lane that led us there.

Birds sang and bees buzzed, and I smiled to myself as the sun warmed my face. Only Willow grabbing my arm with fingers that dug deep into my flesh, dragged me from my happy daze. "Watch out!" she screamed, as she pulled me into the hedge alongside her.

The loud roar of an engine was followed by a flash of red as a large pickup truck sped past, barely avoiding us as we squeezed ourselves against the prickles of the hedgerow. The pick-up came to a screeching halt, and the smell of burnt rubber and diesel smoke hung in the air, filling the narrow lane with toxic fumes and masking the pleasant scent of wild flowers.

A man leaned out of the driver's window and waved at us. "I'm so sorry, girls!" he shouted. "Are you both okay?"

"We're fine," I said, brushing twigs from my short red summer dress, and checking my Doctor Martens for scuffs. "Just watch where you're going in the future."

He leaned further out of the window, his blond hair and thin face barely visible through the cloud of smoke the engine spewed out. "Will do," he said. "You have my word."

His word didn't seem to count for much. He sped away with a squeal of rubber and a scream from the engine, and as he rounded the next bend, some of the loose load in the back of his vehicle spilled over the tailgate and onto the sun warmed tarmac. Neither Willow or I had any requirement for a pile of straw and a few ragged t-shirts, so we kicked the straw off the road and carried the t-shirts with us, throwing them in the rubbish bin at the bottom of one of the farm tracks that led off the lane. Our good deed for the day.

The walk to Granny's house left Willow and I hot and sweaty, and I began to think that Mum had a valid point when she continually insisted I needed a car. Especially since I'd decided to move my shop off the boat and into a proper property. I decided to put it at the top of my list of priorities.

The lean-to attached to the side of Granny's bright yellow cottage was suspiciously devoid of wood. It *had* been stacked high with freshly cut timber which had concealed Charleston

Huang's car, but the logs had been scattered, and fresh tyre marks indicated a vehicle had recently been moved. Willow and I needed no more evidence to prove that it had been Boris and Granny who were guilty of arson that morning. Not that we'd had any doubts in the first place.

The fact that a balaclava wearing goat had been on the scene was not just more damning evidence, but was also proof that Boris and Granny had not only broken the law, but were both stepping teasingly close to the line which separated them from being *relatively* normal — or a pair of raving lunatics.

Granny's front door was unlocked, and Willow and I entered the cottage to complete silence. The kitchen, which Granny spent most of her time in, was empty, and Boris was not in the study where he could often be found writing his blog and drinking brandy.

"Granny!" shouted Willow. "Are you here?"

Hurried footsteps sounded on the ceiling above us, and Granny's face appeared at the top of the narrow stairway, her blue rinse perm recently coloured, and her finger over her lips as she hushed us. "As happy as I am to see you both again, would you keep the noise down, please? Boris and I are *trying* to have a candlelit vigil."

"A candlelit vigil?" I said. "What on earth are you having —"

Granny shushed me with a hiss of air through her teeth. "It's Charleston's birthday," she whispered. "Boris and I wanted to pay our respects. If you two can keep those flapping mouths of yours quiet, you can come up and join us. Boris would appreciate it, I'm sure."

Willow looked at me and shrugged. "Candlelit vigil it is," she whispered.

Granny waited at the top of the stairs for us, and we followed her quietly to the guest bedroom. She ushered us into the dimly lit small room, and Willow's giggle elicited a stern stare from Granny. "It's not funny!" she warned. "Boris is taking this very seriously!"

Boris sat on his haunches with his front hooves on the bed. His head was bowed and he mumbled incoherently under his breath. He looked up at us, and the tea-light candle on the bedspread in front of him almost set alight the long hairs of his beard. Small strands of black wool were visible on his horns, and his white hair was darker than usual — almost as if he'd been near a sooty fire in *very* recent history. "It's good to see you both again," he said in a low voice. "I'm sure we'll catch up later, but for now, please light a candle each and join Gladys and I in celebrating the end of another year in the life of a remarkable man."

"And the beginning of another," murmured Granny, gazing at the acupuncturist who lay in her guest bed.

Only Charleston Huang's head was visible, resting on two plumped up pillows which were scattered with rose petals. The petals matched the colour of the rose plants climbing up the outside walls of Granny's cottage, and tiny aphids crawled off them and onto the white linen pillowcases.

The rest of Charleston's body was covered by a flower print duvet, and his face still wore the shocked expression it had adopted when Granny's witch dementia had switched his mind with that of a goat. His mouth was frozen in a perfect O shape, but his eyelids had been closed — by Granny, I presumed. I tried convincing myself that he looked peaceful, but if I was being brutally honest with myself — he looked like a man who'd been jabbed in the buttock with a long and very sharp pin.

Charleston's body was in complete magical stasis, and the mind of the goat trapped in it was oblivious to anything that was happening. Until Granny cured her witch dementia, the minds could not be switched back, and even then, it was doubtful that Charleston would want his mind to be put back in his own body. He'd become strangely accustomed to living life in the body of a goat, and had insisted that people called him Boris, out of respect for the goat whose body he inhabited.

Willow passed me a candle, and I lit it using the lighter which Granny offered me. Granny had never had a cigarette lighter in the house until she'd moved the goat in with her, but Boris was fond of cigars, and brandy — in large quantities.

Granny peered over her purple glasses. "Kneel down, girls," she said. "Join Boris in his tribute. I'll remain standing. Boris has given me special dispensation due to an injury I acquired this morning… while… feeding the chickens."

"Not while pushing a burning car over a cliff in a quarry?" mumbled Willow, as she lowered herself next to Boris and joined him in his solemnity. Willow had never learned to let Granny's lies go unchallenged.

The candle in Granny's hand dropped to the floor at her slipper clad feet, and she broke the dignified silence with a gasp. "I don't know what you mean! And neither does Boris! Car? Burning? Cliff? None of those words make any sense!" Granny's face paled, and she slowly lowered herself to her knees and crumpled into a heap on the carpet, wrapping her arms around herself. "Nothing happened at the quarry this morning," she mumbled. "I was feeding the chickens. Nothing happened at the quarry."

Her whimpers turned to sobs, and her eyes glazed over, adopting the expression which Willow and I recognised as her thousand-yard-stare. Granny had temporarily shut down.

"Gladys?" said Boris, his face looking convincingly concerned for a goat. "Gladys!" He leapt to his feet, sending wax flying as his beard knocked his candle over. The wax flew in hot arcs which splattered the duvet and the already shocked face of the Chinese acupuncturist in the bed. "Gladys!" he repeated, tapping her with a hoof. "Oh, Gladys! Where have you gone?"

"She's shut down, Boris," I said placing a hand on his back. "It's nothing to worry about, I'm surprised this is the first time you're seeing it, if I'm honest. *Really* surprised."

"Poor Gladys," said Boris. "The shock of what we were forced to do this morning has evidently caught up with her."

"You mean burning a car?" said Willow.

Boris looked into Granny's glassy eyes. "It was necessary. It's my body's birthday, and Gladys and I wanted to begin the next year with a fresh start. Having my car hidden away in the lean-to was just too much of a problem for the both of us. It's only a matter of time before somebody notices Charleston is missing — even though I've been spreading false information over the internet that he's gone away on a vacation. Imagine if they found my body here in magical stasis — your family secret would be revealed to the world before you could say abracadabra."

He was right of course. The fact that my family were witches was a secret known only to a few people, and none of us wanted anybody else finding out. "I can understand you burning the car," I said, "but attacking the firemen was inexcusable."

Granny groaned. "That wasn't Boris," she mumbled, snapping out of her shock induced trance. "It was another goat."

Even Boris rolled his eyes.

"So, you're telling us that there was another goat who just happened to be in the quarry at the same time as you two were there?" said Willow, helping Granny to her feet with a hand under her arm.

"A balaclava wearing goat which attacked the firemen?" I

added. I picked a strand of wool from one of Boris's horns and held it out for Granny to inspect.

"Good grief, Boris!" said Granny. "You just can't hide evidence very well at all, can you?" She sat on the bed, her bottom inches from Charleston's wax splattered face. It seemed that the dignified vigil was well and truly over. "It's your fault we had to send you after the firemen, and now your leaving evidence on your horns! Remind me not to involve you in anything potentially illegal again. You're a liability!"

"Why was it Boris's fault?" I asked.

Granny straightened her glasses. "He said there was nothing with his name on in the car. *Until* the fire brigade arrived and began putting the fire out. *Then* he remembered his passport was in the glove compartment. We had to make sure that car burnt to the ground! I'd been up all night filing the identification numbers off the chassis and engine, and then that daft goat goes and leaves his passport in it! It was imbecilic of him."

"So you sent Boris to distract the firemen until the car was completely burnt out and all the evidence was destroyed," I said. "And you just happened to have a balaclava with you? I'm not even going to ask why you thought it was necessary to make Boris wear it. He's a goat for goddess's sake!"

"Boris is a very distinguished and easily recognisable goat," said Granny, "especially since he won the beautiful farmyard animal competition, and I've always got a balaclava in my bag. You never know when you'll stumble upon a protest. I've needed that balaclava more often than the lipstick I carry in the same bag."

Granny had very rigid political views which had landed her in trouble in the past. It was no shock to me or Willow that she carried a means of hiding her face with her at all times.

"Be warned," I said. "The animal welfare people are searching for Boris, and you'd better hope the police don't find out who the car belongs to."

Granny stood up, bent over Charleston, and began peeling dried wax from his face. "Bah!" she laughed. "The policeman who turned up at the fire was your friend Barney. Forgive me if I say I'm not particularly nervous about the possibility of being found out."

"That's not fair," I said. "Barney did well during the Sam Hedgewick murder investigation."

"Rubbish!" scoffed Granny, gathering up the petals from the pillows. "We all know it wasn't Barney who solved that murder, and I'll go to the foot of my stairs if Barney Dobkins manages to even work out it was a car that was set on fire, let alone link it to me or Boris."

Granny snapped her head upright as a loud knocking on the front door echoed through the cottage. "Who on earth could that be?" she said. "It can't be Maggie, she's preparing for a visitor, and it's certainly not the window cleaner. The cast isn't due to be taken off his leg for another three weeks, and he seemed sincere when he said he'd never clean my windows again. Strange though — most young men would be happy to be confronted by a pair of bare breasts when they reached the top of a ladder. He must bat for the other team… that's the only rational explanation."

There were so many questions to ask, starting with who was visiting my mother, and then moving swiftly onto Granny's indecent exposure incident. Willow prevented me from asking them though, as she moved the curtain aside and looked through the window. "It's Barney," she said, "and he's wearing his uniform. It looks like he's here on official police business."

CHAPTER FOUR

The knocking on the front door grew louder, and Granny pointed to the bedroom door. "Code red! Everybody downstairs!" she panicked. She closed the door behind us as we paraded along the landing. "Boris!" she ordered, "you go straight out of the back door and into the garden, it's time for you to pretend you're a garden goat."

We rushed down the stairs, and Granny pointed to Boris's study. "Willow, it's your job to go in there and make it look like it's not a room that a goat uses to get drunk and write a blog in." She looked at me. "Penny, it's your job to keep Barney's mind occupied. It's obvious he's got the hots for you, and it's time for you to use that to your advantage. We can't let him find Charleston."

As Boris trotted through the house and out of the back door, Willow began work in Boris's study, moving empty brandy glasses and hiding ashtrays. Granny nodded appreciatively at Willow's efforts and put a wide smile on her face as she opened the front door. I stood next to her and smiled at Barney as he gazed down at us. "Penny, you're home!" he said, with a twinkle in his eyes.

The last time I'd seen Barney I'd promised him that we'd go out for a meal together, and I thought that in the circumstances it wouldn't be too manipulative of me to use the arrangement as a means of distraction. Even I knew that it would be no good for any of us if Barney was to discover the magically frozen body of Charleston Huang in Granny's guest bedroom. I could put my principles aside for the time being.

Not used to the intricacies of flirting, I imagined what Willow would do in my position, and pushed my chest out a little as I widened my smile. "Hi, Barney," I gushed. "It's so good to see you. I'm really excited about going out for that meal with you. Did you come here looking for me?"

"Really?" said Barney, his cheeks blushing a deep crimson. "I mean yes. I mean no. I mean I'm looking forward to taking you out, but I'm not here for that."

"Well, just what are you here for, young man?" snapped Granny. "I hope you haven't come here to try and take down *my* particulars."

Barney looked at his feet. His trouser legs exposed far too much of the shiny black leather of his boots, and his stab jacket hung from his skinny frame. He politely removed his hat, revealing his neatly combed ginger hair, and gave Granny a nervous smile. "I am here on duty, Mrs Weaver," he said sheepishly. "But I'm confident there's been a mistake. If I could just clear a few things up, I'm sure I can be on my way."

Granny gazed up at Barney's face, her neck clicking as she struggled to find the correct angle. She shielded the sun from her eyes with a hand, and sighed. "And what things might they be, PC Dobkins? Have I been reported for shouting at that machine in the convenience store again? It keeps telling me I've got an unexpected item in the bagging area. What am I supposed to do? Reason with it? I'll shout at that machine until it finds some manners, and nobody will tell me otherwise!"

Barney shook his head. "No," he said. "No one's complained about that *this* week. I'm here because of an incident that occurred this morning. In the quarry."

"What happened?" I said, hoping that Barney wasn't very good at reading body language. I relaxed my face a little, and gave him another smile.

"There was a fire," said Barney. "A car was set alight, and people normally only set fire to cars when they've got a crime to hide."

Granny grew an inch in height, her head almost level with Barney's chest. "Are you trying to say I'm a criminal?" she blasted, "because if you are, young man, I'd rather you just come right out and say it, than continue beating around the bush."

"Gosh, no!" said Barney. He'd seemed to have lost a few inches in height under the wilting stare of Granny, and he took a half step backwards along the garden path, almost tripping over his feet. "Sergeant Cooper sent me, he's received reports of an elderly woman spotted near the scene, and with the addition of a masked violent goat, I think he's put two and two together and thought that maybe… just maybe, it had something to do with you and that goat you keep in your garden."

Granny placed one of her hands behind her back, and I knew without looking there'd be sparks flying from her fingertips. I couldn't allow Granny to cast any spells, not only because of the danger her witch dementia posed to Barney and anybody else within ten metres, but also because I liked Barney, and I knew Granny did too — she was just panicking.

Granny flinched as I placed a calming hand on her shoulder, but the tension left her muscles. "Elderly!" she said. "Do I look elderly to you, Barney Dobkins?"

"Of course not, Mrs Weaver!" said Barney. "The witness said the suspect had blue hair too, maybe that's why Sergeant Cooper thought of you. You don't look a day over seventy to me."

Granny made a low growling sound in her throat, and I shook my head at Barney with my eyes wide. He understood my message. "I mean you don't look a day over sixty, Mrs Weaver," he said.

Granny patted her hair with both hands and straightened her apron. "Thank you, Barney," she said, "that's very kind of you. I try my best, and isn't it nice to know that Penny will grow into an older woman as beautiful as I am? Good looks run in this family, so you can be assured that if the meal you're taking my granddaughter on goes well, you won't be walking around with a sunken faced old hag on your arm in forty years' time."

"Granny!" I said. "Barney's taking me out for a meal to thank me for my help during the Sam Hedgewick case! Stop embarrassing him." I raised my eyebrows in an apology to Barney. "What is it you need from Granny? I said. "I'm sure she'd be happy to clear her name."

Barney took a notepad from his pocket. "I'm really sorry I have to do this," he said, "but Sergeant Cooper will come here himself if I don't ask you these questions."

Granny sighed. "Ask away, young man, but don't you dare ask for my date of birth. A lady is entitled to *some* secrets."

Barney nodded and touched his pen to paper. "Okay," he said, "would you mind me asking where you were this morning between the hours of eight and nine o'clock, Mrs Weaver?"

Granny placed a hand on her chin and looked at the sky. "Let me think," she said, "where was I between the hours of eight and nine this morning?" She locked her eyes on Barney's. "Where do you *think* I was? I was where I always am at that time of the day! Right here, in my cottage. Next question please, police constable."

Barney scribbled in his notepad and shuffled his feet. "I'm afraid I'm going to have to ask to see your goat… Boris, isn't it?" he said. "And I just need to take a quick look around your cottage."

"What on earth do need to do all that for?" said Granny. "Have you got a warrant?"

Barney sighed. "Mrs Weaver," he said, "this is really awkward for me. I don't want to be asking these questions, and I certainly don't want to infringe on your privacy, but if I don't, Sergeant Cooper will do it himself. I was hoping you'd be more understanding if it was me that turned up on your doorstep. I just want to be able to cross you out of my notebook and tell Sergeant Cooper you've done nothing wrong."

"Of course you can see Boris," I said, pulling Granny aside, and gesturing at Barney to come inside. "And I'd be happy to show you around Granny's cottage. I don't know what you're looking for though."

"Burnt clothing, petrol cans, that sort of thing," said Barney. "Nothing that I'll find here, I'm positive."

Granny's eyes sparkled as her brain leapt into gear. "Take Barney into the garden and show him the goat, Penny," she said. "I'll just go and tidy up a little, it's been a long time since a man has been in my bedroom, and I want it to look nice."

"You're not going to hide something, are you?" laughed Barney. His smiling face quickly transformed into a look of fear as Granny scowled at him. "It was just a joke," he said, moving behind me.

I took him by the elbow. "Come on," I said. "I'll take you into the garden."

Granny scampered up the stairs as I led Barney through the cottage. The back door was open and I was relieved to see that Willow had overheard the conversation on the doorstep and was taking evasive action. Boris didn't look relieved though. He stood with his head bowed, shivering as Willow washed him down with the hosepipe. His beard dripped with water, but as we neared him I was happy to see that his hair was white and any evidence of sooty water had soaked into the lawn.

The chickens squawked as overspray splattered them, and Barney stopped a few feet from Willow with a frown on his face. "Hi," he said, "washing the goat?"

Boris made a spluttering sound as Willow washed a stray strand of wool from one of his horns.

"It's a warm day, Barney," said Willow. "He was getting a little overheated."

Barney studied Boris, and Boris stared back at him, narrowing his eyes. "He does look a little aggressive," said Barney. "Are you sure he couldn't have escaped and found his own way to the quarry? Maybe some kids caught him and put a balaclava on him?"

"Of course not," said Willow. "He's tied to a pole."

Barney gave the goat one last look. "Listen," he said, speaking to both me and Willow, and wiping his brow with the back of a hand. "I know the fire was nothing to do with your grandmother, and to be honest, I wouldn't really care if it was. You two helped me with my last case, and I won't forget that. I'll just have a quick look around the cottage, tell Sergeant Cooper that he's barking up the wrong tree, and get on with my day."

"Coooeee!" came Granny's raised voice. "You can come and have a look around, Barney! Everything's in order now! There's nothing to see here!"

Granny leant from her bedroom window waving at us,

and Barney raised his eyebrows. "*Everything's in order now. There's nothing to see.* What does she mean?"

"She just means she's tidied up a little," said Willow, twisting the nozzle of the hose to the off position, much to Boris's obvious delight. He shook the water from his hair and gave a loud satisfied sigh.

"Is he alright?" said Barney. "He sounds like he needs to see a vet."

"He's perfectly okay," I said, taking Barney by the wrist and leading him down the garden path, both literally and figuratively. "Come on, you can decide which restaurant you want to take me to, while you look around Granny's cottage."

Willow followed us, and together we showed Barney around the bottom floor of the cottage. He gazed around unfazed as we took him into what had once been Granny's prized backroom, but had recently been transformed into a goat's study. Willow had done a good job of making it look almost normal. The empty glasses and half-drunk bottles of brandy had vanished, and the ash trays full of cigar ends were hidden — although the room was still rich with the scent of expensive tobacco. Boris's cushion had been turned upside down, hiding the white hairs, and his computer coffee table desk had been cleared of the technology a goat needed to navigate the internet.

Barney cleared his throat. "Thanks, girls," he said. "I'll just have a quick walk around upstairs, and I'll be on my way."

Willow led the way up the stairs and Barney brought up the rear. "I was thinking of the Golden Wok," he said, as we neared the top, where Granny stood waiting with a smug look on her face. "If you like Chinese food that is."

"That sounds lovely," I lied.

"That way, constable!" said Granny, with her back to the closed door of the guest bedroom, pointing Barney in the direction of her bedroom and the rest of the top floor.

Barney gave an embarrassed smile and poked his head around the open door of the bathroom. "It's okay!" hissed Granny, as Barney moved into the next room. "I've hidden Charleston!"

"Where?" I said. "There's nowhere in that room to hide him, and you couldn't have fitted him under the bed!"

Granny patted me on the shoulder. "Trust me, Sweetheart. Granny knows best."

Barney emerged from Granny's bedroom. "Thank you, Mrs Weaver," he said. "If I could just look in the last room, I'll leave you to enjoy the rest of the day."

Granny swung the door to the bedroom open, and gestured at Barney to step inside. "Be my guest," she said, winking at me and Willow. "I'm sure you'll find everything is in order."

I took a deep breath as Barney stepped into the room, but the air barely had the chance to fill my lungs before Barney gave a panicked cry. "What the —" he shouted. "Who the — what's going on? Come out of there with your hands where I can see them!"

I followed Willow into the room with my heart in my mouth and my mind in slow motion. Willow came to a dead stop, and I bumped into her back as the two of us unravelled what we were seeing.

CHAPTER FIVE

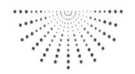

*B*arney stood frozen to the spot with his nightstick raised above his head. "Come out!" he repeated, edging closer to the corner of the room.

Willow gave a choking gasp, and Granny ran into the room and put her hand on Barney's arm. "It's okay," she said. "He's a friend of the family."

Barney ignored Granny. "Come out!" he repeated. "I'm not stupid, I can see you."

The fact that Barney could see Charleston Huang in no way indicated any lack of stupidity on his behalf. When Granny had insisted she'd hidden Charleston, I'd had my doubts, but what I was looking at raised important questions about Granny's level of sanity. Or complete lack of it.

Charleston was unceremoniously propped up in the corner, with one of Granny's spare curtains draped over him. The curtain covered him from the neck down, hanging off him like an ill-fitting moo-moo. I stared in disbelief as Barney approached Charleston and lifted a light-shade from his head, stumbling backwards as the shocked face of the acupuncturist confronted him.

Granny shrugged. "I did my best," she said. "Now, have you two girls been studying my spell book? Or do I have to attempt a spell myself, and risk turning Barney into a standing lamp?"

Barney touched Charleston's face, prodding him with a finger. "What have you done?" he said, slowly turning to face us. "Is he dead? Did you kill him? Who is he? I knew something was wrong here. I saw the tyre tracks near the lean-to, and I wondered why you were washing the goat! You've killed this man and burnt his car to hide the evidence! What's the goat got to do with all this, though? And why does it smell of cigar smoke downstairs? None of you smoke!"

"A spell would be very handy right now," said Granny, leaning against the doorframe, looking far too casual for a woman being accused of murder. "My fingers are itching to cast one, and if I cast it, who knows what will happen. My dementia's feeling very playful today."

Barney reached for his radio, and Willow raised her hand. Purple sparks played on the fingertips, and Barney's mouth widened into an O, matching the expression which was etched on the man's face behind him. "I'm sorry, Barney," said Willow.

"Wh — what's happening here?" stammered Barney. "Am I awake?"

Barney pressed the button on his radio and Willow clicked her fingers. Barney's hands dropped to his sides and he looked around the room in confusion. "Where am I?" he said. "Penny? Willow? Mrs Weaver? Is this heaven?"

I'd have liked to have thought that heaven would have been a little more pleasant than a gloomy guest bedroom containing three witches and a frozen Chinese acupuncturist, but I supposed every mortal had their own personal vision of paradise. I was quite flattered to be included in Barney's.

"No, Barney," said Willow, "It's not heaven and everything's going to be okay. I need you to listen to me, do you understand?"

Barney nodded.

"Put the nightstick away, and pick your hat up."

Barney did as he was told, stooping slowly to retrieve his hat from the floor.

Willow continued. "You're going to walk downstairs, and when you get outside, you're going to believe that you've looked around the cottage and everything was as it should be. You'll forget about tyre tracks, goats, and men in this bedroom. Do you understand, Barney?"

Barney nodded again.

"Tell him to forget about the Golden Wok," I said. "The food there is vile."

"Do you want him to forget about taking you out for a meal completely?" offered Willow.

Barney's confused eyes settled on my face, and he lifted a hand towards me, his fingers trembling, and his voice soft as he spoke. "Penny, have you tried the duck in orange sauce? It's divine."

I smiled. "No, Willow. I'll go for a meal. I want to, just not the Golden Wok."

"Barney," said Willow, her hand at waist height. "You'll remember that Penny said she'd go for a meal with you, but you'll be adamant that she chooses where. Oh, and you'll offer to pay the whole of the bill, including drinks and any taxi fares incurred."

"Half," I said.

"You'll go dutch, Barney," said Willow. She winked at me. "Very modern of you, Penny."

"Can you ask him to ignore any complaints from the window cleaner?" asked Granny. "I'm sure he's the type to try his luck at getting compensation from me."

Willow glared at Granny. "You deserve to pay more than just the window cleaner compensation, and I don't want to hear any more about that whole sorry saga. Some things are best left to the imagination."

"I'll let you keep my spell book for as long as you need it?" pleaded Granny.

Willow and I had acquired Granny's treasured spell book using manipulation and blackmail. It was fittingly appropriate that Granny was now using it as a means to manipulate Willow.

I tried for a better deal. "And let us use your car until I buy one?" I said.

Granny waved a casual hand. "You can have that old thing. Boris is buying us a new one. He wants us to have one of those big Range Rovers."

Charleston Huang was a wealthy man, and Boris had already allowed Granny to use his credit card. It came as a mild surprise that he'd let Granny buy a new car though, especially one that pricey.

"Deal?" I asked Willow.

"Deal," she confirmed. She waved her hand at Barney. "If a window cleaner approaches you with allegations of indecent exposure —"

"Accidental exposure," corrected Granny.

"Of any sort of exposure," continued Willow. "You're to ignore him and tell him to drop any insurance claims against Granny."

Barney nodded, his eyelids drooping. "Indecent. Granny. Understood," he slurred.

"Everyone got what they wanted?" said Willow.

Granny and I both agreed.

"Okay, Barney," said Willow. "Walk downstairs, open the front door, and when you turn to face us, everything will be as it should be, and you'll think everything I've asked you to do is all your own idea."

Barney nodded slowly, dragging his feet as he made his way past us and down the stairs. We followed him closely with Willow directly behind him, sparks still crackling from her fingers.

Sunlight poured into the hallway as Barney opened the heavy front door, and the moment he stepped over the threshold his whole posture changed. He stopped for a few seconds, rolling his shoulders and taking a deep breath, before turning slowly on the spot to face us.

Willow dropped her hand and the sparks disappeared as Barney rubbed his eyes and blinked a few times. "Sorry to have disturbed you, Mrs Weaver," he said, putting his hat on. "I was only doing my job, I hope you understand."

"And a fine job you did too, Barney," said Granny. "Most thorough indeed. It makes me feel safe to know that the constabulary employs officers of such high calibre."

"Just serving my community," beamed Barney. "It's an honour."

"Off you trot then," suggested Granny. "I've got things to do, and you've taken up enough of my time already today."

Barney straightened his hat and pulled his trousers up, showing a flash of white sock above his boots. "Let me know when you've decided on a restaurant, Penny," he said.

I gave him my sincerest smile. "I will," I promised.

"I've got a better idea," said Granny.

I doubted it, but I let her speak.

"My son's arriving for a visit today, Barney." she said. "He's coming to watch the pie eating competition. He loves a nice pie, does Brian. He's staying at Maggie's cottage and we're having a family meal tonight to welcome him and make him feel safe. He's oppressed you see, and he'd love it if an officer of the law was present."

So that's who Mum had been preparing the cottage for. My uncle Brian, her brother. Oppressed though? Uncle Brian was the least oppressed person I knew. Apart from Granny, of course. "I'm sure Barney doesn't want to spend his Friday evening with us," I said, scowling at my grandmother. "He's got better things to do, and anyway, Willow and I weren't asked if we wanted to attend a meal, and Uncle Brian is *not* oppressed."

Granny wiped her hands on her apron and forced her glasses to the top of her nose. "Until the day there's a gay astronaut — Brian is, and will remain, oppressed. And I'm telling you two girls right now that you're coming to Maggie's meal. You haven't seen her for two weeks. She's preparing a feast, *and* she's using her best porcelain. The set with the little blue and white Chinese folk on it."

Barney cleared his throat. "I'd love to come, Mrs Weaver," he said diplomatically. "It would be a pleasure to meet your son, and Maggie *does* know how to cook."

It wouldn't be the first time Barney had been to my mum's for a meal. Last time, she'd cooked lasagne, and she'd glowed for hours after Barney had enthusiastically praised her cooking skills. The ingredients had come from the haven though, and anything cooked with ingredients brought back from the haven was always going to taste good. The magical dimension was off limits to Willow and I until we'd acquired enough magic skills to be given our entry spells, but rumour had it that mine was to be given to me in the near future. If you believed my mother, and Aunt Eva — who was a permanent resident of the haven, and a renowned gossipmonger, that is.

Granny was unable to visit the haven until her witch dementia cleared up, but that was probably a good thing. Granny had caused a lot of trouble in the haven in the past, and it would do her good to stay away for a while.

"Well that clears that up!" said Granny. "Now, off you go, Barney. You need to catch an arsonist, and I need to tend to my goat. We've both got quite a day ahead of us! I look forward to seeing you at Maggie's cottage at seven o'clock sharp."

"Seven it is!" smiled Barney.

He headed down the path towards his car, and I whispered to Willow. "What spell was that?" I said. "It was very impressive."

"A spell of purged memory," said Willow. "Page twenty-four in Granny's book."

"Well done, girls," said Granny, pushing between us. "We averted a disaster back there. He's a cunning one… that Barney Dobkins. I really didn't think he'd spot Charleston. He's got eyes like a hawk and a brain built for policing, that boy!"

"You draped a curtain over Charleston and put a light shade on his head," I said. "Of course Barney saw him!"

"He'll make a fine Sergeant one day," continued Granny. "He'll clean this town up and show the criminals who's boss. You mark my words."

Barney waved at us as he opened the car door, and reached for his radio as it crackled into life. "Okay," he said, speaking quickly. "I'll be straight there. Give Mrs Oliver a cup of tea and tell her to calm down."

There's nothing more infuriating than only hearing one side of what sounds like a very important conversation, and I hated being infuriated. "What's happened?" I asked.

Barney sighed. "The same as yesterday, and the day before," he said. "Birdwatchers complaining about one of the farmers shooting crows. He's not breaking any laws, but you try and tell Mrs Oliver that."

I remembered my promise to Gerald Timkins. I didn't want to get him in trouble, so I feigned ignorance. "That sounds more exciting than looking around Granny's cottage," I said.

Barney put the car in gear and edged forward. "You haven't met Mrs Florence," he shouted through the open window.

"Seven o'clock Barney!" shouted Granny, tapping her watch. "Make sure you're there on time, Maggie's doing a prawn cocktail starter. She'll be as crazy as a dwarf in a stilt shop if you're late!"

Barney waved his acknowledgement, and Granny turned her attention to us as the police car left her property.

"I'd like you two to do me a favour," she said. "Boris is a little upset that he can't come to the meal at your mother's tonight. I'd like you to let him stay on your boat. It will lift his spirits, I'm sure."

"But we'll be at the meal," Willow said, "and I don't like the idea of Boris being alone on the boat. Those hooves of his could cause all sorts of problems."

"Ask Susie to look after him," said Granny. "She and Boris get along like a house on fire. They'll have a wonderful time together, and it will give Susie an excuse to refuse Maggie's invitation to dinner — she said she was going to ask her."

I was absolutely sure that Susie wouldn't want to come to my mum's for a Weaver family meal, and I was absolutely certain that Granny wasn't going to take no for an answer.

"Of course he can stay on the boat," I said. "I'll phone Susie and ask her."

"Good," said Granny. "Take Boris with you as soon as you can. I need to get ready."

"Ready for what?" said Willow.

"There's a gentleman coming from the Range Rover dealership to pick me up. I'm collecting our new car. You two can take my old car and call it your own. I'll miss it, but Boris has ordered a private registration plate for the new ride, and he said the sound system is thumping. I'm rather looking forward to driving it. Boris said it will give me social mobility. I can finally say goodbye to the working-class, and hello to the lower middle-class."

"You've never worked a day in your life though, Granny," said Willow. "You can't really call yourself working-class."

I often wondered why Willow couldn't keep her mouth in the same position I kept mine when Granny made an outlandish claim — firmly closed.

Granny took a deep breath, and the sound I heard was either an animal crashing through the trees surrounding the cottage, or Granny's knuckles cracking behind her back. The look of pain on her face suggested the latter.

"Never worked?" she murmured, her voice taking on the same tone she used for the Jehovah's Witnesses who insisted on knocking her door on a Sunday, even after one of them had almost had a finger severed in a slammed door as he handed Granny a leaflet.

Granny's voice rose in volume, and Willow closed her mouth. She always got there eventually. "Never worked!" lambasted Granny. "When you've pushed two fledgling humans from the space between *your* legs, young lady, and brought them up to be well adjusted adults — while being unpaid and under appreciated… then, and only then, can you tell me I've never worked! Curses of the goddess be upon you!"

Willow's eyes glinted, and her mouth opened tentatively. I shook my head, but it was too late. "Well adjusted?" she said. "Have you had another two children you're not telling us about, or do you *actually* mean Mum and Uncle Brian?"

Granny did well to control herself. Or more likely, it was the fact that a large black saloon car turned into her driveway and parked at the bottom of the garden path which caused the sparks at her fingertips to fizzle out and die.

"My ride's here!" she said, making her way down the path. "You had a lucky escape, Willow. The keys to my car are on the kitchen table, make sure you lock the cottage when you leave and put the keys under the stone chicken."

The stone chicken stood to the right of the cottage doorway, and Granny insisted she'd bought it from a garden centre, although there was speculation that it was the chicken that Granny had insisted had been taken by a fox. The stone egg which protruded from the rear of the chicken, and the look of astonishment on its face, told a different story.

"You can't wear an apron to go and pick up a luxury car," said Willow.

Granny hurried down the path as the driver of the car opened the passenger door for her. "Like I said, I'm still working class. I'll take my apron off when I'm lower middle-class."

CHAPTER SIX

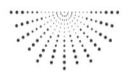

Some people might think that's it's preposterous to have a goat in the back seat of a small yellow Renault hatchback, and I was, without doubt, one of those people. It was more than preposterous — it was complete lunacy, *and* the car smelt like a petting zoo. There was hardly room in the rear of the tiny French car to seat two adults, and Boris was doing a good job of making the car seem even smaller than it actually was.

The tartan rug beneath him was managing to keep the seat fairly free of goat hair, but his rear hooves were leaving scuff marks on the plastic door trims. The window he was looking out of was smeared with tongue shaped swipes of saliva, and he bristled when I asked him to stop licking the glass.

"Penelope, you and Willow have only owned this car for fifteen minutes, and if it wasn't for me being generous enough to buy a new car, you wouldn't own it at all," he said, tasting the glass again. "There's a small part of the goat's brain that continues to control some of my impulses, and unfortunately for you and your window, this is one of those moments. Please give me my dignity and don't mention the subject again. Anyway, when Gladys brings our new Range Rover home you won't need to transport me anywhere again. I'll be riding in style in the future, not in this embarrassingly old yellow tinpot contraption."

The car *was* old, but it held memories that made me smile. Granny had bought it when Willow and I were young enough to believe her when she'd told us that it was a top of the range sports car — the same model that Prince Charles drove when he wasn't being ferried around by his chauffeur. It had a special place in my heart, and the sound the small engine made when it struggled to climb a hill reminded me of my boat. I knew that it wasn't the best looking car on the road, and I'd agree with Boris that it was *slightly* embarrassing, but Granny had given it to me and Willow, and it was our first car. It felt special. Anyway, I didn't think it was too pernickety of me not to want goat drool on my car window.

Willow laughed. "If you can control your impulse to eat Granny's grass, and make her push that heavy lawnmower around, you can control your impulses to lick a window, Boris."

Boris snorted. "Grass tastes vile," he said. "If she wants an animal to eat her grass she can find herself another goat — one with no pride in itself. Anyway, Gladys needs the exercise. You have to keep moving when you get to a certain age or the rot begins to set in."

I laughed. "I dare you to say that to Granny's face," I said, reversing the car into a space in the Poacher's Pocket Hotel carpark, "but please let me watch."

"I have far more sense than that," said Boris, climbing out of the car. "I may be inclined to lick windows, but my faculties are just fine."

Granny had cursed people for far less than an insult about her age, and I very much doubted that she'd hold back from cursing Boris, even though he did seem to have an uncanny ability to bring out the best side in her. I'd not seen Granny treat anyone with the respect she gave Boris since my grandad had died. Boris had far more sense than to incur a curse from Granny, though — especially while she had witch dementia.

Willow led the way through the beer garden towards the path that led to the boat, and I rolled my eyes as several men stopped what they were doing and watched her progress. Her figure was what you'd call "full" and I looked down at my own body, wondering if a spell could enlarge my boobs. Willow and I shared the same black hair as my mother, and you could even say our noses were moulded from the same cast, but from the neck down, all similarities ended.

Willow's bottom *rolled* in her tight shorts, and I was sure mine wobbled, or at least bounced beneath my summer dress. The flip-flops my sister wore on her feet caused her to walk in a way that enhanced her legs, and my burgundy Doctor Marten boots just made my feet feel heavy. Maybe a shopping trip was in order. An *online* shopping trip, I promised myself as I recalled the last time I'd agreed to accompany my sister on a shopping spree. The thought of queuing for a changing cubicle with armfuls of clothes which weren't going to fit, was almost as appealing as admitting to anybody that I was quite looking forward to going out for a meal with Barney. Not that there was anything wrong with Barney, but I'd kept my life free of romantic complications for years, and the thought of the squeals and questions which would come my way from Willow and Susie if I so much as hinted that I liked Barney, made me blush.

Boris trotted ahead of me, ignoring the comments from drunk adults, and allowing children to pat and prod him. I reminded myself that beneath the coarse white hair and curled horns was a cultured man whose life had been turned upside down by Granny's dementia. I almost shed a tear of pity as Boris attempted a bleat to please a young girl who tickled him behind his ear and told him he was beautiful.

As with most things concerning Boris, the precious moment soon passed, and I almost choked on my tongue as Boris spat on the shoes of a woman who called him a mangy old animal as he brushed past her bare legs.

The woman shrieked and kicked out at Boris, and a group of men laughed as she tumbled backwards off the bench she was sitting on and sprawled on the grass, legs akimbo, and covered with the contents of her glass.

Willow placated the angry woman and helped her to her feet, taking money from her pocket to pay for the spilt drink. I ushered the angry Boris through the gate at the bottom of the garden and down the pathway which took us through the trees and down to my boat. "You are *not* a mangy old animal," I assured him. "You didn't have to spit on her shoes though, Boris. They looked very expensive."

"I did not spit," said Boris, as Willow caught up with us. "Llamas, football players, and drunk hobos spit, Penelope. I accidentally spilled a build up of fluids in my mouth. There's a huge difference! I won't be labeled uncouth by anybody, especially a witch who lives on a boat!"

"Chill out, Boris!" snapped Willow. "What on earth's got into you? I just had to pay five-pounds-fifty to buy that woman a fresh glass of Pimms. Five-pounds-fifty! No wonder Tony and Michelle drive a Mercedes!"

Tony and Michelle owned the hotel and the boat mooring I rented, and they'd already asked me to keep Mabel under control when she'd stolen a piece of chicken from one of the customers. I didn't think they'd take kindly to Boris spitting at their patrons. "You need to control yourself, Boris," I said.

Boris led the way across the grass as we emerged from the trees. "I'm sorry," he said. "Gladys has been rationing my brandy. She thinks I drink too much. It's making me feel a little on edge. The smell of the drinks in the beer garden got my dander up. I shall be fine within a minute or two, when you two girls give me a glass of—"

Boris's demand was interrupted by a woman's scream which made my blood run cold. There's more than one type of scream. There's the type of scream a person afraid of spiders makes when they walk into a cobweb, and there's the type of scream that chills the human soul. The scream which resonated across the canal, and made us all stop in our tracks, was the latter. The sky above the fields on the opposite bank of the canal grew dark with crows for the second time that day, and an invisible finger traced a cold line down my spine.

"Help me!" begged the desperate voice. "Somebody's killed him!"

The towpath on the side on the canal I lived on was long overgrown and forgotten, but with Boris leading the way, we tore a path through the briars and shoulder height grass, and scrambled up the crumbling embankment onto the stone bridge which carried the road to Bentbridge across the canal.

Boris pushed through a hedge, and Willow and I climbed over a gate into the field above which the cawing crows circled as the woman continued to scream.

"Over there!" said Boris, already running.

The wheat was still only knee high, and a scarecrow rose from the crops in the centre of the field. At the base of its pole was the hunched shape of the woman, her screams doing a far better job than any scarecrow ever could of preventing the crows in the sky from landing.

"He's dead!" the woman shouted as we neared her. "Someone's killed my Gerald!"

Boris came to a stuttering halt next to her, and turned away from the sight that transformed the field from a quintessential English landscape, into a blood splattered scene of gore.

Gerald Timkins lay dead in the shadow of the scarecrow, and a ragged hole the size of a teacup saucer lay bare the contents of his abdomen. Blood seeped into the soil around his body, and vivid splashes of crimson coated the broken stalks of golden wheat which cradled him. Gerald's shotgun lay abandoned a few feet away from his body, and snapped stems of corn indicated trampled pathways through the crops in more than one direction.

Boris made a strangled cough, and Willow placed a hand on the shaking shoulder of Gerald's wife. "What happened?" she managed, her face white and her hand trembling.

I dialled the police and pressed the phone tight to my ear as Mrs Timkins sobbed her reply. "I don't know," she gasped. "Who would do this to him? He was so happy — he'd just bought some new electronic crow scarers and he only came here to take that old thing down," she said, pointing at the straw stuffed scarecrow that gazed indifferently at the macabre scene below it. "He said it was attracting the crows and not scaring them away. I got worried when he didn't come home for lunch and didn't answer his phone. I found him like this — my beautiful husband. Why would anyone want to kill my Gerald? I don't understand."

I stepped away from the murder scene as I reported the crime to the police, and pocketed my phone when I'd ended the call. "The police are on their way," I said. "I'm so sorry, Mrs Timkins."

Her body shook as she collapsed next to her husband, and her harrowing wails of anguish scared even the most determined of crows from the sky above us.

With the police on the scene, and statements taken from Willow and I, we made our way back to my boat, promising Barney that we were okay. The police had taken note of the time we'd seen Gerald with his shotgun near the canal, and according to Gerald's wife, we were the last people to have seen him alive — apart from his murderer of course.

We hadn't needed to remind Boris not to speak in the company of the police — he was unusually lost for words, and if a goat's face could be described as shocked — Boris looked downright anguished. He'd not uttered a single syllable on the slow walk back to the boat, and I was glad when Granny telephoned me, demanding to speak to the upset goat.

Boris spoke into my phone, which I'd placed on the dinette table next to the bottle of brandy and coffee cups. "Gladys?" he said. "Something terrible has happened."

"You're telling me!" said Granny, her voice edged with anger. "I've never been so embarrassed in my whole life!"

Boris sighed. "There's been a murder, Gladys. An awful, awful murder."

Granny hardly paused. "I can beat that! Your credit card expired yesterday, Boris. I can't pay off the remaining balance for the Range Rover. You'd better sort this out. I want that car. It's beautiful… you should see it… black, shiny, and with leather seats which smell like a fatted calf. It's perfect, and I want it!"

Boris licked at his bowl of brandy. "Didn't you hear me?" he said. "There's been a murder. Gerald Timkins is dead. Shot. With his own gun, and with only a tatty old scarecrow present to witness his violent demise."

Granny's voice took on a no-nonsense edge. "I heard you loud and clear, but did you hear me? Your credit card has expired. There's nothing I can do for a dead man, but I'm standing here in a car showroom which smells like posh candles and fifty-pound notes, looking at a car which I can't pay for. What are you going to do about it?"

Boris snorted and rolled his eyes. "I'll phone my bank and have a new card delivered. It will be sent to my own home though. You'll have to go and collect it for me."

Granny sighed, and said something under her breath. "Make it so, Boris. You telephone the bank right away when I end this call. Oh, and I am sorry about Gerald. He was a good farmer, not like Farmer Bill, who likes to throw around unfounded accusations of sexual assault. I think it's to do with what they farm, to be frank. It's a far more peaceful farmer who grows plants, than one who raises livestock to be slaughtered or milked. I shall visit Mrs Timkins at the earliest opportunity and offer her my condolences."

The sexual assault accusations from Farmer Bill stemmed back to an incident in the Coffee Pot Café. Granny had been adamant she'd been reaching into Farmer Bill's crotch area to retrieve an item of dropped food. Framer Bill said differently, and had embarrassed Granny in front of the other diners. Grammy had never lived down the humiliation.

Granny ended the call with a final reminder that we should still be at my mother's for the meal at seven o'clock, whether a murder had occurred or not, and Boris did as he had promised, telephoning his bank under the guise of Charleston and arranging for a new card to be express delivered the next day.

Susie arrived at the boat at six o'clock and took over guardianship of Boris, and Willow and I got showered, changed, and left the two of them to drink brandy and elderberry wine as they watched *Robot Wars* on the television which Willow had insisted I installed when she'd moved aboard.

A tight ball of tension grew in my stomach as Willow and I headed to mum's cottage. Already that day I'd seen a fat man losing the plot over celery, a candlelit vigil involving a goat, a policeman under the influence of a magic spell, and a dead body.

I took a deep breath and relaxed a little. We were on our way to a civilised family meal, and I very much doubted anything else could go wrong on that day.

That would have just been unfair.

CHAPTER SEVEN

We arrived at Hazelwood cottage with fifteen minutes to spare. Granny had arrived before us, in a taxi, and she took Willow and I aside when we arrived, making us promise we'd take her to Charleston's house the next day to pick up the new credit card.

It was nice to be back at the cottage I'd grown up in, and Willow and I took a short walk around the private woodland which surrounded Mum's home, shaking the gory memories of Gerald Timkins's dead body from our minds before we sat down for a family meal.

It seemed odd to be crowded around a table with my family as a woman on the other side of Wickford mourned the murder of her husband, but Granny had put things in perspective as she'd helped Mum lay the big table. "Life goes on," she'd said, "and we'd all do well to celebrate the living as well as the dead. You never know when a tragedy will strike, so cherish those around you while you still can."

Barney had managed to arrive by seven o'clock as Granny had instructed, and had refused to give Willow any information when she'd asked him about Gerald's murder. "Not tonight, Willow" he said, with an apologetic smile. "The detectives are investigating, but it's early days yet. I'd like to forget about what I saw in that field today and enjoy this meal."

"Nobody's enjoying any meal until that brother of mine gets here," said Mum, diverting the conversation from the subject of murder. "Trust him to be late to his own welcome meal!"

"He'll be here soon enough," said Granny. "Brian would never miss free food without a bloody good reason. He's probably got stuck in traffic."

Barney sat to my right, and I gasped as his hand tightened on my bare thigh beneath the table. There were better ways for a man to let a woman know he was interested in her than groping her at a family meal, and I lifted my hand in readiness to deliver the slap which would indicate to Barney Dobkins that he'd chosen the wrong method to woo me. My hand faltered inches from Barney's face as his mouth opened and he made a sound which attracted the attention of everyone around the table.

"What's wrong, Barney?" I said, worried the gargling in his throat and the tightening grip of his fingers on my leg were symptoms of some sort of seizure, maybe induced by the trauma of what he'd witnessed in the field earlier that day.

"Oh no," said Willow. "Oh no!"

Granny and Mum both turned to look over their shoulders as Barney pointed a trembling finger at the lounge doorway. The deep humming sound that filled the room told me precisely what was happening before I dared to look for myself. A portal to the haven was opening, but as everybody in the room with magical powers was seated safely at the table, it could only mean one thing — it was an incoming portal, and judging by the colour of the light that filled the doorway, there could only be one person who had activated it. Uncle Brian.

The colour of a haven portal was said to reflect the personality of the person who'd conjured it, and the vivid lilac glow that bathed the kitchen in bright light, was certainly a reflection of my uncle's personality.

The doorway quivered and creaked, and the light grew brighter as the throbbing hum grew louder. Barney did his best impression of a fish out of water, and his fingers hurt my thigh as they dug deep into muscle. His other hand shook as he pointed at the doorway, and a sliver of drool hung from his bottom lip. Poor Barney. He'd already been victim to a magic spell earlier in the day, seen a dead body, and was about to meet my Uncle Brian. How much more could one mortal take in one day?

Two matching green suitcases appeared from the shimmering pool of light, and the disembodied voice of my uncle echoed around the kitchen, throbbing in perfect harmony with the spell. "Only me-ee! Anybody home?"

His belly emerged before the rest of his body, and Barney released my thigh from his grip as he stood up slowly and picked up a steak knife from the table, holding it in front of him as Brian's grinning face emerged.

"Who's the ginger ninja with the knife?" said Brian, dropping his cases and removing his hat. "He could do somebody an injury. Oooh, you've got your best china on the table, Maggie!"

"Brian!" said Granny, standing and taking the bright blue Trilby from her son's outstretched hand. "My first born! How are you, my sweet angel?"

Brian wrapped Granny in his arms, and Barney waved the knife in erratic circles as Granny led her son towards the empty seat at the head of the table.

"What are you doing, Brian?" said Mum, taking her

brother's herringbone tweed jacket from him, and tossing it onto the rocking chair in the corner, next to the fireplace. "You said you were coming by car! You know how dangerous it is to attempt a reverse portal, you could have ended up anywhere!"

That was true. It was brave witch indeed who conjured up a portal from the haven to a place they hadn't entered the magical dimension from. Witches could utilise any entrance in our world to use as an anchor point for a portal into the haven, but it was standard, and safe, practice to use the same portal you'd arrived through as an exit point. Conjuring a portal to a place you hadn't arrived from was tempting fate — a witch could end up anywhere if they couldn't *perfectly* picture the place they wanted to arrive at in their mind's eye. One witch had caused widespread panic, and a half-day for the staff at a hardware store, when her portal had inadvertently opened in a display door as a salesman pointed out the finer points of the brass fittings to a young couple hoping to upgrade their new home.

"I didn't fancy driving," explained Brian, "and anyway, I've stood in this kitchen enough times to know I can safely open a portal in it."

"Erm…" I said, laying a reassuring hand on Barney's arm. "There's more to worry about than how Uncle Brian got here." I jerked my thumb at Barney. "What about him?"

Brian leaned across the table and took the knife from Barney's shaking hand. "Doesn't he know we're witches?" he said with a smile. "How exciting! It's been a long time since I've seen that look on somebody's face! Look, he's terrified." He softened his tone. "Don't be scared," he said, "we don't bite… unless you want us to!"

Granny giggled and Barney gurgled.

"Oh, Brian!" said Granny. "It's so good to have you home. It's about time we had somebody with a sense of humour around here again. How are you, my beautiful strapping boy?"

I jerked my thumb at Barney again, who'd begun sweating. "Erm… what about Barney? He looks very peaky."

"Never mind him," said Mum, "we'll sort him out in a moment. One of us will cast a spell on him, and he'll be convinced Brian arrived by taxi — as he should have if he was too lazy to drive."

Brian sat down and stuffed a napkin into the collar of his perfectly pressed shirt. "I'm not lazy — I'm hungry," he declared. "I haven't eaten since four."

"Forget your stomach, uncle Brian," I said, beginning to anger. "There's a man standing next to me in fear for his life. Will somebody please help him?"

Willow stood up and raised her hand. "I'll do it," she said. "I'll use the same spell I used on him this morning."

Barney turned his head slowly and stared at me with pleading eyes. "What's going on, Penny?" he said.

"Sit down, Willow," said Granny, pushing her seat alongside Brian's and placing an empty glass in front of him. "You can't use the same spell on him twice in the same day. You'll fry his wiring. Maggie, you do it, I'm sure Penelope doesn't want to hex her beau." She tapped Brian's empty glass with a long fingernail. "Somebody fetch me a bottle of *Wickford Headbanger*. My little man looks thirsty."

Wickford Headbanger was the town brewery's most infamous and strongest beer. It had won awards all over Britain and was rumoured to be a cure for bunions and an elixir for dying plants. I'd once poured a little into one of my mother's dried out and neglected basil plants, but rather than bringing it back to full health, the plant had immediately wilted into total oblivion. My mother was sure the sound we'd heard had been the wind blowing under the kitchen door, but I was convinced it had been a botanical sigh of acceptance as the plant had finally been able to give up its battle with life.

"That would be splendid," said Brian. "Fetch that tall ginger chap one too. He looks like his whistle needs wetting."

Brian's plump red face widened into a toothy grin, and sparks of rage blossomed in the deepest pit of my stomach. I gritted my teeth and stared at my uncle through eyes which twitched with anger. "His name is Barney," I hissed, "and he deserves your respect, not your ridicule. Can't you see how scared he is?"

Barney slumped into his seat and stared up at me. "Who are you, Penny?" he said. "And why is that fat impeccably dressed man making fun of me?"

"Have a drink, Barney," I said. "You're in shock." I looked around the table. "Okay," I said. "It's obviously only me and Willow who care about how Barney's feeling. You three don't seem to give a damn that Barney's witnessing a dysfunctional witch family having dinner, so I've made a decision. I'm telling Barney all about us, and no-one is going to cast a spell on him to make him forget. He deserves to know the truth after what he's been through today."

Granny tittered under her breath and poured Brian's beer into his glass. "You enjoy good head, don't you, son?" she said as froth rose up the walls of the glass.

"I love *a* good head, Mother! A good head *on* my beer! Good grief, sometimes I wonder if you know what you're saying."

Granny smiled. "Maggie, cast a spell on young PC Dobkins would you. Penelope's right, he shouldn't be witnessing this."

Mum waved an idle hand in front of her, and blue sparks danced at her fingertips.

Barney made a squeak like a balloon vomiting air, and I

placed a hand on his shoulder. "Don't worry," I said. "You'll be okay. Nobody's going to hurt you."

Mum pressed her finger and thumb together, but before she could click them and cast her spell, a swell of rising energy rushed through my body which exited my body through the fingertips of both hands. "I said no spells!" I shouted, crockery and cutlery shaking on the tabletop as magic streamed from me and counteracted Mum's spell with a loud cracking sound which made her shriek.

Mum shook her hand in the air as if she'd been burnt, and her sparks fizzled out. Granny stood up, and Brian gazed at me with a nervous respect. My sister placed her hand in mine as I stumbled backwards, and Barney finally let out his fear in a scream which hurt my ears.

"Where on earth did you learn that?" said Granny. "That was real magic right there!"

"I don't know," I said, my eyes sliding closed with the sort of heavy sleepiness I hadn't experienced since I'd had my first alcoholic drink. What I did know, though, as I gave myself to sleep, was that I knew how to open a portal in a doorway.

I'd been given my entry spell to the haven.

CHAPTER EIGHT

I woke to the gentle touch of Susie's hand on mine and the rancid stench of Boris's brandy breath burning my nostrils. Rosie licked my arm and I tickled her behind the ear.

"What happened?" I said, squeezing Susie's fingers and pushing Boris away from my face with my free hand. I recognised the low white ceiling above me and the softness of the mattress below me. The picture of Granny, Mum and Willow on the wall to my right confirmed it. I was on my boat, in my bedroom. The unmistakeable sound of the bird dawn chorus outside told me I'd been asleep for a while. "How did I get here?" I asked, propping myself up on an elbow. I was certain I hadn't so much as tasted a *Wickford Headbanger* at the meal, and the headache I had was not a hangover. "I remember what happened at the dinner table, but then everything's a blank."

"You passed out," said Susie, moving aside as I swung my legs out of bed. "After you cast your spell. Willow said she'd never seen anything like it, and Barney was worried sick about you. He carried you onto the boat and wanted to stay with you until you woke up, but he had to go to work early this morning. The police are searching the field that Gerald was murdered in for clues."

"Where's Willow?" I said, the smell of bacon being fried giving me a clue.

"Making breakfast," said Boris, "she was very worried about you so we gave her something to do, although I'm beginning to regret it. She tried to *grill* my bacon. She said it was more healthy, or some such hippy nonsense. I had quite the argument with her, didn't I, Susie?"

Susie sighed. "Yes, Boris, you did, and the language you used made Barney blush."

I stared at Boris. "You spoke in front of Barney?" I said. "So he still knows we're witches? Mum didn't cast a spell on him to make him forget when I passed out?"

Susie passed me my dressing gown, and I slipped it over my thigh length sleeping shirt. I hoped it had been Susie or Willow who had undressed me, and not Barney, or goddess forbid, Boris. I was sure his hooves couldn't have undone the laces on my boots, but I wasn't convinced he couldn't have pulled my dress over my head.

"Barney knows everything," said Susie. "Willow stopped anyone from casting a spell on him and he's taking the whole thing remarkably well. Apart from when Boris first spoke to him of course. He was okay after a glass of brandy though."

"I've never seen such a tall man fall over," said Boris. "It was quite spectacular. Quite beautiful, really — he reminded me of a marionette at the ends of a master puppeteer's strings."

Willow appeared in the doorway to my bedroom, her hair tied in a loose bun, and the apron she wore splattered with the evidence of greasy cooking. "You're awake!" she said, looking me up and down and taking me in her arms. "Are you alright?"

"I'm fine," I said. "Really."

"What happened?" said my sister. "How did you cast that spell? Mum and Granny said it was very advanced pure magic, and Uncle Brian said it was better than the Yorkshire puddings Mum had cooked."

My memory was muddled. I could only recall the anger bubbling in my stomach as Barney sat next to me staring at me in fear, and the surge of power through my arms as I'd cast the spell. My mind began putting the pieces together and I caught my breath as the last thing I remembered came flooding back. "I know how to get to the haven," I said, the hairs on the back of my neck standing rigid. "I have my entry spell."

Willow shrieked and Susie clasped her hands together.

Boris snorted. "That's all well and good," he said, "but there's more important things to consider. I can smell black pudding burning."

"Do it," said Willow, pointing at the door which led onto the stern decking. "Make your portal!"

Susie agreed. "You have to! This is so exciting!"

"Black pudding emergency," said Boris, tapping Willow's leg with a hoof.

Willow rushed out of the bedroom to deal with the cooking dilemma, and I took a deep breath. I was sure there had to be more to it than just casting my spell and expecting a portal to open, but I'd seen Mum and Granny do it hundreds of times. Maybe it was that simple.

"Shouldn't I wait?" I said as Willow hurried back into the room, squeezing past Boris and standing next to me at the foot of the two steps that led from my bedroom onto the boat deck. "There's a ritual, isn't there? Mum will come through with me and Aunt Eva will want to meet me on the other side."

"That's only for the first time you go through it," said

Willow. "You can open it and see what colour it is, nobody will mind that!"

Susie smiled. "Go on," she said. "Open it already!"

"If it means I'll get my breakfast any quicker, I wholeheartedly agree," said Boris. "Just open the damn thing before the sausages go cold! They're pork and leek, Susie picked them up from the butcher's for me yesterday. It's an old family recipe, apparently. The leeks are Welsh and the pork is — " The doorway creaking and quivering cut Boris short. "Wow," he muttered.

"It's beautiful," said Willow, "and it matches your personality perfectly."

A soft breeze blew across my face as I took a step closer to the inviting golden glow that filled the doorway. It had been easy to open, far easier than I'd ever imagined — almost an anti-climax after waiting for my spell for so long.

Willow took my hand in hers. "Congratulations, Penelope Weaver," she whispered, her voice hardly audible above the gentle hum of the spell. "You're a real witch now."

I closed my eyes and allowed the portal to close. The temptation to walk through it was too great, but I knew it would devastate Mum if she couldn't open her own portal and enter the haven with me on my first trip. "I am, aren't I?" I said. I squeezed her hand tight. "It'll be your turn soon, Willow."

WITH BREAKFAST EATEN and Boris's beard cleaned of the food detritus that clung to it, Willow and I prepared to take Boris home and pick Granny up for our trip to collect the credit card.

Susie had left to begin the job of reporting on Gerald's

murder. The police were holding a press conference at ten o'clock, and Barney had promised her a front row seat.

Willow had explained why nobody had cast a spell on Barney after I'd fainted. "They wanted to," she said, "but I talked them out of it. Barney promised he wouldn't say a word to anyone, and Granny made him swear on his police badge. Uncle Brian was happy with a pinky promise."

"What about Mum?" I said.

"She was more concerned with finding out if Barney thought the prawn cocktail starter would have been nicer with some melba toast, and checking whether you'd hurt yourself when you fell over."

I put a hand to the back of my head and felt for lumps. "And?" I said.

"He said he wasn't too fussed on any toast, Melba or not. He was in shock though. He could hardly speak."

I laughed. "I meant was I injured at all!"

"Oh! Just a small bruise on your chin. Uncle Brian healed it, but he put on a bit of a show for Barney's benefit. You know how he is."

I nodded. Uncle Brian had always reminded me of the swanky magicians that made their money on TV shows. His three year infatuation with crushed velvet jackets had reinforced that image of him beyond any redemption.

"He draped his polka dot hanky over your face and asked me to be his assistant. I had to swipe the hanky away when he'd waved his hand over you. Barney clapped, but I think he was still in fear for his life at that stage. It was polite applause more than genuine admiration. You were fine though, Uncle Brian gave you a full medical inspection and declared you were in a temporary magical sleep. Mum insisted Barney finished his dinner before she let us take you back to the boat. She told me that the spotted dick she made for pudding would seal the deal on Barney keeping his mouth shut about us. It *was* quite nice, I have to admit. Barney had two helpings."

Fourteen missed calls from Barney were displayed on my phone, and I messaged him to tell him I'd speak to him that evening and answer all his questions. I was sure he'd have a lot of them, and I proposed that we go to the little Italian place on the outskirts of town for a meal. Barney accepted with a text that finished with three kisses, and I sent him one of my own in return. The previous night's events had proved to me that my feelings for Barney couldn't be ignored anymore. I'd experienced a protectiveness for him that had ran deep in my veins, and I wasn't one to ignore my emotions. There was a reason I cared for him, and I wanted to explore it.

It seemed that the previous night had been more than just a catalyst for a new era in my magical life. It had helped move my personal life forward too, and as Willow, Boris, and I, climbed the footpath to the hotel carpark, I allowed the butterflies in my stomach to soar as high as they liked.

It was a good day, and I deserved a good day.

CHAPTER NINE

Granny sat in the passenger seat and Willow sat in the back of the Renault, rubbing white goat hairs from her black leggings. The neighbourhood Boris had give us directions to was in the the most upmarket area of Covenhill. Every tree that lined the pavement was perfectly trimmed and manicured, and it had been at least a mile since I'd seen any rubbish in the gutters.

"Are you sure Boris likes living in your cottage, Granny?" joked Willow. "It looks like he was used to a little more luxury in his life before he met you."

Granny peered between the gap in the two front seats. "Boris is happy where he is," she said, "and if he wasn't, he'd have wanted to come with us today, wouldn't he? Anyway, he'll have all the luxury he desires when I can finally pay for the Range Rover."

"Don't take advantage of him," I warned. "He may have money, but at the end of the day he's trapped in the body of a goat. His decisions might not be good ones."

Granny turned slowly to face me as I took a left turn into Gladiola Drive. "How dare you!" she said. "*How dare you*! Me take advantage of somebody? I've spent my whole life fighting against the injustices of society. I should be applauded for what I've done *for* the disadvantaged, not accused of *taking* advantage of somebody." She shook her head woefully. "I don't know, Penelope. Ever since you got your spell for the haven you've been a different person. A very different person indeed! You've changed. Don't let it go to your head, young lady. Every witch gets their spell eventually — you're not a special case. Bring yourself back down to earth amongst us commoners would you?"

"She only got it last night, and she spent most of that time unconscious," said Willow, leaning through the gap in the seats as we approached the large house at the end of the cul-de-sac. "And we only picked you up twenty-five minutes ago, Granny. Penny has hardly had the time to change her socks, let alone make you think she's changed her whole outlook on life."

"We're here," I said, defusing the tension. Granny muttered something under her breath as I parked the car in the red-brick driveway and peered at the large house. "It's beautiful."

The large house was a modern build, but based on Georgian architecture. Built from cream stone, and with a narrow parapet at the rim of the roof, it loomed against the tall scotch pines which grew beyond it. Pillars framed the wide front door, and the garden was immaculate. "He must still be paying a gardener," I said.

"Boris is paying *all* his bills," said Granny, defensively. "Letting the credit card expire was a simple mistake on his behalf. Come on, let's get inside, pick up his card, and go home. Rich people neighbourhoods make me want to vomit blood. They're so pretentious, and they smell of envy."

"Says the woman who's only here so she can buy a prestigious car," said Willow with a giggle.

Granny chose to ignore Willow, and scampered up the driveway, looking around at the neighbouring homes with furtive glances that made her look every bit like an elderly burglar, or a shy gypsy woman trying to sell lucky heathers to the wealthy. "Around the back," said Granny, leading me and Willow around the side of the house. "Boris said the alarm won't go off if we use the back door. He forgot to set it before he came to my cottage on that fateful night."

"That disastrous night," I mumbled, standing next to Granny as she slid a key from her apron pocket and opened the tall sliding doors which looked out over the large rear garden.

The doors made a gentle whooshing sound as Granny prised them open and stepped inside Charleston Huang's home. "Wipe your feet," she ordered, scrubbing the soles of her sandals on a Persian rug.

"I don't think that's a doormat, Granny," I said. "It looks like it's worth a lot of money."

"Only a rich fool would put something worth a lot of money on the floor next to a door," said Granny. "Boris is no fool, of course it's a doormat. Now come on, don't touch anything, we just have to get to the front door, find the letter from his bank, and pick up the personal belongings he wants me to bring home. We're looking for a silver framed photograph of his parents, and a pair of antique wooden clogs. The clogs are for me, Boris said they'll stop me dragging my feet. He says they force one to lift one's feet *and* force good posture. I'm *not* to drive in them though. Boris said I could cause all manner of accidents."

I'd have loved to have been a fly on the wall at Ashwood cottage when Granny and Boris had a private conversation. How the subject of clogs had ever come up intrigued me, but I decided to help Granny find them nonetheless. "I'll look for the clogs," I said. "Willow, you find the photo, and Granny can get the card. I don't want to be in here longer than we have to. The car looks out of place in this neighbourhood — somebody might phone the police."

"He said the photograph is in the living room and the clogs are upstairs," said Granny sneaking through the kitchen, admiring the huge chrome stove as she passed it, and disappearing through the doorway.

Willow rushed off to find the photograph for Boris, and I headed up the stairs to look for Dutch footwear. Hardwood floors thumped under my boots as I navigated each of the five bedrooms looking for the clogs, and I couldn't help but admire Boris's choice of minimalistic decor. With plain off-white walls dotted with seascapes and modern art, and no clutter to be seen anywhere, it was the sort of home I'd have liked to live in if I was ever persuaded to leave my boat and live on land.

I found the clogs in the third bedroom I looked in, placed on top of a mahogany sideboard, next to a carved wooden duck and a photograph of Charleston standing on the great wall of China. He'd once told us that he'd been to visit the country of his ancestors, but had found the whole experience underwhelming. The sullen face staring back at me from the photograph confirmed he'd been telling the truth. He looked downright miserable.

A photograph on the wall above the sideboard caught my attention. I'd seen the lady somewhere before, I knew I had, I just couldn't place her. The black and white photograph looked very old, and the lady in the picture was dressed in a ballet dancing outfit and was standing alone on a stage. I lifted the photograph from the wall and ran a finger over the old image. I'd definitely seen the woman before, and I decided to take the photograph with me so I could ask Boris about it.

Granny rifled through the stack of letters she'd placed on

the small table next to the front door. "Is the credit card there?" I said, holding out the clogs for her to inspect.

She patted her apron pocket in answer to my question and gave the clogs a cursory glance, nodding her approval. "What's that?" she said, pointing at the photo I'd brought downstairs with me.

I held it up for Granny to inspect. "The woman looks familiar," I said. "I wanted to ask Boris about her."

Granny pushed her glasses closer to her eyes, and took the photo from me. "Heavens above," she said under her breath. "I knew it!"

"Knew what?" said Willow, emerging from the dining room with the silver framed photo of Boris's parents under her arm. She joined Granny in studying the Chinese ballet dancer. "Hey, I recognise that woman, Granny," she said. "She's in your old photograph album!"

Of course! That's where I'd seen her! Why did Granny and Boris both have a photograph of the same woman though? "Who is she, Granny?" I said.

"This explains everything!" said Granny. "I told you that the night Charleston came to me was fateful, didn't I, Penelope? He was brought to me by magic and fate!"

"You said you found him in the phone book, Granny," said Willow, helpfully. "Under acupuncturists. How is that fate?"

"Oh, it's fate alright!" beamed Granny. "There's no such thing as a coincidence. This photo explains so much, girls! The woman you're looking at was a witch. Her name was Chang-Chang, and I know she had secrets. She's one of the very few witches who chose to die in this world. She visited the haven on occasion, but when her time came, she remained in this world instead of choosing immortality in the haven. I'll bet my bottom dollar that the woman in this photograph is Charleston's grandmother, and that would mean that Charleston has magic! If that's not fate, I don't know what is!"

"Why didn't Boris tell you?" said Willow. "Surely he would know something?"

"Who knows?" said Granny. "Maybe he knew, maybe he didn't. But it's fate that brought him to my house that night, and it's fate that sent Penelope up those stairs looking for clogs, and coming down those stairs with this photograph!"

"And the clogs," I reminded her.

"Yes. Yes," said Granny. "And the clogs. Come on, girls, let's get out of here! There's lots to do! First you need to take me to Mrs Timkins's farm so I can offer her my condolences, and then you can take me to the Range Rover dealership so I can pick up my new car!"

"And then you can ask Boris about this photograph?" I said.

"I'll leave that for a day tor two," said Granny. "I'll need to work out how to ask him. It is very personal after all, and you know me… I like to be tactful."

CHAPTER TEN

Two sheepdogs ran to greet us as I parked the Renault outside Gerald Timkins's home. The large house was at the end of a long bumpy track, and the field that Gerald had died in was hidden in the valley below us. The dogs acted as if nothing was out of the ordinary, but the drawn curtains in the windows of the old farmhouse told a different story.

Willow stroked one of the sheepdogs, and Granny shooed another away as she clambered from the car. "When my Norman died, rest his soul, Sandra Timkins came to visit me. Now the shoe's firmly on the other foot. The circle is complete."

"Granny!" snapped Willow. "Do you know how awful that sounded?"

"Nonsense," said Granny. "That's just how it is. Come on, the front door's wide open, Sandra's probably out in the fields, sowing seeds or pulling up lovely fat turnips, or whatever it is that farmer's wives do — baking a cake, I don't know. What I mean is she's probably too busy to let yesterday's tragic murder of her husband get her down."

Granny stomped straight into the house without knocking on the open door, the dogs alongside her. "Coooee!" she yelled. "It's only me, Gladys Weaver, come to offer my condolences! My granddaughters are with me too! We've come in their car, I'm off to pick up a brand new Range Rover when I leave here. Perhaps I should have come to see you *after* I'd collected the new vehicle — it would have dealt with the farm-track a lot better than that shitty little Renault did! Sandra? Are you here?"

Willow and I followed her into the house with a lot more dignity, wiping our feet on the thick doormat as we stepped inside the gloomy hallway. The smell of baking bread hung in the air, and music was being played somewhere in the farmhouse. Maybe Granny had been right. Maybe farmer's wives *were* too busy to spend all of their time mourning when a loved one had passed over.

"Sandra!" shouted Granny. "Where are you?"

"I'm in here," came Sandra's voice. "In the living room. Doing the ironing."

"Told you," said Granny over her shoulder. "Getting on with things. It's the best way."

We followed Granny through the crooked doorway into the living room. It seemed Sandra wasn't coping as well as Granny had imagined. She sat on the sofa, next to a pile of clothes, with an item of clothing clasped in her hands. She brought it to her face and sniffed it, her body shaking as she sobbed. "I'm sorry," she said. "I was doing the ironing, and I could still smell Gerald on this t-shirt," she said. "It's very hard to accept that he won't be wearing it again." Sandra took another long smell of the shirt, and placed it next to her on the sofa. "Sit down, please," she said. "I'll make you all a cup of tea."

"Are you on your own?" said Willow. "How are you coping?"

Sandra sniffed, and dabbed her eyes with a tissue she took from the beneath the sleeve of her jumper. "The police liaison officer wanted to stay with me," she said, "but I sent her away. I'll do better on my own. Gerald's sister is coming tomorrow, she *was* coming to spend a week with her big brother, but now she's going to be helping me arrange his funeral!"

"Oh, Sandra," said Granny, sitting next to the distraught woman and placing her hand on her shoulder. "I'm so sorry. Have the police got any idea who killed him yet?"

"Granny," I said. "Perhaps Sandra doesn't want to talk about things like that."

Sandra smiled at me. "It's okay," she said. "And I hope you two girls are alright, too. It couldn't have been easy for you both to see my husband like that. I was very thankful that you waited with me until the police arrived."

"It was the least we could do," said Willow, looking at the floor. She lifted her eyes. "Let us know if there's anything else we can do to help."

"Thank you," Sandra said, "I know I'll cope. I *have* to. That's what Gerald would have wanted, but I'm not going to pretend it'll be easy. Finding out who killed my husband will help, of course, but things will never be the same without Gerald. We've been together for forty years. Since we met in school."

"Do the police know anything *at all*?" said Granny. "Have they got a suspect yet?"

If Granny was speaking out of turn it didn't seem to bother Sandra. She dabbed at her eyes with the tissue. "Only the people he'd argued with recently," she said. "Gerald wasn't really the type of man to make enemies, though. He just had misunderstandings with folk."

"Who had he argued with?" said Granny, perching on the edge of the sofa and taking Sandra's hand in hers. "Farmer

Bill, by any chance? Don't you think he's got cold eyes, Sandra? Violent eyes, one might say. The empty eyes of an unkind man, almost."

"Granny!" I said. Now was *not* the time to be bringing up her vendetta against Farmer Bill. "Why don't you make the tea? I'm sure Sandra would like a cup."

"That would be lovely, Gladys," agreed Sandra. "If you don't mind, of course. You could take the bread out of the oven for me too? It's been in for ten minutes too long already."

"I *suppose* I could," said Granny, a little reluctantly. "You two can update me when I come back," she said, looking at me and Willow.

I nodded and Willow shrugged. Granny made her way into the kitchen and found the source of the music, switching it off.

"The police don't really have anything to go on, yet," said Sandra, ignoring Granny's outburst about farmer Bill. Most people in Wickford knew Granny, and most people in Wickford knew how to ignore her too. "It's early days. They want to speak to that horrible birdwatching woman... Mrs Oliver," she said. "She doesn't understand the damage that crows can do to a crop, they need to be kept under control, and the scarecrows weren't working. He *had* to shoot at those birds, and that woman wouldn't leave him alone, always shouting at him and running to the police. I doubt she shot Gerald though. She's all bark and no bite."

Sandra picked the T-shirt up and took another smell.

"Had he argued with anybody else?" said Willow.

"Just the buyers for his crops, but that was always happening. That's part of the farming business though, isn't it? And they weren't really arguments... more like negotiations really. Gerald didn't really argue with people, he just got on with life, and let others get on with theirs. He was a good, kind man."

"Tea's up!" said Granny, storming back into the room with a tray balanced in front of her. "Your bread's ruined though, Sandra. It might be alright toasted with a little marmite on it to disguise its inferiority, but I'd not want a cheese sandwich made from it, thank you very much! It looks and smells *vile*."

I hoped I'd never turn out like Granny when I was her age. Watching Granny negotiate normal life was like watching a trained chimp riding a bike — it went through the motions, without knowing why, and without caring what happened around it.

"Never-mind," said Sandra, moving the T-shirt aside so Granny could sit down. "I'll bake another loaf. It will give me something productive to do."

Sandra laid the T-shirt out over the arm of the sofa and took a cup from Granny. "Thank you. Gladys," she said. "I do appreciate you coming to see me."

"Sandra," I said, my gaze still on the t-shirt. "Your husband was the tank?"

Printed on the red t-shirt in a large white font was the simple sentence — *The Tank - Pie-eating champion of South England.*

Sandra smiled. "Yes," she said, with a gentle pride in her voice. "Gerald was unbeatable for years. He retired after winning for three years consecutively — it was a record! Nobody had won for three years in a row before. He retired because he was getting a little podgy from all the practice! I was forever having to let his trousers out and put new holes in his belt." Sandra's eyes twinkled as she remembered. "He only came out of retirement because somebody's getting close to beating his record of three consecutive wins. He just couldn't accept it. That was Gerald for you, though — very competitive!"

"Had he argued with anyone about the pie-eating contest?" I said, glancing at Willow. "Another competitor perhaps?"

Sandra shook her head. "Of course not. It's just friendly rivalry between them." She picked the T-shirt up and held it close to her chest. "Why are you asking these questions?" she said. "Do you know something? Do you know who killed my Gerald?"

Granny looked at me with a raised eyebrow. "Well? Do you? And why am I only just finding out about this? Does gossip not get passed up the chain of command in our family anymore?"

I gave Willow another look. "A man came into the shop, yesterday. He mentioned the tank coming out of retirement and he wasn't happy… was he, Willow?"

"No," said Willow. "He said some quite nasty things about your husband, Sandra, but he didn't use Gerald's real name, or we'd have told the police by now. We didn't know Gerald was the tank, you see."

Sandra stood up and grabbed her phone. "Do you know the man's name?" she said, already dialling the police.

"Felix Round," I said.

CHAPTER ELEVEN

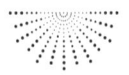

Willow and I dropped Granny off at the Range Rover dealership and headed back to the boat, with the intention of transferring the shop stock from the *Water Witch* to its new home in town.

The police had come quickly to Sandra's house and taken our statements regarding Felix Round and his outburst in the shop. Luckily for me, Barney wasn't one of the police officers who was sent. I was nervous about seeing him. It wasn't everyday that a mortal found out you were a witch, especially a mortal for whom you had feelings. I'd answer all his questions of course, but I was beginning to wonder if I'd done the right thing. Maybe I should have let somebody cast a spell on him at the dinner table. Maybe it would have been easier all round for everybody concerned.

After hearing our stories, the police were eager to speak to Felix Round, and had begun looking for him in town. It made me shudder to think the man who'd stood a foot away from me the day before could have been a murderer.

Mabel ran to greet us as we crossed the grass towards the boat, and Rosie watched us from her vantage point on the roof, sitting next to the tin chimney, licking a paw and swishing her tail.

Willow heard the music before me. "Someone's on the boat!" she said.

"It must be Susie," I said. "I gave her a spare key for the boat and the new shop, and she gave me one for her flat. Maybe she's got news from the press conference."

"That's not Susie," said Willow, as a baritone singing voice flooded from the open bow doors. "That's Uncle Brian!"

As Elton John hit the chorus of *Rocket Man*, Uncle Brian raised his game too, causing Mabel to let out a warbling howl, and making Rosie jump.

"He's found the music channel on the TV," I said, climbing aboard the boat and down into the little room which was still a magic shop, but would very soon be Willow's bedroom.

The aroma of freshly brewed coffee filled the boat, and I could detect the scent of men's aftershave too.

Uncle Brian sat in the built-in dinette area which folded down into the bed which Willow had slept on since she'd moved aboard. The coffee percolator was bubbling away on one of the kitchen counters, and Uncle Brian was singing between mouthfuls of the sandwich he was eating. A newspaper was spread out in front of him, and he gave us a wide grin when he saw us.

"My favourite nieces!" he said, grabbing the TV remote control and lowering the volume. "How are you both today? It was quite the night last night, wasn't it? I hope Barney's alright now. He had quite the scare!"

"Barney's fine," said Willow, "but what are you doing here, Uncle Brian?"

Uncle Brian took another bite of his sandwich. "I came to see if you needed help moving your shop," he said, crumbs spilling from his mouth and onto the dating advert page of the newspaper. "Maggie told me all about your new shop premises in town, and I wanted to help. She said you'd be starting work on it today. It's been a long time since I've been able to do anything for you two."

"And how did you get in?" I asked. "The doors were all locked."

Uncle Brian put his hand in the air and wiggled his fingers. "Nothing's out of bounds to Brian Weaver's magical fingers!" he laughed. "I magicked my way in of course. I hope you don't mind? I waited on the picnic bench for you to come home, but that goose of yours wouldn't leave me alone. It was the last straw when it started humping my leg. I had to get away from it."

"Of course we don't mind," I said. "You're family, Uncle Brian, and Willow told me what you did for me last night — healing the bruise on my chin when I passed out. Thank you."

Uncle Brian smiled. "You are *more* than welcome! I'm that sort of chap, you see… a caring fellow. I've only ever used my magic for good, unlike my mother and sister, and I hope you girls will follow in my footsteps and not theirs. Talking of magic, Penny, when are you going to take your first steps into the haven? We're all very excited about it, you know? Especially me! There's nothing like seeing a witch entering the haven for the first time! It makes me tingle just to think about it!"

"I'm going to ask Mum," I said, sitting down next to Uncle Brian. "She'll want to come with me on my first trip. To show me around I suppose."

Uncle Brian put his hand on mine. "Haven't you been tempted yet? When I got my spell I was through my portal faster than a fat kid does through candy, and I can tell you from experience that a fat kid goes through candy *extremely* quickly," he said, laying a hand on his belly.

Both he and my mother had been overweight kids, and

neither of them had managed to lose their puppy fat, despite Granny attempting to help them both lose weight by casting numerous spells on them over the years. Some of the spells had seemed spiteful rather than helpful, especially the one that had made my mum dislike cake on her own birthday.

"Of course I'm tempted," I said, "I even opened my portal to see what colour it would be, but I didn't go through it. I want Mum to be with me."

"You opened it!" said Uncle Brian."What colour was it? No! Let me guess!" He placed a hand on my head and closed his eyes for a few seconds. "I think it was red. I saw you stick up for Barney last night, you showed real courage, and you have a powerful aura about you, Penelope. I bet it was red! That has to be your colour! It was, wasn't it?"

I shook my head. "It was gold," I said with a grin.

"It was *really* gold," agreed Willow. "Like looking inside a pirate's treasure chest!"

Uncle Brian nodded and smiled. "Gold is good. It shows you have integrity, Penelope. It's an honest colour."

Willow took Uncle Brian's empty plate from in front of him, and put it in the kitchen sink ready to be washed. She rubbed her hands together and grinned. "Right. Are we going to get this shop moved, or sit around chatting all day? I can't wait to have my own bedroom!"

Uncle Brian stood up and straightened the folded handkerchief in the breast pocket of his pinstripe jacket. "I'm ready," he said. "I won't help with the heavy stuff of course, but I can certainly carry some paperwork or light herbs. I'm better suited at helping you work out how your new shop will look." He paused for a moment. "On second thoughts, ladies — I'll be in charge of setting up the new shop, and you girls can do all the carrying. How's that sound to you both? Fair?"

I winked at my sister. "It sounds fair to me," I smiled. I

handed my uncle the key for the shop. "Why don't you head up the footpath and let yourself in, you can start planning where everything should go. Willow and I will do all the lifting."

"I think he's bored," I said to Willow, when Uncle Brian had left the boat.

"I'd be bored too if I had to stay with Mum all day," said Willow, with a grin. She pushed through the purple curtain which acted as a door between the shop and the rest of the boat. "Come on, let's get to work. There's a lot to do."

ALMOST TWO HOURS and four aching arms later, Willow and I assessed the situation. The shop space aboard the boat was almost empty of stock, and the shop at the top of the footpath was beginning to look like a real place of business. Uncle Brian certainly knew how to arrange a shop floor, and he'd displayed the stock beautifully, taking great pride in his work as he showed us where everything was.

"Of course, you can always change things around if you like," he said, "but I think it's perfect as it is."

He was right. The shop not only looked magical, but the various herbs and incenses which Uncle Brian had painstakingly separated into scents and uses, gave the shop a magical smell too.

The sales counter was dotted with smaller items and novelty spells which Uncle Brian called impulse purchases, and the crystals and gem stones shone in the sun near the large window.

A shiver of anticipation ran through me as I looked around. It was really happening. I was leaving my shop aboard the boat behind, and starting a new business on land. All that was needed next was a sign to hang above the door outside and furnishings for the interior to make it feel more cozy.

The three of us stood with our backs to the door, taking a silent moment to admire our handiwork, and we all jumped in fright as a loud bang on the window ruined the moment.

"What on earth?" said Uncle Brian, spinning on the spot with his hand on his chest. "I nearly had a heart attack!"

I turned to face the window and immediately recognised the man who was being pressed hard against the glass. His brown overcoat and balding spot on the back of his head gave him away, but if I'd needed anymore proof it was the greengrocer from the shop next door, the cabbage leaves that were being sprinkled liberally over his head would suffice. "It's Mr Jarvis!" I said.

"And it's Felix Round who's attacking him!" noted Willow.

"Oh my!" said Uncle Brian, rushing for the door. "We must help the poor man! Come on, girls, onward into danger!"

The three of us scrambled out of the door in time to see Felix rubbing cabbage leaves in Mr Jarvis's terrified face. "I want celery!" boomed Felix. "I hate cabbage!"

"You've bought it all," stuttered Mr Jarvis, struggling against the hand that gripped him by the throat. "I told you, I'll have more in tomorrow!"

Uncle Brian stepped forward, looking every inch the chivalrous hero. "Unhand that poor man, you oaf!" he ordered. "Immediately. Or I shall not be responsible for my actions!"

"Help me," begged Mr Jarvis. "He's gone mad with the hunger!"

Felix stared at Uncle Brian. He gave a long laugh and stuffed a leaf into Mr Jarvis's mouth, ramming it home with a podgy finger. "What are you three going to do?" said Felix.

SAM SHORT

"You look like you're on your way to a pantomime... and I don't mean as spectators!" He looked Uncle Brian up and down. "What are you wearing, man? You look like a cross between a farmer and a fancy art dealer!"

Uncle Brian pulled his jacket straight and adjusted his hat, the bright red feather that protruded from the rim swaying in the gentle breeze. I glanced down at myself. I didn't think I looked like a character from a pantomime, and anyway, Felix Round was hardly one to speak — he resembled a TV wrestler from the nineteen-seventies — with his belly on show beneath his pie-eating t-shirt, and his angry red face shiny with sweat.

Uncle Brian raised his hand, and lilac sparks danced at the fingertips. "Last chance, you bearded fiend!" he threatened.

"Sod off, you weirdo!" said Felix, his attention back on the important task of stuffing Mr Jarvis's mouth full of cabbage leaves.

Uncle Brain tilted his head and took deep breath. "Oh well, I gave him a chance."

"What are you going to do?" said Willow. "Don't hurt him. Be careful!"

"I won't hurt him," said Uncle Brian, clicking his fingers. "I'm just going to stop him."

The spell crackled in the air and Felix Round let out a long slow gasp as he turned and gazed at Uncle Brian. "What would you have me do, master?" he drawled.

"Unhand that man," said Uncle Brian, winking at me.

Felix released Mr Jarvis who took a few stumbling steps away from Felix and towards the door of his own shop. "What have you done to him?" he said, staring at Uncle Brian. "Why is he doing what you tell him to?"

"I've hypnotised the rogue," said Uncle Brian, showing remarkably quick thinking for a child of Granny's. He pointed at Felix. "Stay right there until I tell you to move," he said.

Felix nodded. "Affirmative, great lord."

"Wow," said Mr Jarvis. "That's amazing!"

"What happened?" I said, as Willow helped Mr Jarvis pick up the produce that had been knocked from his pavement fruit and vegetable display.

"He came in demanding celery," said Mr Jarvis. "He didn't look well. He was sweating and mumbling a lot, and he seemed very angry."

"He's diabetic," I said. "He's probably made himself poorly by not eating enough."

"He grabbed me by the throat when I told him I was all out of celery," continued Mr Jarvis, "and dragged me out of my shop and down the pavement. It was lucky he slammed me into your window, I really think he might have killed me if you three hadn't come out to help."

"The police are already looking for him about one murder," I said, taking my phone from my pocket and dialling nine-nine-nine. "Another one would be a tragedy."

"Him?" said Mr Jarvis. "Did he kill Gerald?"

"Maybe," said Willow. "We don't know yet. The police just want to question him at this stage."

Mr Jarvis put a hand to his throat. "He could have killed me," he murmured.

"This man is wanted for murder?" said Uncle Brian. "Why didn't you tell me? I may not have been so stupidly brave."

"It all happened so quickly," said Willow. "We didn't have time."

I ended the call. "The police will be here in a minute or two," I said. "Erm, Uncle Brian, do you think you'd better... *de-hypnotise* him?"

"In a moment," said Uncle Brian, stepping close to Felix

and looking him in the eye. "Answer me truthfully, you violent upstart."

Felix nodded. "I'd do anything for you."

"Have you committed the crime of murder?"

Felix shook his head. "No, oh mightiness."

"He didn't do it," said Uncle Brian. "Nobody can tell a lie when they're controlled by the fingers of Brian Weaver! I declare this man innocent!"

Sirens echoed over the rooftops and the roar of an engine announced the arrival of the police in the street. The car screeched to a halt next to us and two young police women leapt out with their nightsticks drawn.

"Quick," I whispered to Uncle Brian. "The spell."

"Oh yes," said Uncle Brian. "Of course." He muttered something under this breath and Felix gasped as he was released from Uncle Brian's control.

"Is everyone okay?" said one of the police women as her colleague read Felix his rights and cuffed the big mans's hands in front of him.

"I'm not," said Felix. "I feel funny. My head hurts. And I'm so, so hungry."

"That'll teach you," said Mr Jarvis, picking up ruined peaches from the gutter. "Attacking a man in his own shop like that!" He pointed at Uncle Brian. "That man deserves a medal, officer," he said to the policewoman. "Or a TV show at least. I've never seen anything like it. He hypnotised him and made him do what he told him to. It was extraordinary."

Uncle Brain beamed. "It was my pleasure," he said with a low bow. "A medal is unwarranted, but a TV show would be splendid. Imagine it — a Weaver on the television!"

"Hypnotised him, you say?" said the shortest of the two policewomen. "Do you think you could help me stop smoking?"

Uncle Brain adjusted his silk cravat. "My dear," he said. "I could definitely stop you from smoking."

"What about eating?" said the other policewoman, guiding Felix into the backseat of the car. "Can you help me get beach body ready for my holiday?"

"Of course," said Uncle Brian. "I am after all, a hypnotist." He took a moleskin notepad and fountain pen from his pocket and scribbled his phone number on a sheet of paper. He ripped it from the book and handed it to the woman who was keen to stop smoking. "Telephone me for an appointment," he said.

The policewomen thanked him and sped off with their prisoner.

"What are you doing?" I said under my breath, as Willow helped Mr Jarvis back inside his shop. "You can't pretend to hypnotise people and use magic on them! It's immoral and probably dangerous!"

"Of course I can" said Uncle Brian. "It's a genius idea, I'm not sure why I've never thought of it before."

I didn't bother arguing. It was never worth arguing with a Weaver. When a Weaver had made a decision, it was practically set in stone. "What spell was that, anyway?" I said instead. "It was quite impressive, although it was strange how he called you his mightiness."

"A spell of subservient adoration," said Uncle Brian. "It's very useful. You should learn it. It can open all sorts of doors for you. I eat for free in a lot of London's swankiest restaurants, thanks to that little spell."

A squeal of tyres and the roar of a powerful engine broke the silence in the street, and I watched in disbelief as a black Range Rover careered around the corner on the wrong side of the road.

"Who's that?" said Uncle Brian. "That's a really nice motor, and a very proficient driver!"

"That's your mother," I said, taking two steps backwards as the large four-by-four came to a screeching halt next to us.

Willow rushed out of the greengrocer's shop as Granny revved the engine and rolled down the tinted window. She waved a hand at us, her face ashen. "Quick. Jump in, I need help. Boris has been kidnapped!" she said.

CHAPTER TWELVE

"What do you mean kidnapped?" I asked, as Granny took a sharp left turn, sending me and Willow sprawling in the back seat. Uncle Brian sat in the front with Granny, and he put his hand over his eyes as Granny barely avoided slamming the Range Rover into the postbox outside the coffee pot café.

"Slow down," said Willow. "Someone will get hurt!"

Granny swung the Range Rover into Church Street. "My Boris is probably undergoing all sorts of hideous experiments and tests as we speak. I can't afford to slow down. I need to get to my goat. He needs me!"

"The famous talking goat?" said Uncle Brian, holding on tight as the car rolled to the right. "I'm yet to meet him, but I'm more than ready to help him in his hour of need! Who's kidnapped him, Mother? And for what manner of nefarious reason?"

"You're such a good boy, Brian," said Granny, slamming the brakes on as a lollipop woman stepped into the highway to allow a gaggle of chocolate and candy eating children to cross the road. "Nobody would guess you were so terribly oppressed. You have such a kind heart! Boris will be thrilled to meet you if we can ever rescue him."

Willow rolled her eyes as Granny gave the engine a burst of revs and pulled away with a squeal of rubber on tarmac. "Who's taken Boris, Granny?" she said.

"Those bastards from the animal welfare department," said Granny. "I got home with the new wheels and found a note on my door. They say they have reason to believe he was the goat present at the quarry fire, and they say he's been mistreated. They've taken him to Applehill veterinary centre for tests! I pray to all that is holy and sacred that they don't still take an animal's temperature by sticking a thermometer up the jacksy! Can you imagine Boris allowing anybody to do that? He's such a proud fellow — he wouldn't let *anybody* near that private spot, let alone a total stranger who kidnapped him!"

Granny made a right turn onto Applehill and gunned the engine with a heavy foot. The Range Rover lurched forward and accelerated quickly up the steep hill towards the red brick building which sat at the peak.

The car park was nearly empty, and Granny brought the car to a halt outside the veterinary centre doors. "Quickly," she said, opening her door and sliding out. "We've no time to waste, and as matriarch of the Weaver family, I grant each of you permission to use magic during operation *free Boris*. He must be rescued no matter what! I'm willing to rack up fatalities if need be — we'll call it collateral damage."

"No one's getting hurt," I said, as Brian rolled up his sleeves and flexed his fingers. "Calm down. We'll just go inside and find out what's happening. I'm sure Boris is fine, and we'll have him home in no time. Everything will be okay. It always is."

Granny led the way along the short path and pushed through the doors into the building. The reception desk was devoid of staff, and three upturned chairs in the waiting room were the first clue that maybe everything wasn't fine after all.

A raised voice came from the corridor to our left, and Granny followed it with the eagerness of a dog on the scent of a fox. Uncle Brian followed her as far as the large animal weighing scales, and took a moment out of his busy schedule to stand on them. "Good gracious me!" he said. "No wonder my boxers are pinching my man eggs! I've put on six pounds since I last weighed!"

"Well, I think you look truly wonderful, my darling," said Granny. "I always said you carried your weight better than that sister of yours. A few extra pounds make you look mayoral and healthy. Maggie just balloons into a big wrinkly mess when she goes over two-hundred-and-fifty."

Another raised voice came from behind a door further along the corridor. "This way!" said Granny.

A woman's scream increased the urgency of the situation, and I quickened my pace as Granny reached the door and swung it open with a push. "What the devil?" she shouted. "What's happening in here? Boris, my gentle goat, are you okay?"

Willow rushed into the room behind Granny, and Uncle Brian and I entered together, jut as a woman screamed again. "Please make it stop!" she begged. "I don't know what's happening. I'm scared!"

The scene in the room was one of complete madness. Pain blossomed in my bottom lip as I bit into it, and even Uncle Brian seemed shocked. He took a step backwards and lowered himself into a plastic chair, loosening his cravat and taking deep breaths as he fanned himself with his hat.

A group of people stood huddled together in the furthest corner from the door. Some held animal crates, and others held onto leashes with terrified dogs at the ends of them.

Two of the people wore white coats, and one of them, a woman with a stethoscope around her neck, was crying uncontrollably.

Boris stood in front of the captive people, baring his teeth and snapping at the air whenever somebody moved. A golden labrador took a tentative step towards Boris, but cowered against its owner's legs when Boris let out a blood curling scream. "Get back in line you filthy animal!"

"Help us," said a man holding a tiny lap dog close to his chest. "He rounded us all up like a dog rounds up sheep, and trapped us in this room. He bit me on the buttock, I'll need a tetanus jab!"

The trembling woman next to him pointed a finger at Boris. "It speaks too," she murmured. "The goat speaks! I only came here to get worming tablets for my cat, and now I'm trapped in a horrific nightmare." She looked at the floor. "I took acid in the seventies, maybe it's come back to haunt me."

Granny dropped to her knees next to Boris. "My poor, poor Boris," she said, wrapping an arm around his neck. "What have they done to you?"

"Gladys," said Boris, quite calmly considering the circumstances. "I have a thermometer inserted where the sun doesn't shine. Be so good as to remove it for me, would you? Ive tried, but I can't quite get my mouth around that far, and I've been hesitant to take my eye off these people. One of them has already tried to inject me with what I can only imagine is a sedative of some description. Who knows what they'll do to me if they get the chance."

"I only wanted some eyedrops for my gerbil," said a tall wiry man with thick black rimmed glasses. "I just want to go home. I won't hurt you, Boris."

"I'm sorry you've been dragged into this, Nigel," said Boris. "But I had to take you all hostage until help arrived. I knew Gladys would come for me eventually, it was only a matter of waiting long enough."

"How do you know his name is Nigel, Boris?" said Willow.

"He did a meet and greet," said a young girl dressed in the green uniform of an animal nurse. "He made us tell him our full names, starsigns, and our ambitions."

Boris snapped at the leg of a man as he attempted to move towards a table with a telephone on it. "Get back, Larry," he growled. "Or you'll never see the Niagara Falls."

Granny pointed at a table. "Penelope," she said, "pass me something I can use to pull this thermometer from out of Boris. There's barely any of it visible. It's really gone deep, Boris. It can't be comfortable for you."

I rifled through a tray of medical implements and settled on a pair of forceps. Granny took them from me and held Boris still as she carefully slid the glass tube from his rear end.

Boris let out a contented moan of pleasure as the thermometer left his body, and snarled at one of the vets. "I will *never* forgive you," he said. "You took my dignity from me."

Granny stood up and stared at Boris's prisoners. "You should be ashamed," she said. "Stealing a goat from his own home and forcing him to endure horrific medical experiments."

"We were worried about him," said a woman. "We followed the footsteps of a goat that was involved in an incident in a quarry, and they led to your home. We needed to make sure he wasn't being mistreated. The last time he was seen he was wearing a balaclava, and that's animal cruelty."

"As you can see, he's perfectly fine," said Granny. "I do not mistreat him."

"He talks," said a female vet. "That's not fine. There's something very wrong about this whole situation, and we need to get to the bottom of it, so if you'd just allow us to do our jobs, we can find out what's wrong with the poor animal."

Uncle Brian had recovered, and carefully placed his hat on his head as he stood up. "Mother, would you like me to work a little magic?" he said, wriggling the fingers on both hands. "I think these people need to forget what they saw here today."

Granny clapped. "Go on, son," she said. "Give them what for! Show them who's boss!"

Sparks crackled at Brian's fingertips, and a woman made a break for the door, clutching a basket which contained an injured crow.

"Stop right there, Mrs Oliver!" said Boris. "It will be easier if you don't resist."

"Mrs Oliver?" I said. "The birdwatcher? The woman who kept complaining about Gerald Timkins?"

The woman's face froze in an expression midway between a smile and a scowl. "Yes that's me, and I'm still clearing up his barbaric mess. I found this young crow today with a broken wing and pellets embedded in its abdomen. I'm sorry about what happened to him, but I'm not sorry he can't shoot at defenceless birds anymore. Who knows? Maybe he had it coming. Anyway, the police have already spoken to me about it. They had the audacity to ask if I knew anything. I told them the truth. I didn't see anything or hear anything, and that's the end of the matter."

Uncle Brian waved his hand in the air, trailing bright sparks behind it which mesmerised the crowd of people huddled in the corner. "What are you?" said one of them. "Who are you people, and why can that goat talk?"

Mrs Oliver made another panicked attempt at reaching the door, and Brian cast his spell. The air in the room seemed to heat up, and my eardrums popped as the people huddled in the corner sighed in unison and froze in position.

"Very good, Brian," said Granny, getting to her knees in front of the male vet.

"What are you doing?" gasped Willow. "Pull his trousers back up and put that thermometer down!"

"I'm just repaying him," said Granny, grasping a buttock and pulling it aside. "Let's see how he likes a glass tube in *his* bottom."

"Boris," I whispered. "Please stop her. Nothing good can come from this!"

Boris snorted his contempt. "He deserves it."

"I'll buy you a bottle of brandy every week for a month," I negotiated.

"And a packet of cigars?"

I nodded. "Deal. Just make her stop, she hasn't even put any lube on it!"

"Gladys," said Boris. "Stop that. He was only doing his job. Two wrongs don't make a right."

"But, Boris," said Granny, taking aim. "I need my revenge. You know it's my weakness."

Boris stepped slowly towards Granny and placed a hoof on her shoulder. "Your revenge will be knowing you're a better person than he is, Gladys."

Granny hesitated, but released the buttock and withdrew the tip of the thermometer from near catastrophe. "Can I leave his trousers and underwear around his feet? That will steady my lust for revenge."

I shrugged and Willow nodded. "Yes," said Boris. "Leave him as he is."

"Okay, Brian," said Granny. "Make them all forget what happened."

"Wait," said Willow as Uncle Brian lifted his hand. "Can you ask Mrs Oliver if she killed Gerald Timkins? You know, the same way you asked Felix Round if he was a murderer? Let's be sure she's innocent while we've got her trapped here."

Brain smiled. "Of course I can," he said. He waved his right hand in front of Mrs Oliver's face as his left hand kept the other people under control. "Did you murder a man?" he said. "Speak the truth and speak it freely!"

"No," mumbled Mrs Oliver. "I've not killed a man."

"Does she know anything about it at all?" I said.

"Tell me what you know about Gerald's death," said Uncle Brian.

"Nothing," said Mrs Oliver. "But you should ask the scarecrow making man."

"Who?" said Uncle Brian.

"The scarecrow man," said Mrs Oliver. "He told me he was angry with Gerald."

"Did you tell the police?" said Uncle Brian.

"No," said Mrs Oliver. "I won't help the police. Gerald Timkins had it coming. He shot innocent animals, and someone shot him. It's poetic justice."

"Who's the scarecrow making man?" said Uncle Brian.

Mrs Oliver furrowed her brow and groaned.

"Hurry," said Granny. "You can't keep two spells going at the same time like this Brian, they're beginning to weaken."

Granny was right. The other people in the room were starting to regain some control over themselves. One woman moved her nose and another blinked. The vet with his dignity around his ankles began bending at the waist to reach for his trousers.

Uncle Brian nodded. "Sorry, girls," he said, speaking to me and Willow. "I can't ask her anymore questions." He clicked his fingers and everybody fell still again, including Mrs Oliver. "You'll all wake up in three minutes," said Uncle Brian. "And have no memory of what's happened here today.

You'll forget about goats and mistreatment, and everyone will think it's perfectly normal to all be in this room together. They'll be suspicions as to why the strange male vet has his tackle on display, but you'll carry on with your day as if nothing's happened." He clicked his fingers again. "We've got three minutes," he said.

Granny rubbed her hands together in glee. "Everybody into the car," she said. "I've always wanted to be a getaway driver!"

CHAPTER THIRTEEN

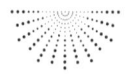

"I look ridiculous," I said. "Surely I can wear shoes without heels. Barney won't care."

Willow seemed more excited than I was about the fact that I was going out for a meal with Barney. She'd almost forced me to borrow one of her dresses and a pair of matching shoes.

"Penny," said Willow. "You're below average height for a woman, and Barney is ridiculously tall — for a man *or* a woman. There's nothing wrong with adding a couple of inches to your height. You don't want to strain your back when it's time to snog him, do you?"

Willow expertly avoided the make-up brush I threw at her. "There'll be no kissing, thank you very much! We're just friends. Anyway. Barney is a gentlemen. He wouldn't expect me to kiss him on a first date."

Susie looked up from her laptop. "So it *is* a date!"

"Who rattled your cage?" I laughed, sitting down to take the strain off my calves. Heels may have added a little height, but they certainly couldn't be described as comfort wear. "I thought you were supposed to be doing some investigative journalism, not helping my sister tease me."

Susie tapped at her keyboard. "There's nothing about scarecrow making men," she said. "According to google, farmers make their own scarecrows. There used to be people who made them for a living, but the art died out years ago. Maybe Mrs Oliver got muddled up."

"Maybe," I said. "I'll tell Barney though. It might mean something to him."

I tugged the hem of the black dress a little further down my thigh. I was sure it was too short, but both Susie and Willow assured me it was fine. Yes, they enjoyed teasing me, but neither of them would see me going out in a dress which looked terrible on me. I trusted them.

My hair was gathered high on my head and held in position by numerous hairpins which Willow had studiously applied, and the matching earring and necklace set which Mum had given me on my eighteenth birthday twinkled in the light as I checked my makeup in my compact mirror. Mum had insisted the diamonds had been bought from a shop in our world, but I was convinced they'd come from the haven. It seemed impossible that earthly diamonds could shine with so many colours. They even looked magical.

Wherever they were from, they only came out on very special occasions, and I classed the meal with Barney as being a very special occasion. Not only was it a chance for the two of us to share some time alone — it was also the first time I'd be seeing Barney since he'd found out I was a witch. It was a new situation for us both and things could get awkward, and I at least wanted to look nice in case Barney said something which made me angry enough to storm out of the restaurant.

Willow accompanied me along the path into town to wait for the taxi. We stood outside our shop and made plans for the sign which would hang outside and make the shop official.

"Don't be late home and don't do anything I wouldn't do," joked Willow as the taxi appeared at the end of Bridge Street.

Barney climbed from the car and opened the door for me, much to Willow's delight. "Aww, that's nice of you. Barney," she said. "And I must say — you do scrub up well. Look at you, Wickford's very own James Bond! I don't think I've ever seen you in a suit."

Barney blushed, ignoring the compliment. We weren't so different, me and him — neither of us dealt very well with compliments or praise. A compliment may have made Barney blush, but they made my skin crawl and my jaw tighten. Especially if I didn't feel good about myself.

"You look really nice, Penny," Barney said, helping me balance on my heels as I climbed into the back of the car. "Really pretty."

Instead of the familiar awkwardness, Barney's genuine compliment made me smile. "Thank you," I said, as Barney climbed in beside me. "You don't look too bad yourself."

He didn't look in the least bit bad. In fact, he looked amazing. The suit he wore fitted him better than any other clothes I'd ever seen him wear, and he'd obviously taken time to make his hair look stylishly messy. I'd be proud to walk into a restaurant with him.

Willow stood on the pavement waving as the taxi pulled away, and Barney reached between his feet and handed me a bouquet of flowers which he'd been hiding. "I wasn't sure when to give them to you," he said. "Before or after the meal. I've never really given a woman flowers before, apart from my Mum and Nan obviously. But I think that's different. I mean —"

Barney's face tightened with anxiety, and I quietened him

with a kiss on his cheek. "They're really lovely, Barney," I said. "Thank you."

"I wanted to add a flower that would suit you, some sort of witchcraft flower, like hemlock or something, but the woman in the shop looked at me like I was mad. She put a sprig of elderflower in though. I think that's supposed to be magical, isn't it?"

I put a finger to my lips and nodded at the back of the driver's head. "Don't talk about that here," I said. "Wait until the restaurant. It'll be more private."

BARNEY HAD BOOKED the table in advance, and he'd chosen the perfect table for a couple who required privacy. As the name suggested, The *Cosy Cucina* was not a large restaurant, and most of the dozen or so tables had couples or small families already seated at them.

The waiter led us to a secluded cubical table in a corner near the large window. The view across the countryside was breathtaking even in the dying light, and the canal was still visible in the distance as the sun gave way to the moon.

Barney ordered us some wine, and I licked my lips as the aroma of garlic and mussels flooding from the kitchen made my mouth water. We ordered our meals, and with a full wine glass each, Barney's bottom lip already staining red from just a few small sips, I looked him in the eye. "You're taking the whole thing very well, Barney," I said, "I'd have thought you'd have had a lot of questions for me. I know I probably would if *I'd* just found out that witches existed."

"Of course I have questions," said Barney, breaking a small piece of bread from one of the rolls in the wicker basket in the centre of the round table. "But I understand how it is for you, Penny. And Susie, Willow, and erm.. Boris were very patient with me. When I had to rush off to work and leave you in that *trance* in your bed, I was scared and I wanted to know everything. It took all my self control to stay away from you until now, but I thought you'd need to think about things just as much as I needed to. It's not everyday your secret is laid bare like it was that night at the meal. It must have been very difficult for you too."

It had been difficult, but I'd have thought what Barney had gone through would have been worse. "It was," I said. "But I'm happy that you know the truth. I just need to know that you can handle the truth, Barney. Finding out that witches exist must have turned your world upside down. I know some people wouldn't be able to handle it."

"Can I handle knowing that witches exist and that the woman who's sitting opposite me sharing a bottle of wine can do magic? Hell, yeah, I can handle that! It's awesome, Penny, and Susie told me how your magic helped with the Sam Hedgewick case. Imagine it — I've got a witch as a… friend, who can solve crimes! It's amazing."

I took a long gulp of wine. "I can't really solve crimes, Barney. I can help you, but the leg work still needs to be done by the police."

We stopped speaking as the waiter slid our starters in front of us. Seared scallops for Barney, and mussels with white wine sauce for me. I knew that drinking red wine with fish went against every piece of food advice I'd ever read or been given, but it seemed that Barney's and my relationship was breaking a lot of normal conventions. Drinking the wrong wine with a meal was the least of them.

"How do you do it, Penny?" said Barney. "I mean how do you actually do it… like how do you cast a spell or whatever it is you do?"

"Wiggle your fingers on your left hand," I said.

Barney gave me an enquiring look, but laid his fork down and did as I'd asked.

"How did you do that, Barney?" I said. "How did you wiggle your fingers?"

"I don't know. I thought about doing it and it just happened."

"That's how magic works" I said. "When you first learn a new spell it takes a little more effort, but after that, it's just a case of thinking about what you want to do. Just like wiggling your fingers."

Barney asked me more questions, and I answered each one as honestly as I could. We were onto the subject of the haven by the time Barney's lamb shank with rosemary gravy and my paella had arrived at the table.

"You can go to the haven, but you haven't gone yet?" said Barney. "Why?"

"I've waited so long," I said. "I can wait a day or two longer while Mum arranges a simple ceremony for me. It would be unfair of me to enter without Mum. She'd take it very badly, and to be honest, I'm a little nervous about going alone."

Barney nodded and put a hand to his head. He rubbed his temple with two fingers and winced. "Ouch," he said. "I've had a terrible headache all day. It's wearing off though. Thanks to the wine, I think."

"It's because of the spell you had cast on you," I said. "It will go away soon enough."

"What spell," said Barney. "You stopped them casting one, remember?"

I sipped my wine. "The spell that Willow cast on you to make you forget. At Granny's cottage. That was powerful magic, it was bound to give you a headache."

"What are you talking about?" said Barney, placing his

glass on the table and staring at me. "What spell at Granny's? Making me forget what?"

I swallowed hard. I'd assumed that Willow, Boris, and Susie had told him everything… including the fact that we'd wiped his memory clean. "Nothing," I said, my cheeks warming from the lie. "I've had too much wine."

"Penny," said Barney. "I'll ask you once more, and I'd like to think you trust me enough to give me an honest answer. What spell at Granny's?"

I dabbed my mouth with a napkin. "You came to Granny's house to investigate an arson, Barney, remember?"

He nodded. "Of course I do, everything was okay. I crossed your grandmother out of my book and told Sergeant Cooper she had nothing to do with it. Or that goat of hers. It seems quite weird now I know the goat can speak though, but I definitely found nothing amiss at Ashwood cottage."

"It didn't quite go down like that," I said.

"How did it go down then, Penny? What happened to me."

"You'll be angry," I said, "and we probably broke the law too. How will you deal with that?"

"Just tell me," said Barney. "I'll deal with it the same way I deal with everything… calmly and rationally."

"I can do better than tell you," I said. "I can show you. If you trust me to cast a spell on you, that is."

After watching Willow cast the spell, I'd taken the time to learn it myself. It was simple to learn a spell from Granny's spell book. A spell was s series of numbers, letters, and symbols, which imprinted themselves onto a witches mind when she read them. It had taken me less than a minute to learn the spell Willow had cast, and I'd spent a further half an hour learning more spells, including one which could bring back memories.

"Do it," said Barney. "Make me remember."

"Here?" I said. "It might be too public here, Barney. You might have a shock when you remember what happened."

Barney narrowed his eyes. "Just do it," he said.

I glanced around the room. The other customers were either preoccupied with eating, or deep in conversation with their dining companions.

"Okay," I said. "Prepare yourself. I'm not sure how it will work."

Barney gripped the edge of the table with both hands. "Go for it. I'm ready. I want to know what you did to me, and why you did it to me."

The spell came easily. I sucked a little air between my lips and tasted copper in my mouth. The spell tingled in my fingertips, and I hid my hands beneath the table as I clicked my fingers.

Barney closed his eyes and gasped, the table rocked a little as he tightened his grip on it, and I put my hand on one of his. "It's okay," I said. "You're safe."

"Goat in garden," he mumbled. "Cigar smoke in strange backroom. No one in cottage smokes though."

"That's it," I said, unsure if he could hear me. "Let the memories come back slowly."

Barney smiled, his eyes still closed. "Penny's bottom on the stairs in front of me. Nice. Mustn't touch though, however tempting."

I wondered why I was blushing — Barney had his eyes closed and I doubted he had any idea about what he was saying. There was no reason to be embarrassed, but my cheeks burned hot nonetheless.

"Mad Gladys Weaver," murmured Barney. "Look in her bedroom. Why does she keep a baseball bat under her bed? None of my business. It's not illegal. Forget what you saw in her top drawer — never think of it again — it might mentally scar you. Leave Barney... go and look in next bedroom."

I promised myself I'd never look in Granny's top drawer, however tempted I was, and watched Barney's face closely. The important part was coming up. He was about to remember discovering Charleston Huang's hiding place.

"What's in the corner?" said Barney, his voice becoming louder. "A man! In the corner! Get out!"

Barney's eyes snapped open and he stared through me. "Come out with your hands up!" he shouted, standing up and knocking the bread basket off the table. "Light-shade on his head! Chinese fellow in the corner! Is he dead?"

People stopped eating and lowered their cutlery as a waiter scampered towards us, placing the tray he was carrying on the nearest table and putting his hand on Barney's back. "No dead Chinese man in here," he said in broken English. "This Italian restaurant! No dead men at all in corner!"

Barney ignored him. "Am I in heaven?"

"No, sir," said the waiter. "Food good here, but this not heaven!"

I attempted to stop the spell, but it seemed that when the memories which Willow had purged from Barney's mind had been replaced by my spell, there was nothing to do but let it run its course and wait for Barney to recover.

"He's okay," I said, as the waiter looked in Barney's wine glass, possibly for drugs. "He's just very tired."

"Too much wine?" said the waiter. He looked Barney up and down. "He very tall man. Should be able to drink lots."

"Yes, he is tall," I said. "But he doesn't drink very often."

Barney laughed, his eyes closed again. "I'll only pay for half of the meal! Perfect!"

"No, sir," said the waiter. "Not perfect. You pay full price."

Barney gasped, and the waiter took a hurried step away from him.

"Are you alright?" I said, as colour flooded Barney's cheeks.

Barney sat down and waved at the spectators he'd acquired. "Show's over," he laughed.

The waiter smiled at Barney. "You fine now, sir?" he said.

"Everything's fine," said Barney. "Thank you."

When the other diners had started eating again, and the bread and basket had been picked up from the floor, the waiter retrieved his tray and continued with his business.

I leaned across the table. "I'm so sorry, Barney," I said. "I feel awful about everything that happened at Granny's, and now I've put you in terrible position — you have to decide whether you're going to charge Granny with arson or not, now you know the truth."

"Charge Gladys?" said Barney, his eyes sparkling. "Of course not. How can I possibly apply laws which are meant for humans, to witches? I understand everything now... that spell did more than give me my memories back... it filled in the blanks too. I know who Charleston Huang is and I know why Gladys and Boris burnt that car. They had to protect themselves. The secret is safe with me, Penny. You have my word."

"I'd have thought you'd have been angrier," I said. "We stole your memories."

"For a valid reason," said Barney. "And anyway, how could I be angry? I was just given a beautiful memory."

"What on earth was beautiful about what happened to you in that cottage?" I said. "Scary, yes. Hideous, maybe. Beautiful — I'm just not seeing it."

Barney took my hand in his. "When Willow asked you if you wanted me to forget about the meal, you said no. You said you wanted to come with me, and you even offered to pay half which was a lovely gesture! I've never been happier, Penny. I wondered if you were just coming for a meal with me out of pity, but now I know the truth, and it's the best feeling I've ever had. It certainly takes the sting out of the shame I feel for the comment I made about your bottom."

I laughed. "You remember saying that?"

Barney nodded. "I remember everything that happened in your grandmother's cottage, and to my shame…everything that just happened here — it will be a long time before I eat in this restaurant again." He paused momentarily, and squeezed my hand. "There's no secrets between us anymore, is there, Penny?"

"I wish the comment about my bottom was still a secret, Barney," I giggled. "But no, as far as I'm concerned there are no more secrets between us."

Barney leaned across the table, and despite a few of the other customers and the waiter still watching us, I sat forward in my seat, smiled at him, and allowed him to kiss me.

It was how I'd imagined it would be, and the fluttering in my belly stayed with me long after Barney had pulled his lips from mine and ordered dessert.

CHAPTER FOURTEEN

"The scarecrow man," said Willow, seemingly out of nowhere.

I looked up from the box of novelty spells I was sorting through. "What about him? I told Barney last night and he said he wasn't aware of anyone who makes scarecrows. He's asking around though, but because we got the information from Mrs Oliver by using magic, he has to be careful what he says."

Willow placed a cast iron cauldron on a low display shelf near the door. "You told Barney about what happened in the vets?"

"Yes," I said. "There are no secrets between us anymore."

"What did he say?"

"He didn't really want to talk about the Gerald Timkins case. He was more interested in the fact that I'm a witch, Willow, but he laughed and asked how Boris was after his ordeal… he's very taken with him. He wants a boys night in… just him, Boris, and a bottle of brandy."

Willow smiled. "I can't think of anything that could go wrong with that," she said. "Not a thing at all."

"My thoughts precisely," I said, allowing myself a giggle as I pictured Boris and Barney drinking into the small hours of the morning. "But Barney's a little like me. He doesn't have many friends. It will be nice for him to be able to relax and have some fun with Boris."

Willow stood up and joined me at the sales counter, flipping through a brochure from the sign writing company we'd chosen to make the sign for the shop. "As I was saying," she said. "The scarecrow man."

"And as I said — what about him?"

"Remember that pick-up truck? The one that nearly knocked us down in the lane on the way to Granny's?"

I nodded, realisation dawning. "Yes, I do. The one that seemed to be in a real hurry, probably around the time Gerald was killed!"

"The one that dropped old clothes and straw from the back," added Willow. "It doesn't take a huge leap of faith to suggest that he might be the scarecrow man, does it?"

I already had my phone to my ear. "I'll tell Barney," I said. "The police are still questioning Felix Round, but Barney doesn't think he did it. He has a strong alibi — he said he was at a yoga class to help stretch his stomach for the pie eating competition. Barney's checking it out."

"Tell him I remembered it," said Willow. "I could do with a little praise."

Barney answered the phone. "Hi," I said, blushing as Willow doodled a heart on the notepad next to her, writing *Penny luvs Barney*, inside it.

I told Barney what had happened in the lane and explained our suspicions, adding that it had been Willow's suggestion, much to her delight. "I don't," I said, when Barney asked if I remembered a registration plate number. "Maybe willow does."

Willow was no help either, and Barney ended the call

with only a vague description of the pick-up truck and driver to help with his investigation.

"He's checking out CCTV footage in town," I said, "looking for the pick-up, but there's not many cameras. He says the police are releasing Felix this morning, too. His alibi checks out, and Mr Jarvis doesn't want to press charges either."

"I was sure he'd done it," said Willow. "He seemed so angry."

"It's the quiet ones you have to watch out for," I said. "According to Granny, but she's not quiet and you have to look out for her."

Willow laughed, and glanced at her watch. "Speaking of Granny, we'd better lock up the shop and get going. She wants us there by ten o'clock."

Willow switched off the lights and I closed the door behind us. The shop was going to be opened officially when our new sign had been delivered and fitted, and Willow and I were both excited about running a business together. "Granny can't demand our presence when the shop is officially open," I said, locking the door. "We can't just open and close when we feel like it. We'll get a terrible reputation."

Willow nodded. "Of course, but you must admit you want to go to Granny's this morning, though? I know I do."

I slipped the keys into my short's pocket. "I do too," I admitted. "I'm intrigued about —"

"Girls! Could I have a moment of your time please?"

The woman's voice cut me off mid sentence, and Willow and I turned to see a short woman running across the road towards us.

"Mrs Round," said Willow.

"Im sorry to bother you both," said the tiny woman with the big hair. "But I wanted to apologise for my husband's behaviour outside your shop. I've already apologised to Mr

Jarvis, and he kindly agreed to drop the charges of assault against Felix. I've been told that you two and a man had to come outside and stop Felix from hurting poor Mr Jarvis. A hypnotist, a policewoman told me?"

"Yes, that was our uncle," I said. "But there's no need to apologise. We're just happy that Felix is okay, and that the police have cleared him of murder. It can't be easy to have that sort of accusation hanging around your neck."

Mrs Round shook her head and offered us a narrow smile. "Murder and Felix don't even belong in the same sentence," she said. "He's normally as mild mannered as a stoned vicar, but when it's pie eating competition time, he turns into another man completely — not violent though, you understand? Just hungry and grumpy. What he did to Mr Jarvis was completely out of character for him. It's his health, he really needs to stop with these stupid food eating competitions before they kill him."

"Is he still taking part in the pie eating competition?" said Willow. "After what's happened?"

"Yes," said Mrs Round, wiping a tear from the corner of her eye, her green nail polish matching her eye shadow perfectly. "He says if he wins it will be his last one. He'll have set a new record, and he'll be happy. I've got my fingers crossed for him, I don't think he'll be alive in two years time if he carries on eating the way he does. The doctor says he needs to make changes now."

"We'll cross our fingers for him too," I offered.

Mrs Round smiled. "Thank you," she said. "It's such a shame that the competition has been overshadowed by the death of The Tank, though. Felix had a lot of respect for Gerald, even though it may not have seemed like it sometimes. It really is awful. All the money that's raised this year is going to his wife."

"I'm sure Sandra will be grateful," I said.

"Poor lady," said Mrs Round. "I can't imagine what it must be like for a woman to lose her husband. I don't know what I'd do without Felix. That's what makes me so angry about this whole eating for competitions nonsense. He doesn't seem to care that if he drops dead from a heart attack he'll be leaving me on my own."

I glanced at my phone, trying not to seem rude, but aware that Granny would be waiting for me and Willow to arrive. "I'm really sorry," I said. "We have to be somewhere. We'll see you at the pie eating competition, though. We'll be there to support Felix."

GRANNY TAPPED her watch as Willow and I strolled into the kitchen. "What time do you call this? I said ten o'clock sharp, not seven minutes past ten."

"Sorry, Granny," said Willow. "We got held up, but we're here now. That's all that matters isn't it?"

Granny stood up. "I suppose so. Come on then girls, Boris is in his study writing his blog. Let's go and ask him about this photograph."

Granny retrieved the black and white photograph of the ballet dancer from her apron pocket, and Willow's eyes lit up. "I thought you weren't going to wear the apron when you got the Range Rover," she said with a grin, pointing through the window at the large black car. "You're lower middle class now, aren't you?"

"I said I wouldn't wear it when I go somewhere," said Granny. "Of course I'm going to wear it at home — it's very handy. You girls should try one. I got my first apron at eighteen, and I've never looked back."

Granny took two steps towards the door, her footsteps like somebody hammering a nail.

"Heavens, Granny!" said Willow. "You're wearing your clogs, I see. They're very loud."

"Aren't they lovely, though?" said Granny, lifting one foot for us to inspect. "They fit perfectly, and Boris says they make me look very continental. My back feels better too… I walk with a far straighter gait, don't you think?"

"Maybe, but you sound like a horse on this slate floor, Granny," I said.

"They're better on carpet, I'll be the first to admit," said Granny, clip clopping through the kitchen.

Granny led us to Boris's closed study door and knocked on it gently "Let me do the talking," she said, as Boris called us in. "I'm a little more sensitive than you pair. You two would go at it like a bull in a china shop, and personal family matters like this require a little more finesse and understanding — such as I can offer."

Willow tittered, and I rolled my eyes. "Why did you want us here then, Granny?" I said. "You could have asked him on your own."

"Moral support," said Granny, "and I know you two are just as nosy as me."

Boris nodded a greeting as we entered, and spoke into the microphone next to his laptop. "Go to sleep," he said. The voice activation software did as it was told, and Boris's laptop screen flickered and turned black. "My three favourite ladies," he said, turning around on his cushion until he faced us. "Something tells me you haven't interrupted me to ask how my blog is going…. although it's going very well, thank you. I've got quite a fanbase building, and the Golden Wok delivers free food for me and Gladys once a week in return for me advertising them."

"Very nice it is too," said Granny. "I ate some squid last time didn't I, Boris? Even though I didn't want to!"

"You did, Gladys," verified Boris.

Granny puffed out her chest. "Boris said it's good to try new foods, and that he was very proud of me, didn't you, Boris?"

Boris chuckled. "I did indeed, Gladys. I did indeed. You're a brave woman. Not everybody would try squid."

"Erm... well done, Granny," I said. "I suppose." I pointed at the photograph in her hand. "Go on then, show him."

"Show me what?" said Boris. "What's that you have there, Gladys? A photograph? That frame looks familiar. Let me see it."

Granny turned the picture around, and Boris gave a gentle sigh. "It's Nanna Chang-Chang when she was young. She was a beautiful woman and an expert ballet dancer. Those clogs you're wearing were hers, Gladys. She used them to improve her posture and strengthen her feet." Boris tilted his head and twitched an ear. "Why do you have that picture? I only asked you too bring me the photograph of my parents, which I'm very grateful for incidentally."

The other photograph we'd brought back from Charleston's home was on the mantelpiece overlooking Boris's coffee table desk. His mother and father were pictured outside, beneath a large tree, and both of them looked happy.

Boris gazed up at the picture of his parents. "Nanna Chang-Chang didn't pass her dancing skills down to her daughter though — my mother had two left feet and no rhythm whatsoever."

"Boris," said Granny, sitting on the sofa and laying the picture on her lap. "I have this picture because I recognise the woman in it. In fact, I knew Chang-Chang personally... not very well, but I did know her."

"How did you know her, Gladys?" said Boris. "She died when I was ten, she got ill."

A tear ran the length of a thick hair near Boris's eye, and

Granny wiped it away with a thumb. "Did you ever think she was special, Boris?" she said. "I mean differently special."

"Of course she was special," said Boris. "She was Nanna. She was a wonderful woman. Kind and considerate, but you didn't want to cross her, oh no! She had a vicious tongue in her mouth and she knew how to use it. She didn't speak English very well, but you got the meaning from her facial expressions — she was very elastic in the face department, and very gifted at impressions too. My mother told me she could do a perfect Chairman Mao, although she did get in trouble for it once or twice."

Granny sighed. She was thinking… looking for the right words to tell Boris he came from magical ancestors. I sat next to her and put my hand on her forearm. "Tell him, Granny," I said. "Just be honest."

Boris sat higher on his cushion. "Tell me what, Gladys?"

"Boris, I don't know how to tell you, or how it say it." Granny put her hand on Boris's shoulder and looked him in the eyes. "Oh sod it!" she said. "Boris, your grandmother was a witch."

The tip of Boris's tongue slid from his mouth, and he looked at me with shocked eyes. "Is… is this true, Penelope?" he stammered.

"I think so, Boris," I said.

Boris stood up and walked to Granny, gazing down at the photograph in her lap. "Nanna Chang-Chang was a witch? Are you certain, Gladys? That's quite a thing to say if you're not totally sure of it."

Granny slid another photo from her apron pocket. "This picture is from my own photograph album," she said. "It was taken in the haven, not long before your grandmother died. That's me on the right — you won't recognise me, I got given my entry spell when I was in my early twenties."

In the haven, a witch was always the age at which he or

she had been given their entry spell. I'd remain twenty-three whenever I entered the haven, even if I lived to be one-hundred. Many witches waited until they were close to death in the mortal world before moving to the haven permanently and gaining their immortality in a younger body.

"But Nanna looks so young in this photo. This couldn't have been taken just before she died. She was almost seventy when she passed," said Boris.

"The photograph was taken in the haven, Boris. She's at the age when she was given her entry spell."

Boris looked up from the picture. "So she's alive? In the haven? Isn't that where witches go when they get old? So they don't have to die?"

"Most witches," said Granny, placing a hand between Boris's horns and rubbing his head. "Your grandmother was different though, Boris. In China, witches were considered devils. Chang-Chang probably brought that belief with her when she moved to Britain, and when your mother was born she would have done everything in her power to prevent your mother from knowing the truth. She didn't like being a witch, she didn't like the haven either, she chose to die in this world, and because she didn't help your mother develop her own magic skills, your mother would never have known that *she* was a witch either."

"And if she didn't know she was a witch, Boris," I said. "Then you wouldn't have known that..."

Boris looked at each of us in turn. "That I'm a witch," he whispered.

"Precisely," said Granny. "It makes so much sense, Boris. Fate sent you to my door, and you said yourself that you'd always believed in magic."

"I always have done," said Boris. "Since I was a little boy."

"That's because you are magic, Boris," said Granny. "And fate had everything planned out for you. Why do you think you came to me in the first place and ended up in the body of a goat? So you'd have to stay with me, that's why! Then your credit card just happened to expire, and we went to your house, where Penny recognised the photo of your grandmother."

All the talk of fate seemed very addictive, so I joined in. "Because I went looking for the clogs which belonged to your grandmother," I said. "The photo was above them. As if I was led to it."

"Why did you want the clogs, Boris," asked Willow. "What made you think of them?"

"I had a dream!" said Boris. "My grandmother was wearing them! She was telling me how they helped her posture. I woke up and thought of Gladys's back problems, and because you three were going to my house to collect the credit card, I asked Gladys to bring the clogs back too… and as you rightly say, Penelope, they led you to the photo of Nanna."

"You see?" said Granny.

Boris gasped. "Jumping Jehovah!" he said. "It is fate! But why? Why was I sent to you, Gladys? What does this mean?"

"I'm sure fate will let us know, Boris," said Granny, stroking the goats back. "We just have to be patient. The answer will come eventually."

CHAPTER FIFTEEN

The four of us stood in Bridge street. Barney stood on my left, and Willow and Susie stood to my right. We all looked up at the sign which ran the length of the the shopfront. The sign company had done a good job. Bright red lettering on a green background made the shop stand out, and even Mr Jarvis had popped out to have a look, convinced that our new shop would bring him additional business too. "I don't know much about witchcraft," he'd said, "but surely witches need vegetables for some spells? If they do, just send them next door to me. I'll give them a discount!"

Willow and I agreed, on the condition that if any of his customers complained about not being able to find love, or not being promoted in work, he'd send them to our shop for a spell or a potion.

Barney had lowered his voice when Mr Jarvis had gone back inside *The Firkin gherkin.* "You don't give people real spells do you?" he said. "I'm not sure how I'd feel about that. It could be dangerous. Or illegal."

Susie put his mind at rest. "I've known the Weaver family were witches since I was eleven," she said, "and in all that time they've never used magic for anything but the best of intentions."

I could have listed at least three-hundred times that Granny had used magic for less than good intentions, but I chose to keep quiet. Barney could discover the dynamics of the Weaver family is his own good time. I was in no hurry to expose the inner workings of a dysfunctional magical family to him.

The four of us stared at the sign. "What a fantastic name," said Barney. "Boris really hit the nail on the head when he came up with that."

Willow and I had asked everyone we knew to offer suggestions for the name. I'd wanted to name it after my floating shop of course, but *The Water Witch - Floating emporium of magic,* was hardly an apt name for a landlocked shop. At least the boat would remain named *The Water Witch.*

Granny's idea for the shop name had not even made it onto the shortlist. *Wicked witches of Wickford,* sounded more like a film, or a gang that Granny might have been a member of as a teenager — or an elderly woman, I supposed. Boris had really come up trumps though, and surprised us all when he'd suggested his idea.

"*The Spell Weavers — Emporium of magic,*" read Barney. "I love it."

"It's really clever," agreed Susie. "And it looks so professional."

Barney placed his hat back on his head. "I'd love to stay a little longer, but duty calls. The fingerprint experts have lifted a partial print from Gerald Timkins's shotgun. They say the murderer wiped the gun, but not well enough."

"That's good news, isn't it?" I said.

Barney nodded. "It's not always simple, even with a print. We'll see if it matches Mrs Oliver's or Felix Round's prints which we took when we brought them in for questioning, if they don't match, which I'm assuming they won't, I'll run them through the system. If there's no match there, it'll be a question of finding the so called scarecrow man, or another suspect. It could take a while to solve the case."

"I'm sure you'll find out who did it, Barney," I said.

Barney looked at his feet. "I was going to ask a favour," he said, lifting his eyes.

"Yes?" I said. "I'll do anything I can for you."

"You know how you all helped me solve Sam Hedgewick's murder, using… magic?"

"You want us to use magic to solve this case for you, don't you, Barney?" said Willow.

"Something like that," muttered Barney. "If you can. Please. It would be a great help."

"It doesn't work like that," I said. "We can't just use magic to find out who committed a crime. We can help if you have a suspect, you know… with helping them open up a little."

"Making them talk, you mean. Like you did with Mrs Oliver," said Barney. "Can't you look in a crystal ball or something like that? You sell them in the shop, maybe you can find out who murdered Gerald using one of those? It's very important that this case is solved quickly."

"I'm afraid not, Barney," said Willow. "We'd love to help, we want to know who killed Gerald as much as you do, and we'll always be here for you, but you need to point us in the right direction before we can do anything. Why has it suddenly become so important, though? I mean — I know it's a murder and it needs solving, but why the sudden urgency?"

Barney sighed, and gave me a look I couldn't interpret. "No reason," he said, looking away. "And I'm sorry if I offended anyone by asking for magical help — I'm still coming to terms with what it means to find out that magic is real and... witches are real. I suppose I was hoping you'd be able to perform miracles."

"Not those sorts of miracles," I said, "but come to Mum's cottage tonight, and you'll see a different sort of miracle."

Barney raised an eyebrow. "Oh? What would that be?"

"She's going to the haven, Barney," said Willow. "And the miracle will be that all our family will be in one room, but the attention will be on Penny, not Granny or Mum."

"That *will* be a miracle, Barney," I said. "Believe me."

IT FELT odd allowing Barney to kiss me in front of my family, but even Granny looked happy that Barney and I were an item, and saved any sarcastic comments she may have had for another day.

Uncle Brian was dressed as stylishly as usual, although I was sure his choice of a blue crushed velvet suit would look better on the streets of Soho where he lived, than in Mum's country kitchen surrounded by four other witches, a magical goat, a journalist, and a very tall ginger policeman — still in his uniform.

Mum was wearing her best dress, and had obviously visited the hairdressers earlier in the day. Her hair looked freshly dyed, although everyone pretended not to know that most of the rich black was from a bottle. It was always tempting to point out grey hairs to her when they began appearing, but most people had learnt never to mention Mum's appearance to her unless it was a compliment.

Barney was a quick learner. "You look amazing, Maggie," he said, standing at my side. "Really lovely."

"Thank you, Barney!" gushed Mum. "You're a real gentleman. You look very smart too, I've always liked a man in uniform."

Barney left my side to speak to Boris and Granny, and Mum lowered her voice a notch or two. "I don't think that young man *is* of Scottish heritage after all," she said. "He's far too polite and well mannered. And I've yet to see him start a fight in a pub. I can admit when I'm wrong, and I *was* very wrong — there's less Scottish in Barney than there's sense in your grandmother, and that's not a lot at all. I think he's perfect for you, Penelope."

Mum had been convinced that Barney was Scottish due to his red hair and the way he walked. We'd explained that Barney wasn't swaggering as Mum had suggested, he was simply uncomfortable because all his trousers were a little too short and dug into his nether regions. We didn't question Mum's unique view of the Scottish — she was a complicated woman — although she had alluded to the fact that Scottish witches had once caused a lot of trouble in the haven. She also believed that Shakespeare had been accurate and completely validated in his portrayal of Scottish witches in *Macbeth*.

"Thanks, Mum," I said. It was the nicest thing she'd said about any boy I'd ever dated. "We're taking it slowly, but I feel good about him. He's the same as me in so many ways."

"The way he acted the last time he was here sent him sky rocketing in your grandmothers estimation," said Mum. "There's not many mortals who would be so calm when confronted with magic. He was more concerned about you than the fact that your Uncle Brian had just magicked up a portal, and that we were talking about casting a spell on him. When you passed out, he was beside himself with worry."

I smiled. "I'm glad he knows we're all witches," I said. "It would have been hard to get close to him otherwise. It's not the sort of secret that's easy to hide from someone you're close to."

"Very true, Penny, and it's obvious you care for each other," said Mum. "That's the reason you got given your haven entry spell."

"The fact that I like Barney is responsible for me getting my spell?" I asked. "How does that work?"

Mum smiled. "No, the fact that you stuck up for him is the reason. That spell you cast to stop me hexing Barney was powerful magic. It was completely pure and was cast from a place of love. You put yourself at risk for the sake of Barney and proved that you're a good witch. That's why you got your spell."

Mum moved towards me, and I let her hug me. It was rare that she showed me any physical affection, and I settled into her arms with a sigh, enjoying her smell and each moment of closeness she allowed us.

"Are you ready to go to the haven?" she said, pulling herself from me. She turned away briefly, but I saw her wipe a tear from the corner of her eye.

"I'm ready, Mum," I said. "And I'm so proud and happy to be going with you on my first trip. It means a lot to me."

"Me too, sweetheart," said Mum. "I remember the day I first went to the haven. Your grandmother knitted me a lovely red pullover and bought me a new pair of shoes for the trip. It was the proudest day of my life. Until today of course — being able to accompany her own daughter to the haven for the first time is every mother's wish. Well, every *witch* mother's wish, I should say. Today is the proudest day of my life so far, and I'm sure I'll feel the same when Willow gets her spell too."

Barney arrived at my side and Boris trailed behind him.

"Such exciting stories," said the goat. "You really have had a marvellous life, Barney."

"Thanks, Boris," said Barney. "I'll save the rest of them for another time. Remind me to tell you about the time I took Mavis Henshaw down in the greengrocers shop. She was stealing lychees. Slipping them into her bag when Mr Jarvis wasn't watching. He saw her from out of the corner of his eye and called the police. They sent me, and it was quite the struggle, I can tell you."

I swallowed my laughter. I knew full well what had happened on that day. Eighty year old Mavis Henshaw had almost broken Barney's finger with her walking stick, forcing Barney to call for backup. I wouldn't make Barney look stupid in front of his new friend though.

"Barney's quite the hero," I said, drawing an approving nod from Boris.

The loud sound of smashing glass grabbed everyone's attention, making Mum spin on the spot and Boris jump with fright.

"What have you done?" said Mum. "That's one of my best crystal whisky glasses!"

Granny stared at the shattered glass at her feet, and put the spoon she was holding down on the table. "Sorry, Maggie. I was trying to get everyone's attention, like they do in the films. I only tapped it gently — either these glasses are not real crystal and you got seen coming a mile away, or I don't know my own strength! I'm sorry though, I suppose."

"It was an accident," said Mum, unusually diplomatically for her. "Don't worry about it. What did you want to say?"

Granny cleared her throat, and looked around the room, her gaze finally settling on me. I returned the gentle smile she gave me and let her speak.

"I wanted to say that I always knew Penny would grow into a wonderful young woman," she said, "and that I've been waiting for this day for a long time. It's a wonderful moment when a loved one steps through a portal into the haven for the first time. Today is a truly wonderful day."

"Hear! Hear!" said Boris, stamping his front hooves on the slate floor. "Well said, that woman!"

"Don't interrupt!" snapped Granny. "I haven't finished!" Granny put her arm around Brian's shoulder and pulled him close to her. "I'd also like to take this moment to congratulate my eldest child... my first born... my little gay angel... my beautiful Brian. A big round of applause for Brian please, everybody!"

"Stop it, Barney," hissed Mum.

Barney managed one more clap, and looked at me. "Don't clap," I urged, putting my hand on his.

Mum scowled at Granny. "What exactly are we congratulating Brian for, Mother?" she said. "This is Penny's special day!"

"Well," said Granny, "it's all very exciting! My big boy has decided that he's going to move from London back to Wickford, and start a business as a hypnotist, here in town! Isn't that wonderful!"

"But he's not a hypnotist," said Willow. "He can't just practice as one. It's probably illegal. Isn't it, Barney?"

Barney shifted uncomfortably from foot to foot, no doubt refereeing a fight between his policeman's mind and the part of his brain that knew he should be terrified of confronting Granny. Luckily for Barney the sensible part won, and he kept quiet. He offered Willow an apologetic shrug.

Granny fixed her gaze on Willow. "Don't you dare tell Brian what he can and can't do, young lady," she said. "He's fought hammer and tongs to get where he is today. Do you think it's been easy for him to live in Soho as a gay man? Of course not, he's been oppressed at every turn, but here he is today, standing before us... loud and proud and more queer than ever!"

"It's not particularly hard living in Soho as a gay man, Mother," said Uncle Brian. "It's quite fun actually, and I can't recall being oppressed by anybody if I'm being perfectly honest with you. In fact, I've only ever been treated with respect."

"You've internalised the oppression, dear," said Granny, patting her son's hand. "It's quite normal. You've been oppressed so often that you've come to accept it as the norm, but it isn't, and you're a survivor, Brian!" Granny put her hands together. "A round of applause for my son please, everybody!"

"Stop clapping, Barney. I won't tell you again," snapped Mum. "That's enough of that for today, Mother. It's Penelope's day, and we've already wasted enough time. It's time for Penny to enter the haven!"

This time Mum allowed Barney to clap, and everybody else joined in too, including Granny.

"Just one thing," said Brian, "before the main event. What did you mean, Mother... when you said I was more queer than ever?"

"The suit, son," said Granny looking Brian up and down. "It's very, *very* camp. Crushed velvet should really only be seen on furniture, my darling."

"Really?" said Brian. "Is it camp?"

"A little," said Susie from her seat at the table. "But you do wear it well, Brian."

Mum slammed her glass down on a kitchen counter. "That's enough! It's time for Penny to open her portal." She put a gentle hand on my shoulder. "Go on, darling. Open your portal."

"I'm a little nervous," I said, standing closer to Barney. "I don't know why."

"I was the first time I stepped through my portal," said Mum. "But there's no need to be, honestly. You use the lounge doorway and I'll use the hallway doorway. You step through your portal first and then I'll step through mine. We'll appear close by one another in the haven, there's nothing to be scared of. I'll be with you every step of the way."

Barney held my hand. "It is safe, isn't it?"

Mum touched his shoulder to reassure him. "Barney, I know you don't know us very well yet, but you can be assured that nobody in this room would allow Penny to come to harm. We wouldn't let *anyone* in this room come to harm, and that includes you, young man. She's perfectly safe."

Susie got up from the table and stood next to Barney. "I've seen Maggie and Gladys open hundreds of portals," she said. "And I've never seen anything dangerous happen. She'll be fine, Barney."

I slipped my hand from Barney's, and stood on tiptoes to kiss him on his cheek. "I'll be okay." I promised. "Don't wait here for me though, I don't know how long I'll be away. I'll phone you when I'm back."

I stood before the lounge doorway, and Mum crossed the kitchen to the doorway which led into the hallway. Taking a final look around the room at the smiling faces, and Boris's yellow toothed grimace, I cast my spell.

The doorway creaked and quivered and filled with a bright shimmering light.

"Whoa!" said Barney. "That's amazing. It's beautiful. I can't believe what I'm seeing."

"I've seen it before," said Boris. "On Penny's boat. It's no better the second time."

"Very gold," said Uncle Brian. "Very you, Penelope."

"So, so," said Granny. "I've seen prettier portals."

"That's my girl," said Mum, opening her own portal.

"Go on, Penny, step through it," said Willow. "I want to hear all about it when you get back."

Taking a deep breath, I placed a foot over the threshold, shuddering as hairs stood on end and a breeze ran up my leg. I took one last glance at Barney, smiled at him, closed my eyes, and stepped into the light.

CHAPTER SIXTEEN

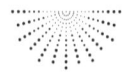

*E*very muscle in my body tensed, and a loud whistling sound in my ears made me wince. A scary sensation of falling passed within a second, and I stumbled forward with my eyes closed and my arms held out to break my fall.

Somebody caught me almost immediately. "I've got you!"

"Mum," I said, opening my eyes and blinking. I shook my head a couple of times to rid my ears of the whistling, and stepped back from my mother. "Wow. You look… different!"

Mum looked at least twenty years younger, and the black of her hair was obviously not from a bottle. She was still overweight, but nowhere near as heavy as she'd been in her kitchen a couple of minutes before. She was younger than I was, I needed to remind myself. Mum had acquired her entry spell when she was twenty-one, and I was twenty three. It was unsettling having a mother who was younger than me, and it must have shown on my face.

"Oops, sorry!" said Mum. "I forgot to change."

In less time than it took to blink, Mum had transformed

into the woman I knew, complete with recently dyed hair and a few extra pounds around her thighs and midriff.

"How?" I said. "I thought you always remained the age you were when you got your entry spell, when you're in the haven? That's what you've always told me and Willow."

"This is the haven, Penny," said Mum. "Anything's possible. We tell youngsters they'll always be the age they are when they get their spell so they'll work harder to acquire it. It worked for you didn't it? Every time you enter the haven, you'll be the age you were when you got your spell, but you can transform into any age you like when you're here, as long as it's between the age you were when you got your spell, and the age you are in the mortal world. There are plenty of witches here who don't want to look young again, they're happy in the body they have, but they'll never age if they stay in the haven, and if they want to be young again, even if it's just for a day, they can be. I prefer looking this age if I'm honest. I hated my body when I was younger, I was far too thin. I think I looked sickly. Your grandmother didn't feed me enough — I was a hungry girl."

I stumbled and Mum grabbed me. "Are you okay?" she said.

I shook my head. "Not really. Coming through the portal wasn't as easy as I thought it was going to be," I said.

"You must have closed your eyes when you stepped through," said Mum. "I'm sorry. I forgot to tell you to keep them open, Penelope. Your brain can't cope with what's happening if your eyes are closed. Next time keep them open and it'll be a lot simpler."

I blinked again, and looked left and right.

"Close your portal," said Mum. "It's still open."

Sure enough, the familiar hum of an open portal throbbed behind me. I allowed the portal spell to slip from my mind and the sound stopped. "Where are we?" I said. "It smells damp."

Mum and I stood together in a stone archway. The moss covered stone walls were a few feet apart and the curve of the ceiling seemed low enough to touch if I jumped. It was like standing in a dark and dank soldier's sentry box.

"This is an entry arch," said Mum. "You use it to leave and enter the haven. Every town and village has a few of them, and the big cities have thousands."

"Cities?" I said. "There are cities here? In the haven?"

"Not cities as you know them," explained Mum. "There's no skyscrapers or busy roads, but thousands of people live in them, and there's lots to do. They're fun places to visit, but I wouldn't like to live in one. I prefer the peace and quiet of the countryside."

I'd regained my bearings, and couldn't wait to leave the damp arch I was standing in. "I want to see," I said, looking past Mum's shoulder at the light behind her.

Mum smiled. "Come on, I'll show you," she said. She took me by the hand and pulled me from the arch.

I squinted as Mum guided me into the bright light, and turned to look at the arch I'd come through. Five stone arches were built side by side in a row, and dim light still flickered in the two arches through which Mum and I had arrived.

I turned on the spot slowly as the sun warmed my face, and gasped as I took my first look at the haven. Mum slipped her arm through mine and squeezed my hand. "It's nice isn't it?"

"It's amazing," I said.

We stood on the peak of a grassy hill, and stretching before us in all directions, as far as the eye could see, was scenery so beautiful I wished I could climb inside it and wrap it around myself like a blanket — just looking at it wasn't enough. I wanted to be enveloped by it.

Butterflies danced in my stomach, and my ears and nose worked overtime to distinguish between smells and sounds as my eyes flitted from snow capped mountain top, to sparkling lake. The soft peach colour which lightly tinged the sky, painted the scenery in a gentle glow which brought the vivid green of the vegetation to life and gave the scenery a warmth which made me happy to be alive.

"'It's huge," I said.

"They say it's as big as the world we just left behind," said Mum. "But I wouldn't know how true that is. I tend to stay here in this area, where my friends and family live, but your grandmother has travelled extensively — and has probably caused trouble in every corner of the haven."

What about getting home?" I said. "How do I get back to the door in your kitchen?"

Mum pulled me closer to her. It was the longest that Mum had held me for as long as I could remember. "Whichever arch you use will open a portal to the last doorway you used to enter the haven through," she said, "unless you specifically think of somewhere else you want to go to, like Uncle Brian did when he appeared in my kitchen, but that's definitely not advisable. Wherever you go in the haven, Penny, even if you stay here for years and find yourself thousands of miles away from this spot — any of the archways you use will take you back to exactly where you came from. It's that simple."

I remained silent, appreciating the view, and enjoying feeling so emotionally attached to my mother. Birds soared high in the sky and a sheep bleated somewhere in the distance. The fragrant scent of wildflowers and grass was underlaid with the salty aroma of an ocean, but the only water I could see was in rivers and lakes. The haven was a welcome assault on my senses, and I smiled as a warm breeze blew a strand of hair from my eyes.

"Can you feel it?" said Mum. "I could when I first came here."

"Feel what?"

"The prickles," said Mum. "Like pins and needles on your skin."

I nodded. I could. "I thought it was a residual effect from the portal."

"The sensation will pass in minute or two, but what you're feeling is magic, Penny. *Real* magic, not like in the world we just left behind. When Maeve created the haven, she used almost all of the magic in the mortal world to create this dimension. The haven is how our world used to be before most of the magic was sucked from it. You'll find it a whole lot easier to cast spells here than it is in Wickford."

I shielded my eyes from the sun and studied the valley below us. Smoke rose from chimneys on thatched roof cottages in a quaint village to our left, and a sprawling urban development was visible in the far distance.

"Look at the size of that forest." I said, squinting. "On the horizon. It's huge."

"It's a rainforest," said Mum, "like the Amazon Jungle."

"A jungle? In the haven?"

"Yes," said Mum with a smile. "This place is like the mortal world, Penny, but without the same rules. Here there might be a rainforest next to a desert, or a glacier next to a tropical beach. The haven creates the environments where witches lived in the mortal world, but not in the same geographic locations. Somewhere in the haven there's an ice cap where Inuit witches live."

Mum allowed me a few more minutes to soak up the atmosphere, before removing her arm from mine. "Come on," she said. "Aunt Eva can't wait to see you. She was going to meet us here, but she decided to cook you a welcome meal instead. She'll be waiting for us at her cottage."

THE WALK down the hill was nicer than any walk I'd taken at home. Rabbits hopped across the narrow path in front of us, and butterflies with vivid patterns flitted between wild flowers which grew from the lush green grass. Our surroundings were unspoiled, and I knew without asking that it would be perfectly safe to drink water from the little stream which bubbled and splashed down the slope alongside the path.

A fat dragonfly settled on my shoulder and I placed a finger in front of it as it spread it's wings to dry them in the breeze. It climbed onto my finger and I looked at Mum. "Aren't you nervous?" I asked. "There's a huge insect on my hand."

In the world we'd just left behind, Mum was terrified of insects, particularly insects which she considered capable of landing on any food she was about to eat. It was a serous condition, and one which had forced her to wear a beekeepers hat when she'd visited my boat on the canal.

"I'm not nervous here," she said with a smile which lit up her face. "The haven has a way of making you feel calm... most of the time anyway." The dragonfly flew from my finger and Mum watched as it zig-zagged away. "This way," she said, leading us towards a stone bridge which spanned the stream where it widened into a river at the base of the hill.

Mum paused halfway across the bridge and called me alongside her as she leaned over the wall to look at the sparkling water below. "Look," she said. "You don't see trout like that in Wickford."

Long fat fish swayed rhythmically in the crystal clear

water, inches below the surface. A fly broke the surface tension of the water above one of the trout, and the plump fish moved quickly, taking the fly before resuming its position in the current. "They taste good too," said Mum. "All food tastes good in the haven though."

I'd tasted food that Mum had brought home from the haven on many occasions in the past, and I was beginning to see why everything she brought back with her was so wholesome. It wasn't because of magic, as I'd thought — although some of the food she'd brought home in the past *had* been enhanced with magic — it was because the haven was unspoiled by mankind. The haven was how the world had once been, before humans began poisoning it with chemicals and clouding the atmosphere with pollution.

"How do you travel long distances?" I said, looking at the track we walked along. The ruts that were imprinted in the dirt surface looked like they'd been formed by the narrow wheels of a cart. "Are there cars here?"

"There's no cars," Mum said, "But there's steam trains and horses and carts. We have bikes too, and boats of course, and if you really wanted to be a little maverick, there's enough magic in the haven to fly a broom, although hardly anybody does — a broom is far too narrow to sit on. People have been injured very intimately while trying. I'm told that when one drunk male witch attempted to fly a broomstick, he hurt himself very badly when he flew into turbulence. I don't know who started the rumour that witches always fly around on broomsticks, but it certainly wasn't a witch, and definitely not a male witch — it was probably the same person who started the rumour that we have wart susceptible skin."

The dirt track we walked on gave way to cobblestones, and Mum hooked her arm through mine. "We're here," she said, as cottages with thatched roofs and neat gardens appeared around the bend. "Your home from home."

CHAPTER SEVENTEEN

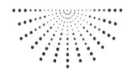

The little town was so painfully quaint it was as if Mum and I had stepped back in time, rather than through a magical portal — although for all I knew — we'd done both. My understanding of the haven had already been questioned by Mum's off the cuff admission that people could choose the age they were in the haven — it went against everything I'd ever been told about the place, but I supposed there was lots about the dimension that I was yet to learn, and lots that Mum had yet to tell me.

Cottages with thatched roofs lined the wider roads, and small shops were squashed tightly against one another in narrow lanes which were fragranced with the aroma of baking bread and pastries. People said hello as we made our way past the bustling town square, and I laughed as a small child in old fashioned clothing ran ahead of us with a hoop and stick. A toy I'd only ever seen in pictures.

"Why are there children here?" I asked. "Did they get their entry spells when they were really young? Were they really that good at magic?"

Mum guided us to the left and into an alley which led

between two shops and brought us out in a park with a duckpond, a bandstand, and beds of vibrantly coloured flowers everywhere I looked. "People can have children here," said Mum. "The portal isn't like an x-ray machine — too much of it doesn't mess with a person's... special bits. Some of the children came here when the portal was first created, when Maeve conjured it up to stop witches being burnt at the stake. Some of the witches that fled here had children who they were allowed to bring with them, and those children will never grow up. They'll always be young if they don't leave the haven, and some of them don't want to — they remember the outside world as a cruel place which murdered people like them."

Two elderly men played chess on a board which was set up on the green painted bench between them, and both of them smoked long pipes. The shade of a large oak tree gave them protection from the warm sun, and they smiled as we neared them.

"Who's this, Maggie?" said one of them, removing his flat cap in a polite greeting. "Another one of the Weaver coven?"

"This is my eldest daughter, Herman," said Mum. "Her name's Penelope. This is her first time here."

The other man smiled. "Come here, Penelope," he said, peering at me through spectacles with lenses so thick they magnified his eyes to somewhere approaching the size of golf balls. "What's that behind your ear, young lady? Let me get it for you."

Mum sighed. "She's twenty-three, George, not five. She doesn't want to know what's behind her ear, and she's seen plenty of magic. No trick that you can do will be anything she hasn't seen before. You can't impress a witch with mediocre magic."

I giggled, and smiled at the old man. "Of course I want to

know what's behind my ear," I said. "Go on, what's there? Get it for me."

I stood in front of George and bent at the waist as he reached for my ear. His calloused fingers brushed my face, and he laughed as the crackling sound of a spell being cast reverberated next to my head, and a glass full of black liquid with a white frothy head appeared in his hand.

"Oh! It's just a beer… for me," he laughed, his wrinkles tightening around his mouth. "Want a sip?" he asked, offering me the glass.

I pushed his hand away with a smile. "No thanks," I said. "If it had been elderberry wine, I might have said yes, but I have to be in certain mood for beer, especially when it's been behind my ear."

"You're just like your grandmother," said Herman, staring at me as he puffed on his pipe, the spicy pungent aroma of burning tobacco reminding me of my grandad. "You've got those mischievous eyes of hers. And the little smirk. Where is she anyway? I haven't seen Gladys for weeks and weeks. I miss her, and I'm sure she misses me just as much."

"She's taking a break from people like you, Herman," said Mum. "I can assure you she doesn't miss you."

George sipped his pint, and moved a chess piece on the board. "We heard she got witch dementia so she can't get through her portal, and that she turned three grown men into singing horses," he said. "Or donkeys. I don't remember which. Some species of farmyard animal anyway."

"Chinese whispers," said Mum, walking away. "It's nonsense, my mother's just staying away from the haven for a while." She smiled at me. "Come on, Penny, Aunt Eva's cottage is just around the next corner. She'll be wondering where we are."

"Goats!" said George. "That was it, she turned them into talking goats! That's what I was told!"

I laughed. One Boris was enough, three of them would have been a nightmare. "You've had too many of those beers," I said with a wink. "You're drunk."

"As witty as your grandmother too," said Herman, patting my hand. "Go on, get on your way. If your Aunt Eva's waiting for you, you don't want to be late. She's worse than her sister."

"Worse than Granny?" I laughed, following Mum as she hurried off.

"Maybe not worse," shouted George. "But they're as bad as each other, that's for sure!"

"Ignore those old codgers," said Mum, as we left the park and turned right onto a long lane, the warm air fragranced by the sweet perfume of a large honeysuckle bush which grew in the small front yard of a cottage. "That's what happens if you don't try hard enough to get your entry spell when you're young. Those two men spent their lives in the mortal world drinking and playing cards, they were only given their spells because Maeve thought they'd die before they earned them the traditional way. Producing glasses of beer is about the only spell that George can manage, and they're stuck in those bodies however much they wish they were young again."

"I liked them," I said, watching a red squirrel bounding through the branches of the beech tree which spread its thick limbs across the road, offering us shade from the hot sun. "They reminded me of grandad."

Mum crossed the cobbled lane, and pointed at a beautifully maintained white cottage which was set back from the road and surrounded by colourful flowering bushes and leafy trees. "That's your Aunt Eva's home," she said. "She'll be thrilled to see you."

The crooked gate creaked as Mum pushed it open, and a fat bumblebee buzzed past my ear on its way to the apple tree which stood in the centre of the small lawn, heavy with bright red apples which begged to be picked.

The cottage door swung open, and Aunt Eva stood in the doorway, her apron covered in a light dusting of flour, and her smile as happy as her voice. "Penny!" she said, rushing down the path to meet me, pushing Mum aside without so much as a smile. "I've missed you! How you've grown — you were no higher than my waist when I last saw you!"

"Hi, Aunt Eva," I said, melting into her embrace. "You haven't changed a bit!"

Aunt Eva looked just as I remembered. No taller than Granny, but wider at the hips, and without the blue rinse perm. She was the older of the two sisters, but the reddish tint to the light in the haven took the age from her wrinkles. The folds of skin looked as soft as a peach.

"I made myself look this way just for you, darling," she said. "You don't want to see me as an nineteen year old just yet, it would be too much for you to take in." She released me from her hug, but kept her hands on my shoulders as she took a step backwards and looked me up and down. "You look just like Gladys did when she was your age," she said. "The resemblance is uncanny. You have her eyes."

I didn't know whether to take that as a compliment or an insult. In all the pictures I'd seen of Granny as a young woman, she'd always had the same glint in her eye — a glint which hovered midway between mischievous and evil. I was sure I didn't have the glint, but I *was* aware that when I was angry, people seemed to cower internally when I stared at them. Maybe I'd not fallen far from the tree where Granny was concerned. I smiled at Aunt Eva. "Thank you," I said, accepting it as a compliment.

Aunt Eva's mouth curled into a wide grin. "Come on, there's people waiting to meet you. I hope you're hungry. I do like baking, you see, and I got a little carried away with myself today. They'll be plenty of cakes for you to take home with you."

Aunt Eva's cottage smelt like the French patisserie which had recently opened in Wickford. The scents of cinnamon and vanilla vied with each other for my attention, and I licked my lips as I followed Mum and Aunt Eva into the large kitchen, where a long table was hidden beneath plates of cakes, scones, and breads.

"Wow," I said. "You baked all this today?"

Aunt Eva wiggled her fingers. "With a little help," she smiled. "I have a few spells which speed the process up. If you think the microwaves you have back in the other world are fast, you should see my pronto-pastry spell!" She picked up a tray laden with sandwiches, and passed it to me. "Would you be so kind as to carry this into the back garden please, Penelope? We're eating in the sun today."

Bright sunlight spilled through the kitchen window, and another realisation dawned on me. "It was evening when we left Wickford," I said, taking the tray from Aunt Eva. "Why is it still daytime here?"

Mum picked up a plate of scones and two pots, one brimming with cream and another full of jam. She balanced the pots on the edge of the plate and led the way out of the kitchen. "It's dark somewhere in the haven," she said. "We have time zones here too, they don't match perfectly with our world back home though. You get used to it the more you visit."

Aunt Eva pushed past us, carrying a large cake on a stand. "I can't wait to introduce you to my friends," she said. She lowered her voice as she pushed the back door open with a flick of her thigh. "Take whatever Hilda tells you with a pinch of salt, dear."

"Who's Hilda?" I said, following Mum and Aunt Eva into the sunlight.

"She's a seer," said Mum. "But she's very old. She came to the haven a long time ago, when Maeve first conjured it up. She was old when she got here, and she'd lost a few of her marbles already. Do as Eva says, and take what she says with a *big* pinch of salt."

Mum and I followed Aunt Eva past the flower beds and bushes which teemed with bees and insects, and along the short pathway which snaked through a tiny orchard which was planted with two plum trees and three apple trees, all laden with fruit bigger and brighter than any I'd seen in a supermarket at home.

The scene beyond the orchard where wild grasses and flowers prevailed and a small fountain trickled water into the pond that surrounded it, reminded me of the Mafia films I'd enjoyed watching with Granny when she'd baby sat me as a young child. Mum had not been impressed at Granny's choice of entertainment for a five year old, but I had lovely memories of snuggling up to Granny on her sofa while one crime family slaughtered another on the television. Aunt Eva's guests looked like they'd be perfectly at home in the countryside of Sicily, and I smiled at the small group of people as Aunt Eva began her introductions.

Three people sat at the long wooden table, the legs protruding from grass and flowers, and the top already laid with plates, cutlery, and big wooden bowls of salad next to jugs of iced water. The whole scene screamed rustic Italian, and I placed the tray I was carrying on the table as I said my hellos.

At the head of the table, wearing a black knitted shawl which seemed overkill for such a lovely day, sat an elderly woman who peered at me with one eye. The other eye was covered with a bejewelled eyepatch which glinted in the light as she tilted her head to study me.

Next to her sat a muscular young man wearing a white

shirt with the sleeves rolled up to his elbows, and the top three buttons undone. His blond hair glowed in the sun, and dimples gave a mischievous element to his smile as he greeted me. "Hello," he said, his voice as soft as the butter which was melting on a little plate in front of him. "I'm Gideon. Gideon Sax."

He stood to shake my hand and I gazed up at his handsome face, knowing right away that Willow would be infatuated with him. "Hi," I said. "I'm Penelope."

He chuckled. "We know who you are," he said, releasing my hand. He indicated the elderly woman at the head of the table with a nod. "This is Hilda Truckle," he said, "and the old rogue opposite me is Alfred Stern."

I said my hellos and sat down to the right of Gideon in the chair he politely pulled out for me.

Hilda remained quiet, studying me with one eye, as Aunt Eva and Mum took a seat each. Mum sat to my right and Aunt Eva sat next to Alfred who poured me a glass of water and passed it across the table. "Gideon calls me an old rogue," smiled Alfred, his old eyes still managing to sparkle with young joy. "But would you believe me if I told you he was two-hundred years older than me?"

"One-hundred-and-ninety-three to be precise," said Gideon, nudging me playfully with an elbow. "That's how many years I came to the haven before you did. And you are rogue, Alfred. You were a highway robber in the other world, before you got too old to ride a horse. There's nothing more roguish than a highway robber. Especially one who used magic to commit his crimes."

"A rogue I may be," said Alfred, offering me a conspiratorial wink, "but I never hurt anyone, and I was better at highway robbery than you were at piracy."

"You were a pirate?" I said, glancing at Gideon. "A real pirate?"

"Aye," said Gideon. "That I was. I was caught though, when I was twenty-four. They were going to hang me, and I hadn't developed enough magic skills to stop them. The walk to the gallows is a long one, let me tell you."

"How did you escape the hangman?" I said.

Gideon laughed. "I'd done no real evil as a pirate, I enjoyed the women and rum, and the loot of course, but like Alfred, I'd never hurt anyone — so Maeve granted me my entry spell — a little late for my liking, but I like to think I left that world in style."

"How did you leave that world?" I said.

Gideon gave a sly grin, and closed his eyes for a moment. "As they were placing the hood over my head and preparing the noose, Maeve granted me my spell. The only doorway I could use was the trapdoor they were about to drop me through. It was still open after the unfortunate soul before me had passed through it — on the end of a rope — to whatever place waited for him. I cast my spell and a portal opened. I took a single step forward and shouted 'farewell cruel world' as I dropped. It was quite the show, I'm sure — it *must* have been — although I was very disappointed to be told I never made it into your history books."

"Enough!"

The piercing shout from the head of the table made Alfred jump, and I did well not to spill my glass of water.

Aunt Eva put a theatrical hand over her chest. "Hilda!" she said. "You darn near gave me heart attack! Could you show some manners and let us know when you're going to shout like that? What will Penelope think? You haven't even said hello to her yet."

"I've seen," said Hilda, her eye rolling in its socket as she studied my face. "I've seen."

"What have you seen?" said Mum, touching my arm briefly in what I assumed was an attempt to reassure me.

"Have you seen another jumbled vision? Don't you go filling my daughter's head with your nonsense now, Hilda."

Hilda lifted a trembling hand and pointed at me. "You hold the heart of a lawman!" she said, her voice quivering. "A tall lawman with hair like the very fires of hell. Tell me it's so!"

"Let the girl eat, Hilda," said Aunt Eva. "You can read her fortune later."

"It's okay," I said. "I want to know what she means. She's talking about Barney."

Aunt Eva shrugged, and Gideon bit into a chunk of ham.

I smiled at Hilda. "Yes," I said. "It is so. Although his hair's more like a ginger bird nest, than the very fires of hell."

Hilda's finger remained where it was, pointing at my face. She spoke slowly. "The lawman will be gone from your life. Taken from you by malevolent forces while he's still young and virile! Such a shame, but it will be so! It will be so! I have seen and I have spoken!" Her eye widened, and she lowered her arm. She pointed to the small yellow dish in front of me. "Pass me the olives would you? I like the black ones."

CHAPTER EIGHTEEN

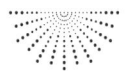

"*H*ilda!" said Aunt Eva. "You can't just tell Penelope that the man she's involved with is going to die, and then ask for the olives. Have some etiquette would you — at least tell her *how* he's going to die. I don't know — you seers, you're all about *you*."

I understood what George and Herman had meant when they'd said that Granny and Aunt Eva were as bad as each other. Neither of the sisters had an ounce of tact.

Mum put a hand on my shoulder and Gideon put his hand over mine. "What do you mean, Hilda?" I said, aware of the shaking in my voice and the cold finger that touched my spine. "What's going to happen to Barney?"

Impatient of waiting for me to pass her the olives, Hilda popped a sun dried tomato in her mouth and took a sip of water. She chewed as she looked at me thoughtfully. "I did *not* say he was going to die." She looked at the elderly man to her left. "Did I, Alfred? You've got your head screwed on right and your ears clear of wax — did I *once* say that anyone was going to die?"

Alfred buttered a piece of crusty bread. "You did imply it,

Hilda. We've warned you about it in the past, and you keep promising that you're not doing it for theatrical effect, but I have to admit, Hilda… I really think you take pleasure from scaring people."

Gideon, Mum, and Aunt Eva mumbled their agreement.

"Tish-tosh!" snapped Hilda. "I say it as it comes to me. I *see*, you see? My visions must be delivered to their rightful owners, and the last one was for Penelope. I make no apologies for my style of delivery." She lifted her eye patch and gazed around the table with both eyes. "Where's the soft cheese? I don't see it."

Aunt Eva saw me staring at Hilda. "It's a style statement," she said, shrugging. "Those stones she's used to decorate it with aren't real diamonds either — they're as fake as most of her prophecies, I wouldn't take any notice of what she says."

I moved my stare from Hilda to Aunt Eva. "I wasn't looking at her because she's wearing an eyepatch she doesn't need," I said. "I'm staring at her because I want to know what she means about Barney! For goddess's sake — will someone please tell me what she means about Barney?" A warm tear spilled onto my cheek, and I looked at Hilda again. "Please," I said. "What did you mean, Hilda? I have to know. I feel sick."

"Honey baked ham?" said aunt Eva, pushing a plate of sliced meat over the table at me. "It goes wonderfully well on the rye bread, and it'll take the sickness away. The ham itself comes from a part of the haven where they really know how to breed good meat, and the honey's from a delightful woman who lives not a mile from here. Her bees are as fat and healthy as a chubby baby."

My eye twitched. "I *do not* want fat baby bee honey ham. I *do not* want to hear one more word from anyone, unless it's to tell me what the heck is going to happen to Barney! Hilda, I'll ask you one more time — what did you see?"

Hilda swallowed what was in her mouth, replaced her

eyepatch, and sat back in her chair. Gideon and Alfred pretended to be more interested in the food which was on their plates, than the tension which was rising with each second that Hilda kept the information she had about about Barney from me.

I fixed Hilda with a stare which I imagined resembled Granny's sternest scowl. "Go on."

Hilda cleared her throat. "The lawman isn't going to die. Not yet anyway, but I can see with hindsight how you may have misconstrued the meaning of what I said. But that's on you, not me. I can't help what images you attach to the simple words I speak."

"Hilda," warned Mum. "Tell the girl. I want to know too, I've got quite the soft spot for Barney now I know he's not Scottish."

Hilda spoke slowly. "He will be taken away from you by the people who tell him what to do — his superiors. If he doesn't solve the terrible crime he's investigating — a murder, I see. The fiery haired lawman will be sent to a distant land, far from you and your love for him." She popped an olive into her mouth from the bowl I slid towards her. "A green and pleasant land with mountains which touch the sky and people who speak in riddles."

"What are you talking about?" said Mum. "What land? Barney lives in England, not a fantasy novel setting."

Hilda furrowed her frown and concentrated. "The land is known as Wales, and it will be the new home of the lawman if he doesn't complete his quest. He hides this knowledge from you."

"Barney will move to Wales if he doesn't solve the murder he's investigating?" I said. "Because his superiors will tell him to, and he knows about this, but has kept it secret from me? Is that what you're trying to tell me?"

Hilda nodded. "That's about the crux of it, I suppose. The

messages come in pictures and I do my best to translate them into words you will understand."

Aunt Eva slid another plate across the table. "Hard boiled egg, Penny? They go very well with the spicy chorizo dip."

I took one out of politeness not hunger, and thanked Gideon as he passed me a fork. Alfred reached for the ham, and Hilda gave me a wry smile.

"I don't understand why Barney will have to leave if he doesn't solve a crime," I said, looking at Hilda. "That makes no sense."

"I can only tell you what I see," said Hilda between chews.

"Can you help Barney solve the murder?" I asked. "Can you see anything which will make his job easier?"

Hilda shook her head. "I can't see the past, only the present and the future. The past is a wall of impenetrable fog, which no seer can penetrate."

"Can you tell me anything that will help?" I said. "Please try."

Hilda stared at me for a few moments. "Give me your hand, witch."

Gideon sat back in his seat as I offered Hilda my hand, which she took in hers. Her fingers closed on me with more strength than her thin body suggested she'd possess, and a faint electric current seemed to pass between us as she closed her eye and concentrated.

Hilda's eye opened suddenly, and she squeezed my hand. "You seek a man!" she said. "A man who makes men of straw!"

"Yes! A scarecrow man! Can you tell me who it is?" I urged. "Can you tell me his name? What is the name of the man who makes scarecrows?"

Hilda mumbled incoherently and dipped her chin. "I can't see. The image is murky, but — wait!"

"Yes?"

"I see a horned man with cloven feet who can help you!" said Hilda. She stared at me with a nervous eye. "Who are you that the lord of darkness himself would help you? Who are you that he who has many names would help you? Who are you that Beelzebub himself, master of demons and lover of fire would speak to you with news of the scarecrow man?" I gasped as Hilda snatched her hand from mine. Her voice trembled and she took a deep breath. "Who are you, friend of the cloven footed bringer of doom?"

I sighed. "Erm... could it be a man who's been turned into a goat you're talking about?" I said.

Hilda tilted her head as she considered. She nodded sagely. "That makes so much sense," she said. "That would explain why the devil in my vision was white and didn't have a thrice pronged fork. Does this goat man have a grin of teeth most yellow?"

I nodded. "They are very yellow, yes."

"Then you must ask the goat man what he knows. He harbours information, and what he knows will guide the lawman to the man he so urgently seeks."

"Boris — the goat man, knows who the scarecrow man is?" I said.

"Harfa bell!" yelled Hilda, startling the birds from the trees. "Ask him of harfa bell!"

"Half a bell?" said Gideon. "Is that what you're saying, Hilda?"

Hilda shrugged. "Harfa bell — half a bell. I can't be sure which. Penelope must ask the goat man, and he will reveal his knowledge." Hilda reached over the table. "Give me your hand one more time, young witch."

I did as she asked, and Hilda concentrated as she squeezed my fingers. She muttered something under her breath and released her grip on me. "You're more than you think you are, Penelope Weaver," she announced. "The goddess has seen fit to bestow upon you a gift which will reveal itself to you when the time is right."

"Gift?" said Mum, spooning cream onto the big dollop of jam which crowned the scone on her plate. "What gift, Hilda? Penelope's never show any signs of been gifted."

"Thank you," I breathed. "It's lovely to know my mother thinks I'm not gifted."

"You know what I mean," said Mum. "Don't be so tetchy, young lady. Hilda's told you that Barney's going to be okay. Bring it down a notch or two would you?"

"Hilda's told me that Barney knows he may have to leave Wickford, and he's hidden it from me while at the same time beginning a relationship with me. I think I can afford to be a little *tetchy*, Mother."

Mum snorted. "That's men for you. Always keeping important secrets to themselves. Get used to it, or stay single — that's my advice."

Birds had begun returning to the trees since Hilda had stopped yelling, and Aunt Eva tossed a piece of bread to a brave one which flew to the ground and pecked around for scraps of food near the table. "That's enough arguing for today," she said, looking between me, Mum, and Hilda. "Penelope — I'm sure things will work out with this Barney gentleman you've met. Maggie — your daughter is bound to be upset by her boyfriend keeping secrets form her, and Hilda — what gift does Penny possess? Please tell me it's the gift of alchemy."

"It's a gift far greater than that of alchemy," said Hilda, with a sparkle in her eye. "She is a witch of the highest calibre, a witch born to lead, a witch who will touch people's lives in positive ways and who will be held up as an example of greatness in every land she steps foot in. She is a force to be reckoned with."

"Oh, no," said Mum. "She's a bloody seer isn't she? That's

all I need — a prophet in the family. I've got enough problems with my mother, without adding a jumped up fortune teller to the mix."

Hilda took my hand again. "You are indeed a seer, Penelope. The gift will make itself shown when you need it most. Use it wisely and do no ill with it, for it is a gift of great power, to be sure."

Mum tutted. "Great power. More like trouble with a capital t."

"I'm a seer?" I said. "I'll be able to see into the future?"

Hilda nodded. "Indeed, Penelope Weaver. You will."

A cherry tomato bounced off my nose and Alfred laughed. "You didn't see that coming, did you?" he chortled. "You can't see very far into the future at all."

"She will, Alfred," said Hilda, arming herself with an olive which she tossed in the cheerful man's direction. "Just give the gift time to make itself shown."

Alfred's cheeky smile and mischievous demeanour broke the tension which was building, and after a few barrages of olives and tomatoes from everyone around the table, including Mum who even managed a full belly laugh as an olive she threw bounced off Gideon's forehead, we all settled down again.

"I don't mean to be rude," I said, "I know you made this meal to welcome me, Aunt Eva, but I really think I should get home now. I need to speak to Barney."

"And ask the goat man for his information," added Hilda.

Aunt Eva stood up. "Make sure to come back soon, Penelope. It was lovely seeing you, and remember to take some food back with you. I'll plate some cakes and scones for you. Willow will enjoy them."

"Not this time," said Mum. "I don't like the idea of carrying plates back up the hill to the portal arches."

"You're not going to make the poor girl use the arches are

you?" said Hilda. "I told you, she's a talented witch. She'll be able to use a doorway in Eva's cottage. She's more than capable. I've seen it."

"Use a doorway in Aunt Eva's cottage?" I said, turning to Mum. "You told me I had to use one of the arches we arrived through."

"That's what they tell newcomers," said Gideon. "It's safer to use an arch they say, but I wouldn't know. I've never left the haven since the day I arrived, this place is much nicer than the world I left behind. A little more mad at times, but nicer."

"Penny can't use a doorway in the cottage," said Mum. "I won't let her risk it. She's not experienced enough. She could end up anywhere."

"Give the girl a chance," said Alfred. "She seems as bright as a button to me. I'm sure she'll manage it without a problem."

"Yes," I said. "Give me a chance. It can't be that hard."

Aunt Eva smiled. "It's not hard, sweetheart, come on inside with me, and I'll explain how to do it."

"Be it on your head, Eva," said Mum. "If she ends up in Australia, you can pay for her airfare home."

"It won't come to that," said Aunt Eva, leading the way back through the orchard. "And if she does end up in Australia she can open another portal which will bring her back here."

Hilda, Gideon, and Alfred followed us into the cottage, and we all stood in the kitchen together as Aunt Eva explained how to open a portal in Mum's kitchen back home. "You need to picture the room you want the portal to open in," she said, "really focus on it. Smell the familiar smells and picture the colour of the walls, and when you're ready, cast your spell. The portal that opens here will take you straight home, and if it doesn't, just open one wherever you end up and step back through, you'll find yourself in one of the arches at the top of the hill. There's nothing to worry about, your mother's over concerned."

Mum sighed. "I'm not *over* concerned, Eva, just concerned." She put her hand on my shoulder as I stood in front of Aunt Eva's kitchen doorway, holding a tray of goodies and ready to open my portal. "Penelope, I try and focus on three permanently placed things in the kitchen, it really helps to stabilise the spell. I use the Lionel Richie clock above the door, the magnet on the fridge which your grandmother brought back from Cuba, and the aga stove. Can you see those things clearly in your mind?"

Lionel Richie was Mums's favourite singer and one time crush. It was no problem to envision the Lionel Richie clock. The singer's cheesy grin and perfect hair had haunted me since I was old enough to tell the time. The internal mechanics had stopped working long ago, but Mum kept the clock hands showing the time as half past six, so they didn't interfere with Lionel's good looks.

The aga stove was similarly easy to picture, and the fridge magnet depicting Fidel Castro beneath a halo was an easily remembered bone of contention in the household, but an item which Granny insisted stayed where it was under threat of a curse on the person who dared to remove it.

Granny had given up on her plans to move to Cuba one day, and when her cat, Che Guevara had died, she'd finally agreed to discontinue her habit of wearing an ill-fitting beret whenever she attended protests.

I pictured the three items in my mind and looked at Mum. "I'm ready," I said.

Aunt Eva kissed me on the cheek, and Hilda, Gideon, and Alfred said their goodbyes as I cast my spell and the doorway flooded with shimmering gold.

With a final warning from Mum to be sure to open

another portal immediately if I didn't end up in her kitchen, I stepped through the doorway, this time with my eyes open.

I stepped out of the other side with far more dignity and balance than when I'd taken my first portal journey, and for the first time in my life was happy to see Lionel Richie gazing down at me. Nobody was waiting for me in the kitchen, and I shut my portal.

No sooner had I closed mine than Mum's opened in the same doorway, and she stepped through with a look of relief on her face when she saw I was safe.

"I knew you could do it," she said, placing the tray she'd brought with her on the table. "I had every confidence in you."

"That's so good to hear," I said, hoping the sarcasm was evident in my voice. "It's lovely to know that your mother has confidence in you."

I placed the tray I'd brought with me next to Mum's and saw the note on the table.

Penny — Barney's been called into work — forensics have found something interesting on Gerald Timkins's shotgun. Me and Susie have gone back to the boat. I had a phone call from the delivery man — my new bed's arrived — so me and Susie are going to move it aboard.
Can't wait to hear all about the haven.
See you soon,
Willow x
P.S. Remember it's the pie eating competition tomorrow. I thought we could go in the boat as it's taking place so close to the canal.
P.P.S Boris and Granny want to come with us on the boat. I said that would be lovely. (I didn't mean it, but I wanted to be a little more like you, and show some manners.)

CHAPTER NINETEEN

I'd got back to the boat late at night and spent an hour telling Susie and Willow all about my trip to the haven. Susie had seemed jealous that I had such a beautiful place to visit whenever I wanted to, and Willow was excited about gaining her own entry spell — promising herself, me, and Susie, that she was going to practice her magic every day in an attempt to gain her spell as soon as possible.

The next morning, Willow and I shared breakfast on the picnic bench next to the boat, tossing Mabel and Rosie scraps of bacon and sausage as they begged at our feet.

It was going to be a busy day. Barney was on his way to the boat to find out what Hilda had meant about Boris knowing something about the scarecrow man. Barney, Willow, and I were going to visit Boris ourselves to find out what he knew — Barney had been sensible enough not to tell his superiors that he was going to be interviewing a goat — he'd say the information had come from elsewhere if Boris did prove to be helpful.

With the pie eating contest in the afternoon, we had a full day lined up.

I hadn't mentioned anything to Barney when I'd spoken to him on the phone about everything else Hilda had said. I wanted to ask him to his face if he was hiding anything from me. I knew our relationship was still young, but if there'd been a possibility that *I* was going to be moving away, I would have told Barney before taking the next step in our relationship. Maybe that was the traditionalist streak in me, but I thought I was well within my rights to question Barney on something he was evidently hiding from me. Something that might affect me as much as him.

Susie had told me and Willow that the police had questioned Sandra Timkins again, and she'd confirmed what Mrs Oliver had said — Gerald *had* had a disagreement with a man, but Sandra didn't know who he was, or what the argument had been about — only that it concerned the new crow scaring devices Gerald had bought to take the place of his scarecrows. She'd considered it so minor an altercation that she'd forgotten about it until the police had jogged her memory.

Willow squirted ketchup onto the sausage sandwich she'd made. "I'd have thought you'd have been more excited about finding out you're going to be a seer some day," she said. "I know I would. Imagine the possibilities that could come from being able to see the future."

I smiled. "If you'd seen Hilda, you'd understand. If all seers end up as batty as her I rather hope my gift doesn't make itself known to me for a long time to come. Preferably never."

"If she's that batty, why do you think she's right about Barney? Maybe she's mixed up."

I shook my head. "No. I believe her. I'm not saying she's wrong about what she sees, just that she's batty in the way she explains it to people. Imagine what Granny would be like if she could see the future and you'll have some idea of what Hilda's like."

Willow bit into her sandwich and nodded towards the pathway which led from the hotel. "Barney's here," she said.

"Would you think it was rude if I took him aboard *The Water Witch* to speak to him about it?" I said.

"Of course not!" said Willow. She pointed at my plate. "Does that mean I can have your bacon?"

I stood up, laughing. "Help yourself," I said. "I'm still full from all those cakes we ate last night."

Willow, Susie, and I, had devoured the baked treats I'd taken back to the boat, but I'd had the presence of mind to save a few cakes for Barney. He could have them if it transpired he'd not been hiding something from me. Who was I kidding? He could have them even if he *had* — Aunt Eva's baking was far too tasty to keep from anybody — even a boyfriend who'd been obtrusive with the truth.

Barney said hello to Willow as he followed me onto the boat. We entered using the bow decking doors and Barney ducked low as we stepped down into Willow's bedroom.

Willow's new bed was in place, and she'd begun painting the walls a calming duck egg blue. It was surprisingly upsetting to smell fresh paint as I entered the room in which the shop had once been — instead of smelling herbs and incense — but I reminded myself that not more than two hundred yards away was the shop which Willow and I owned. The grand opening was scheduled for the beginning of the forthcoming week, although grand was perhaps not a word we should have been using to describe a gathering of less people than could be counted on two hands.

Barney followed me through the boat to the living area, keeping his head low. "I thought we were going straight to your grandmother's to speak to Boris," he said as he took a seat at the dinette table. "It's urgent we speak to him a soon as possible. We need to find out who the scarecrow man is."

"Just how urgent, Barney?" I said, sitting down next to him and staring out of the window at Willow, who was over-feeding the two animals who had her wrapped around their figurative little fingers.

Barney put his hat on the table and placed his radio next to it. "There's a murderer to be caught. I think that's pretty urgent," he said.

"I'll get to the point," I said, not wanting to waste time. Finding out who'd killed Gerald was more important than my feelings, but I needed some sort of answer before carrying on with the rest of the day. "I told you what Hilda said about Boris, but that wasn't all she said. She also told me something about you."

I studied his face for clues, but his expression was as friendly and open as ever. I resisted the urge to wipe the dried toothpaste from his chin and waited for him to answer.

"What about me?" he said. "Something good I hope."

"Barney, are you hiding something from me? Something about you *really* needing to solve this crime — like, if you *don't* solve it, you'll have to go and live in Wales. That sort of thing."

Barney's eyes narrowed. "Wow. Hilda knew about that? She really is talented."

"So?" I said. "It's true? Don't you think you should have told me before I let you kiss me in the restaurant? I wouldn't have been so keen to start a relationship with you if I knew you might be moving away from here. I'm not sold on the whole idea of long distance relationships."

"I didn't know then," said Barney. "I only found out yesterday morning. I didn't tell you because I didn't want you worrying about me, and anyway, Hilda's not entirely correct — I won't be going to live in Wales whatever happens. It was just an option, and it's not just me who's being pressured to solve the crime — it's all of the Wickford police."

"Tell me," I said. "I don't understand."

Barney sighed. "Wickford's a small town. It hardly needs a police station of its own — a larger one in Covenhill could cover most of the county, and that's what the moneymen want, but they need us to mess up before they can get their way. They want us to fail at solving Gerald Timkins's murder so they can make us admit failure and accept outside help."

"They want to prove the Wickford police are not fit for purpose?" I said.

"Something like that," said Barney. "They want everything centralised these days, but they need a good reason to implement their plans. A failed murder investigation is the perfect excuse."

"But where does Wales fit into this? Why would you need to move away?"

"If they close down the station in Wickford, those of us who still have years left to serve could either resign from the police or agree to being posted elsewhere. They can't just sack us."

I understood. "So they'll tell you to either accept a position in Wales or resign?"

Barney nodded. "Yup," he said, "but I won't move away whatever the outcome. I love my job, but I'm loving getting to know you even more, and your family — mad as they might be. I couldn't imagine having to go and live hundreds of miles away from you."

"You'd leave your job for me?" I said, taking his hand in mine. "That's a lovely thing to say, but I'd never want you to do that. You enjoy being a policeman too much. I couldn't live with the knowledge that you gave it up for me."

Barney put his hat on and grabbed his radio. "So what are we waiting for? I've got a crime to solve. I need to show that the Wickford police are worth keeping — come on, I've got a goat to interview, and I need your help."

I followed Barney through the boat and climbed ashore with him. Willow joined us as we headed up the footpath to the hotel where Barney had parked the car, and Rosie and Mabel wandered off to bully a family of brave swans who'd made the mistake of considering the patch of grass next to the boat as being a good place to relax.

We could still hear Mabel barking as we got into the police car, and a scrap of paper on the dashboard reminded me of the note Willow had left for me at Mum's cottage. The note had said that the forensics department had discovered something on Gerald Timkins's shotgun, but with all the excited questions coming from my sister and Susie about my trip to the haven, it had slipped my mind the night before.

"They found a microscopic piece of dried paint," explained Barney when I asked. He took a right onto Church street, and an immediate left into the lane which would take us to Ashwood cottage. "Green paint, on the trigger guard, but it's so small it will take them some time to work out exactly what paint it is. Mrs Timkins said Gerald was always painting too, and his tractor's green — so there's a good chance it came off that. It's something and nothing, but it needs to be investigated."

Barney took the right turn onto Granny's property and parked next to the lean-to. He looked at the cottage and gave a little shudder as he laughed.

"What's so funny?" said Willow.

Barney looked up at the guest bedroom window. "I'm remembering the last time I was here, thanks to the memories Penny gave back to me. I'm still coming to terms with the fact that there's a man's body in the bedroom who's mind is in a goat. It's like a dream, and to think that for all the years I've known your family… you've been witches. It's hard to get my head around."

I'd tried to put myself in Barney's position. I thought I could empathise with him, but I'd never truly know what it would feel like to discover that magic and witches existed after spending my whole life thinking they were mere fantasy. Magic had always been a part of my life. My earliest memory was of Mum opening a portal in the kitchen doorway, and some of my best memories involved magic of some kind. Barney was doing really well to take it all in his stride so easily.

"Come on," I said, opening the car door. "This time it'll be easier. There's no secrets anymore."

"Where are they?" said Willow. "We told Granny we were coming, but the Range Rover's not here."

The roar of an engine from the woodland behind the cottage gave us a clue, and I took my phone from my pocket. Granny answered on the third ring, and after boasting she was speaking to me using the cars bluetooth technology, as if it were more special than magic, she told me where she was and that she'd be back at the cottage promptly.

"They're off-roading," I explained, slipping the phone into my pocket. "I could hear Boris screaming, so I don't think Granny's very good at it."

"Or too good," suggested Willow.

The sound of the engine grew louder until the Range Rover appeared at the end of one of the narrow trails which led into the woodland that spread for miles behind Granny's cottage. It's black paintwork was splattered with mud, although the private registration plate was still visible. It read B1TC HY, and never had a registration plate been more fitting for the person who drove the vehicle.

Barney and Willow jumped backwards as Granny

skidded to a halt in front of us, and I held a hand up to protect my face from the gravel which the tyres spat at us.

Granny gave us a wave before climbing from the vehicle and rushing around to the front passenger door. "Quick! Help me get him out. The carpet in this car cost more than all the carpets in my cottage put together, and I do not want sick on it!"

Boris had obviously been using the door for support, and he thudded to the gravel as Granny opened it and he fell out of the vehicle.

"It's all okay," said Granny. "He wasn't sick. Well done, Boris."

Boris groaned and got to his feet, he took a step forward and Barney caught him before he slipped and fell again. "Careful, Boris," he said. "Get your balance before you try again."

"I begged you to slow down, Gladys," murmured Boris, his eyes closed as he wobbled on his four legs. "I begged you."

Granny slammed the door shut and took the large sunglasses from her face and replaced them with her regular purple spectacles which she took from a pocket.

"What are you wearing, Granny?" said Willow. "I think I preferred it when you wore an apron everywhere you went."

"I told you before, sweetheart," said Granny, sauntering past Boris, who dribbled from his mouth and took a deep breath. "I'm in a different class now. I need to look the part."

"You look like a posh farmer," said Willow.

Granny's waxed jacket and expensive wellington boots over tweed trousers certainly gave the impression that she was a wealthy landowner, but the insistence in keeping her blue perm kept the top fifth of her body firmly grounded in the working class.

"Thank you, darling," said Granny. "I appreciate the compliment."

"Don't worry, Gladys," said Boris, regaining his balance. "I'm fine. Don't you worry about me. I'll just stand here with my stomach in knots as a result of your atrocious driving."

"Quiet! Know your place!" snapped Granny. "Don't you dare speak to me in such tones! Take the Range Rover away and clean it. I want to be able to see my face in it when you've finished, and when you've done that, you can water the horses and bring me my drink — a Gibson cocktail, and don't you dare forget the onion this time or I'll have your job, and then who'll put food in the bellies of that fat family you insist on keeping? I'll make sure you never work for the landed gentry again! You'll be down the mines before you can say 'please, Lady Weaver, I won't do it again — I suggest you think on that."

"Not in front of them, Gladys," said Boris. "I told you I'd play along, but only in private."

"Ooh. I got carried away. Sorry, Boris," said Granny. She looked at our puzzled faces. "Boris and I like to play aristocrat and commoner," she explained. "It's just a little fun. We enjoy role playing."

"Is that how you think the aristocracy speaks to their employees?" said Willow, following Granny into the cottage.

"I certainly hope they do," said Granny. "Otherwise what's the point of privilege? Anyway, enough of that depressing talk— you came here to speak to Jeeves, erm — I mean, Boris, didn't you? Come on in, I'll put the kettle on."

CHAPTER TWENTY

With her waxed jacket and wellington boots removed, Granny looked half normal again, and when she slipped her apron on as she served us tea, she was completely herself once more.

"How can I help?" said Boris, fully recovered from his car sickness, and with the remains of a saucerful of brandy around his lips. "Gladys says I was mentioned during your trip to the haven, Penelope?"

"A seer told me you may be able to help us find the man the police want to speak to about Gerald Timkins's murder," I said.

Granny sat in her favourite seat near the unlit fire, and Boris stood next to her. The paintings of family ancestors looked down at us from their places on the walls, and Barney seemed to wilt under their oil painted gazes. I didn't blame him — some of my ancestors looked like the type of people you wouldn't like to meet in a well lit high street, let alone a dark alley.

Boris looked at me with interest. "Me? I may have information which will help apprehend a murderer?"

"Murder suspect," said Barney. "At this stage he's just a suspect, but I'd be extremely grateful for any help you could offer."

Granny put a hand on Boris. "Hold it right there, Boris. Don't say anything that will implicate you. I know how the police work." She looked at Barney. "What do you want to know, fed? Are you trying to butter Boris up with your good cop act? It won't work in this cottage. I've been around the block too many times to be taken in by good looks and a truncheon."

"Granny," said Willow. "This is Barney you're talking to. Penelope's boyfriend and friend of the family. Show him some respect!"

"Right now, I'm talking to the badge," said Granny. "I only see a uniform, not the man beneath, and the uniform *screams* violent fed."

Barney smiled. "This... fed, let you and your goat get away with the very serious crime of arson, Mrs Weaver. Remember?"

Granny smiled. "Call me Gladys, Barney, please. None of this *Mrs Weaver* — we're practically family now, we can afford to be a little courteous to each other. More tea?"

Barney shook his head. "No thanks, Gladys. This is urgent, I need to find out what Boris knows."

Boris gazed up at Granny. "Gladys. Could this be why fate brought me to you? Did fate want me here to right a wrong? Was I sent here to help solve the riddle of the four-and-twenty blackbirds murder?"

"The what?" said Barney.

"It's a tongue-in-cheek name I came up with for the murder," said Boris. "You know — from the nursery rhyme? I thought it was very fitting as your first suspect eats pies, and we found Gerald's body beneath a flock of crows — or birds which are black, if you'll allow me the artistic licence."

"Very good, Boris," said Willow. "I'll tell Susie. Maybe she can use it for a newspaper story."

"No hack's using anything Boris says unless he gets financial compensation," said Granny.

Boris winked at Willow. "Of course she can use it," he said. He turned his attention to Granny. "Calm down, Gladys, you're being very confrontational today. Have a chamomile tea, and relax. Now… do you think this is why fate brought me here?"

"I'd be highly disappointed," said Granny. "I was hoping for more, to be honest. Something earth shattering, you know?"

Barney coughed. "This is all very nice," he said, "but do you think we could move the topic of conversation back to what Boris may or may not know? This is *very* important."

"Of course," said Boris, "ask of me what you will, and I'll do my very best to answer truthfully and factually."

"Boris," I said, "the seer in the haven knew Barney was looking for a man who makes scarecrows. She told me to repeat a phrase to you — does half a bell, or harfa bell mean anything to you, Boris. Anything at all?"

Boris laughed. "Of course it means something to me, but something's been lost in translation. You mean *Arthur* Bell. He's an artist and he *has* been known to make the occasional scarecrow for the local farms."

"Why haven't you said something before, Boris?" I said. "You were in the vets when Mrs Oliver mentioned a scarecrow man — didn't you think to mention you knew a man who made them? It *was* sort of important."

"Trigger warning!" yelled Granny.

Boris gasped and dropped to his knees, struggling to breathe.

"Don't mention the vets!" said Granny. She placed her hand between the goats horns. "Boris, it's okay, deep breaths, deep breaths. Think of nice things. Think of brandy, cigars, and Chinese food."

"Is he okay?" said Barney, leaning forward.

Granny shook her head. "No. It's some sort of PTSD," she said. "We don't mention what happened in the vets. He's still very sore from the experience, both emotionally and anally. I'm having to apply both physical and emotional salves to help him heal. He'd almost wiped it from his mind until you brought it up, Penelope. How very uncaring of you."

"I'm sorry, Boris," I said. "I didn't know."

Boris looked at me through tearful eyes. "It's not your fault, Penelope. It's the fault of those barbarians and their glass probes. I'll be okay in moment or two. Pass me my cigar would you?"

I placed Boris's cigar holder in front of him, and Granny lit the cigar which Boris greedily sucked on. The cigar stand had once been my grandad's fishing fly tying vice, but it worked admirably as a cigar holder for a smoker without opposable thumbs.

"Is that better, Boris?" said Granny. "Would you like some brandy now?"

Boris regained his composure and blew a large smoke ring. "I'm okay, Gladys, thank you." He looked at Barney. "You're looking for a man named Arthur Bell. He lives out in the woods on the road to Bentbridge. He made a living as a mediocre artist and subsidised his income by making scarecrows for local farmers. He used my services as an acupuncturist for a hand injury which prevented him from painting, and he began relying on income from making scarecrows until the time he was well enough to paint again. He was barely making enough money to feed himself, let alone pay me for acupuncture."

"An artist," I said, looking at Barney. "And a scarecrow maker."

Barney nodded. "The green paint on the shotgun!" He stood up. "Thank you, Boris. You've been a great help. I'll go straight back to the station and tell Sergeant Cooper. We'll have Mr Bell in custody within an hour."

****

Barney left in a rush after promising to keep us updated on events, and Granny drove the remaining four of us to the Poacher's Pocket Hotel, stopping off at the carwash on the way to remove the coating of mud her off-roading expedition had created.

She parked the gleaming Range Rover next to the little Renault she'd given us, and we made our way through the beer garden and down the footpath to the *Water Witch*.

Granny hadn't forgotten that she'd invited Boris and herself on our boat trip to the pie eating competition, and as Boris's face lit up when Rosie and Mabel ran to greet him as we approached the mooring, I was happy they were with us. Mum had phoned to let me know that she and Uncle Brian were on their way to the pie eating contest, and I looked forward to a day out with the whole of my family.

Family trips were a rare occurrence in the Weaver family, and they'd been made a lot harder to arrange by Granny's lifetime bans from a lot of the popular venues in the area. Her most recent ban — from Bentbridge great ape and owl sanctuary, had even made it into the newspapers. Granny had denied the accusations of course, arguing that it must have been one of the keepers who'd left the chimpanzee enclosure open after feeding time. Even when PETA claimed the chimp liberation as one of their operations — and pictured a jubilant Granny on their website with only her purple spectacles visible beneath her balaclava — she still denied the charges. I doubted Granny could cause many problems at a pie eating contest, but it was always wise to be a little vigilant in her presence.

The contest was being held near the brewery which was sponsoring it. As with all old businesses in a town built around a waterway, the Wickford brewery was built on the banks of the canal, and an adjacent field had been transformed into the setting for the afternoon's competition.

Granny took the controls of the boat for the last five minutes of the short journey, and she giggled as she increased the power, wetting Boris with spray from the propeller.

Willow took over driving duties as we approached the brewery and guided the boat alongside the bank as I leapt ashore to tie it off. Four other boats were already moored up next to the field, and the vehicles in the makeshift carpark glinted in the sun.

The field contained a few small colourful marquees and a low stage which was home to a long table which the competitors would sit at while eating their pies. In a small town like Wickford, a lot of people could be relied on to attend most planned events, and the pie eating competition was no exception. Children ran round playing and bouncing on the inflatable castle which had been erected, and adults drank beer and ate the pies which were being baked on site for customers and pie eating professionals alike.

The smell of food being cooked and the music which came from speakers on the stage had an uplifting effect on all of us, and Granny hurried towards the tent which housed the bar, to meet Mum and Uncle Brian, with Boris trotting alongside her on the end of the dog leash they used when Boris was in the public eye.

Susie waved at us from across the field and made her way over to join us, her camera hanging around her neck, and a notebook in one hand. We told her about the developments in the murder case, and she scribbled down notes as she listened, promising not to alert her newspaper about the developments concerning Arthur Bell until Barney had given her his permission. "Of course not. Barney knows he can trust me. Anyway, I'm here to cover the contest," she said, looking around the field. "I've just been interviewing the competitors for a piece I'm writing, they're all in the little tent behind the stage. Felix Round doesn't look too well — he stuck to his celery diet, but he really needs to eat something more substantial before he faints."

Willow laughed. "I've said it before and I'll say it again — salad is not real food, and a man like Felix needs more than just celery to keep him going. I'm surprised he's still alive."

"His wife's so angry with him," smiled Susie, "but she's happy that Felix will be retiring from competition eating if he wins today — which I'm sure he will — none of the other competitors look like they have a chance of out eating Felix. I think *I* could beat some of them. They take it all far too seriously if you ask me, it's only a bit of fun."

"One man's fun is another man's passion," I said, hoping I sounded wise.

Susie and Willow seemed to agree, and before either of them had the chance to question my wisdom, Granny and Boris hurried towards us with Mum close behind them. Granny clutched a plastic glass of beer and Mum carried a wine glass, while Boris complained about not being able to finish his drink.

"There's plenty of time for another drink, Boris," scolded Granny. "But a moment like this will never be repeated. Today's the day I get validated as a mother and get to watch my first born triumph victorious. Today's the day that Brian will bring the Weaver family name into the spotlight where it so rightly deserves to shine."

"What's happening?" said Susie.

"My thoughts exactly," I said.

Granny pointed at the stage. The competitors had begun

to climb the short flight of stairs and take their seats at the long table as plates laden with freshly baked pies were placed in front of them.

His bright red suit and green cravat made Uncle Brian stand out like a clown among vicars, and Granny clutched her chest as she watched. "That's what's happening," she said with a quiver in her voice. "He entered without telling me — as a beautiful surprise. My son has risen from oppression and is about to win the Wickford pie eating competition. If any higher accolade could be bestowed upon a mother, I'd like to know what it is."

"I gave you two beautiful grand children *and* I did very well in university," said Mum.

Granny sighed. "Maggie, Maggie, Maggie," she said, shaking her head. "It can't always be about you. I'm very proud of you, of course, but you had it easy, dear. Brian has had to fight hard to smash his way through the layers of oppression which society has put in his way. Has he been burned in the process? Many times. Too many times to count, but look at him up there on the stage — transformed into the beautiful phoenix we see before us — transformed so the whole world may marvel at him. You and he are in different leagues, sweetheart."

Uncle Brian waved and smiled at us, putting two beefy thumbs in the air as Granny blew him a kiss.

The speakers on stage went quiet and the music was replaced by the voice of the mayor, who stood centre stage with a microphone in hand, dressed in his full ceremonial regalia. "Ladies and gentleman," he said, his booming voice matching his large stature. "Welcome to the Wickford pie eating contest, kindly sponsored by The Wickford Brewery — home of the world renowned Wickford Headbanger, *and* the locally renowned, but considerably weaker, Wickford Tallywhacker. Both fine ales, but only one of which finds a home in the little cupboard under my oven, although I'm told the Tallywhacker is a beer which grows on you, although, frankly, life's too short to be trying to force oneself to enjoy a beer which is not to one's taste. Drink what you enjoy is my motto."

A man hurried onto the stage and spoke into the mayor's ear.

"I digress, *apparently*," said the mayor. "So let's get on with the competition!"

The crowd applauded, and Granny put her fingers in her mouth and blew a piercing whistle. "Go Brian Weaver!" she yelled. "Give em hell! That's my boy!"

The mayor continued, reading from a small card he held close to his face. "The competition rules have changed this year after advice from the British Foundation of Obesity and Heart Health. No longer will the contestants be expected to eat as many pies as they can in order to win. This year will be a timed competition — the contestants will have ten minutes in which to eat as many pies as they can!"

Granny wolf whistled again. "You've got this, Brian! Glory awaits you! Fill your face!"

"But before we begin," said the mayor. "Let us have a minute's silence for a man whose place at the table behind me is empty, and a man who was a legend in the highly competitive world of pie eating. Please be silent and remember Gerald Timkins, or as he was known in pie eating circles — The Tank."

The crowd fell dutifully silent for the prescribed sixty seconds, and when the minute was up, the mayor thanked the competitors and organisers and passed the microphone to the compère as the contestants stuffed napkins into their shirts and pulled their pies close.

Felix Round sat to the right of Uncle Brian, and I realised what Susie had meant when she'd said he looked ill. He pallor was far too pale to be healthy, and his hands trembled as he pulled a plate in front of him.

The other competitors appeared as if they were only there to make up the numbers, with one man in particular looking far too thin to finish one pie, let alone the pile in front of him. It seemed that the competition was firmly between the two fattest men on stage — Uncle Brian and Felix Round.

A hand tightened on my wrist and I gasped as the painted finger nails dug into my flesh. I looked into the face of Felix Round's wife who pulled me close to her. "That's your uncle on stage isn't it?"

I attempted to tug my wrist from her fierce grasp as Granny pushed between us. "Take your hand off my granddaughter. Nobody touches a member of my family in that way," she warned.

The look in Granny's eyes could have melted ice, and it had the desired effect on Mrs Round, who released her grip and took a step backwards. "I'm sorry," she said, "I didn't mean to hurt you, but you have to help me. You have to tell Brian to throw the competition. Felix has to win!"

CHAPTER TWENTY-ONE

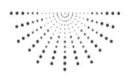

Mrs Round's eyes were those of somebody who had not been sleeping well, and her hair was thoroughly neglected. She took a step away from Granny and allowed her arms to drop by her sides. "Please tell Brian to throw the competition," she urged. "My husband *has* to win. If he doesn't win today he won't retire from pie-eating, and the doctor has told me he won't be around for more than three years if he carries on like he is. It's literally life and death that he wins today."

Granny smiled. "Then he'd better win, hadn't he? My son has been oppressed his whole life, and a win today would show him that he's a valuable person. He needs the validation. I must warn you though, Brian can put way food with the best of them — I'd be very surprised if he didn't give Felix a run for his money."

Mrs Round scowled. "Felix would have this competition in the bag if they hadn't changed the rules. He's trained for eating slowly over a period of time, not for stuffing as many pies as he can in ten minutes. It's not fair — a change of rules this late in the game must be illegal."

"It's only a bit of fun," said Susie. "Don't take it so seriously."

Mrs Round's face reddened. "My husband's health is not just a bit of fun!" She turned to Granny. "You'd better hope Felix wins, you have no idea how important this is to me. I'd do anything to make sure my husband has a long life. Anything."

"That sounds like a threat to me," said Granny. "And I'd advise against threatening me."

Mrs Round looked Granny up and down, and rushed away. She stood directly in front of the stage as the compère gave a countdown from ten and declared the competition had started.

Granny handed me her beer and began clapping with the rest of the audience. "Eat! Eat! Eat!" she chanted, urging Brian on, who stuffed a second pie into his mouth as Felix finished his first.

The other four competitors took sips of water between bites, but Felix and Uncle Brian devoured their pies quickly, with the colour returning to Felix's face as he ate his first proper food in days.

The minutes ticked by, and the competitors ate pie after pie as the compère encouraged them with words of support. As the crowd's shouts grew louder, Boris tapped me on my leg. "Put Gladys's beer down here for me, would you, Penelope? All this excitement is making me thirsty."

I placed the plastic cup on the floor for the goat, and as I stood up straight again, a dizzy sensation made me stumble. Willow caught me with a hand under my elbow. "Are you okay?" she said. "Do you need to sit down?"

I tried to speak, but my throat tightened and my heart bounced against the walls of my chest. Images swirled around my mind and instinct told me that the pictures I was seeing were not conjured up by my imagination — I was having a vision. What Hilda had told me was true — I *was* a seer — and the story which unraveled in my mind was as vivid as any Hollywood film.

My phone vibrated in my pocket, and I didn't need to see it to know that the message was from Barney, telling me that Arthur Bell was in custody and awaiting an interview by detectives. I also *knew* that Arthur Bell hadn't killed Gerald Timkins, and that the ten minutes allocated to the pie-eating competitors was about to elapse, with Uncle Brian being declared the winner.

With a clarity that shocked me, I saw a picture which made my blood run cold and my legs tremble, and I attempted to clear the swirling images from my mind and warn people of what was about to happen. Mum and Susie helped Willow lower me to the ground while Granny's excited chanting grew louder as the compère counted down from ten and declared the competition over.

"He's won!" said Boris, his voice distant and his outline a blur.

Mum put her face inches from mine. "Sweetheart, are you okay?" she said. "Someone phone an ambulance."

"No ambulance," I said, aware that Barney would be arriving in a few minutes to enjoy the rest of the day, and that his presence would be required to arrest the *real* murderer of Gerald Timkins — and If I didn't do something to stop events unfolding as my vision told me they would — the murderer of Uncle Brian too.

"What's wrong?" said Granny, finally noticing her grand-daughter sprawled on the floor at her feet.

"Stop Mrs Round," I muttered, beginning to regain my composure and pushing myself into a kneeling position. "She's going to attack Uncle Brian."

Granny didn't need telling twice. A threat of violence towards her son may as well have been an attack on her very soul. She hurried through the crowd as Willow pulled me to my feet, and made her way towards the stage where the compère was announcing Brian as the winner and picking up the tall metal trophy from the table. Felix Round was magnanimous in defeat, and gave Brian heavy congratulatory slaps on the back as the cup was presented to him.

Mrs Round was not so magnanimous, and she took the steps onto the stage with one long leap and snatched the cup from Uncle Brian's hand, lifting it over her head with two hands and bringing it down in a sweeping arc which was aimed at Uncle Brian's head.

The images my new found gift was presenting me with involved blood, gore, and a dead Uncle on the stage above me, but Granny had obviously not been taken into consideration when the vision had been conjured. She screamed as the heavy trophy swung nearer to Uncle Brian, who had no time to cast a spell, but instead shielded his face and head with his hands. The crackle of Granny's spell was evident even above the shouts and screams of the crowd, and nobody warned her about her dementia — if ever there was time when *any* spell would suffice, this was it.

Mrs Round paused at first, the swing of the trophy slowing dramatically until it stopped with a fraction of an inch between the jagged handle and Uncle Brian's head.

Felix Round stepped forward, his shock giving way to an anguished shout of fear as his wife transformed to stone before his eyes. The compère scurried across the stage, dropping the microphone, and the onlookers began running — putting as much space between themselves and Granny as they could manage.

My vision had shown me that Barney would be arriving at any second, and right on cue, his police car appeared through the gateway which led into the field. Seeing the panic unfolding before him, he leapt from the car and ran towards the stage, not knowing what had happened, but looking in every direction in an attempt to piece the events together.

Granny climbed onto the stage and hugged Brian as a loud throbbing hum from somewhere behind me sent the sound system into a feedback loop which produced ear piercing whistles and whines.

"What on earth!" said Boris, staring past me. "What on earth?"

The throbbing grew so loud that the ground vibrated, and the crowds of people grew even more panicked, rushing for their cars or taking cover in the tents that dotted the field.

Nobody ran for the tent behind me though, and I didn't blame them. A dazzling sliver light filled the wide entrance, and the guide ropes strained as the striped canvas shook. Barney reached my side, and helped steady me on my feet as the portal fully opened and two figures walked through, one of them a beautiful woman in a flowing red robe, and the other a short portly man with a head of gold hair and a staff in one hand.

"What's happening?" said Barney, his breathing strained and his face white. "Who are they, and why is everyone screaming?"

Mum smiled. "Don't worry, Barney. The woman is Maeve, the creator of the haven" she said, "and she's with the copper haired wizard of the west. Everything will be alright now."

Maeve said something to the wizard, and he slammed his staff into the ground, making the ground swell and the crowds of fleeing people freeze on the spot.

"An EMP," explained Mum, "an extremely magical pulse."

People were frozen in time everywhere I looked. Some were frozen as they clambered into cars, and others were attempting to climb over the hedge which surrounded the field. Three particularly brave children were frozen in mid bounce on the inflatable castle, and one old man still clutched a pint of beer in his hand as he relaxed in a deck chair, unaware, or not caring that armageddon surrounded him.

Silence replaced the screaming and shouting, and Barney gazed around the field, extending his nightstick. "Should I be concerned?" he mumbled.

Mum put a hand on his shoulder. "Everybody will be okay," said Mum. "The spell will just wipe their memories."

"Why am I not frozen?" said Barney.

"The spell will only affect those who are not magic or don't know about our existence," said Mum. "You're one of us now, Barney, like Susie is… a member of the magical community."

A crow called somewhere in the distance, and Maeve looked out over the frozen crowd, her long blond hair framing her petite face. "This is a bit of a mess, isn't it?" she said, making her way towards us, with the wizard close behind, his multicoloured patchwork jacket reminding me of a clown. "Quite a mess indeed."

The wizard lifted his staff and pointed it at the stage. "Don't you dare push her, Gladys Weaver," he shouted. "The lawman will deal with her!"

Granny paused, and removed her hands from the petrified body of Mrs Round which teetered on the edge of the stage. "She tried to kill my son!" she shouted. "Nobody tries to kill Gladys Weaver's son and gets away with it!"

"Who tried to kill who?" said Barney, his eyes wide. "What the hell is going on here?"

"Arthur Bell didn't kill Gerald. Mrs Round did, and she just tried to kill Uncle Brian." I said quickly. "So Granny turned her into stone," I added, as Barney gazed at the statue on the stage.

"Anyway!" shouted Granny, descending the steps from the stage, with Brian behind her. "Since when does the copper haired wizard of the west give orders around here?"

"I don't go by that moniker anymore," said the wizard, looking at his feet. "People just call me Derek these days… or Derek The Great… if they so desire."

"Just Derek will do," said Maeve, winking at me.

Granny joined us, and bent down to check on Boris, who licked the last drops of beer from the bottom of the plastic cup, and burped. "This is all very exciting," he said. "But could somebody explain what's happening please?"

CHAPTER TWENTY-TWO

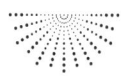

Maeve's presence demanded respect. She was every inch the formidable woman I'd been told she was in the countless stories Mum and Granny had told me over the years, and we all stood still as she studied us, with Barney on one side of me with a protective hand on my shoulder, and Willow on the other, holding my hand.

Granny stepped forward and spoke to Maeve, her glasses on the end of her nose and her face still reddened by the anger that had enveloped her when her son was attacked. "Why are you here?" she said.

Maeve laughed and the wizard smiled. "Gladys," said Maeve. "You just turned a woman into stone with a field full of people as witnesses. You have witch dementia, and you risked seriously injuring or killing a human. You could say we're here for damage control. Somebody's got to clean this mess up."

"How did you know I'd done that?" said Granny. "Are you spying on me?"

"I know whenever a spell is cast in the mortal world," said Maeve, "but it just so happens that I knew this incident was going to occur. Fate never lies, and fate told me a long time ago that I'd be standing here today with you people before me."

Granny put a hand on Boris. "I told you," she said. "Fate is a powerful mistress."

"She is indeed," said Maeve. "And fate made sure you two would meet, and she certainly had a hand in Charleston's transformation into a goat. In fact, everything that's happened since the day you developed witch dementia, Gladys, has been to ensure that you found the portal clogs which belonged to Charleston's grandmother."

"Portal clogs?" said Granny.

Derek the wizard nodded. "The clogs you found are very powerful. They allow the wearer to pass through any witch's portal into the haven… even a mortal can enter the haven if he or she wears the clogs. Charleston's grandmother owned them, and when she died we never knew were they were, until now."

"But why did fate want us to find the clogs?" I said.

Maeve smiled, and looked at Barney. "So the lawman can come to the haven," she said. "To help us with a little problem. If he so wishes to of course."

"Problem?" I said. "What sort of problem could Barney possibly help you with?"

"We don't have time for explanations," said Derek. "My EMP will only last for another two minutes or so. Just know that we have a problem in the City of Shadows that magic can't solve. We need an old fashioned mortal lawman who can look past magic and see a crime."

"The City of Shadows?" said Susie. "That sounds ominous."

"Don't be fooled by the name," said Maeve. "It's a beautiful city where the sun always shines and long shadows are cast."

"Very imaginative," said Boris. "Why not just call it Sun City, though? It sounds a lot more friendly and welcoming."

"Or Solar City," offered Willow. "That sounds lovely. I'd book a holiday there."

"Enough!" said Derek. "Please… it's always been The City of Shadows, and that's what it will remain known as. I think it's a very nice name."

Somebody in the crowd groaned and another person moved a foot.

"Quickly," said Maeve to Derek. "We must be leaving soon. Reverse the spell Gladys cast on the stone woman and open a portal, the people here will forget what happened, and all evidence of witchcraft will be removed from any of their modern recording devices." She looked at Barney. "Lawman, think about what I said, and let us know if you'll help us. The clogs will allow you entry into the haven."

"They won't fit him," I said. "They're very small clogs, and Barney has huge feet."

"Like slabs of meat," agreed Boris, looking at Barney's boots.

"They're *magic* clogs," said Granny. "They'll be one size fits all, won't they Maeve?"

Maeve frowned. "Actually, no they're not, but he doesn't have to wear them, he can carry them. It's the magic they contain that's important, not the fact that they're on someone's feet or not."

"A key would have been better in that case," said Boris.

"What?" said Derek, pointing his staff as he prepared to reverse the spell on Mrs Round.

"If you don't need to wear them to enter the haven, then it seems pointless to have imbued the clogs with magic. A key would have been more symbolic," explained Boris. "Don't you think?"

"Enough of this nonsense," said Derek. "Clogs, key… does it matter in the grand scheme of things?"

"Just saying," said Boris.

Derek sighed and cast his spell. "The petrification spell will wear off in a minute, the woman won't remember being turned into stone, but she'll be confused." Derek pointed his staff at the tent the portal had opened in, and the entrance shimmered with silver as the portal formed again.

Maeve slipped her hand into a long pocket in her robe. "This is for you, Gladys," she said, handing Granny a small bottle with a cork stopper. "It will cure your witch dementia, and you'll be able to put Charleston's mind back into his own body and the mind of that poor goat back where it belongs."

Granny took the bottle and slid it into her own pocket. "Thank you, Maeve."

Derek gave a last look over his shoulder before entering the portal, and Maeve paused for a moment before following him. "Think about what I ask of you, lawman," she said to Barney. "Your help would be greatly appreciated and fairly rewarded."

Barney nodded. "I will," he promised.

Maeve stepped into the light, and the portal closed after her, leaving us surrounded by people who were beginning to regain their senses and stare at each other in confusion.

"Ignore them," said Granny. "They'll be as right as rain soon enough. They'll think they all got collective sunstroke or something. It's a very hot day."

"You need to make an arrest," I said grabbing Barney by the wrist and leading him towards the stage where Mrs Round was standing with her head in her hands, fully transformed back into flesh and bone, and with a blank look on her face. "Come on."

"How do you know she did it?" said Barney, following me. "What evidence do you have?"

"I saw it," I said. "With my new gift. I also know that Arthur Bell told you he argued with Gerald because he was buying electronic crow scarers instead of paying Arthur to make scarecrows for him. He needed the money and was upset with Gerald."

"That's exactly what he told me," said Barney.

"He's telling the truth," I said, "He didn't hurt Gerald. His fingerprint won't match the partial print on the gun, and I'll bet that the green paint on Gerald's gun is actually nail polish which matches the colour of Mrs Round's nails perfectly. She's the murderer, and before you got here she tried to crack Uncle Brian's skull open with that trophy at her feet. She's a maniac who needs locking up."

Barney followed me onto the stage where Felix was still regaining his composure and the compère was huddled beneath the table where he'd hidden when Granny had transformed a woman to stone before his eyes.

"What's happening?" said Felix. He looked at the trophy on the floor. "Did I win?"

"Im afraid not, Felix," I said. "Brian won. You must have fainted. It's very hot."

Barney pushed past me and stood in front of Mrs Round. "Why did you kill Gerald Timkins?" he said.

Mrs Round narrowed her eyes and rubbed her head. She still looked confused, but the seriousness of the situation was beginning to show in her eyes. "I didn't!" she said. "That's an absurd accusation!"

Barney grabbed Mrs Round's hand and inspected her bright green fingernails. "We found green paint on the shotgun, Mrs Round, and I'm willing to bet it's a perfect match for the paint on your nails. We also have a partial fingerprint. I'm sure we'll clear things up soon enough."

"Ridiculous!" said Felix. "My wife wouldn't kill a man... would you, darling?"

Mrs Round took a deep breath. She put a hand on Felix's stomach and sighed. "I'm sorry, Felix," she said.

"Why did you kill him?" said Barney, taking his handcuffs from his belt.

Mrs Round looked at me swallowed hard. She turned her gaze to Barney. "It was an accident," she said, her voice low. "I went to see Gerald to beg him to withdraw from the pie-eating competition so Felix would win. I was so scared about Felix's health, I wasn't thinking straight. Gerald was in his field and his gun was on the ground, and I just picked it up. I had no idea it would go off, I just wanted to scare him."

"But you killed him instead," said Barney. "And left him there for his wife to find."

Mrs Round sobbed. "It was an accident and I couldn't allow myself to be caught — if I'd gone to prison who would have looked after Felix? He'd have eaten himself into an early grave with me not around to control him."

Felix gasped. "You killed Gerald Timkins. How could you?"

"And why did you attack my son?" said Granny, joining us on stage and peering over her glasses.

"I lost control," said Mrs Round. "All the years of watching Felix get fatter and fatter, and more ill, took their toll on me. Today was the day I thought Felix would stop. I thought that if he won today he'd never enter another competition — he promised me he'd retire if he beat Gerald's record, and I believed him. When Brian won, I lost my temper. I'm so ashamed."

"Well, you'll have a long time to come to terms with what you've done," said Granny. "In prison."

Mrs Round stumbled, and Barney caught her. "Who will look after Felix?" she said. "He won't be able to help himself when I'm locked away, he'll eat himself to death."

"I can look after myself," said Felix. "And don't you dare

use me as the reason you murdered a man. That's not fair." He turned to Barney. "Take her away, officer. I can't look at her again."

The clinking sound of handcuffs being locked brought home the reality of what she'd done, and Mrs Round sobbed loudly as Barney led her from the stage and to the waiting police car.

Granny and Boris sat together on the grass near the water's edge, and Willow, Susie, and I sat at the picnic bench, listening to the radio and drinking wine. Mabel sat at our feet, and Rosie was curled up on the roof of the *Water Witch*, enjoying the last of the evening sun.

Barney had telephoned to tell us that Mrs Round had made a full confession and that her fingerprint matched the partial print on the gun, and Arthur Bell had been released from custody with an apology.

All in all, it had been a good day. Susie had got a scoop for the newspaper, Barney had arrested a murderer and been invited to the haven, and I'd had my first vision. The only thing we couldn't understand was why Granny hadn't immediately taken the cure for witch dementia that Maeve had given her.

Boris and Granny had excused themselves from our company and had been speaking in hushed tones for at least twenty minutes, but finally they both got to their feet and joined us at the table, with Boris standing next to granny as she pushed onto the bench beside me.

"We've come to a decision," said Granny.

"A joint decision," said Boris.

"Yes?" said Willow.

Granny sighed. "Today my witch dementia nearly got my son killed when my spells got muddled up."

"Erm… what are you talking about?" I said. "The spell you cast was perfect — it stopped Mrs Round in her tracks. Literally."

"You don't understand," said Granny. "That was an accident. I was trying to turn her heart to charcoal. She would have died on the spot — *should* have died on the spot — nobody tries to kill my son. Nobody! Nobody! Nobody!"

"There, there, Gladys," said Boris. "Keep it real. Think happy thoughts."

Granny shifted her weight and cleared her throat. "My apologies. I didn't mean to shout. As I was saying — today a near catastrophe happened because of my dementia, and I know I need to cure it, but…"

"But what?" I said.

Granny continued. "But, I've — I mean *Boris and I* have decided, that I won't cure it for another few weeks. Boris and I have a holiday booked, you see. In Wales — we've booked a beautiful static caravan for the week and we're looking forward to going. As soon as I drink that potion Maeve gave me, I'll be cured, and all my mistakes will be righted — which means Boris and Charleston will swap places immediately. That goose will turn back into a real bird too — all manner of little things might happen."

"That's good though isn't it?" said Susie. She looked at Boris. "You want your old life back, don't you?"

"Truth be told," said Boris, "not just yet. I'm happy, and as Gladys said — we want to go on holiday, and we've paid for one adult and one well behaved pet. That's me by the way."

"I'm sure they mean dogs," I said. "Not goats."

"Well *they* should check their small print in the brochure," said Granny. "It says *pets* not *dogs*, and anyway, Boris is far more well behaved than any dog could ever be."

Boris puffed out his chest. "I try my best," he said.

"You could go as Charleston, Boris," said Willow. "You could go on the holiday in your human body."

Granny sucked in air and shuddered. "Share a caravan with another man! Norman would turn in his grave. Rest his soul. No, Boris and I will go as we are. We're driving to Wales in the Range Rover next week, and we're going to have a wonderfully restful holiday. When we get back we'll further discuss curing my dementia."

"And find out what favour Maeve wants from Barney," said Susie.

Willow nodded. "Imagine what we can do with those clogs. Maeve said any mortal can get into the haven with them, so that means you can go too, Susie, and me — even if I haven't got my entry spell. We can all go to the City of Shadows. Together. It'll be an adventure!"

"Do you think Barney will agree to go?" said Susie. "He looked a little terrified today to be honest. I don't think he's processed the whole magic thing very well yet."

"He's not used to it, Susie," I said. "He's only known that magic exists for a few days, you've known for twelve years. I think he's doing very well, and I'm sure he'll be happy to come to the haven."

"You'll find out soon enough," said Granny. "If Maeve and the copper haired — I mean *Derek,* think it's fate that led us all to where we are today, then I can only imagine that the favour they want from Barney is a big one. Fate wouldn't interfere in trivial matters."

I sipped my wine and smiled. "Well, let's wait and see what fate has in store for us next," I said. "I can't wait to find out."

The End

An Eye For An Eye

A Water Witch Cozy Mystery – Book Three

Sam Short

Copyright © 2017 by Sam Short

All rights reserved.

No part of this book may be reproduced in any form or by any electronic or mechanical means, including information storage and retrieval systems, without written permission from the author, except for the use of brief quotations in a book review.

❧ Created with Vellum

For Mum and Alan. Thank you for everything - I love you both more than words could ever say.

CHAPTER ONE

Rosie purred and curled into a tight ball on my lap as Mabel the goose gave a low growl and lifted her head in response to an owl's hoot which echoed over the water outside.

"You don't own the canal," laughed Willow, placing a hand on the goose's back. "There's plenty of room for other animals here too. Quieten down."

I studied the goose. Or dog — depending on how you perceived the situation. The white bird had been made to think she was a dog when my grandmother had accidentally cast a spell on her. My sister and I had become accustomed to welcoming the goose aboard the boat we lived on together, for affection or scraps of food. It would be odd to see her acting like a normal goose again if Granny decided to take the potion she'd been gifted by another witch. The potion would cure her rather serious case of witch dementia and reverse any disastrous spells she'd cast while her magic had been affected. Mabel the goose was a lovely creature, but I supposed she'd be happier when she was a normal bird again and not some sort of hybrid creature with a beak and wings who cocked her leg when she went to the toilet.

Granny would be returning to Wickford in the morning, along with Boris the enchanted goat. They'd been on holiday together in Wales for a week, and I dreaded to think how an elderly witch and a sixty-something year old Chinese acupuncturist — trapped in the body of a goat by another of Granny's errant spells — could possibly have lived together peacefully in a caravan for seven days. As Willow had pointed out though — we'd seen nothing on the TV news or read anything in the newspapers, so if Granny and Boris *had* drawn any attention to themselves, at least they'd managed to keep themselves away from any media attention.

Willow stood up and made her way through the narrow canal boat. "Hot chocolate?" she offered, standing in the galley kitchen. "It'll help us sleep. I don't know about you, but I can't wait for tomorrow. I'm as excited as I used to be when Mum took us on holiday when we were little!"

I smiled. The trip was hardly going to be a holiday, but I understood what she meant. Tomorrow was going to be a big day. Maeve — the powerful witch who'd conjured up the magical dimension known as The Haven, had asked for the help of my policeman boyfriend, Barney. It was unprecedented that a mortal person be allowed to cross from our world into The Haven, but Maeve had said the problem she needed help with could not be solved by magic. She needed the help of an old fashioned mortal policeman. "I am excited," I admitted. "Even more so since I found out Mum's arranged with Maeve that we can take the boat into The Haven. *The Water Witch* has been moored up for too long, she deserves a nice cruise."

Willow nodded her agreement and repeated her offer of hot chocolate, a carton of milk in one hand and her other hand on a shapely hip.

I nodded. "Make mine very milky, please," I said as my sister lit the gas stove and began heating milk in a small pan. She added chocolate powder to the milk and the boat filled with the complimentary aromas of burning gas and warm chocolate. I sighed and stroked Rosie. Living on a canal narrowboat with my sister was awesome at the best of times — but when it was dark outside and we sat next to one another on the small sofa drinking late-night hot chocolate — life was as near to perfect as I could imagine. It would have been nice to have Barney next to me too, but inviting Barney to stay on the boat overnight wouldn't have been fair to my sister. Willow had only moved aboard a few weeks ago — before Barney and I were *an item.* Giving Willow the space and privacy I'd promised her when I'd invited her to move aboard with me was the right thing to do. Anyway, she'd have to get used to a crowded boat for the foreseeable future. Barney, Mum, Granny and Boris were all joining us the following day as we took the boat into The Haven. I hadn't worked out *exactly* where everyone would sleep, but I'd already resigned myself to the fact that my bed would be handed over to Granny. She might have acted like she was still in her teens, but she was way past the age I'd expect anyone to sleep on furniture which folded down into a makeshift bed.

Willow carefully poured the drinking chocolate into two mugs and passed me one as she sat down. She pointed at the pair of wooden clogs on the dinette table. "They don't look very powerful, do they?" she said.

The clogs were a magical artefact that allowed anybody to enter The Haven — even a mortal with no magical powers, but Willow was right — they didn't look very impressive.

I laughed. "No, but then again, Granny doesn't look very powerful either, but she's managed to cause havoc throughout her lifetime!"

Willow snorted as she laughed, and squealed as the hot liquid in her mouth dribbled down her chin. "Ow! I burnt my lip!"

I clicked my fingers and cast a minor healing spell.

"Wow," said Willow, touching her lip and sounding as impressed as I felt. "You're turning into a magical dynamo! You stopped the burning."

I'd been studying the big spell book that Granny had given Willow and me, but even I was impressed at how much I'd learnt in such a short time. I wasn't big-headed though, and certainly didn't think of myself as a dynamo of any type — let alone a magical one. "That spell's pretty easy to be honest," I lied. "You could learn to cast it in no time at all."

It hadn't been easy to learn. As Granny had told me — spells which change the physical biology of a human being or animal were the hardest to master. I'd had a few mishaps attempting to learn the healing spell, including growing an extra toe which had throbbed with as much pain as the toe I'd stubbed and was attempting to heal. I didn't tell her, but the spell which I'd just cast on my sister was my first successful attempt at a healing spell.

Willow drained the last of her drinking chocolate and stretched her arms towards the low ceiling. "I'm ready for bed," she said through a yawn.

I was tired too and I was certain that the next day would demand I was well rested. "Me too," I acknowledged. "I'll let you use the bathroom first, you look even more tired than I feel."

When we'd both cleaned our teeth, and Willow had applied the moisturiser she insisted on using every night — even though her skin had always been smoother than a Frenchman's chat up lines — we went to our bedrooms at opposite ends of the boat. I opened the doors that led from

AN EYE FOR AN EYE

my room to the bow decking and knew that Willow would be opening the doors that led from her room onto the stern decking. It was a warm night, and there's something truly beautiful about falling asleep with a breeze on your face and listening to the splashes and calls of the nocturnal canal wildlife. Sleep came quickly, and I dreamed of navigating *The Water Witch* along the rivers of The Haven as we made our way to The City of Shadows and whatever mystery Maeve required help in solving.

BEING WOKEN by a tall ginger haired man, grinning inanely, and wearing a policeman's uniform, is not everyone's idea of the perfect start to the day, but as Barney gave me a kiss and handed me a steaming mug of black coffee, I was as content as I'd ever been.

"Breakfast's on," said Barney, quite unnecessarily — my nose was already twitching as the salty aroma of frying bacon reached my bedroom. "Willow's gone to the shop to make sure it's locked and secure, and your grandmother and Boris are waiting for your mother to finish cooking breakfast. We're all set to go!"

I looked Barney up and down. "Why the uniform? We're going to The Haven, you can wear whatever clothes you like — you're not on official Wickford police business."

"Gladys said it would be best if I arrived in uniform," said Barney. "She thinks it will give me some credentials and authority. I've packed a suitcase full of other clothes too — don't worry."

Granny had a valid point. If Barney was to gain the trust of the magical community in The Haven, and have them accept him as a figure of authority, it was best that he at least looked the part. I sipped my coffee and squeezed his hand. "And you look so handsome in your uniform too, so there is that added bonus," I said.

Barney raised an eyebrow. "You've always said my trousers were too short."

I laughed. He was right. I had said that — and meant it, but Barney was so tall that the police uniform department didn't stock a pair of trousers which fitted him correctly. It was hard to get any clothes that fitted him well. As well as being extremely tall, Barney was thin for his height. Not *too* thin, but a few extra pounds around his waist and a few inches of additional width across his shoulders would have allowed clothes to fit him, rather than hang off him. I smiled at him. "You look extremely handsome in your uniform," I said. "Now go and sit with the others while I get dressed. I won't be long."

I listened to Barney laughing with my family as I got dressed, and joined them on the shore just as Mum brought out plates of food and a large teapot adorned with a colourful knitted tea-cosy. The teapot was from the boat's kitchen, but I'd never seen the cosy before. I knew that when Mum packed to go away, she liked to pack as many home comforts as she could fit in her suitcase. I guessed that somewhere amongst her luggage would be a Lionel Richie CD and possibly even a full set of silver cutlery.

I hugged Granny and tickled Boris behind one of his horns as I took a seat at the picnic table next to Barney. Boris grunted a *good morning* and Granny reached across the table and squeezed my hand in hers. "Hi, sweetheart," she said. "It's lovely to see you. Ignore Boris's grunting. He's in a foul mood today."

"What's wrong with you, Boris?" I asked. "It's not like you to be in a bad mood."

The goat looked up at me. "Let's just say that your grandmother has a heavy foot, Penelope. She sped all the way home from Wales, and it was through good luck and *not* through any skill on her behalf that we didn't die in a fiery car wreck. I'm still trembling inside, Penelope — it will be nice to spend a few days cruising slowly along rivers in your boat."

Granny smiled. "You bought me a powerful Range Rover, Boris. If you think I'm going to potter about in it you've got another thing coming. I intend to make that bitch burn rubber!"

Barney cleared his throat. "It's probably not a good idea to admit to a speeding offence while you're in my company, Gladys. I am an officer of the law after all."

Granny fixed Barney with a stare that made the policeman gulp. "I dare you, Barney Dobkins! I double dare you to even suggest that you'll do so much as tell me what the speed limit on the motorway is. Go on, Barney... I'll bloody —"

"That's enough!" barked Mum. "We'll have no language like that at the breakfast table. We're all about to take a trip together on a small boat, so I suggest we learn to be polite to one another!" She turned her attention to Barney, and frowned. "But seriously, Barney. No one likes a grass. What were you thinking?"

Barney nodded and dropped his gaze. "It was habit," he said. "But it's hard to listen to people telling me they've committed crimes, especially crimes which could hurt somebody else." He looked at Granny. "Try and keep the speed down okay? I don't want to be called out to a car wreck one day and find you at the wheel. That's all."

Granny raised an eyebrow and sipped her tea, but said nothing.

Willow chose the opportune moment to emerge at the bottom of the path which led to the magic shop we ran together. She broke the silence with a shout and gave us a cheery wave. "Save some bacon for me, I'm hungrier than ten men on a diet!" she demanded.

Mum spoke under her breath. "How she keeps that figure is a mystery to me," she said. "She eats more than I did at her age and I had a heck of a job keeping the pounds off."

Granny gave a laugh which echoed across the canal and startled a moorhen. It flapped its way through a vibrant raft of lily-pads and sought refuge in the slender reeds which covered the opposite bank. "You were a little fatty from the day you could *say* food, Maggie! It's no mystery that you couldn't keep the pounds off. The only mystery is how I managed to find clothes to fit you!" she said.

Barney gulped.

Boris snorted.

Granny laughed again, and Mum shook her head. "Your parenting skills are second to none, Mother," she said, buttering herself two thick slices of bread and sandwiching four crispy bacon rashers between them. "But you do make a good point. I *have* always enjoyed my food."

Willow took a seat at the table and helped herself to breakfast. She watched mum bite into the sandwich and lick her lips. "Mum!" she said. "You're eating outside and there are insects everywhere!"

Mum smiled. "You can thank Boris for that," she said, speaking as she chewed. "He worked really hard to get me to where I am today. He's a fine psychologist, and an even finer friend."

The man trapped inside Boris the goat's body was an Oxford educated gentleman who had done many things in his life, including almost finishing a psychology course. He'd offered to help mum overcome her fear of eating outside when insects were present, and as mum took another bite of her sandwich and waved a fat dragonfly from her face, it seemed that he'd accomplished what he'd set out to do.

"I was happy to help," said Boris, "phobias can be awful to live with, but are often surprisingly easy to cure. Yours was a simple case, Maggie." He looked at *The Water Witch*. "Are we leaving soon?" he said, "I'm considerably excited about visiting The Haven. It sounds so perfectly wonderful, and maybe I'll find out more about who I am whilst I'm there."

Boris, or Charleston to be precise, had recently found out that he came from a family of witches — a secret which had been hidden from him by his family. We weren't sure if he possessed the gift of magic, and we wouldn't know until Granny had cured her dementia and put Charleston's mind back into his own body, but a trip to the haven might be beneficial nonetheless.

I wiped my greasy hands on a paper towel. "We'll leave soon," I said. "Uncle Brian and Susie will be on the bridge at half past nine. They'll wave us forward when there are no people or cars nearby. Then I'll open the portal and the bridge will become our way into The Haven!"

"Brian should be on the boat with us," said Granny. "Not on look out duty. He's far more important than that."

"Brian wanted to stay," said Mum. "He's focusing on opening his *business*, remember?"

Granny narrowed her eyes and her purple glasses threatened to slide from the bridge of her nose. "Did you put sarcastic emphasis on the word *business*, my dear? Because if you did, I'll enjoy hearing why, you jealous upstart."

Mum sighed. "My brother is pretending to be a hypnotherapist and using magic to help people break their bad habits. It's a very dubious *business* model if you ask me." Mum looked at Barney. "What do you think, Police Constable Dobkins? Surely it's illegal too? Gaining money by misrepresentation, or something like that?"

Barney blushed for the first time that day. Barney had a problem with blushing, but even I'd have blushed — or withered — under the gaze which Granny had fixed him with "Well?" she said. "Is what my first born is doing illegal, young man?"

Barney slumped in his seat. "I don't know! Probably, but there are no laws regarding magic in the British legal system. We used to have laws a long time ago, but the outcome was always miserable for the witches involved. It usually ended up in a drowning or a burning at the stake."

"Are you threatening to burn Brian at the stake?" shouted Granny, getting to her feet and holding a hand before her with sparks dancing at the fingertips. "Cos' I'll burn you first, you ginger muppet!"

"Calm down, Gladys," said Boris placing his front hooves on the table. "You're suffering from witch dementia! You shouldn't even be threatening to cast a spell — anything could happen! Now put your hand away and sit down! Barney wasn't threatening Brian, and you know it. Anyway, you like Barney. You told me he would make a fine grandson-in-law."

Granny smiled. "Yes, I did, didn't I?" she looked around the table with pride replacing the expression of anger. "It was a pun! Do you all get it? He'll be my grandson-in-law if he makes an honest woman of Penny, and he's a dirty fed, hence the *law* part of the pun!"

"Very good," said Willow. "Very clever, Granny."

"Funny," I acknowledged. "Don't anyone arrange a visit to a hat shop just yet though. Barney and I have only been together for a few weeks."

Barney cleared his throat. "I'm not a dirty fed, Gladys. I'm a police officer, and anyway the term *fed* is American."

"I didn't want to call you a pig, Barney. Not in the presence of bacon and sausages anyway. It seemed disrespectful," said Granny. "So I went yank on your ass."

"Why do our conversations always end up so far away from where they started?" asked Mum. "Let's focus on the task in hand for once. Is everybody ready to go? Is all the luggage on the boat, and is the boat prepared?"

The last question was aimed at me. "The boat's ready," I confirmed. "*The Water Witch* has a full fuel tank, fresh gas canisters, a full water tank and a greased stern gland. She's ready to go when everybody else is."

Willow looked at her watch. "It's nine o'clock," she said. "Uncle Brian and Susie will be making their way to the bridge. We'd better get going."

"Any more questions before we leave?" asked Mum. "Just remember — the most important thing is that everybody is touching the clogs when we pass through the portal, apart from Penelope of course, as it's going to be her portal we're passing through. The magic clogs will ensure we all get through safely as long as we're touching at least one of them, okay?"

Everyone nodded, and Barney cleared his throat. "I have a question," he said.

"Yes?" said Mum.

"How does it work? The portal I mean. I've seen Penny going through hers, and it looks a little scary. I'm the only one among all of us who doesn't have magic. Will I be safe? I don't understand what a portal is."

"I don't have magic," said Boris. "As far as I know at this juncture in time anyway."

"You come from a family of witches though, Boris," I said. "I'm sure that when Granny takes the cure for her dementia, and you find yourself back in your body, you'll have magic. I know it."

"When will you take the cure, Granny?" said Willow. "Maeve gave it to you almost two weeks ago."

Boris looked away and Granny fiddled with her necklace. "I don't want to talk about it right now, thank you. I'll take it in my own good time." She pointed a finger at the breast pocket of Barney's jacket. "Pass me a piece of paper from your police notebook, and your pencil, and I'll show you how a portal works and put your mind at rest, Barney."

I handed Granny a white paper towel. "Use this. Barney can't remove pages from his police notebook, Granny. He could be accused of destroying evidence. Even I know that."

Granny sighed and took the pencil from Barney as she smoothed out the paper towel on the table. "He's wearing his uniform to a magical dimension, Penelope. I'm sure the police authorities would have a bigger problem with that than with a missing page from a notebook."

"Just show him what you want him to see, Mother," said Mum. "We must get going."

"Do you look at the stars, Barney?" said Granny, using her finger to test the sharpness of the pencil point.

"Of course," said Barney. "I like stargazing."

Granny smiled. "Those stars are not there anymore, Barney, but they're so far away that the light from the explosions which destroyed them is still reaching us, millions of years later. That's all a lot of the stars are, Barney — the light from an explosion long ago."

"I know," said Barney. "It's amazing."

Granny nodded. "Space is vast, Barney. It's why a lot of people argue against the existence of aliens who have the technology to visit our planet — space is just too huge. It would take them millions of years to cross the void."

"I've read about that," said Barney.

Granny licked her lips. "What if they didn't need to cross

that distance though, Barney? Maybe they could get here quickly if the distance wasn't so great?"

"That make sense," said Barney.

Granny folded the paper towel in two and held it up for us all to see. "Imagine The Haven is a long way away, Barney."

Barney nodded. "Okay."

Granny held the pencil near the paper. "Imagine this pencil is the boat we're going to be traveling through the portal on, Barney."

Barney nodded again.

Granny struck the folded paper viciously with the pencil point and held the impaled paper aloft. "Boom!" she said. "That's how it works."

"Huh?" said Barney.

"How does it work, Granny?" said Willow. "What does the paper represent?"

"Well, I don't know. Willow," snapped Granny. "That's what the scientists do in films when they need to explain cross dimensional travel, and nobody questions them!"

"It's because they offer an explanation too, Granny," said Willow. "They don't just poke a hole in some paper and expect people to understand what they're talking about."

"It's because they're men! Isn't it?" spat Granny, throwing the pencil and paper at Barney. "Curse the patriarchy! Curse the scientists in films, and curse space travel! I've had enough of the lot of them!"

Mum put her hand on Barney's shoulder. "Relax, Barney," she said. "Traveling through Penny's portal is new to all of us, you're not the only one who's trying something new."

Mum was right. She could have opened her own portal to travel through if she'd wanted, but Granny couldn't open hers while suffering from witch dementia and Willow and Boris had no way of opening their own portals — Willow was yet to earn her Haven entry spell, and Boris was a goat. Trusting the magic clogs would be a leap of faith for everybody on the boat apart from me.

My phone beeped. "It's a message from Susie," I said, defusing the tension. "Her and Uncle Brian are at the bridge. They're waiting for us, we should get aboard the boat. Next stop — The Haven."

CHAPTER TWO

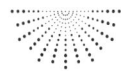

The engine vibrated beneath my feet as I gave *The Water Witch* a burst of power and guided her around the final bend in the canal as the bridge appeared in the distance. Barney stood to the right of me at the steering tiller, and Granny and Mum sat below deck at the dinette table, with the magical clogs in front of them.

Boris peered up at me through the open doors of my bedroom and gave as close to a smile as a goat could manage. The goat's teeth had been yellow and grass worn when the animal had existed purely as a goat, but had become further discoloured since Charleston Huang had inhabited Boris's body and continued to satisfy his penchant for brandy and cigars. Even Boris's coarse white hair carried the aroma of cigar smoke, which I had to admit, was more agreeable than the odour the goat had emitted when it had been tied to a stake in Granny's back garden.

With the sun in my eyes it was hard to make out the shapes of anyone standing on the bridge, but as the trees on the bank thickened their uppermost branches into a canopy which stretched across the narrow canal, it became easy to make out the spherical figure of Uncle Brian. Susie stood next to him, dwarfed by my uncle's bulk, waving a hand in the air. "It's all clear!" she shouted. "No cars or people in sight, and Brian has cast a spell which will keep people away! It's safe to open a portal!"

I waved my acknowledgment, and sent Barney below deck. "You'd better go and take hold of a clog," I said. "And when we go through the portal make sure to keep your eyes open, it becomes very disorientating otherwise."

I'd learnt from my first trip through a portal that closing your eyes when passing from one dimension to another confused the brain and brought on a dizzying case of vertigo.

Barney kissed my cheek. "I'll see you on the other side," he said, rather ominously, as he descended the three steps into my bedroom where Boris waited.

"Be sure to put a hoof into a clog, Boris," I said, reminding him of our plan. "And make sure Rosie's paw is touching them too."

We'd been sure to leave Mabel the goose safe at my mooring in Wickford, but I wouldn't go anywhere without Rosie on board. She'd been my constant and loyal traveling companion ever since I'd bought my boat.

Boris grunted. "Don't worry about us, just concentrate on steering the boat in a straight line."

He made a valid point. My boat was seven feet wide, and the space below the bridge was just a couple of inches wider. It could be tricky to navigate a narrowboat beneath one of the smaller canal bridges on the best of days, without the addition of a magical portal masking the route. "Don't worry," I said, "I'll get us through safely. You have my word."

"Have you seen that in a vision, Penny?" asked Boris. "Or is it just a guess to make us feel safer?"

I'd recently found out that I possessed the gift of seeing, and my first vision had helped solve a murder. I'd had no more visions since then, and had been told by my mother that I may not have another for years to come. I laughed. "No vision I'm afraid, Boris," I said. "You'll just have to take my word for it and put your trust in me."

Barney smiled. "We trust you, Penny."

Barney and Boris disappeared as they made their way through the boat to the dinette table, and Mum shouted to confirm that everybody was in position. "We're all set, Penny!" she said.

The bridge neared and I prepared to cast my haven entry spell. Susie leaned out over wall of the bridge and smiled. "I'll keep an eye on your shop!" she said. "I really wish I was coming with you!"

Susie lived in a flat directly above *The Spell Weavers* — the magic shop which Willow and I ran. She'd been unable to take the time away from her job as a journalist to join us on our trip into the haven, but had been consoled when I'd pointed out that now we possessed the magic clogs which allowed mortals safe passage into The Haven, she'd be able to join us on a future trip. "Thank you, Susie!" I shouted.

"Have a fabulous time!" yelled Uncle Brian, looking as dapper as he always did, in a bright red jacket which I knew would be fashioned from crushed velvet. "And don't do anything I wouldn't do!"

I gave him a smile and a wave. Uncle Brian had only recently moved to Wickford from London, but was a welcome addition to the Weaver family. "We'll have a great time," I assured him, my fingertips crackling with magic as I prepared to cast my spell.

The bow of the boat, sixty feet to my front, neared the bridge, and I concentrated hard. Portals were normally opened in doorways, but Maeve had promised my mother that a portal could be opened in anything which was considered an entrance. I tasted the familiar metallic copper flavour in my mouth which accompanied any spell I cast, and forced the build-up of magic from my fingertips.

The water beneath the bridge churned and a warm breeze blew from the space between the cold damp walls of the archway. A soft gold light hovered in the entrance, and spread slowly until it filled the space below the bridge. "It worked!" I shouted.

"Good luck!" yelled Susie, as the bow of the boat slid into the light.

I concentrated on keeping the steering tiller in position as I nudged the power leaver forward a fraction, giving The Water Witch the extra power she'd need to remain on a straight course. The breeze grew stronger and my long dark hair lifted from my shoulders. I shielded my eyes from the leaves which the wind blew from the trees, and shouted a final farewell to the two people on the bridge as *The Water Witch* was completely enveloped by the shimmering wall of gold.

WIND and bright light made it hard to keep the boat's course straight, but almost as soon as I'd entered the portal, I was steering the boat along an unfamiliar but beautiful stretch of water. "Is everyone okay down there?" I shouted, slowing the boat and guiding the bow towards the bank-side.

"We're just dandy!" shouted Boris. "Are we there yet?"

"Yes!" I shouted, "come on up."

The bow of the boat nudged the bank and I leapt ashore with two iron mooring hoops which slid easily into the soft earth. I hammered them home with the mallet Willow tossed ashore, and tied off the bow and stern ropes.

"It's beautiful here" said Barney stepping ashore and

offering Granny a steadying hand as she climbed from the boat. "It's *really* beautiful."

He was right. The stretch of water we were on was wider than the narrow canals I was used to navigating at home, reminding me of the River Thames in its middle course. The banks were alive with lush foliage and fragrant wildflowers, and a fat trout leapt for a fly which hovered suicidally close to the surface of the pristine water. Swallows dipped and dived as they caught insects on the wing, and a frog croaked from its hidden position in a clump of bull rushes.

On my first trip to The Haven I'd noted how clean and alive with life the magical dimension was, putting me in mind of the paintings I'd seen of England in the days before pollution had poisoned the landscape and waterways. It truly was a beautiful place, and a peaceful serenity washed over me as I imagined journeying along the river. I closed my eyes and took a deep breath of the sweet-smelling air, enjoying the sun on my face and the sound of birds and insects.

"Why does the sky seem a little red?" said Boris, leaping gracefully from *The Water Witch* and gazing at the scenery.

The peachy tint to the sky was strongest where the snowy peaks of distant mountains touched the sky, but the whole vast sky had a slight reddish hue to it. I'd noticed it when I was last in The Haven, but there had been far more important things to concentrate on than the colour of the sky.

Mum joined us on the shore and scooped her long dark hair behind her head, gathering it into a ponytail which she tied with a bobble she took from her pocket. "The sky is red," she said, "because as Maeve was being burned alive at the stake — she closed her eyes and prepared to die. The red of the sky is the colour of the flames which she could see through her eyelids. It's said that the pain she experienced as the flames began burning her is what caused all her magic to explode form her in a fraction of a second — creating The

Haven and transporting her to safety. She's lucky to be alive, but what she created when she thought she was going to die, not only saved her life, but the lives of countless other persecuted witches who fled to The Haven after her. It's quite a story, and we should feel very honoured to be standing here."

Granny gave a low snigger. "It's okay here, but it's certainly no Oz. Now *that's* a place which would impress me. If I was to conjure up a magical land I'd fashion it after Oz, populating it with a mixture of folk, but I'd most certainly throw in a few short fellows who'd dance, sing, and jump at my every command. It does the soul good to look down on others every now and again — both figuratively and literally. No flying monkeys though, those buggers would cause havoc with a banana plantation, and I'd be sure to plant a few of those. And a pear orchard. I like pears. I like Oz."

Boris lifted his nose from the flower he was smelling. "Is that how you see me, Gladys? As somebody you can look down on?"

Granny placed a hand on the goat's back. "You know that's not how I feel about you, Boris. I treat you with the respect and dignity you deserve."

Boris stamped a hoof and snorted. "Then why didn't you take the dementia cure when I asked you to?"

Granny bristled. "This is not the time or place for this conversation, Boris. We're in the company of others."

Mum frowned and gave Granny a stern stare, but just as she was about to speak, the air around us crackled and fizzed. Boris took a few stumbling steps backward and Barney jumped. Two billowing clouds of red smoke swirled into existence in front of us, and in a fraction of a second, with a loud popping sound, there were two extra people in our group.

Maeve and Derek stood side by side, up to their knees in grass, the smoke dispersing around them. Derek carried the staff he'd used to cast a spell over a field full of people the last time we'd seen him, and Maeve gave us a wide friendly smile. "Thank you all for coming," she said. She turned her attention to Barney. "Especially you, lawman. Our need is dire, and you are the only person equipped with the skills to solve a mystery which no amount of magic can help us with."

"Skills," muttered Granny. "I've seen more skills in a circus monkey."

Derek slammed his staff into the river-bank. "Silence, Gladys Weaver. Show some respect to the creator of The Haven!"

Granny narrowed her eyes. "I respect Maeve," she said, "but I find it hard to respect a man who until very recently called himself The Copper Haired Wizard of The West." She turned her back on Maeve and Derek and clambered aboard *The Water Witch*. "Would you be so kind as to accompany me, Boris?" she said. "We should talk."

Boris gave Maeve what was an attempt at an apologetic grin, but was a grimace of yellowed teeth. "Please excuse me, your honour," he said.

Maeve tilted her and gave a gentle laugh, her long blond hair shining in the sunlight. "Call me Maeve, please. We don't stand on formalities here."

Boris bent his front legs and lowered his chest to the ground in a bow, and Willow hid a giggle behind her hand. The white goat leapt aboard the boat and followed Granny below deck, grumbling to himself as his hind quarters disappeared.

"Gladys Weaver is a rude woman," said Derek. "I don't know why you invited her here, Maeve. It was a blessing when she was struck with dementia and couldn't open her own entry portal. Things have been… peaceful around here without her. If I had my way she'd still be banished from The Haven."

"Well you don't have it your way, Derek!" snapped Maeve. "Every witch is special in my eyes and Gladys is no exception. You'll have to put the past behind you and make your peace with her."

Derek and Gladys had butted heads in the past when Derek, during his time as The Copper Haired Wizard of The West, had cast a community of Haitian Voodoo witches from his lands and conjured a wall of magic to keep them out. Granny had not liked the injustice and had formed a group of witches known as the SJW's — or Social Justice Witches — eventually forcing Derek to tear down the wall. Granny's time as a social justice activist had culminated in her being banished from The Haven for a period of time, and it seemed that Derek still held a grudge.

Derek huffed. "Don't you find it odd that she hasn't taken the cure for her dementia yet, Maeve?" he said, twisting his staff into the ground, the jewels set in the carved knob glinting in the sun. "It was very kind of you to give it to her, I'd have thought she'd have used it by now — don't you?"

Maeve closed her eyes for a moment. "It's her choice, Derek, but yes, I happen to agree with you. I was surprised to see the Chinese acupuncturist still trapped in the body of a goat — as soon as Gladys takes the cure he'll be freed, and I'd have thought that would be best for all concerned. Things will happen in their own time, though. We should allow fate to run its course."

"But —"

"Enough, Derek. We can't force our will on people." Maeve looked at each of us in turn. "Rumour has it that Eva has prepared a welcome feast for the hungry travellers, and Derek and I have been invited. How about we all climb aboard that beautiful boat of yours, Penelope? Eva's village is only two miles downstream and I'd love a trip on *The Water*

Witch. We can discuss the reason I've asked for your help over a plate of your aunt's fine cooking."

"I'll meet you there," said Derek, straightening his colourful patchwork jacket. "I'll not be getting on that contraption. Why not use magic if you have it?"

Derek vanished in a cloud of smoke, and Maeve smiled. "I'm sorry about Derek," she said. "He's old fashioned. He doesn't feel I should be asking for the help of a mortal to solve a haven problem." She smiled at Barney. "No offense meant, Lawman Barney. You're a fine mortal indeed."

"None taken," said Barney, offering Maeve his hand. "Let me help you aboard. You'll love the boat."

CHAPTER THREE

On my first visit to The Haven I'd eaten a meal at the table situated amongst the trees in the orchard at the bottom of Aunt Eva's cottage garden. I'd had no idea that beyond the orchard ran a river, and as I steered the boat alongside the bank I found myself looking forward to the day in the distant future on which I'd move to The Haven on a permanent basis. I'd live in a cottage just like Aunt Eva's, and moor my boat at the foot of my garden — ready for the regular trips along the river I imagined myself taking during my immortal existence in the magical dimension.

Maeve had driven the boat for most of the short journey and had laughed with joy as *The Water Witch* had responded to the instructions she gave it through the steering tiller. Her face was tinted with a happy red blush as she climbed ashore and helped Barney tie the boat to the trunks of two trees whose lowest branches dipped their leaves in the water. "That was the most fun I've had in a long time!" she said, tying a firm knot in the rope and moving aside as Boris leapt ashore.

AN EYE FOR AN EYE

Boris and Granny had spent the journey in Willow's bedroom, at the bow end of the boat, speaking about the issue they so obviously had between them. I didn't ask them what was wrong, neither did Mum, Barney or Willow — we'd been enjoying ourselves far too much to worry about a disagreement between Boris and Granny. Over the last few months, since Charleston had been magicked into the body of Boris the goat, the pair had had at least three disagreements a week. The only thing different about this one was that it seemed more personal. I made a mental note to bring it up with Granny when I had her on my own.

I studied Barney as he gazed around. He was still coming to terms with the fact that he was in a magical dimension, the existence of which he'd only been made aware of two short weeks ago. We'd told him to curb his excitement a little when he came to The Haven, because if he wanted to be taken seriously, he couldn't act like a child on his first trip to a toy shop. He was doing a good job so far, but it was easy to sense his awe. His eyes glinted with excitement and his nose twitched as the aroma of cooking drifted through the trees which hid Aunt Eva's garden from view.

Boris was way ahead of Barney. "I smell Italian food," he said, licking his lips and wetting the hairs which formed his beard. "I'm quite the fan of Italian food." He gave Granny a sideways look. "If it's prepared correctly of course."

Granny's blue rinse perm bounced as she approached Boris at speed. "Was that meant as a dig at me, Boris?" she said, bending at the waist and staring the animal in the eyes. "It had better not be, because I put everything into making that spaghetti bolognese for you. I can't help it if you're a fussy eater!"

Boris took a step backwards. "You used child's spaghetti in tomato sauce, Gladys. From a tin! The type shaped like letters, and you didn't even ensure I had the letters on my plate to spell out *this meal sucks big time*. It was hardly fine Mediterranean dining!"

"We were on holiday. In a caravan," said Granny. "I did what I could, besides — I never got much practice at making fancy nancy dishes — Norman, rest his soul, was a simple man. He liked his meat and two potatoes, and he didn't whine if the gravy had lumps in it! He didn't pester me for posh nosh. He was happy with what he got!"

Maeve clapped, the sound startling a frog from a lily pad. "Please," she said, "stop that at once. The Haven is a place of peace, most of the time. Save your arguments for later and concentrate on being nice to one another." She took a step along the overgrown pathway which disappeared into the trees. "Come on. If we're not quick, Derek will have eaten all the food before we even get to the table."

We formed a line behind Maeve and followed her along the narrow pathway as the sound of a woman's laughter grew louder.

"That's my sister's flirting giggle," said Granny from behind me. "I may not have seen her for some time, but I can tell from a mile away when she's trying to get her claws into a man. She's in her young body too — that laugh gives it away."

The pathway opened into a clearing and it seemed that Granny's observation had been correct. Sitting at the large wooden table among the fruit trees and wild flowers was Hilda — the elderly seer who had foretold of my power to see the future, Derek — who was chewing on a mouthful of food, and my Aunt Eva — looking more beautiful than I'd ever seen her. When a witch is given their Haven entry spell, they're also afforded the gift of being able to transform themselves between the age they were when they moved

AN EYE FOR AN EYE

from the mortal world for good, and the age they were when they were granted their haven entry spell, *and* any age in between. Aunt Eva had been nineteen when she'd acquired her spell, and she'd chosen to be young today, unlike the last time I'd visited The Haven — when she'd remained in the body of the eighty-nine-year-old she'd been when she chose to make The Haven a permanent home. She looked to be in her early twenties today — a good couple of decades younger than the man she was trying to impress. Though most of Aunt Eva's body was hidden by the table, it was apparent from whom Willow had inherited her shapely figure. Aunt Eva's cleavage burst at the low-cut blouse she wore, and she pressed up close to Derek, filling his plate with offerings from the many dishes and plates which filled the table top.

"Look at that alleyway hussy!" hissed Granny. "All over Derek like he was the last man alive. It's disgusting!"

Mum pushed passed us, spurred on by the sight of the feast. "Try not to be jealous, Mother. Just because your dementia stops you shifting to a younger body, doesn't mean everyone else has to stay old and wrinkly."

Granny laughed. "At least you're admitting you're wrinkly, dear. It's about time."

"I wasn't talking about myself," snorted Mum. "I'm hardly old, and I'm staying this age out of respect for my daughters. They don't want their mother outshining them in the looks department."

"And the weight department," said Granny. "You were even tubbier when you were younger. Like a fatted piglet. A cute one, but a wobbly one too."

Mum chose to ignore Granny and took a seat at the table, giving the young Aunt Eva a kiss and smiling at Hilda who adjusted the bejeweled eye-patch she wore. I'd learned on my first meeting with Hilda that the eye-patch was for purely decorative purposes, but I had to admit that it did a good job in giving her the aura of mystery which I imagined was a great aid in her existence as a seer of the future.

Granny sat down and scowled at her sister. "You're looking… nice today, Eva. Ashamed of your real age?"

Eva smiled. "It's lovely to see you too, dear sister. How's the dementia?"

Granny mumbled something and helped herself to a large scoop of lasagne. "It's a good job for you that I can't take on my younger form," she said. "I always was the better looking one."

"Granny," said Willow. "You're sisters. You shouldn't be competing with each other!"

Eva laughed and Derek rolled his eyes, popping an olive in his mouth and pushing Aunt Eva's hand away from his arm. "Enough bickering," he said. "I'm trying to eat."

Boris's hooves scrambled for purchase in the grass as Hilda slammed her fist into the table top and screeched. "Danger!" she warned. "Danger!"

Barney leapt to his feet and drew his nightstick, brandishing the weapon above his head. "Where?" he said, twisting his head left and right.

"Calm down everybody," said Maeve, her voice as soft as butter. "Hilda's had a vision." She looked at the old woman. "Is that right, Hilda?"

Hilda nodded. "I see danger greeting you on your journey," she half whispered, looking at each of us in turn.

I grabbed Barney's wrist. "Sit down," I said as he put his nightstick away. "It's okay."

Hilda closed her one visible eye and sighed. "I see romance blossoming too. I see pure love on the horizon."

Barney took my hand and squeezed it, making me blush.

Maeve picked up on my unease and ushered the seer on.

AN EYE FOR AN EYE

"The danger you spoke of is more relevant, Hilda. Tell us more," she said.

Derek grunted. "Are we really going to listen to the ramblings of Hilda?" he said. "If we took everything Hilda said seriously we'd all be hiding under our beds."

"Yes, we are, Derek," snapped Maeve. "Show some respect."

Hilda continued, slowly swaying her torso from side to side as she spoke. "I see danger and love, and I see a man with coal black hair. Beware of him, for he means ill-will to all." She paused for a moment and took a deep breath. "I see great power too, power greater than Maeve's. The power is so great that the person who wields it will rule The Haven if they so choose."

Derek leaned forward in his seat. "Tell us more, Hilda."

"You've changed your tune," said Granny.

"I've heard of this power before," explained Derek. "In an ancient prophecy. If the power Hilda speaks of threatens Maeve's control over The Haven, then it's prudent that we listen."

"I see no more," said Hilda with a shake of her head. "Though you must heed my words."

"Duly noted," said Derek, pushing his plate way from him and taking a small metal tin from his breast pocket. He prised it open and withdrew a small twig which he placed between his teeth and began to chew.

Boris raised his head from the plate of cold meats and salad he was eating. "Liquorice root?" he said, sniffing the air. "Would you be so kind as to allow me one, Derek? I've not had one in years, and I find they cleanse the palate rather well."

Derek raised an eyebrow and took another twig from the tin, tossing it into the grass in front of Boris. "Be my guest," he said, as the goat gripped the stick in his mouth and settled down in the wild flowers to chew. Derek held the tin out. "Anybody else?" he said.

He put the tin away when nobody else took him up on his offer, and watched Barney with amusement as the policeman took his notebook and pencil out and cleared his throat.

"I feel it's my duty to ask some questions," he said, with a nervous strain in his voice. "After all, I was asked to come here to help solve a mystery, but so far, I've been given no indication as to what that mystery is, and we've just been told by a fortune teller that there's danger waiting for us."

Hilda gasped. "I'm no fortune teller, fire haired man of the law. I'm a seer! I require no recompense for my visions. A fortune teller would demand you cross her palm with silver before telling you of your fate, but I do it from the goodness of my heart. I've never been so offended."

"He meant no offence, Hilda," said Maeve, gently. "But Barney is right — it's about time I told everyone why I've asked for their help."

Maeve's forehead creased and everybody quietened down, even Granny, who was informing Aunt Eva that her makeup was sixty-years out of style. The powerful witch took a breath and began speaking. "As you all know." She looked at Barney and Boris. "As *most* of you know, I'm aware of most things that happen in this land. I'm tied to the very essence of the place by invisible strands of energy which keep me informed of happenings." She looked at Granny with an accusatory gleam in her eyes. "That *doesn't* mean I spy on people, despite some folk organising protests in the past which falsely stated the opposite. It means I know if people are in trouble, or if somebody new arrives in The Haven... or, if somebody leaves."

"Yes, we get it," said Granny. "You're the all-seeing eye."

Maeve took Granny's comment in her stride, and chose not to respond. "I should say, I *normally* know when some-

AN EYE FOR AN EYE

body has left The Haven. It's just a feeling I get — one less soul feeding on the magic in the air." Her face darkened. "But recently, some people have been reported missing by their families. You must understand that this sort of thing never happens. People report other people for crimes they've committed, but not for —"

"And for crimes they *haven't* committed," interrupted Granny, her arms crossed and her purple glasses teetering on the tip of her nose.

"You were found guilty of every crime you were ever accused of, Gladys Weaver," scoffed Derek. "*And* some you weren't accused of, but boasted about when you'd had too much wine to keep your mouth shut."

"Enough... please," said Maeve. "People are missing, and they may be in danger."

Barney put the tip of his pencil to paper. "Can you give me some more details please?" he said, his eyes narrowed with concern.

Maeve gave a small nod. "As I said, this is new to us in The Haven. I'm glad to see you're eager to help us, lawman Barney."

"I'm happy to," said Barney.

Maeve continued. "Six witches have vanished off the face of the..." She looked at Derek.

"Radar," he obliged.

"Yes, radar. I try to keep up with the modern parlance of the other world, but it becomes confusing. Anyway, witches began disappearing five months ago, and the sixth one went missing just yesterday. They all resided in The City of Shadows, but aside from that we have no other information. I'm sure they couldn't have left The Haven, as I'd have been aware that they passed through a portal, but neither do I feel like they're *in* The Haven. It's a mystery. There are places in The Haven that my magic can't penetrate for reasons unbeknown to me, but people have searched those areas, and have found no sign of the missing witches." She stared at Barney. "Would your investigative skills be of use to us, lawman?"

"I can do my best," said Barney, "I'd need more information of course."

"We have no more information, Lawman. I would suggest you make your way to The City of Shadows and do what you must do to help. We'll pay for your services of course — whether you solve the mystery or not."

Barney put his notebook away and shook his head. "I don't want your payment," he said. "Helping you would be a pleasure."

"We'll discuss it again at a later date," said Maeve. "Meanwhile, let me give you all something to take with you." She handed each of us a small black stone and passed Granny a silver ring to hang from Boris's red collar. "Although I can sense where you'll be while you're in The Haven, I'd like you to carry these. They'll allow me to find you quickly if anything should happen," she said. "They won't work in the parts of The Haven in which my magic can't penetrate, and no magic can be used in those places, but there is only one such area on your route along the river — the Silver Mountains, it should take you half a day to reach them, and then a further half day to reach The City of Shadows."

"Or we could just magic them all there and leave the boat here," said Derek. "That would be my decision."

Maeve sighed. "It's not your decision, Derek. They want to see the sights of The Haven along the way, I'm sure, and it will give them the chance to look out for our missing witches along the route."

Barney stood up. "We should leave right away. Those people could be in trouble."

"I'm ready to go," said Willow, arranging her knife and

fork on her empty plate. "I can't wait to see more of The Haven."

I agreed. "We've still got hours of daylight left, we'll travel until dusk and find somewhere to moor up for the night."

Maeve got to her feet. "Although The Haven is a safe place," she said, "be aware of your surroundings. There are dangers here — some I'm aware of and, others I'm yet to experience."

"What sort of dangers?" said Willow.

"When I magicked this land into existence," said Maeve, "everything I knew about the world was recreated here, and you must understand that back in those times, we had a very different understanding of your world."

"She means she believed in dragons," sniggered Granny, "and dwarfs — and I don't mean real dwarfs like Big Jim back in Wickford. He's harmless enough when he's not drunk and angry. I mean dwarfs like the ones in books — the type who live in mines and chop people's heads off for looking at them wrong."

"I'm afraid it's true," said Maeve. "Everything I believed in during my time in the other world, now resides here. Don't be alarmed though. The last dwarf war ended three-hundred years ago, and no dragons have ever been seen — their existence is pure speculation based on my belief system when The Haven was conjured into being."

"Could any of these creatures be responsible for the disappearance of the witches?" said Barney, his voice catching in his throat. "Because I'm a policeman, not a dragon slayer, and I'm far too tall to pick on a dwarf. It wouldn't be fair!"

"It would be oppressive," agreed Granny.

Maeve put a reassuring hand on Barney's arm. "Be calm, lawman. If that were the case I would know. The missing witches have the magic to protect themselves from such creatures, as do the witches you travel with. The answer to the mystery of the missing witches will be found among other witches. Of that I'm sure. Worry not, Barney. The creatures spoken of are rare, and most of them mean no harm anyway. Go now, and travel well. Find my missing witches."

CHAPTER FOUR

Maeve, Aunt Eva, and Derek waved us off, with Maeve reminding us that if we needed her help all we needed to do was think about her while holding one of the stones she'd given us. Derek and aunt Eva headed back towards Aunt Eva's garden as soon as the boat was a few metres downstream, but Maeve remained on the bankside, watching us until we'd rounded a bend in the river.

"Brandy time!" said Boris, as the river widened and the banks thickened with trees. "Gladys, my good lady, would you do the honours please?"

It seemed that Granny and Boris had put their differences aside, and Barney helped Granny onto the flat roof of the boat and lifted Boris up after her. Granny moved a few of the potted plants and herbs aside, and laid a blanket on the sun-warmed roof for the two of them to sit on. With a bottle of brandy between them, and clouds of smoke billowing from the cigar which was clamped safely in the vice which had once been used by my grandfather to tie fishing flies, but had been commandeered by Boris as a smoking aid, the two of them laughed and joked as *The Water Witch* swallowed up the peaceful miles.

"This is nice," said Barney, standing next to me at the steering tiller.

He'd changed out of his police uniform on the sage advice of Maeve. Contrary to what Granny had said, Maeve had explained that it would be better if Barney drew no attention to himself in The Haven. People had an innate nervousness around anybody who represented authority — in our real world, and in The Haven, she'd said. He looked far more suited to a trip along a river on a sunny day while dressed in a t-shirt and shorts anyway. His stab jacket had begun to make him sweat, and his boots had trampled dried soil all over the boat's clean decking. The flip flops which adorned his feet would necessitate a lot less sweeping up after him.

"It is nice," I agreed, raising my voice to compete with the throb of the diesel engine beneath our feet. I took a sip of wine and enjoyed the warm tendrils which spread through my limbs. My homemade elderberry wine was strong, and I'd never have drunk any while driving my boat in the mortal world, but despite the fact we were on a journey to look for missing witches, we were all in vacation mode. Besides, the river was a lot wider than the canals I was used to navigating, and I was certain that I'd be able to polish off a whole bottle of wine before I turned the boat into a collision risk.

Mum and Willow were below deck, finalising the sleeping arrangements, and their raised voices could be heard every now and again as each of them tried to assert dominance over the other. It would be hard for Willow — she'd only been living on the boat for a few weeks, and already she was having to give her bedroom up for somebody else. We'd decided that Granny and Mum would share Willow's bedroom, and Willow would sleep with me. Barney would have to make do with the fold down dinette furniture, and Boris would be happy to curl up on a blanket.

Barney pointed into the distance. "Is that a village?" he asked, squinting his eyes against the bright light of the sun.

He was right. It was a village. The riverbanks had been steadily opening up into rolling pastures on one side of the river, as the opposite bank gave way to the foothills of the looming mountains, which had been getting nearer as every minute passed. The slight silver colouration of the rock formations gave us a clue that we were approaching the Silver Mountains which Maeve had told us about.

The small village was comprised of a handful of thatched cottages, some of them with smoke pouring from the chimneys, unchallenged by wind until it reached high into the sky. Children gathered on the sandy beach, shouting greetings and waving at us as we passed.

An elderly man in a fishing coracle paddled out of our path and tipped his hat as he reeled in a trout, which he tossed at his feet to join the others which were soon going to be somebody's dinner.

"I'd have thought it would be a little more magical here," said Barney, as we left the village behind. "Everyone seems to be living normal lives, surely they could magic the fish out of the river if they wanted to?"

"Where would the fun be in that?" said Granny, watching us from the roof of the boat. "These people accept magic as normal, it's more of a novelty to them to do things without magic. That's why handmade things and food grown from scratch rule the economy. If anybody can conjure up a nice hat, then one that's been handmade is worth a lot more. Possessing a practical skill goes a long way in The Haven. They'll enjoy eating those fish far more than they would if they'd blasted them from the water with a spell."

Barney sipped his wine. "I understand that," he said.

"There's something primal about catching your own food. I used to love fishing when I was a child. I kind of miss it."

I smiled. "In the storage compartment on the roof, there's a fishing rod and tackle. It was there when I bought the boat. I've never used it, why don't you try it out?"

Barney's eyes lit up. "I'll catch us some trout!" he said. "We can cook it over a campfire when we moor up for the night!"

He scrambled onto the roof and opened the storage box, the hinges giving a squeaking protest. "I'll use bread as bait," he said, jumping down next to me with the rod and tackle.

As Barney went about assembling the rod, I glanced at the sky. Dusk was falling and the mountains to our left cast a dark shadow over the river. "I'm going to take us ashore when I find a suitable spot," I said. "We're at The Silver Mountains. We'll stay here tonight and if we leave early enough in the morning, we'll be in The City of Shadows by midday."

A LARGE FLAT rock made a perfect natural jetty to moor the boat alongside, and a sandy beach surrounded by ancient trees with an open pasture beyond, made the perfect spot to relax in. The Silver Mountains rose from the ground about a mile away, and the river gurgled gently as it meandered past. Barney had dug up some worms when it quickly became obvious that the trout in the river weren't big fans of bread, and he'd proudly delivered three fat fish which he'd cleaned and de-scaled ready for cooking.

Mum had been the first to try and light a fire using magic, and then Willow and I had both tried, none of us being able to conjure a single spark from our fingertips.

"Remember what Maeve said," commented Boris,

watching us with amusement. "Magic doesn't work in the Silver Mountains. You'll have to do it the old-fashioned way."

With firewood collected and with the use of matches from the boat, we soon had a roaring fire lit, which we sat around watching the fish cook on spits while we drank.

"Would anybody like some elderberry wine?" I offered, as dusk gave way to a starry moonlit sky.

Several bottles of my homemade wine still filled a storage rack aboard the boat, and it seemed that it was only me who truly appreciated its deep natural flavours. The berries had been picked under a full moon, and I was beginning to think that my sense of taste was vastly more advanced than the people's around me.

Boris snorted and looked up, the reflections of the flames dancing in his eyes. "I'll stick with my brandy, thank you, Penelope," he said.

Granny giggled, the brandy she'd been drinking all day cheering her up. "I'm very proud of you, Penelope, you know that, don't you?"

I raised an eyebrow. "I think so."

"You're a trier," she said, "but please don't try your hand at wine making again. That stuff is just filthy."

I ignored everyone's laughter and took a long swallow of wine. It meant more of it for me, and I was sure it was healthier than the array of drinks which everyone else was sipping.

I licked my lips as Barney turned the trout, the skin splitting and browning as the flesh softened. It smelt better than any shop bought fish I'd cooked. Barney glanced behind me at the open grassland at the foot of the mountains. "What are they?" he said, standing up for a better view. "Fireflies? I've never seen a firefly!"

I turned to look. Rising from the grasses and floating

from the shadowy silhouettes of trees were dozens of bright lights which dropped, rose and bobbed left and right.

"Do they bite?" said Boris. "They'd better not bite! It's no fun being a goat when there's biting insects around." He looked at Granny. "Did you bring my antihistamine cream, Gladys? I really don't want a repeat of the horsefly incident, and I truly don't relish the thought of you slavering ointment on my… *you know whats* again."

"You should have seen how the bite swelled up," said Granny, smiling at us. "It was like he had three balls, wasn't it, Boris?"

"Thank you, Gladys," said Boris. "You've painted a pretty picture in the minds of my peers."

"You're welcome," said Granny, ignoring Willow's laughter.

"Wait!" said Mum, sitting up straight and staring at the lights which were slowly approaching. "Those aren't fireflies. They're… fairies! I'd heard they lived in The Haven, but I've never seen one before!"

Glee bubbled in my stomach. I'd spent hours as a child searching for fairies at the bottom of Mum's garden. "Fairies! Really?" I said. "Oh, my goddess!"

The lights stopped moving when they were less than ten metres away, and when I squinted I was able to make out the blur of tiny wings through the bright lights. A small female voice called out to us, the vowels in the words rising and falling in pitch like a song. "May we approach?"

Boris leapt to his feet and clamped his rear legs together. "Do you bite?" he asked. "Because if you do, there's a fly swat aboard the boat which Gladys won't be afraid to use!"

A gentle sing-song of murmurs spread between the fairies. "We are not heathens," said the female voice. "We are the fairy clan of the Silver Mountains, and we've been drawn to you by the fragrant perfume you possess."

"That'll be my Chanel number five," said Granny, sniffing her wrist. "I won it in a bingo game on holiday, didn't I, Boris?"

"You pulled the chair from beneath the old man sitting next to you and stole his full house ticket, Gladys," said Boris, "but if we're not splitting hairs, then yes, you won it."

Granny stood up. "You may approach, fairies of the Silver Mountains, and appreciate my perfume further."

More murmuring spread through the swarm of fairies, until two small shapes broke free from the rest of the group and tentatively approached us, heading in my direction. As they neared, their forms became clearer, and I swallowed a delighted giggle when I realised they were just how I'd always imagined fairies to be. One fairy was female, her skin a silvery blue and her tiny dress sparkling with incandescent light, and the other was male, dressed in a silver robe which flowed behind him as he flew. Both wore delicate necklaces of intricate designs, and the female's golden hair was adorned with tiny jewels. Their shimmering light dimmed as they neared me, and their wings buzzed slower as they came to a halt. They stopped inches from my face and studied me, their smiles wide and their small eyes kind. The female bowed in the air. "I am Breena, queen of the Silver Mountain fairies, and this is my king, Trevor."

"Trevor?" said Boris. "Is that even a fairy name? That's the name of a pub landlord, or a used car salesman."

The king span in the air and pointed at Boris. "Your livestock insults me," he said. "Silence the beast. Or he'll be on my spit before this night is over."

"How dare you!" said Granny. "You jumped up little flying bastard! Boris isn't livestock, he's a wonderful and kind spirit."

Breena put a small hand on Trevor. "Don't start arguments, Trevor, or you'll be sleeping on the chaise lounge tonight. Apologise to these people and their goat right away!"

Trevor blushed a pinky red. "I'm sorry," he said, lowering his voice. He cast a glance at the fairies who still hovered a short distance away. "I have to look the part in front of my clan," he nervously explained. "I was showing off. Please accept my humblest apologies."

"Accepted," said Boris.

"Y'all are forgiven," said Granny, slipping into the American slang she had a habit of using when she was drunk.

Breena raised her voice and addressed the other fairies. "Leave us, clan. We are safe among these kind people and their spirited goat. Go about your night, and know we are safe."

"You'll bring some back for us, won't you?" came a male voice, which was surprisingly deep for such a small life form. "It was me that smelt it in the first place. I should get a share!"

"We'll see!" said Breena. "Now go, and be on the lookout for the horsemen of the deep. They may travel tonight."

The remainder of the clan did as their queen asked and their lights dimmed as they flew into the distance.

"Urm," said Barney, staring at the two fairies with childlike wonder in his eyes. "The horsemen of the what now?"

"Horsemen of the deep," said Trevor, his eyes on my glass. "Dear lady," he said, bringing his eyes to mine. "Would it be rude of me to ask that my queen and I may sample some of the fragrant perfume you possess?"

"Urm," repeated Barney. "Horsemen of the deep? They sound…scary?"

"The worse," said Breena. She dropped from the sky and landed on my knee, standing next to my wine glass. "May I taste some?" she said. "It smells divine."

"It's alcoholic you understand?" I said. "It's a drug."

AN EYE FOR AN EYE

"Horsemen?" said Barney.

Breena looked up at Barney. "We will speak with you of the horsemen of the deep when our mouths have been wet with the divine liquid captured within this good lady's drinking receptacle."

Trevor dropped from the air and joined his queen on my knee. "I'm gagging for a taste," he said. "It smells so good. May I partake?"

"If fairies can handle alcohol, you're welcome to some," I said.

Trevor laughed. "How else are we supposed to get shit-faced?" he said.

"Language, Trevor!" snapped Breena. "These are refined people. They won't enjoy your foul mouth."

Willow laughed and passed me the lid from a bottle. "Pour some in here for them, Penny," she suggested.

The two fairies fluttered to the floor as I filled the lid and laid it on the sand. Trevor tasted the wine first, dipping his lips to the surface and taking a long swallow. "Delicious," he said. "Who is the winemaker responsible for this drink of the gods?"

Breena took a sip and sighed. "This is fine wine indeed. It was made by the hands of an expert."

"I made it," I said, brimming with pride. "I picked the berries under a full moon!"

Granny snorted, and Barney put an arm around my shoulder.

"I can taste the moonlight," said Trevor, licking his lips. "And a hint of vanilla?"

"Yes!" I said, smiling at Barney. "Can you taste strawberry too? I added a little to sweeten it."

Trevor took another long gulp. "The strawberry makes it what it is, young lady. You possess a remarkable skill."

"Good grief," said Mum. "The wine tastes vile. What's wrong with you, fairies?"

Trevor and Breena ignored her and continued to sip the wine, making appreciative sounds and smiling up at me.

"The fish is done," said Granny. "Who's hungry?"

As Granny passed plates of fish around, including a small portion for Breena and Trevor to share, an echoing horn blew in the distance, startling the two fairies and making the hairs on the back of my neck rise.

"The horsemen of the deep!" shouted Trevor, a tremor in his voice. "Tonight, they hunt!"

CHAPTER FIVE

"We must leave," said Breena, taking a last sip of wine. "Would you be so kind as to send us on our travels with a little of your fine wine? The rest of the clan would truly appreciate it." She flew to an unopened bottle of wine which lay in the sand, and landed on the cork. "This bottle would do nicely. It would last us for days."

"I'm not sure you could carry it," I said. "It's very heavy."

"We are imbued with a strength far greater than our stature would suggest," said Breena. "Transporting this bottle will be an easy feat for us."

"Then you're welcome to it," I said, happy that at last I'd found wine connoisseurs equal to my own high calibre.

The horn sounded again, echoing over the grassland and reverberating in my ears.

Trevor's face whitened. "Hurry," he said, fluttering to the bottle to join his queen. "The horsemen approach! We must take our prize and leave."

Breena withdrew a length of silver strand from a pocket hidden deep in her dress, and proceeded to wrap it around the neck of the bottle while Trevor scanned the dark distance for danger. When the twine was firmly in place, the fairies each held an end, and with no visible exertion, lifted the bottle into the air.

"Wait a cotton-picking minute!" said Granny, leaping to her feet and grabbing the wine bottle, stopping the fairies in mid-flight. "You two aren't going anywhere until you tell us who the horsemen of the deep are! Who do you think you are? Fluttering over here like Mr and Mrs fancy pants, manipulating my granddaughter into handing over her wine, and then leaving when the going gets tough! Not on my nelly! You tell us if we're in danger from these horsemen, or I'll put you both *in* that wine bottle and keep you as pets!"

"You don't want to be her pet," said Boris.

Breena and Trevor tugged on the twine, their wings buzzing so quickly they were barely discernible. "At first, we thought you had come to trade with the horsemen," said Breena, giving the rope another tug. "This is where the horsemen meet the other boat to sell their goods. We assumed you were traders until you lit a fire. The horsemen deal in secrecy, and wouldn't allow a fiery beacon to draw attention to their dealings."

"They are a fearsome people indeed," said Trevor. "They wear clothes of metal and ride great steeds. They hunt us fairies, but have yet to capture one of our type. I would not like tonight to be any different. Give us our wine, and allow us to flee, for I hear the hooves of their stallions in the dry grass. They approach at speed!"

Barney took a step towards the grassland and cupped a hand to his ear. "I hear something," he said. "Like metal clanking."

"Their clothes of protection!" said Trevor, with panic in his voice. "Release the wine, old lady, and let us leave!"

"Let them go, Mother," said Mum. "They're terrified! Poor little things."

Granny reluctantly released the bottle, and the fairies flew away, dragging the wine between them. "Good luck, travellers!" shouted Trevor, as the two lights flitted between trees and were swallowed by the darkness as cloud cover hid the moon. "You will need it!"

Barney grabbed my wrist, pulling me to my feet and dragging me towards the boat. "Come on!" he said, "I'll start the engine. Let's get out of here. I didn't sign up for this mission to end up being murdered by horsemen!"

"Too late," said Boris, staring into the gloom. "They're here. I can smell them."

A loud snort from an animal shrouded in darkness confirmed the horsemen's presence, and the scraping sound of a sword been drawn from a scabbard made my blood run cold. "What do we do?" I said. "Magic won't work here! We're unprotected!"

"Everybody calm down," said Granny. "I'll deal with this." She took a few steps along the beach and spoke into the darkness. "Make yourselves known, vile horsemen!"

A low voice answered, the words muffled and echoing as if spoken from within a helmet. "I wouldn't say we're vile. Some of us may be a little uncouth, but vile is a very harsh word. Take it back at once!"

"Make yourselves shown!" said Granny, "and I'll reconsider my choice of word. Until I see you, I consider you vile."

"Don't antagonise them, Granny," said Willow. "They'll kill us!"

"We'll do no such thing!" said a high-pitched voice.

"Quiet, Bertram!" said the voice in the helmet. "Let me do the talking."

"Sorry," said Bertram, the sincerity evident in his tone.

Barney stepped next to Granny. "We heard a sword being drawn. If you mean us no harm, why are you armed?"

"That was me," said a third voice. "It wasn't a sword being

drawn, it was the pipe of peace. It's very long so I store it in a sword scabbard. Sorry for the misunderstanding. It's not the first time its happened."

"Who are you people?" said Granny. "Who are you, horsemen of the deep? Show yourselves!"

"You've been speaking to the fairies, haven't you?" said Bertram. "Only the fairies call us the horsemen of the deep. We live beneath the mountains, yes, but deep? Not really. We live in caves, I'd say we live just below ground level if I'm being totally transparent. Gossiping fairies — they really are a pain."

"Why do you hunt the fairies?" said Granny. "If you are a peaceful people, why would you pursue such small folk?"

"Were the fairies drunk?" said the helmeted person.

"They were on their way to being drunk," said Willow.

"The fairies of the Silver Mountains have a complicated relationship with alcohol," came a voice from the dark. "They like it a little too much, and the only time we chase them is when they steal our mead. It takes us months to make, and they'd clear us out in a night if we didn't see them off. Those fairies are their own worst enemies, and they leave a terrible mess after a night on the sauce. We once found King Trevor's underwear floating in a vat of our mead. We had to pour the whole batch away."

The clouds finished their journey across the moon, and Granny laughed as the area was bathed in a silver glow. "Stand down, everybody. I think we're safe."

Boris snorted. "Horsemen of the deep, my hairy backside!"

I stifled my own laughter. I was politer than Granny and Boris, but it *was* an amusing sight. Standing in a small semi-circle were three bedraggled donkeys, each carrying a dwarf on its back. Each dwarf wore a mismatched ensemble of dull silver armour, which clanked as they shifted nervously in

AN EYE FOR AN EYE

their saddles. The dwarf in the centre wore a helmet with a small slit to see out of, and the other two wore leather hats, buckled beneath their chins.

"You're dwarfs!" said Granny. "On donkeys! How wonderful!"

"And you're strangers on our land," said the helmeted dwarf, climbing from the saddle and jumping to the ground with a clang of metal. "Please, tell us who you are and what you desire. Are you here to buy our wares?"

Granny smiled. "I am Gladys Weaver, and these people are my family. I apologise for trespassing, sir, we needed somewhere to moor our boat for the night, and this was the perfect spot. We have no wish to buy your wares."

"Sir? I am no sir!" said the dwarf, removing the helmet and bowing. "I am Gretchen the bold of the Silver Mountains."

"You don't look bald," said Boris. "You've got a fine head of hair going on there, madam dwarf."

"Bold!" said Gretchen. "Not bald!"

"My apologies, your boldness," said Boris.

Granny wrung her hands and frowned. "I'm so sorry," she said. "How dare I assume your gender! You *must* believe that this isn't something I do regularly!"

"Be at peace, Gladys Weaver," said Gretchen. "You are forgiven." She addressed the other donkey riders. "Dismount, companions."

The other two dwarfs hopped from their donkeys and stepped into the golden ring of light cast by the fire. "Allow me to introduce Bertram and Ulric," said Gretchen. "My most trusted companions."

Bertram held up a long silver pipe. "It is our custom to welcome strangers with the pipe of peace. Would you do us the honour of joining us for a smoke of some happy herb?"

Granny rubbed her hands together. "I'm in," she said. "I

haven't had a good toke since January the first, nineteen-eighty-four."

"What?" said Mum. "You used to smoke cannabis?"

"It was a one off," said Granny. "Norman and I were celebrating the year we thought George Orwell's book would come true. It never did of course, unfortunately, but the ganja was good, and the living was easy."

"I'd like some too," said Boris. "Beats a cigar."

"Light the pipe of peace, Bertram!" said Gretchen, placing her helmet on the sand near the fire and sitting next to it. "We have new friends to make."

"Have they had too much?" said Bertram, throwing the skeleton of the trout he'd eaten into the fire. "They *look* like they've had too much."

"I'd say it looked that way," said Mum, shaking her head.

Gretchen took a long puff on the pipe and blew a perfect circle of smoke, scattering the mosquitoes which had gathered above her head. "We brought the strong stuff," she said. "It's not meant to be taken in such large quantities."

Boris and Granny had both taken drag after long drag on the pipe, while the rest of us had politely refused — with Barney needing to be reminded that he couldn't confiscate the drugs, or press charges against dwarfs of the Silver Mountains. He'd finally relented and sat back to watch Granny and Boris get high. It had been quite the show, and it seemed that they hadn't yet reached the crescendo. They lay in the sand, side by side, a few feet from the fire, Boris's hooves pointing heavenward, and Granny marvelling at the size of the moon. "I feel like I can touch it, Boris," she murmured. "I feel like I can touch the moon."

AN EYE FOR AN EYE

"You can do anything you put your mind to, Gladys," said Boris, waving a hoof left and right. "You're a special woman."

"Special, my foot," said Mum. "Irresponsible more like."

"Leave them to it," said Willow. "They'll frazzle out and fall asleep soon enough." She looked at Gretchen. "You mentioned selling wares. Are you dealers in the happy herb?"

Barney made a strangled sound in his throat, but managed to compose himself.

"No," said Gretchen. "We don't sell our happy herb. We give that away to anybody who requires it — happiness should be free for all. We sell the metals we mine from the mountains. The metals which give our home its name — the Silver Mountains."

"You sell silver?" said Mum. "You must be rich!"

"No, not silver," said Bertram. "We have no name for the metal we sell." He rapped his knuckles on his armoured chest plate. "This is made from the metal we mine."

"And that's only a recent development," said Ulric, the plait in his long beard swinging dangerously close to the fire as he tossed another log into the flames. "Nobody wanted our metal until a few months ago."

Barney leaned across me. "May I?" he said, forming a fist over Ulric's armour.

Ulric nodded. "Be my guest."

Barney tapped the metal and dragged his fingernail across it. Satisfied, he sat back. "I bet it's heavy to wear, isn't it?" he asked.

"Very heavy," said Gretchen. "But we're strong enough to shoulder the burden."

"It's lead," said Barney. "You really shouldn't be wearing it. It's poisonous if ingested."

"Those rules don't apply here, Barney," I reminded him. "Nobody gets ill in The Haven."

"Well, lead is not very protective either," said Barney,

undeterred. "It's too soft to stop a sword. It doesn't make very good armour."

"We do not wear it to deflect the blade of a weapon," said Gretchen. "We wear it to look good."

"It works," said Willow. "You look lovely."

Gretchen couldn't hide the smile that crept over her face. "How very kind of you to say," she said. "You're certainly people of high standing and fine manners." She passed the pipe of peace to Bertram, and looked at Mum. "Pray tell, what brings such well-mannered folk to our lands?"

"We're investigating a mystery," said Mum. "On behalf of Maeve. We're searching for six witches who have gone missing. They were last seen in the City of Shadows. We plan to arrive there tomorrow and begin our search."

Barney took the opportunity to exercise his policing muscles. "Have you heard or seen anything? Anything suspicious that might help us?"

Gretchen shook her head. "I'm sorry," she said. "Our lands are quiet, we are a simple folk who rarely see strangers, and we stay out of the business of the rest of The Haven. I'm afraid your questions are wasted on us."

"I understand," said Barney. "I'm sure we'll have more luck in the City of Shadows."

Ulric frowned. "Gretchen," he said. "What about those three lady witches who were bound and gagged in the boat of the man who buys our metal?"

Gretchen sighed and rolled her eyes. "I'm sorry," she said to Barney. "Forgive his stupidity." She knocked on Ulric's leather hat with her knuckles. "Hello? Anybody home? He asked if we'd seen anything suspicious, you silly dwarf."

"That is quite suspicious," said Barney, sitting up straight.

"Really?" said Gretchen.

Barney frowned. "You don't think that seeing three women tied up and gagged is suspicious?"

Gretchen's eyes clouded with confusion. "Why would it be? We assumed he was having trouble with his wenches. When our wenches misbehave, we tie them up and gag them until they *can* behave. Doesn't everybody?"

"Aren't you a wench, Gretchen?" said Willow. "What if you misbehaved? Would you be tied up too?"

Ulric and Bertram gasped in unison. "Gretchen is not a wench!" said Bertram, spittle flying from his mouth. "She is a lady! From a high family! How dare you!"

Barney held up a hand. "Stop, please. She didn't mean to be rude. We come from different cultures. In our culture, we don't tie women up, but that's not the point. What you've told us is *very* suspicious... please tell us more. Who is the man on the boat?"

"Don't tie naughty wenches up?" muttered Bertram. "Heathens."

"It was almost half a year ago when he first arrived," said Gretchen. "In a boat, as red as the morning sun. We were happy to sell him our metal — nobody had ever asked us for our metal before."

"Were the captive witches in his boat the first time he visited you?" asked Barney.

"Oh no," said Bertram. "He came a few more times before that night."

"What does he want your lead for?" asked Barney, his notebook and pencil in hand.

"He does not tell us," said Gretchen. "He buys a tonne in weight each time he visits."

"How does he pay for your metal?" said Willow. "With gold?"

"We don't swap metal for metal. We have no use for gold," said Ulric. "We are paid in condiments that are hard to come by in The Haven. Spices, pepper, mustard... all the things that finish a nice meal off. The mustard is particularly good

— especially on a salt baked trout. His payments have certainly changed our diets."

"They *certainly* have," said Bertram, rubbing a hand over his armour protected belly. "I've put pounds on since I discovered spicy food, and doesn't my donkey know it."

"He pays for the metal you've risked life and limb to mine from the mountains, with spices?" said Mum. "That hardly seems a fair swap."

"Not just condiments," said Gretchen. "He pays us with his promise too. The promise that when he acquires the one true power, he will bestow upon us such glory that the name of the dwarfs of the Silver Mountains will be forever enshrined in the folklore of The Haven. We will be a people to be reckoned with — his words, not mine, although I do like the way they roll off the tongue."

"Power?" said Barney. "What power?"

Gretchen shrugged. "We only know what he tells us."

"One true power!" said Mum. "Hilda warned us of a power! Her vision was correct!"

"Does the man have hair as black as coal?" said Barney, recalling Hilda's prophecy.

"I do not know. He shrouds himself in a hooded cloak as black as the depths of the night sky," said Gretchen. "But if he matches his clothes with his hair, there's a good chance his hair *is* black."

"And the witches in the boat?" said Willow. "Can you tell us anything about them?"

"It was a few weeks ago, and it was a very dark night," said Bertram. "They were chained up in a corner of the boat's hold. We didn't really pay them much attention. We assumed they'd been *very* mischievous. We helped the man load his metal and went on our way."

"How is it possible to imprison a witch?" said Barney. "Surely they could use magic to escape?"

AN EYE FOR AN EYE

"Not if the man had more powerful magic than the witches," said Mum. "It would be easy. He wouldn't need chains; a simple spell would capture them. The chains were to stop them escaping when he brought them here, where no magic can be used."

"Do you know where he takes his metal?" said Willow. "Do you know where he took the witches?"

"He speaks of a ten-hour journey, and he comes from, and returns west along the river," said Gretchen. "I would guess that he travels to the City of Shadows."

"We should leave now," said Barney. "Hearing of witches chained up in a boat has made this whole thing seem far more urgent!"

"The lamp on my boat isn't bright enough for night travel," I said, "and we can't use a magical light until we're clear of these mountains. It would be far too dangerous. Besides, I don't think we'd have much luck getting Boris and Granny aboard."

"What on earth are they doing?" said Mum.

At the rim of the circle of light cast by the fire, Granny stood on tiptoes, her fingertips grasping at the air above her head. "I can't reach it, Boris," she wailed. "I can't touch the moon!"

Boris reared up on his hind legs, his front hooves waving. "Me neither, Gladys. I can't touch it either. There's only one thing for it. You must ride me to the moon!"

"You're a genius, Boris, a genius," murmured Granny.

"Thank me when our feet touch cheese, Gladys," said the goat. "Climb aboard, dear lady, and ride me hard and fast. Ride me like there's no tomorrow!" He dug all four hooves firmly into the sand and tilted his head rearward. "Use my horns to steer, and trust in my abilities, Gladys, for I am your steed tonight. I will fly you to the moon."

"Oh, Boris," said Granny, swinging a leg over the goats

back and taking a curled horn in each hand. "I'm to be the first astronaut in my family, and it's all thanks to you. I'll never forget this night."

Boris looked skyward. "Settle in, Gladys, for the flight will be long and arduous."

Granny leaned forward and lifted her knees, allowing Boris to take her full weight. The goat shuddered for a moment, before emitting a wailing gasp of pain and collapsing into the sand, his legs akimbo and his head at an odd angle.

"Fly, beautiful Boris, fly!" shouted Granny, slamming her heels into Boris's quivering hind-quarters. "Make haste!"

Boris took a rattling breath. "Are we there yet, Gladys?"

"Almost, Boris, almost. Fly faster!"

"It's hard to breathe," gasped Boris, his snout slipping below the sand.

"It's the altitude," said Granny. "You'll soon get used to it."

Barney leapt to his feet and crossed the sand in three long strides. He lifted Granny from the back of the goat, ignoring her protests and dodging her flailing fists. She fell to the sand and stared into the night sky. "So close," she murmured. "Yet so far."

Boris took a deep breath as Barney rubbed his flanks. He blew chunks of sand from his nostrils and sighed. "We'll try again tomorrow, Gladys," he said.

"Tomorrow," repeated Granny. "Sleep à la carte with me tonight, Boris, we'll dream of flying to the moon."

Boris giggled. "You mean al fresco, dear Gladys, and I'd be happy to share the blanket of stars with you."

Gretchen stood up. "Bertram, put that pipe of peace away," she said. "It's done enough damage for one night." She smiled at me. "We shall leave you now. Good luck with your quest." She glanced at Boris and Granny before sliding her helmet over her head. "I fear you'll need all the luck of the Silver Mountains."

The dwarfs mounted their donkeys, and will a final farewell, rode into the night, their laughter echoing across the plains.

"Help me get Granny aboard, Barney," I said. "I'm not leaving her in the sand."

Mum and Willow helped Boris stumble to the boat as Barney and I each slid a hand beneath Granny's armpits and helped her to her feet. "Come on," I said. "It's time for bed."

"I've got a secret," mumbled Granny.

"Come on, Gladys," urged Barney. "It's getting cold and the fire will go out soon. I've never seen anyone get so stoned before."

"Do you want to know why I won't take my dementia cure?" slurred Granny.

"Why?" I said, supporting her as she tripped over a log.

"I love him," she said. "I love Boris. Not the goat you must understand — I'm a progressive, but even I draw the line somewhere. I love the man within him — Charleston Huang, and when I take my cure and he leaves the body of the goat, he'll leave me for ever. He's in his sixties, and I'm at least… ten years older. He won't want to be with me. I'll lose my soul mate." Her eyes slid closed and her breathing became laboured.

"Wake up, Granny!" I said. "What do you mean you love him?"

"Watcha mean?" she mumbled. "Watcha talking about? Are there munchies on the boat? I'm hungry."

CHAPTER SIX

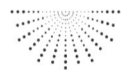

We'd been traveling for almost four hours when Granny finally woke up, the remains of the three chocolate muffins she'd eaten the night before lining her lips, and her eyes bloodshot. "My head hurts," she said, emerging from Willow's bedroom and approaching the narrow galley kitchen where I was preparing hot drinks. "Why is it you only become ill from over indulgence in The Haven? It doesn't seem fair."

"Probably so people think twice before doing it again," I said. "Sit down, I'll make you a coffee."

"Where's everyone else?" she said.

"Willow's driving the boat and the others are on the roof, sunbathing. We're half way to the city of Shadows, they wanted to relax a little before we arrive," I said, handing Granny a mug.

Granny sipped the coffee and smiled. "That stuff the dwarfs gave us was far stronger than the weed me and Norman smoked back in eighty-four, all we did back then was dance to Norman's favourite song — Pass the Dutchie —

and eat too much cheese. I can't remember *what* I did last night!"

"I can help you out with that," I said, "you told me and Barney that —"

Granny out a finger to her lips. "And I don't want to know, thank you, sweetheart."

"But —"

"No buts, Penelope," snapped Granny. "I *don't* want to know."

The thud of a skull on a low door frame, followed by a swear word that made Granny wince, marked Barney's arrival into the belly of the boat. He rubbed his head as he smiled at Granny. "Morning, Gladys," he said. "Did you have a good time last night?"

"I'm sure I did," said Granny, "but as I've being telling Penny — I don't want to know what happened last night."

"Fair enough," said Barney, giving me a knowing glance. "Anyway, I've had an idea. We need to summon Maeve. She should know about what the dwarfs told us. She's almost like my police superior if you think about it, and superiors should always be informed of a breakthrough in a case."

"Breakthrough?" said Granny with a raised eyebrow. "What breakthrough? Why don't I know anything about this development?"

"You were otherwise occupied when the dwarfs gave us some information," I said with a smile.

Granny put her mug down. "Well fill me in then."

Without speaking over one another, Barney and I repeated the story the dwarfs had told us. When we'd finished, Granny nodded at Barney. "I agree, Barney," she said. "Maeve must be told. Knowing that three witches were being held captive in a boat changes everything. I must admit that I thought the six witches had simply decided to become outsiders — there are communities of people throughout The Haven who live in places similar to The Silver mountains, where magic doesn't work. They shun society and they shun magic, but I'm now led to believe the witches are being held against their will… or worse. Summon her, Barney, and we can only hope that Derek doesn't come along for the ride. Ghastly man that he is."

Willow stayed above deck, driving the boat, as the rest of us gathered in the living area. Barney remained standing, with the stone Maeve had given him in his hand, and the rest of us sat on the dinette furniture, with Boris at Granny's feet.

"What do I do?" said Barney, inspecting the small black stone.

"Just think of her," said Mum, "and she'll appear."

Barney closed his eyes and wrinkled his nose. He muttered Maeve's name under his breath, and cautiously opened his eyes. "Is she here yet?"

His answer came in the form of a swirl of smoke which materialised before him. Mum leapt up and turned on the extraction fan above the small gas cooker as Maeve took on her solid form and smiled. "You require my presence?" she said.

"Is Derek not with you today?" said Granny. "You two seem to have been joined at the hip recently."

"Derek is otherwise occupied, Gladys," said Maeve. She lowered herself gracefully into the comfy wicker chair opposite us, threading a hand through her golden hair. "With your sister."

"What's Eva doing with that hideous man?" snapped Granny. "The silly woman! She should know better."

"You don't give Derek *or* your sister enough credit, Gladys," said Maeve. "Eva is wise, and Derek isn't as bad as you like to assume he is." She looked at Barney. "Why did you summon me, lawman? Surely not so that Gladys can question me about Derek's whereabouts?"

"No, of course not," said Barney, retrieving his notebook from his pocket. "We have information about three of the missing witches."

Maeve's playful expression moulded into concern. "Speak," she said abruptly.

For the second time that day, Barney retold the story. When he'd finished speaking, Maeve leaned back in her seat with her eyes closed and let out a long breath.

"Well?" said Granny. "What should we do?"

"We should hurry to the City of Shadows," said Maeve. "I have great concern for the missing witches. I have a home in the city, we'll gather there and formulate a plan."

THE STRETCH of river which led into the city was busier than any I'd seen in the mortal world. It seemed that not all of The Haven was a vision of calm tranquillity after all. Boats vied for mooring spots along the quays and wharfs which made up the port area of the city, and traders transported wares from their boats onto the dockside where horses and carts waited to take them away. We could have been in London during the eighteen-hundreds, and the sight of a young boy running alongside the river pushing a hoop in front of him with a stick, solidified that vision. The abundance and array of different colours and types of boats immediately shot down any plans I'd formulated of simply looking for a red boat and finding the person responsible for taking the missing witches.

Mouth-watering cooking aromas filled the air, and a large market area was loud with the sound of traders shouting over each other as they each attempted to attract customers with their bargains. It was a completely different haven than the one I'd witnessed so far, and I looked forward to exploring the city.

Maeve guided me past the busy port area, pointing to a channel of water which took us to a secluded harbour. I maneuvered *The Water Witch* into the mooring which Maeve indicated, and cut the engine as a man on the wharf side caught the ropes which Barney tossed ashore, and tied us off.

"This is a rarely used harbour," said Maeve. "Traders don't use it. Your boat will be safe here, and more to the point, so will you."

"Secure from what?" said Willow. "I've always thought The Haven was a safe place."

"It used to be," said Maeve. "And the countryside still is, but in recent decades some people have tired of the old magical ways. They miss the world they left behind when they came to live in The Haven, and have sought to recreate it here. A little too well for my liking. Even I have no control over some cities and towns."

"Why don't you take back control?" said Boris, navigating the narrow gangplank which a dock worker had laid between the boat's hull and the low stone quay. "It's your haven."

"I'm not a dictator," said Maeve. "And I have no wish to be. I believe in allowing people to achieve their own destiny, even if I don't always agree with that destiny. If I was to rule The Haven with an iron fist, I'd be no better than the people who tried to burn me alive at the stake." She followed Boris along the plank and drew her hood over her head as she stepped onto the quay. "I will hide my identity. Many people in the city reject authority, and if you're seen with me they may not trust you when you begin searching for our lost witches. Your questions will remain unanswered."

"Aren't you going to help us search for the witches?" said Granny, slapping a man's hand away as he attempted to help her off the plank. The elderly man took a startled step backwards and narrowly saved himself from slipping into the gap between boat and land.

"I'll be more of a hindrance than a help," said Maeve. "People are wary of me, and will not seek to aid me. Come to my home, and I'll tell you more about the city and suggest some folk you may want to speak with. Some people in the city have their ears closer to the ground than others."

"Like the dwarfs!" said Granny, lifting a hand for a high five, which everybody ignored.

A drably coloured carriage, drawn by four black horses, drew to a halt above us at the top of the narrow set of slippery stone steps which led from the mooring to the main quayside.

"Our transport awaits," said Maeve.

"It's not very grand, is it?" said Granny, with an upturned nose.

"I don't want to draw attention to us, Gladys Weaver," said Maeve. "Come, climb aboard, everybody. My home is a short drive away."

The carriage was cramped, but everybody managed to find a seat. Barney's thigh pressed against mine and Granny put a hand on Boris's head, lazily twirling her finger through his hair. As the goat gave a contented sigh, Barney nudged me and winked. With a roll of my eyes, I looked away from Boris and Granny and instead concentrated on the streets of The City of Shadows which moved past the window next to me like a strange period drama on the TV screen. The period drama I was watching outside was a mismatch of historical eras, with some people dressed in clothes which I guessed had been practical in the medieval period, and others dressed in clothes which were of the same style as the ones I wore.

Men in world-war two soldier's uniforms sat outside a tavern drinking beer and three women in dresses straight out of the nineteen-sixties chatted to them, batting their eyelids and sipping cocktails. I reminded myself that people in the magical dimension had been arriving for centuries, and modern witches from the mortal world visited regularly, bringing their own styles with them. I gave a low giggle as I compared the view outside the carriage to the fancy dress party Willow and I had attended the summer before. Willow had dressed as a sexy pirate, and I'd hidden my figure with a Pikachu outfit. The unflattering costume had not only ruined any chance I'd had of attracting any male attention, but had also been responsible for three embarrassing falls on the dance floor, and at least four pounds of weight loss due to excessive perspiration and a small mouth hole through which I could only squeeze the tiniest of finger foods.

Street vendors cooking all manner of food lined the dusty pavements, and I licked my lips as the sweet aroma of barbecued meat filled the small carriage. A small tree filled park bustled with people, and children laughed as they watched a man on stilts juggling five balls, his vintage clown costume a throwback to a time long ago. The City of Shadows was not named for the dark underbelly which it undoubtedly possessed, but took its name from the shadows which were always cast due to the year-round sun, and true to its name, the city was awash with sunlight which lifted my spirits.

"It's a beautiful city," I said, to no one in particular.

"It has its beauty and it has its ugly side," said Maeve, "but I think you'll enjoy your time here."

The sprightly clip-clop of the horse's hooves slowed in tempo as the driver took a turn, causing us all to lurch to the left. "We're here," said Maeve, as the carriage passed through a set of tall wrought iron gates. "Welcome to my home in the city."

CHAPTER SEVEN

Maeve's home was impressive. It wasn't the castle on the hill which I'd been expecting a witch who was powerful enough to conjure up a magical dimension to live in, but it was most certainly worthy of a person of great importance.

The driveway snaked through perfect lawns and tall trees, and the large house, built in the style of an Edwardian manor, was guarded by stone lions and dragons. Two flights of steps led to the marble pillared entrance, and a short portly woman dressed in a flowing black dress stood at the top to greet us. "Miss Maeve!" she said. "It's a pleasure to have you home. When I knew you were arriving with guests, I ordered the cooks to roast a whole pig. I trust you're all hungry?"

Maeve handed the carriage driver a silver coin, and waved at the red-faced woman. "Hello, Mildred," she said, leading us up the steps. "I'm sure we could all do with a bite to eat, thank you."

The large woman hurried into the house, clapping her

hands and barking orders. "Prepare the dining room," she shouted. "Miss Maeve is home! Chop, chop!"

"I wish they wouldn't treat me this way," said Maeve. "The staff were all servants in the mortal world, and they seem to enjoy continuing to perform their jobs in this world. I don't enjoy the fuss, but they insist on it."

"They know their place," said Granny, handing a butler her cardigan and patting him on the head as he bowed. "Keep them on their toes, Maeve. If they sense any weakness from you, they'll be rifling through your family silver before you can say, *shine my Sunday shoes, you common piece of shi* —"

"Mother!" snapped Mum. "Have some respect!"

"They don't want respect," said Granny. "It would only confuse them. They're simple folk with no self-esteem."

"This way, please," said Maeve, frowning at Granny and leading us across the large entrance hall, her heels clicking on the granite floor. "Let's eat, and discuss our missing witches."

AFTER FRESHENING up in one of the many bathrooms, I joined the others in the large dining room. A long mahogany table took centre stage, and the tall walls were decorated with large paintings and intricate embroideries, some of them over six-feet in length. A crystal chandelier hung from the ceiling, the candles which gave off the light burning brightly, and a tall unlit fireplace took up most of the space in the wall opposite the doorway.

I took my seat between Barney and Willow as Matilda wheeled in a long wooden stand on which lay a whole pig, its skin a crispy gold and its body surrounded by cooked vegetables and a large pot of what smelt like the finest gravy I'd

AN EYE FOR AN EYE

ever shared a room with. Matilda began slicing the pork, and Boris closed his eyes, making a sobbing sound. "It seems so cruel now I'm in the body of an animal," he whimpered. "Poor, poor pig."

Boris sat on a smaller table which had been drawn alongside the main table to perform as a makeshift seat, and Granny pulled it a little nearer to her side. "There, there," she said. "You don't have to eat any, Boris. I'm sure the cooks can make you something else." She raised an enquiring eyebrow in Maeve's direction.

"Of course!" said Maeve. "What would you like, Boris? Salad… grass?"

Boris shook his head. "No. The cooks have gone to so much trouble — it would be rude of me. I'll put my feels aside and eat what's been prepared."

"I wouldn't hear of it," said Maeve. "Nobody should eat out of guilt! I'll get Matilda to bring you in some lovely hay, and maybe a nice rosy red apple."

"Of course, Miss Maeve," beamed Matilda. "It would be my pleasure."

"I want the pork," murmured Boris, a spark of annoyance in his eyes. "Give me some pork."

Granny scowled. "You fickle little attention seeking bast —"

Willow and Mum gasped, and Barney blushed.

"Apple sauce, sir?" said Matilda, her voice loud enough to drown out Granny's profanities.

"That would be divine, lovely Matilda," said Boris. "And maybe a nice bit of crackling? From the belly of the beast?"

"Your wish is my desire, sir," said Matilda, piling Boris's plate high with food.

Boris tucked in, gravy dripping from his beard, as everyone else was served and Matilda left the room, pushing the pig before her. "Ring when you'd like coffee, Miss Maeve," she said as she left the room.

The food was delicious, and nobody spoke for a few minutes as the clank of silver cutlery on fine china echoed around the room, interspersed by sounds of appreciation and the occasional belch from Granny, who shifted the blame onto Boris with covert sideways jerks of her head. When the plates were empty, and Matilda had wheeled in coffee and the drinks cabinet for Boris, Maeve leaned forward. "If everyone's had their fill of food, allow me to make a suggestion as to how you approach the search for the lost witches."

Barney slid his notebook and pencil from his pocket. "That would be a great help," he said. "It's always a good idea to have local knowledge."

"If it's local knowledge you want, lawman," said Maeve, "then you need look no further than a particularly shady business premises in the city. *The Nest of Vipers* — a tavern, as the name suggests, has a reputation for quenching the thirsts of some of the less desirable characters in the city. You'll find it near the clock tower. Be cautious though, and don't mention my name. You'll get no help if you do. A conversation with some of the tavern's patrons may point you in the right direction"

"Got it," said Barney, writing in his book.

"I must admit to having a great feeling of unease," said Maeve, "and not just for the safety of the lost witches, but for The Haven itself."

"Why?" said Mum.

"The power that the dwarfs told you of, and that Hilda spoke of," said Maeve, "troubles me immensely." She drained her coffee cup and sat back. "When I created The Haven," she said, "there was nothing here. I had to magic a home to live in, and as time went on and more witches arrived, we began building our homes — we were prouder of homes we'd constructed with our own hands than homes conjured up by magic." She paused for a moment, deep in thought. "And then I found it."

"Found what?" said Boris, pushing an empty saucer towards Granny who topped it up with brandy from the impressive drinks cabinet.

Maeve frowned. "The only building in this land that nobody built or conjured into existence. A castle… hidden in the mountains to the west, overlooking a great lake. It's a beautiful building, and one I tried to enter repeatedly, but alas — I couldn't."

"You can't get into it?" said Willow. "Why?"

"It is protected by a spell," said Maeve. "A spell so powerful, that even I, the creator of The Haven, cannot break."

"If you didn't create the castle or cast the spell… who did?" asked Mum, reaching for a third biscuit from the plate Matilda had supplied with the drinks.

Maeve shook her head. "I do not know, but I found a stone nearby, hidden from view, with an inscription gouged into its surface."

"What was written on the stone?" said Granny.

Maeve sighed. "It says, *the holder of the one true power will come from the east bearing a jewel, and the castle will be claimed. Only the true ruler of this land can break the spell.*"

"You're the true ruler of The Haven, Maeve," said Mum. "You created it. There must be a mistake."

"I thought as much, Maggie," said Maeve, "but things are happening — witches are vanishing and people are speaking of a power that only I should know of — I put my own spell around the castle *and* the existing spell, so nobody else can get near to it — nobody but me knows of that stone or the castle, I'm the only person to have been there, and the only person who knows of its existence." She looked around the table. "Until now, but I know in my soul that I can trust each one of you with this information… even you, Gladys Weaver."

"Your words cut me deep, Maeve," said Granny. "How rude. How very rude, and to think I could have been back in Wickford, showing off in my new Range Rover and tending to my chickens, but yet I chose to come here and help you solve the mystery of the lost witches! I'm offended, Maeve. Off-en-ded."

Electric buzzed in the air around Maeve, and her whole demeanour changed. "As offended as I was when you chopped down the magic rose bush, or fought a guerrilla war against Derek, in the west? The poor man had to move to the east and change his name from The Copper Haired Wizard of The West, because of you, Gladys. You have a colourful history in The Haven, Gladys, and you should be pleased that I ever lifted your banishment and allowed you back in. The fact that I now trust you is a bonus indeed. I even gave you the cure for your dementia, which for a reason known only to you, you still haven't taken."

Granny filled Boris's saucer again, her cheeks showing the gentle blush of embarrassment. "My apologies, Maeve," she said. "I spoke out of turn."

Barney gave me a sideways glance. We both knew why Granny had backed down so quickly, but we'd promised one another we'd keep it a secret between the two of us. If Granny still hadn't taken the cure by the time we got back to Wickford, we would confront her. It wasn't fair on Charleston to be trapped inside the body of a goat because Granny had fallen in love with him, although he looked pretty happy lapping up the brandy which Granny was feeding him. He'd last another few days.

Granny pointed at the wall behind Maeve, completely changing the subject. "Who's that handsome hunk of man?" she said, gazing at a portrait of a young muscular man with thick dark hair. "I wouldn't throw him out of bed for playing the bagpipes."

Mum bristled. She had an irrational dislike of the Scottish, and the image of a man playing their national musical instrument in a bed had obviously hit a nerve.

"Granny!" laughed Willow. "He's far too young for you! I wouldn't mind meeting him, though!"

"He's nothing special," grunted Boris.

Maeve turned to look at the portrait. "You've met him, Willow" she said, turning to face Granny. A smile played on her lips. "That's the man who's currently wooing your sister, Gladys," she said. "That handsome *hunk* of man is Derek."

Granny got to her feet and hurried to the painting. "Derek does not have black hair," she protested, standing below the oil painted portrait and pushing her glasses further up her nose, as if by moving the lenses closer to her eyes she would make sense of what she was seeing. "He has dirty blond hair, which is never styled very well. He's always reminded me of a scruffy scarecrow, and the man in this picture reminds me of a lovely librarian, or a high-class gigolo."

"Those two professions don't even belong in the same sentence," said Boris. "Anyway, he's not that good looking, his nose is too small for his eyes."

Granny looked down at the goat who stood next to her, a little unsteady on his feet after downing nearly half a bottle of brandy. "Jealousy will get you nowhere, Boris," she said. "Anyhow, if the portrait is of Derek, then I feel sick for even suggesting he's good looking. Disgusting man that he is."

Maeve gave a gentle laugh. "I can assure you it's Derek,"

she said. "He dyes his hair with magic these days, but that's what he looked like when he was first granted his haven entry spell, Gladys, many hundreds of years ago. And that's how he looks right now as he takes your sister to his home in the east. Derek is shy of reverting to his younger age in front of most people, but not when it comes to impressing pretty young ladies like Eva."

"The little harlot!" said Granny. "She knows Derek and I don't get along, and she's chosen to go gallivanting with him! Why she'd want to go to the east with him, I'll never know, only farmers and failures live in the east!"

"Farmers?" said Willow, "why would farmers live in the east?"

"The climate," said Mum, eating the last of the biscuits. "It's wet and humid in the east, but dry and hot in most of the west. It's no good trying to grow crops in the west without magic. The east is where most of the crops are grown. I'm not sure why your grandmother mentioned failures, though."

Granny shrugged. "Farmers — failures, same difference."

"Derek enjoys growing things from seed," said Maeve. "He's a simple man really, who got dragged into the politics of The Haven. I hope he and Eva enjoy themselves, Gladys. I'm sure they both deserve some happiness. Anyway, the east is a nice place to live. I have a home there myself, as does Hilda. She likes the peacefulness of the hills, it helps her to hone her visions."

"Good for Hilda," said Granny, "and Derek and Eva are welcome to each other. They can be farmers together. I always was the classiest sister."

"Class comes in all types," said Maeve, with a wink in my direction. "Would you all like to see more of my paintings? I keep the best ones in the library."

"I'd love to," said Willow.

"I'm quite the art critic," said Boris, with a belch. "I'd like to cast my eye over your pieces, Maeve."

"I'm sure you would," said Granny, running her eyes along Maeve's slim figure.

"Then follow me this way, please," said Maeve, heading for the doorway. "You'll like my library."

CHAPTER EIGHT

The library smelt of leather and old books, which was no surprise, as long rows of old books lined the tall shelves, and leather furniture provided the seating. The huge book shelves filled two of the four walls and four sliding ladders made it easy to pick a book from even the highest shelf. The wall opposite the doorway was reserved for art, and Maeve had made sure to utilise every available piece of space with oil painted portraits, landscapes and stunning waterscapes.

"Impressive," said Boris, wandering across the thick carpet and gazing up at the pieces. "Very impressive."

Willow and I focused on the books, craning our necks to scan the shelves, noticing books we recognised from our world, and books with titles such as *'Portal Travel - A Step Into The Unknown,'* which had obviously been written by an author from The Haven. Maeve stood at my side, smiling as I scanned the thousands of book spines. "I'm happy to see that you two appreciate books," she said. "Books are the sturdy foundation that any advanced civilisation is built upon."

"I love books," said Willow, opening a leather-bound tome

on ancient spell-craft and pressing her nose into the yellowed pages. "Mmmm," she murmured, closing the book and sliding it back into place on a shelf. "You can't beat the smell of old paper."

"My word!" shrieked Mum, from the other side of the room. "You have a macabre taste in art, Maeve."

"I think it's wonderful," said Boris, gazing at the wall above him. "It speaks of death and rebirth, and the evil that mankind is capable of. It's a fine work of art indeed."

"It reminds me of where I came from," said Maeve, crossing the room. "Although on some days I'd rather not remember."

Willow and I followed her and stood beneath the painting that had shocked Mum. It wasn't as macabre as Mum's reaction had made me believe, but it wasn't the sort of painting I'd have liked on my wall either. Framed in dark wood and painted with an accomplished hand, the painting filled a huge portion of the wall, with life sized figures filling the canvas. The painting portrayed Maeve as she burned at the stake, and I gave her arm a gentle squeeze as a tear bulged in the corner of her eye. "It hurts every time I look at it," she said, laying a soft hand over mine. "But it serves a purpose. It reminds me of why I don't wish to become a dictator in my own land. Nasty things happen to good people when one person has too much power."

"It's barbaric," said Barney. "Truly barbaric, and to think that this was allowed to happen in the country I enforce the law in, it makes me shudder."

The painting showed Maeve tied to a stake surrounded by a tall pyre of logs. Bright orange flames licked at her legs and her face was contorted in pain as people in the background looked on in horror, with some women covering their children's faces, and men staring at the ground in helpless despair. The second life sized figure in the painting couldn't have been more different than the onlookers in the way he was portrayed as behaving. A tall black hat hid most of his long dark hair, and his face showed a horrific expression of glee, his teeth bared in a savage smile and his eyes wide and excited as he watched a woman burn.

"What an evil man," said Granny.

"The Witch-finder General," said Maeve, her hand still on mine, her fingers gripping me tight. "He was responsible for searching out and killing many witches, most of them with a trial which was only ever going to end in a verdict of guilt, quickly followed by the punishment of death by drowning or burning."

"Dark times indeed," murmured Boris. "Dark times indeed."

Barney leaned closer to the painting, his height affording him a better view than the rest of us. "There's something about his eyes," he said, "something very evil."

Maeve's fingers closed tighter. "Not only was his cruelty rarer than most people's," she said, "but so were his eyes. Look closely, lawman, beneath his brows, and you'll see his eyes are of different colours. He claimed they were a gift from God which gave him the ability to see witches where nobody else could. Those eyes were the last thing I saw before I closed my own and prepared to die."

"You're right," murmured Barney, moving even nearer to the painting. "One eye is brown and one is green."

"The artist did a good job," said Maeve. "It was painted by a male witch who watched my near demise. He came into The Haven not long after my fortuitous escape from the jaws of fiery death. He told me that the Witch-finder General dug through the ashes of the pyre for one full day and one full night, searching for my ashes and bones, desperate to prove that God had not saved me from death as the other onlookers believed when I vanished in a flash of light."

"But really, you'd been able to cast a spell so powerful that you created this wonderful land," said Boris. "Remarkable."

"And purely fate's doing," said Maeve. "I was prepared to die. Using magic to save myself would have resulted in more witches and innocent people dying when the Witch-finder took his revenge. I did not cast the spell, my magic did that for me."

"How awful," said Maggie. "We witches don't know how good we have it these days."

"I'm glad it is that way," said Maeve, finally releasing my hand and wiping a tear from her cheek. "And I'm happy to be able to offer refuge in this land to anyone who should need it. The Haven has saved many a witch's life in the centuries since it was created."

The heavy door creaked behind us, and Matilda stepped into the room. "Do you require anything else, Miss Maeve? It's getting late and I should be leaving for home."

Maeve's mood lifted. "No, Matilda. I need no more from you. Go now, and thank you for what you did for us today, the pork was heavenly, and your service was divine."

Matilda performed a half bow, and left the room with a smile. "Thank you, Miss Maeve."

Maeve glanced at a window high in the wall. "It is nearly dark, perhaps you should be getting back to your boat. I will be gone by the morning. I have my own investigations to carry out. While you good people search for the missing witches, I will be scouring the land for information on the great power that has been spoken of. Should you discover anything, do not hesitate to summon me again. I will come quickly." She turned her back on the paintings. "I'll summon my carriage."

"I don't know about everyone else," I said, "but I'd like to walk."

Barney agreed. "That's how you get the feel of the pulse of a town — you walk the beat. I'll walk with you, Penny."

"As will I," said Boris.

With all of us in agreement that an evening walk through the city would be pleasant, we said our goodbyes to Maeve on the steps outside the house, and promised to keep her updated about any developments in our search for the witches. Maeve had insisted we took the pouch of coins she offered us, explaining that currency would go a lot further than magical ability in a city such as the one we were in.

"Do we know the way?" said Boris, as we reached the end of the driveway and followed the dusty road downhill. "I didn't take much notice on the way here, but to be fair on myself, I couldn't see out of the carriage window."

"I offered you a place on my lap, Boris," said Granny, watching an elderly man light a street-lamp with a spell cast from the tip of a wand. "You chose to sit on the floor at my feet."

"I'm way ahead of you all," said Willow, walking half a pace in front of us. "It's so easy to use magic here. I've cast a spell of direction — and used the boat as a beacon, it will lead me right to it."

"Or we could just head in that direction," said Barney, pointing at the twinkling lights of the docks below us. "Basic cub scout skills — walk downhill until you find water."

Willow gave Barney a playful slap on his arm. "Spoilsport," she said. "I don't get to use magic much in the mortal world. Let me have my fun!"

"Lead the way," said Barney. "I'm sure your way will take us via a quicker route than I would have."

After a few minutes of walking the quiet streets soon gave way to the bustle of city life at night. Smells of food and the upbeat sounds of live music excited my senses, and I leaned into Barney as he slipped his arm through mine. "I love it

AN EYE FOR AN EYE

here," he said, watching a man playing an accordion outside a small tavern. "Everything is so… simple."

Fireworks exploded in the sky above the city and Granny clapped her hands as the explosions morphed into the glowing shapes of a huge dragon and a phoenix, which flew into the night together, heading for the distant snow-capped mountains which glowed silver beneath the moon. "Magical pyrotechnics!" she said, laughing. "You don't get those in Wickford!"

"And a good job too," said Mum, ever the realist. "I've heard stories about those firework creatures causing untold damage. They don't just fizzle out like a catherine wheel, you know! They fly around for weeks, setting fire to hay-barns and scaring animals."

"Lighten up, you miserable lump of lard," said Granny. "Breathe the air, and feel the magic running through you. If I didn't have dementia I'd launch a few of my own fireworks. My griffin would put that phoenix to shame, *and* give the dragon a run for its money too."

The crowds of people jostling for space became louder as we reached the centre of the city, and the malty aroma of real ales pouring from the open doors of numerous taverns caused Boris's nose to twitch. "Anyone for a taste of the local brew?" he suggested. "Gladys… I'm sure you'd like a snifter or two?"

"You don't need to ask me twice," said Granny.

"I'm in," said Barney. "Why not?" He pointed across the wide street. "We'll go in there for a drink," he said, "we may as well mix business with pleasure."

"The Nest of Vipers," said Boris. "Maeve warned us it was frequented by ruffians; do we really want to go in there tonight?"

Granny rubbed her hands together and scurried towards the open door. "Just you try and stop me, Boris," she said. "I'm yet to meet a ruffian who could scare Gladys Weaver!"

Boris trotted after her, narrowly avoiding being run over by a man on horseback who veered right at the last moment. "Keep your goat out of the road!" the rider shouted, as Barney and I walked hand in hand after Boris, with Mum and Willow behind us.

The Nest of Vipers looked a friendly enough place from the outside. Even the snakes which formed the letters on the hanging name sign were smiling as their tongues searched the air, and warm light spilled from the two large windows. The hum of conversation and music grew louder as we approached the open door, and a man sitting on a bench outside tipped his hat in our direction.

Inside the tavern, a roaring fire burned in the large hearth at the far end of the room, and the long tables were occupied by a diverse crowd of people, some of who looked up as we made our way towards the bar. A small raised stage in a corner took the place of the customary juke-box I was used to seeing in the pubs at home, and the three-man band who sat on it played folk music on guitars and an accordion, accompanying a beautiful woman who sang in a buttery voice which sent shivers along my spine.

A large man laughed as Boris passed the table he sat at with a dwarf and three women, all of them drinking foaming beers from earthenware flagons. "You can't bring that in here," he said pointing at Boris, and jerking a thick thumb at the sign which hung over the bar behind him. "Timmy won't allow it."

"No magic, no animals, and no weapons," read Willow.

"We'll see about that!" said Granny, rapping her knuckles on the oak bar to attract the attention of the thick set barman with his back to us. "Service please! This moment!"

The man turned slowly and smiled. Barney took a step

backwards, pulling me with him, his fingers digging into my wrist. "What the heck is that?" he said. "What on earth?"

"I could say the same about you," said the barman, scowling at Barney. "You're a little freakish yourself — you're taller than a horse, and we don't see many gingers in these parts. It's said that ginger hair indicates a soul of blackness, but I'm willing to judge a person on the merits of his or her character. But to answer your insensitive question — I'm Timmy, and I'm unapologetically a troll."

Boris tapped Granny on her foot. "Urm," he said, gazing up at her. "I'm a goat and that's a troll. In the stories my mother used to read to me, there was always a little friction between the two, with goats usually coming off the worse. Far worse."

"Relax, little goat," said Timmy, peering over the bar, his voice far gentler than the mouth of sharp teeth, and narrow yellow eyes set deep in a twisted green tinged face, would have suggested. "I won't eat you. I will ask the people you're with why they thought it acceptable to bring an animal into my tavern, though. Can't any of you read?"

"I've read your sign," said Granny. "And I find it to be highly problematic. Since when did it become acceptable to discriminate based on gender, body weight or shape, IQ, culture, religion, physical ability, age, sexual preference, race, or in this despicable instance — species? I'll have you know that I've spent many years of my life fighting against social injustice, in and out of The Haven, and I will not tolerate your bigoted attitude — especially since you're of a species which has experienced its own fair share of discrimination over the centuries. You should be ashamed, sir! Ashamed!" She folded her arms and gave Timmy the practiced glare which normally made people cower.

Timmy gave Granny a grin which exposed a second row

of teeth set behind the first. "Don't you come in here spouting that nonsense, old lady. You —"

"Oh!" said Granny. "You can't help yourself can you, you crusty disgusting creature. How dare you comment on my appearance, *and* get it so very wrong. You will serve us all with a beer each, and you shall serve Boris — the goat you've insulted, with some of your finest brandy, and we'd like it on the house, or my wrath will be swift and decisive!"

The troll gave a low laugh, and his eyes glowed a brighter yellow. "Crispin! Tarquin! Come here please!"

"Granny," said Willow. "Be careful."

From a door behind the bar appeared two hulking shapes, both of them with eyes as yellow as Timmy's, but with considerably wider shoulders and thicker necks. "Yes, boss?" said the tallest of the troll pair.

"Time to earn your money, boys," said Timmy. "We've got trouble makers in the tavern. The angry one with blue hair and purple glasses has threatened me with swift and decisive wrath if I don't let her goat stay and give them all a free drink."

"Go on then," said one of the bouncers, staring at Granny down a recently broken nose as he adjusted his long black coat. "Show us your wrath."

The music stopped and I became aware that everyone in the room had stopped talking to train their eyes on us.

Granny looked slowly around the room and took a deep breath. "Okay," she whispered, reaching into a pocket.

CHAPTER NINE

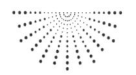

"Let me see those hands!" said one of the bouncers.

"Relax," said Granny, retrieving the pouch of coins Maeve had given her. "It's just a money pouch, and I'm hoping it will buy me out of the unfortunate incident I've found myself embroiled in."

"What are you talking about?" said Timmy. "Where's the wrath you promised? My boys are dying to release some of their pent-up energy. It's been a little quiet in here recently. We could do with seeing a few people being tossed out of the door."

The two bouncer trolls grunted their agreement, and Granny put her hand on the largest one's arm. "Calm down, beefy," she said. "You won't be doing any tossing tonight. I find myself in a bit of a predicament. You see — nobody has ever stood up to me when I've threatened them with my wrath, but it seems you fellas are made of sterner stuff than the normal folk I cross words with. Add to that the fact that I'm suffering from a severe case of witch dementia, and it becomes clear that my threats were nothing more than crassness and bluster. For that, I apologise, and I'd like to offer you each a shiny gold coin in way of recompense, and to buy my companion Boris, the goat at the centre of this misunderstanding, his rightful place in your fine establishment."

Timmy laughed. "We don't need your gold!"

The shorter bouncer cleared his throat. "I could do with a little extra gold, boss," he said. "Jemima's going to give birth soon. She's expecting a large litter this time round, and us trolls don't have the privilege of being able to magic up food. Between this job and the new building job, I hardly earn enough to keep a roof over our heads. That gold would keep us fed for a month."

"I feel the same as Tarquin," grunted the other bouncer. "I need a new pair of boots. I dropped a metal sheet on my foot today and it went right through. My toe hurts, boss. I could use that gold."

Timmy rolled his eyes, the thick wrinkles in his forehead creaking like a leather jacket being folded. "That'll teach you for working in the depths then, won't it? I told you it wasn't safe down there, and I don't trust the man you're working for. He's sly."

Granny rolled a coin between finger and thumb. "Come on, Timmy," she teased. "You know you want it. You trolls love hoarding wealth, and one of these gold pieces is worth more than a hundred flagons of your beer."

"Gladys," said Barney, smiling nervously at the trolls. "Why don't we just leave? It would be cheaper and simpler. I'm sure we can find a tavern that will allow Boris inside."

"Principle, dear boy," said Granny. "Boris has as much right to be here as everyone else in this room, and I want to prove to the management that he won't cause any problems. I can't leave here knowing that the next enchanted animal that walks into this tavern will be given the same treatment as Boris has received. I like to make positive changes wherever I go, and if it takes handing over money to achieve that change, then so be it. Plus, it's not really my money, is it? If Maeve is silly enough to hand over a bulging purse of coins to *me*, then she should know that some of it will be squandered foolishly. It's only right and proper."

Timmy sighed, the sickly aroma of pickled something — possibly eggs, rolling across the bar in a gross invisible mist. "We'll take your gold, but that won't be enough." He nodded towards the corner where the band sat in nervous silence. "Tonight is open stage night. If any member of your group has a talent which will keep my customers entertained for a few minutes, then you're welcome to stay. If not, I'll take the gold anyway and *still* get the boys to toss you out."

"Thanks, boss," said Crispin. "You're a kind troll. Always thinking of others."

"Too kind sometimes," muttered Timmy. He ran his eyes over us. "Now, can any of you perform, or are my lads going to show you the door?"

"This is your chance, Boris!" said Granny. "Your chance to show these people, and trolls, that animals are not all dumb beasts of the field." She lay a hand on the goat's head. "Dance for us, Boris! The band will play a lively tune, and you can dance a lively jig! Bend those limbs and move that head, and wow us like you wowed the crowds at the animal show. I regret not being there to witness your moves that day, my dancing, prancing, sure-footed friend. But you can show me now! Get on stage and dance like you've never danced before!"

Boris looked at me and Willow for support.

"You've got the moves," said Willow.

"You did dance well at the show," I admitted, "and it seemed like you had fun at the time. Not to mention the trophy you won. It's still got pride of place on Granny's mantelpiece. You must have been proud of your performance."

It had been almost eight weeks since Boris had won the Wickford and Covenhill best farm animal contest. His win had been clinched by the pirouette he'd performed at the judge's table, which had surprised Susie, Willow and I as much as it had surprised the judges and spectators. There had been just one small difference on that day, though. Boris had been extremely drunk. He still had alcohol in his veins from the brandy he'd drank at Maeve's house, but he was nowhere near as drunk as he'd been on the day of his victory.

"I *was* proud, Penny," said Boris. "It was a fine day."

"Have a brandy or two," I suggested. "Then dance." I looked at Timmy. "I'm sure the barman won't mind serving you a brandy if it means he can watch a dancing goat."

Timmy bit the gold piece Granny had handed him. "The gold's good," he said. "I suppose I can give the animal a few brandies — but be warned, if he fails to please the audience, you're all getting thrown out."

A man in the crowd shouted. "Get on with it! We want a show!"

Timmy took a large bottle of brandy from a shelf and handed it to Granny. "Satisfy your goat's thirst, but go easy — that brandy doesn't come cheap."

Granny tugged at the cork, removing it with a pop. "Open wide," she said, tilting the bottle towards Boris. "Take your fun juice."

Boris suckled at the bottle like a piglet at a teat, his throat contracting as he swallowed the amber liquid.

"That's enough!" said Timmy. "And wipe that bottle before you hand it back to me. That animal's teeth are disgusting!"

"You're a fine one to talk," said Granny, wiping the bottle rim on her sleeve and replacing the cork. She placed the brandy on the bar next to Timmy's muscled arm. "Was that enough, Boris? Have you lost your inhibitions yet?"

"Almost," said Boris. "I'll need to hear some music to help release my inner dancing beast."

Timmy clapped. "You heard him," he said, speaking to the band. "Play!"

One of the guitarists struck a melancholy chord, and the accordion player dragged out a long vibrating note. Boris shook his head, drops of brandy dripping from his beard. "No, no, no," he said. "That won't do! This ain't no funeral — this is a party!" He hurried to the stage and clambered up the two low steps, joining the confused band. He looked out over the crowd. "Any beatboxers in da house?" he shouted.

"I'll beat you into a wooden box and bury you alive in it if you don't hurry up and dance!" shouted Timmy, to loud guffaws from the crowd.

"What's a beatboxer?" called a woman from the back of the room.

"It's somebody who wants to be a musician, but hasn't got the self-discipline or skill to teach themselves to play a musical instrument," said Granny, raising her voice. "I know it sounds strange in this world, but imagine somebody invited you to dinner and using magic to prepare it instead of cooking it themselves. It's very, very lazy. A little like when my daughter tries to trick me into thinking she's cooked a curry, but I find the empty glass korma jars at the bottom of her bin, underneath the family sized chocolate bar wrappers, that she *apparently* doesn't eat anymore. Although her increasing clothing size tells a different story. A very different story indeed."

"Have you been going through my bins again, Mother?" said Mum. "I've told you before, you won't find any evidence of drug use in there. I like dancing naked to Lionel Richie music because it feels liberating — not because I'm stoned, and if you didn't keep spying on me on a Sunday morning, you wouldn't have to witness it!"

The cottages Mum and Granny lived in were each built on the peak of a hill — one at either extremity of Wickford. With a valley between them, the two women had long been spying on each other, with Mum utilising a high-powered telescope, and Granny using binoculars. The last I'd heard, they'd come to a truce, but it seemed Granny wasn't honouring it.

"Somebody has to look out for you, sweetheart," said Granny. "You're your own worst enemy."

"Erm, I can do a little," said Barney.

"A little what?" said Granny. "What are you talking about now, young man?"

"Beatboxing," said Barney. "I was into the hip-hop scene at school for a few months. I'm sure I could still knock out some killer beats."

"Well don't just stand there boasting," snapped Granny. "Get up on stage with that brave goat and drop some sounds."

I gave Barney a nervous smile. "School was a long time ago," I reminded him.

He took a deep breath. "I still practice now and again, it helps me bond with some of the young street gangs in Wickford. I call it cultural policing. You'd be surprised how easy it is to diffuse a crisis with a little mouth bass. I once stopped a potential blood bath between the Bus Stop Massive and the Duck Pond Posse by spitting chords. Young Charlie Wilkinson, leader of the BSM, had ripped the name tag out of Freddy Simpon's — leader of the DPP's, school gym shorts. The teacher had already punished Charlie by not allowing him to play football at lunch time, but Charlie was having none of it. He wanted blood, so I bought them both an ice cream and knocked out a few ghetto beats. Problem solved. Freddy went to Charlie's for a sleepover a week later, and now the two gangs have joined forces against the Playground Proud Boys."

His beaming smile told me he wasn't joking, and I put a gentle hand on his arm, pushing him in the direction of the stage. "I'm sure you'll do great," I said, ignoring Granny's snorting laughter.

"Go, Barney!" said Willow. "Show them what you can do!"

Barney climbed onto the stage and stood next to Boris, cupping a hand over his mouth. He began rocking from foot to foot, his long legs gaining a little rhythm as he made a repetitive deep bass drum sound, interspersed by higher pitched sounds which reminded me of the laser weapons used in Star Trek. His lips vibrated and his mouth opened and closed, and Boris's rear end swayed in time to the sounds as Barney increased the tempo.

Boris turned to the band. "Play!" he said. "In time with the beat-meister!"

The guitarists looked at one another, and with their feet tapping in time to Barney's sounds, began playing rhythmic chords. The accordion player joined in, playing low notes and nodding his head to the beat. When the singer joined in, her voice complimenting Barney's beatboxing perfectly, even my foot tapped to the beat, and a smile slid over my face.

A loud whistle from somebody in the crowd and a round of applause spurred the band on, and Boris began shaking his whole body, his head nodding faster and faster as the band played louder. People began thumping the wooden tables with their flagons, in time to the beat, and Boris threw himself into the air, his legs making a star shape and his spine arched in a curve.

"What's he doing?" shouted Timmy, as Boris crashed into the stage and began writhing like a dying fish. "Is he possessed by a demon? Should I call an exorcist?"

"It's called the caterpillar," I said. "He's performing what we call break-dancing."

Boris threw himself onto his back and the crowd roared their appreciation as he began spinning, his legs drawn close to his body and his chin close to his chest.

"He'll break his legs if he's not careful," said Timmy, his hand tapping out the beat on the bar. "They're too spindly for that sort of exertion."

Boris leapt to his feet as Barney rocked from side to side, beatboxing with obvious enthusiasm and pulling his shorts down a few inches to expose the elasticated band of his red underwear.

"Is he a stripper too?" shouted a woman. "I hope so. It's been too long since I saw a gentleman's ding-a-ling. My Harold's been at the pies a little too much lately. His belly gets in the way."

"No! He's *not* a stripper," I shouted. "Some people in our world who enjoy this sort of music wear their trousers like that. It's a fashion statement."

"It's a blight on humanity," said Granny. "Gone are the days of the Rockers and Teddy boys. Now those young cats dressed with dignity, not like narrow waisted ruffians."

As the music got faster and Boris slid seamlessly into the move I knew as crazy-legs, Crispin stepped from behind the bar and approached me. The huge troll strutted toward me in time with the music and reached for my hand, gripping it in his shovel sized palm and tugging me toward him. "Dance with me, female!" he demanded.

I pulled my hand from his and stepped backwards. "That's not how you speak to a lady," I said. "I'm sure you're a hit with the girls, aren't you?"

"That's how we trolls show our affection for the weaker sex," said Crispin. "The lady trolls love it."

"Weaker sex?" said Granny. "How dare you! You misogynistic animal! When I get my magic back I'm going to pay this tavern another visit and cast a spell on you — so powerful that your kidneys will pop out of your ears! Now step away from my granddaughter and thank your lucky stars that my magic is not accessible now."

"Stop the music!" shouted Timmy, his roaring voice scaring the band into silence and stopping Boris mid moonwalk. "I've had enough. You troublemakers should leave now."

Mum tapped me on my shoulder and passed me her handkerchief. "Wipe your hand, darling," she said. "You've got some sort of disgusting troll bodily fluid on it."

I took the handkerchief and looked at my hand. It was dark with a dusty deposit which stained my fingers.

"That's not bodily fluid!" said Crispin. "That's the dust from an honest hard day's work in the depths. That's what that is!"

The white handkerchief darkened as I rubbed my hand clean. Barney joined me, pulling his trousers up and wiping an accumulation of spittle from his chin. "Beatboxing is a messy business," he said. "Let me use that hanky after you."

He took the dirty piece of linen and studied it for a second. "This looks familiar," he said, examining the stains. "My granddad was a roofer and his white t-shirt looked like this when he'd been working with lead and wiped his hands clean on it. I'm no Sherlock Holmes, but I know a clue when I see one." He looked at Crispin. "Why do you have lead dust on your hands?"

Crispin frowned. "From working in the depths. I already told the female. It's the dust from the same metal that almost took a toe off my foot when I dropped a sheet of it on my boot."

"What work?" said Barney. "And what are the depths?"

"We're building a —"

"Quiet!" said Quentin, putting a huge hand on his fellow bouncer's shoulder. "Stay your wagging tongue and say no more! The man we work for told us to speak to nobody of our work, and there's something about him which tells me he should not be crossed."

"It's important," said Barney. "We're looking for —"

"Enough!" shouted Timmy. "This isn't an establishment in which people gossip to strangers. This isn't Twiggy's General Store and Tattoo Parlour! The people who sit in her chair to be decorated may be liberal with their tongues, but secrets spoken in The Nest of Vipers stay within these walls. Now be gone — I'm itching to see if that goat can fly as well as he dances, and my boys are itching to be the trolls who launch him."

Knowing we'd more than outstayed our welcome, we left the tavern quickly, with Granny reiterating her threat that she'd return when her magic was back.

Willow led the way to the boat, her spell leading her quickly along side streets and through narrow alleyways until the harbour opened up before us. The Water Witch's bright red and green paintwork shone in the yellow light emitted from the street-lamps, and distant sounds of people having fun bounced across the water's surface.

Boris stopped as we approached the boat, his head cocked to the side and his ears twitching. "Something is wrong," he said. "I can hear footsteps on the boat. Somebody's aboard the Water Witch!"

Barney broke into a run, shouting at us to stay back. His warning to us served as a warning to whoever was on the boat too, and with a thumping sound on wooden steps and a slam of the bow decking door, the dark shape of somebody wearing a flowing cloak appeared on the Water Witch and glanced in our direction.

Barney approached the gangplank at speed, almost slip-

AN EYE FOR AN EYE

ping on the damp stone surface of the dockside, but regaining his balance as the intruder lifted an arm in our direction. "Stop right there!" shouted Barney. "Stay where you are!"

The intruder stood still and gave a low laugh.

"It's a man," said Granny, as the intruder laughed again.

Barney reached the gangplank just as the man lifted his arm and emitted a shower of colourful sparks from his fingertips. The buzz of electric in the air accompanied the light show, and Barney let out a cry of pain as he was thrown backwards through the air, his arms flailing and his head thudding on stone as he slammed into the hard floor.

"Barney!" I yelled, as the man climbed over the bow railings on the water side of the boat.

"He's jumped in the river!" said Mum.

The thud of feet on wood disproved Mum, and as I arrived at Barney's side and cradled his head in my hands, the roar of an engine starting drowned out Barney's groans.

"He's on a boat!" said Granny.

The long hull of the Water Witch had afforded the stranger's boat a perfect hiding place, but as it slid into view with the man at the controls, it was obvious even in the darkness that the hull was painted a vivid red.

"I'll stop him," said Mum, magic sparking at her fingertips. The spell left her hand at speed, the golden stream of light flying straight and true until it neared the boat where it spread over the hull in an umbrella shape, before fizzing and spluttering out of existence.

"A forcefield," said Granny. "It's powerful magic."

Barney groaned again, and I watched helplessly as the boat slid into darkness. "Forget it," I said, as Willow and Boris hurried along the dockside in a pointless attempt at following the stranger. "Help me with Barney. I can't lift him on my own."

CHAPTER TEN

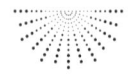

Barney took a bite of toast and sipped his tea. "Amazing," he said, rubbing his head for the umpteenth time since he'd woken up. "The lump has totally vanished and there's no pain at all."

"You can thank Penny for that," said Willow, tossing Rosie's stuffed toy mouse along the length of the boat. "Her healing spell is second to none."

Rosie chased the mouse through the boat and pounced on it as it landed next to Willow's bedroom door, giving a satisfied mewl and settling down to chew on her prey.

"Should we check again?" said Willow. "Surely he must have taken something. Why else would he break in?"

The intruder hadn't even damaged the door he'd used to gain entry to the boat through, using magic to unlock it rather than brute force, and if we hadn't arrived at the boat when we had, it was doubtful we'd have ever known somebody had been aboard. As far as we could tell, after an exhaustive search which went on into the early hours of the morning, nothing had been taken and nothing had been damaged. Mum had done a sweep of the boat checking for sleeper spells which may have been cast. She and Granny had explained that some spells could be cast and left to fizz away in the ether, unseen until they were triggered by the person who'd cast them. Mum had found nothing, and with the bright sunlight spilling in through the boat's windows, and music playing on the CD player, we all felt safer and more cheerful than we had the night before.

Barney buttered another piece of toast. "We're all in agreement that the person on the boat last night must be the person who's responsible for taking the witches, and we can safely assume that the boat he was on is the boat the dwarfs told us about."

"Agreed," I said. "And we can be equally sure that he's the same man the trolls are working for in the depths — whatever they are — and that lead has a big part to play in it all."

"And that the lead is being used to deflect magic," said Boris. "We're all in agreement on that front too."

"What?" said Willow. "When did we speak about that?"

"We didn't," said Boris. "Did we need to? Are you all telling me that it hadn't crossed your mind that lead works against magic in the same way it does against radiation in the mortal world? Why do you think magic can't be used in the Silver Mountains? Because of the lead, and I'd bet a bottle of the finest brandy that there are lead deposits in every part of The Haven where magic can't be used." He looked around the table. "Really? Nobody picked up on it? I assumed it didn't need saying as it was so blatantly obvious."

Granny gave Boris a pat on the head. "You forget that your Oxford education affords you a far greater intellect than the rest of us, Boris. Think of us as village simpletons and yourself as Einstein — the chasm between our intelligence levels is that glaringly wide. I'm so proud of you."

"I thought of it," mumbled Barney.

"You did?" said Granny. "So why didn't you mention it?"

"I wrote it in my notebook."

Granny held out a hand, tapping the palm with a finger. "Let me see."

"It's in my other shorts," said Barney.

"I'll get them," said Granny. "Where are they."

"Okay, I put my hands up," said Barney. "I didn't think of it, but I would have got there eventually. I have a process, and I trust that process."

"Well put some more fuel in the process's tank," said Granny. "It's running on fumes at the moment."

Barney pushed his plate away and stood up. "Excuse me," he said. "I'm going to take a shower."

I waited for Barney to enter the small bathroom and close the door behind himself before I narrowed my eyes and stared at Granny. "It was Barney who realised it was lead on the handkerchief last night," I said. "And it was Barney who ran towards danger when we found somebody on the boat. I think we're doing well as a *team*, and anyway, Granny — what has your contribution been towards the solving of the mystery? All you've done is get stoned and cause an argument with trolls."

"I've got other problems too," said Granny. "I can't be using all of my grey matter on the problem of the missing witches, I've got to save some brain power for coming up with a way to split my sister and Derek up. There is absolutely no way that that pair are ever becoming an *item*. So, forgive me if I haven't *contributed* to solving the mystery *just* yet. I'm sure my time will come, and I'm equally sure that when it does I will shine. Brighter than you lot. That's for sure." She gave Boris another gentle pat on the head. "Not you of course. Nobody can shine brighter than you, Boris."

"The gesture is appreciated, Gladys," said Boris, getting to his feet, "but undeserved. We all deserve praise, and we all shine in different ways. I consider myself lucky to be able to call you all friends. Now, as it seems you three have bickering to carry on with, I'm going to take a leaf from Barney's book and leave you to it. I fancy a walk along the waterfront. I need a breath of fresh air and some time to think."

"Don't go too near the edge of the river," shouted Granny, as Boris climbed the steps up to the decking. "And don't go speaking to strangers!"

"I won't," came the distant reply.

"I'd prefer it if you didn't speak to me in that way in front of Boris," said Granny, glaring at me. "Asking me what my contribution to solving the crime has been — you made me look silly."

"Oh, stop worrying what that goat thinks about you," said Mum. "You act around him like you used to act around Dad. You're like an old married couple, and it's embarrassing!"

"How dare you call my relationship with Boris embarrassing," said Granny. Sparks rolled from her fingertips and her eyes glazed over.

"Careful, Granny," said Willow. "Dementia, remember. Don't do anything you'll regret."

Granny watched the sparks at her fingers and took a deep breath. The sparks vanished as quickly as Granny's mood shifted from angry to upset. "Why is everything so difficult?" she said, a tear forming in her eye. "Why did I have to get witch dementia? It's not like it runs in our family. It's my dementia's fault that Charleston is trapped in the body of a goat!"

"Well take the damned dementia cure for goodness sake!" said Mum. "What's wrong with you? It's a simple fix!"

Granny seemed not to have heard Mum. "And it's my dementia's fault that I've fallen in lov —" She stopped speaking and put a hand to her mouth, as if to stop anymore words tumbling out, and her body shook as she sobbed.

"What did you say?" said Mum.

"Don't, Mum," I said, putting an arm around Granny. "She's upset."

"Oh, Penny," gasped Granny, pushing her head tight against my chest. "I've got a secret that will make you all hate me if I reveal it."

"What secret?" said Willow. "Are you okay, Granny? What's wrong?"

Granny seemed to have shrunk in my arms, and her bony shoulder dug into my flesh. I put a hand on her head, and pulled her tighter to me. "It's okay, Granny," I said. "I know your secret, and so does Barney. You told us after smoking the pipe of peace, and Barney and I don't hate you. We love you."

"I told you?" she said, looking up at me through teary eyes. "And you don't hate me?"

"You did," I said, squeezing her tight. "And of course I don't."

"It had to come out at some point," she said, hiding her face in my bosom. "I couldn't hide it forever! It's been burning a hole in my very soul! What would Norman, rest his soul, think? He'll be spinning in his grave knowing he had a harlot for a wife!"

"Mother?" said Mum, her voice soft. "What's going on?"

"I'm worried," said Willow. "Granny, you know we love you. You can tell us anything."

"Anything," said Mum.

Granny looked up, her cheeks puffy and her eyes bloodshot. "Anything?" she sobbed. "Even that I've fallen in love with another man and betrayed your grandfather, Willow?" She turned her gaze to Mum. "I can tell you that I've betrayed your father, Maggie? Because that's what I've done. I've gone and fallen in love with a Chinese acupuncturist. I've gone and fallen in love with Charleston, and when I take my dementia cure I'll lose him. I can't tell him of course, he harbours no romantic feelings towards me. Why would he?" She wiped her cheeks with a shaking hand, and stared up at me. "What would Norman, rest his soul, think? It's a saving grace that Charleston is Chinese and not Japanese. Norman, rest his soul, loved Chinese food, but hated what the Japanese did in Pearl Harbour. That's the only positive I can draw from this terrible mess!"

"The only positive you can draw from all this is that Granddad was a little racist?" I said. "What about the fact that you've fallen in love? That's a beautiful positive."

"Mother," said Mum. "We're not the sort of family who judges one another in matters of the heart. We never have been. I loved Dad, yes, but I love you too. I want you to be happy."

"I'm sure Granddad would too," said Willow. "He's probably looking down on you, happy that you're happy."

"What?" said Granny. "Your grandfather once made a man cry because I commented on how nice his suit was. Norman, rest his soul, was a jealous man, a very jealous man indeed. He won't be smiling down on me, he'll be bubbling with rage. I can picture him now, his right eyebrow arched and his knuckle duster ready for action."

"Knuckle duster?" said Willow. "Granddad?"

"Oh yes," said Mum. "You'd be surprised, Willow."

"How else do you think he made a grown man cry?" said Granny. "He wasn't big or strong, he needed back up for the occasions on which his mouth wrote cheques that his body couldn't cash."

"You can't base your future life on what Dad was like," said Mum. "That was the past. Your future is your future, and if you want my advice, you'd tell Boris, I mean Charleston, how you feel about him. You might be surprised. He speaks of you in very high regard, and I think I speak for everyone else when I say that we're all very fond of him too."

Willow and I nodded our agreement, and Granny gave Mum an affectionate smile. "You fatties are always very optimistic," she said, resting her hand on Mum's. "Maybe it's the raised cholesterol playing havoc with the thought process, I don't know, but I admire your outlook, Maggie. On this occasion, I think your optimism is misplaced, though. Charleston won't look twice at me when he's back in his real body. He'll be gone from my guest bedroom the second his body is no longer frozen by magic. That room will be empty without him. I like to go in there sometimes to comb his hair and polish his ring. It's got a lovely stone in it – a *real* diamond, I think."

The bathroom door opened, spewing a cloud of steam into the boat. "That's better," said Barney, emerging from the mist. "There's nothing like a hot shower to get the blood pumping."

Granny sat up straight and wiped her eyes with a paper towel. "Not a word to anyone else about what just happened at this table," she hissed.

"Barney knows," I reminded her.

"He doesn't know that *I know* he knows," whispered Granny. "And I want it to remain that way. This is woman talk. I won't discuss emotions with a man — it makes them flighty and hungry. That's why men with over emotional wives tend to be anxious and fat. It's not fair on them. Men aren't built to speak about love as openly as us women."

The sound of hooves thudding on the decking put a stop to anymore conversation concerning Granny's love life, and Granny wiped the final tear from her cheek as Boris pushed past Barney and stood next to the table. "I've found the shop that the trolls mentioned last night," he said. "Twiggy's General Store and Tattoo Parlour. It's just around the corner. Shall we go? If Twiggy is as much of a gossip as the trolls made out, then you never know what she might be able to tell us."

"Clever goat!" said Granny. "Let's get going, right this moment. We've got a mystery to solve! There are six witches out there who need our help. Time is of the essence!"

CHAPTER ELEVEN

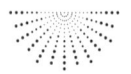

Two hours and twenty minutes later, we all stood outside the shop. Granny had wasted an hour insisting on finding the hairbrush she'd misplaced, finally admitting reluctantly that she may not have brought it with her, and even more reluctantly using Mum's brush instead, pulling handfuls of black hairs from the bristles before taking the risk of running it through her blue hair. The second hour had been taken up by carefully removing tiny splinters of wood from Rosie's gums. She'd discovered a small twig in Willow's bedroom while searching for her stuffed mouse, and had chewed it into a yellow mush which Willow scooped up with a paper towel and tossed in the bin.

The final twenty minutes had been spent strolling along the waterfront, taking in the atmosphere of the city by day, and looking out for the red boat we'd seen the night before. Mum had cast a spell over the Water Witch before we'd left, making it impossible for anyone to get within a foot of the hull. If the man on the red boat did return, he'd have no luck if he tried illegally boarding my boat again.

Twiggy's General Store and Tattoo Parlour stood on a

corner, the open door spewing the tantalising aromas of spices and herbs which mingled with the yeasty smell of fresh baked bread. The term *General Store* seemed a little tame as we stepped inside. Twiggy's seemed to stock everything — more a universal store than a general store. Shelves brimming with huge ripe melons sat opposite shelves crammed with thick woolly sweaters, and a glass cabinet placed next to a rack full of wine bottles was filled with magic wands of various lengths and aesthetic appeal.

A huge oven stood near the doorway, and I watched fascinated as a man dressed in traditional baker's clothing withdrew a large brown loaf, using a long wooden paddle to retrieve it from the hot interior. Women and men browsed the aisles, and children gathered around a stand displaying hand carved wooden puppets — some of them painted and dressed as clowns and others as witches and wizards. One child had removed a particularly colourful clown from the stand, and with expert control of the strings, was making it dance, much to the delight of the other children. The whole shop smelt delicious, and I had already decided that the evening meal was going to consist of one of the fat honey roast hams which stood on the meat counter, accompanied by a few of the soil covered freshly harvested new potatoes which filled a wooden barrel.

Barney pointed towards the rear of the shop. "That's where we should be," he said. "The trolls said people gossip while they get tattoos."

Twiggy's Tattoos, read the sign hanging from the ceiling, painted with an arrow which pointed to a staircase leading to the upper floor. The staircase creaked as we trudged up it and took a turn to the right near the top before opening into a spacious room, the high walls adorned with tattoo designs and fantastical paintings of dragons, and other strange creatures, which I hoped were mythical and not accurate representations of haven residents.

Old leather sofas and chairs provided seating for customers awaiting a tattoo, and a single seat beneath a bright light was the chair in which customers were inked. Nobody was waiting, but a huge man with a bare chest and full beard was currently being worked on by a tall woman with a body that ran straight up and down, with no discernible bumps or curves beneath the green velvet body hugging dress she wore. "No prizes for guessing that she's Twiggy," I said under my breath.

Twiggy leaned over the man in the chair, and with a wand in hand, made shapes in the air a few inches above his bulging pectoral muscle. "Wow," said Boris. "No needles."

Colours and shapes appeared on the customer's sun browned skin as the wand danced through the air, and as I approached the chair for a better look, the shapes shifted on the man's skin. The tattoo was of a ship, but what was remarkable was the way the vessel rode the incandescent blue waves which Twiggy was working on. The galleon dipped into deep troughs of water and rode the peaks of tall waves, tilting from side to side as it ploughed through the rough sea, going nowhere on the man's chest.

"That's amazing," I said, standing behind Twiggy. "Do you mind if I watch?"

"I don't mind," said the tall woman, her eyes resting on me briefly. "Do you mind, Jimmy?" she asked, returning her attention to the magical tattoo she was creating.

The big man smiled at me. "Watch all you want," he said. "You thinking of having one?"

"No, she is not!" said Mum, standing beside me.

"I'll have one if I want, Mum," I said. "But I don't think I'm ready for one just yet. If I ever get one I want it to mean something special."

"Like this one," said the big man, tapping his chest with a wide finger. "The ship you're looking at is the galleon that I took my last voyage aboard. It went down with all hands lost apart from me. I was lucky. It happened in the mortal world and I'd already been given my haven entry spell. The ship was completely underwater and sinking fast when I manged to open a portal in the captain's cabin doorway. I was almost out of air when I swam through. The other poor souls had no chance."

Twiggy made a final mark on the man's skin, adding a sailor to the crow's nest at the tip of the tallest mast. "There," she said. "All done."

I moved nearer to the man's chest for a better look. The sailor in the tattoo was small, but the thick beard which blew in a non-existent breeze gave away his identity. "That's you, isn't it?" I said, resisting the urge to touch the tattoo as the ship dipped and rose on the man's chest — going nowhere, but giving the illusion it was moving at speed through the swelling ocean.

"Aye," said the man. "That's me. I was on look-out duty. I never saw the iceberg that broke the bow, and I'll never forgive myself either. This tattoo is a reminder of how I failed all those men I sailed with."

Mum drew a sharp intake of breath as an iceberg floated into view in the path of the boat. I was almost convinced that I heard the splintering of wood as the boat was torn apart by the sharp ice and began sinking, the broken bow sliding quickly beneath the surface. The man drew his shirt over his tattoo. "There's no need for you good ladies to see the worse part. That's my penance. Each time I look in a mirror I'll be reminded of the people I let down that day."

Twiggy put a hand on the man's shoulder. "Try to forgive yourself, Jimmy, and when you do, come back so I can remove it. You'll be alive a long time in The Haven, and having that reminder on your chest will do no good for your soul. It'll send you mad."

Jimmy smiled and handed Twiggy some coins. "I don't want to forgive myself," he said. "I want to remember. It keeps those men alive in my heart."

Twiggy and Jimmy hugged, and when the large man had left, Twiggy looked around the room. "Who's next?" she said, with a smile. "The goat? I've never tattooed an animal before, it could be fun."

"I'm sorry," I said. "We're not here for tattoos. We were hoping you could help us. We're looking for six witches who have gone missing."

Twiggy looked down at me, her thin neck decorated in swirls of black ink, and her eyes piercing and thoughtful. "How do you think I can help?" she said. "I know nothing of the missing witches. I've heard about them, of course, but I don't think I can be of help to you people — whoever you are."

Barney joined us and stood at my side. He withdrew his notebook and looked at Twiggy. "We're just people who want to help," he said. "Would you consider answering some questions?"

"I don't know where you come from," said Twiggy. "But nobody likes a loose tongue in the City of Shadows. They don't tend to stay in the mouth for long, and I'm quite attached to mine. I'm sorry, but you'll be getting no help from me."

Barney glanced at his notes. "It really would help," he said. "Just a few simple questions."

Twiggy ignored Barney and stared over my shoulder. "Who's that woman?" she said. "The one sneaking down the stairs. The one who hasn't turned to face me since she came in here and saw me? The one with blue hair. I know her. I'd recognise that plump bottom anywhere. I recognise all the

AN EYE FOR AN EYE

flesh and bone canvases I've worked on." She took a few steps towards Granny. "It's you, isn't it... Gladys...Weaver?"

Granny paused on the third step down. "My name is not Gladys," she said without turning around, her voice a few octaves higher than usual. She took another step. "I am a simple woman. My name is... erm, my name is.... John Jones. No! Joanne Jones, my name is Joanne Jones and I am but a simple washer woman who wandered into your place of business by accident. Please forgive me, I should be going now. I have washing to... wash."

"I'd know you anywhere, Gladys," said Twiggy, crossing the room. "Why do you hide from me? Do you not remember me? We spent time in prison together. I tattooed your right buttock using a sewing needle and the red ink you stole from the warden's office. Of course it's you, Gladys — I'd never forget the person I created my first ever tattoo on."

"You have a tattoo, Gladys?" said Boris. "How exciting."

"I'm not Gladys," said Granny, her shoulders slumping.

"The game's up, Granny, come on," said Willow. "And what's she talking about... tattoos and prison? We knew you'd spent an hour or two in the Wickford police cells in the past, but you've never mentioned prison!"

"We spent a terrible time together in prison," said Twiggy, holding a hand to her chest as if to calm herself. "Here in The Haven. We shared a cell, and during our incarceration we became blood sisters, cutting our flesh and mixing our lifelines with the promise that we'd always be there for one another." She took a step closer to Granny. "Why do you hide your face from me now, Gladys? Does our pact no longer stand? Are we no longer sisters of blood? I tattooed you, Gladys, you bare my artwork on your fleshy behind, surely that still means something to you?"

Granny turned to face Twiggy. "Of course it means something," she said, her eyes shimmering with tears. "I didn't want my family to know my shame, that's all, and I certainly didn't want them to know I wear a tattoo. I'd have never come in your shop if I'd recognised the name, but you weren't known as Twiggy when we were held in that prison hell-hole, like rats in a trap."

"I took the name after leaving prison," Twiggy said. "I needed a change. I wanted to feel reborn when I felt the first breath of free air on my cheeks and the grass beneath my feet. Twiggy was the name my brother gave me when I was young, due to my build. I thought it fitted quite well."

"It fits beautifully," said Granny, climbing the stairs and approaching her old friend. "Illyria never really rolled off the tongue. Twiggy is simpler."

"Tattoo?" I said, staring at Granny. "What tattoo do you have on your arse, Granny?"

"It's nothing," said Granny. "Forget it was ever mentioned."

Twiggy gasped. "Nothing! How can you say that? It meant so much to you back then!" She looked at me, her eyes twinkling. "Its meaning was lost on me of course — I left the mortal world centuries ago and never kept up with developments, but your grandmother assured me that one day the symbol and slogan I inked on her derriere would be known throughout your world, and worshipped by all." Twiggy smiled at Granny. "Did it happen, Gladys Weaver? Did the red-heaven you spoke and sang of come true? Is your world a place of equality and peace as you predicted it would be?"

Granny looked at the floor. "Not quite," she said.

"What's the tattoo?" said Willow.

"It was beautiful," said Twiggy. "It was never my best work of art, of course, but it was my first, and the fact it was a prison tattoo made it so much more special. It was a simple design, but with great meaning to your dear grandmother. I can see it now, a crossed hammer and sickle, above the slogan — Rise, Comrades! The cleverest part was the phrase above it though, wasn't it, Gladys?"

Granny grunted.

"Unroot evil, it reads," said Twiggy. "An anagram of revolution! Beautiful."

Granny blushed. "It was a long time ago. My politics have changed a little since that time."

"I think it comes as no surprise to most of us that you lean very much to the left, Gladys," said Boris. "Maybe just a tad *too* far on some occasions, but it seems the revelation that you were incarcerated in a haven prison is news to your family. What did you do, Gladys? What crime did you commit?"

"What crime did *we* commit?" said Twiggy, laying a hand of solidarity on Granny's shoulder. "Gladys was the founder and leader of our movement — the Social Justice Witches. We made great changes in The Haven, until one night we were betrayed." She lowered her eyes. "Betrayed by one of our own."

"Big Bertha," spat Granny, her fist clenched. "The big bitch."

"Yes," said Twiggy. "Big Bertha let it be known that we were planning an operation — *Gladys* was planning an operation, she was the mastermind behind all our actions after all. Gladys planned to disrupt a man only event, in protest against the patriarchy and their refusal to allow female participation. Sexist pigs!"

"What was the event?" said Barney.

"A competition," said Twiggy. "To see who could grow the fullest beard in two weeks without the use of magic. We never got close enough to the event to disrupt it though, did we, Gladys?"

"No," muttered Granny, a vein in her forehead pulsating with angry blood. "Big Bertha had given the game away.

Derek and his cronies were waiting for us. They confiscated our scissors, eggs, and hair removal potions — and tossed us into prison without trial. That was the end of the SJW's. The prison system tore us apart as a group and broke us as individuals."

"It did," said Twiggy. "But here we stand, Gladys Weaver — reunited after all this time, and with a bond between us so strong that only people who've been prison inmates could ever hope to understand it."

"Good lord," said Mum, pulling Granny close to her in a fierce hug. "I never knew. You poor, poor woman. How long were you locked up for, and why did I never know? Was it before I was born? Did you try to shield me from the shame? You needn't have! I'd have understood!"

"Two nights and almost three long days," said Granny, her voice faltering. "The worst weekend of my life. You were fourteen years old. Your father told you I'd gone to visit cousin Beryl in Cleethorpes. He couldn't tell you that your mother was a lag. I wouldn't allow it!"

Granny stumbled as Mum pushed her away. "A weekend! A bloody weekend!"

"A long weekend," interjected Twiggy, "and they ran out of teabags on the Sunday. It was awful. It was inhumane!"

"You sang communist songs, became a blood sister, had a prison tattoo, *and* were broken by the system over a weekend?" I said. "It must have been some prison."

"It was terrible!" said Granny. "You'll never understand — not until your liberty is snatched from you by force!"

"Take comfort that I understand, Gladys," said Twiggy. "I know your pain, and as your blood sister I will do all I can to help you and your family." She turned to Barney. "Ask your questions. I will answer them."

CHAPTER TWELVE

*A*fter Granny had introduced us all to her old prison friend, Barney reeled off a series of questions. Twiggy looked around the room before answering, as if to search for eavesdroppers. "The depths," she said quietly. "I've heard talk of it. Some of the men who sit in my chair come from work dirty with dust from their labour, and speak of a place known as the depths."

"What is it?" said Granny. "I've never heard of it and I've been around The Haven a bit."

"It's said that The City of Shadows is built upon another city, a smaller city, a city that sank in swampland and was lost to time, a city that now hides beneath our feet... in the depths. The men who work there speak of it being discovered by a strange man who possesses great power. He employs people to build for him, beneath our feet, but *what* they build... I do not know."

"Do you know what the man looks like, and if he has a boat?" said Barney. "A red boat to be specific."

"What I've told you is all I know," said Twiggy. "If you'd

like to know what despicable man is having an affair with whose despicable wife, and where the finest happy herb can be had for cheap, then I could talk all day, but most of the people who sit in my chair know when they've said too much. They seem nervous of speaking of the depths and the man who employs them. I do not push them for more. Until today it's never been of great importance to me, but now you tell me it may be connected with the missing witches. Do you think they are down there? Trapped in the depths, like Gladys and I were trapped in Sunny Mountain Open Prison and Recreation Centre?"

"I think it's a *little* worse than that," I said. "They could be in *real* danger. Can you tell us how to reach the depths? Is there a doorway? A hidden tunnel?"

Twiggy shook her head. "I'm sorry," she said. "I don't know. Though if I were to search for the depths myself I'd begin at the lowest point of the city."

"The docks." said Barney. "The same level as the river."

"No," said Twiggy. "There is a lower place. Before the dock side walls were built higher, the river used to be held back by magic when heavy rainfall poured from the mountains. If it wasn't controlled, the flood water would find its way to the old part of the city, where the spire of light is built. It sits in a dip, at the edge of the city."

"Spire of light?" said Barney, adding more notes to his book. "What's that?"

Twiggy looked at Granny. "He's a lawman you say? You would think he would have more sense." She smiled at Barney in the way a teacher smiles at a child who can't grasp a simple concept. "It's a spire," she said. "With a light atop it… the spire of light."

Barney scribbled another note in his book, his eyes flickering with annoyance for a moment. The pages in his book were beginning to fill up with random notes, and I wondered just how close we were to being able to help Maeve solve her mystery and find the missing witches. It seemed that although we had some clues, the investigation — if we could call it that, was disjointed, almost like it needed a metaphorical lynch pin to hold it together. Finding the depths was of paramount importance.

Twiggy looked towards the stairs as heavy footsteps approached. A man appeared, glancing around at the artwork which covered the walls. "Have you got time to do a tattoo, Twiggy?" he said.

Twiggy gave us an apologetic smile. "I'm sorry, I can't help you any further — duty calls, but before you leave," she said, "please allow me to make you a gift. Take what you will from the shop downstairs." She handed Mum a metal token. "Take this — it will tell my staff that it's free of charge. I had some fresh eggs delivered this morning, laid without magic, and my baker is working on a new bread recipe — spell free of course, and using only the finest whole grains. Take what you will." She pulled Granny into a lingering hug. "And now you know where to find me, Gladys, don't be a stranger. You are my blood sister after all."

With Granny promising to return, we left Twiggy with her customer and browsed the shelves downstairs. Deciding we didn't want to take advantage of Twiggy's kind offer, we filled a single paper bag with half a ham, a dozen eggs, and a loaf of warm bread. It would make a lovely supper, and the Water Witch was already stocked with the non-perishables we needed. There was no need to be greedy.

The young girl behind the sales counter brimmed with happy energy and with a smile, took the token Twiggy had given us. "The ham is lovely," she said. "You'll enjoy it, and the eggs are fresher than a breeze from the northern sea."

Boris glanced behind the counter, his eyes on the large metal safe which was bolted to the wall. "What's in there?" he asked.

A sign was propped on top of the safe, the words on it written in large red letters.

Please ask a member of staff if you wish to make a special purchase. This safe is locked with magic, and only Twiggy has the power to open it.

"The valuable things," said the girl. "We had a problem with thieves, so Twiggy was forced to use a safe."

"What sort of valuable things?" said Willow.

"Just the normal stuff," said the girl. "Jewels from the ice-caps of the north, love potions made by the elderly voodoo witches, and liquorice root."

"Liquorice root?" said Barney. "That's rare?"

"Very much so," said the girl, twirling a strand of curly brown hair around a finger. "It's very rare indeed. It only grows in one part of The Haven — The Ridge of The Morning Sun. Few people can grow it, and many people love it. Good liquorice can't be grown with magic, it spoils the delicate taste. It's used for making alcoholic drinks, and chewing. Having a tin full of liquorice root is a sign of high status indeed. It's only become available for sale in Twiggy's shop in recent months — since Twiggy formed a trading agreement with the dwarfs of the Silver Mountains. I do not know how they come by it — they live where no crops will grow and no farmed animals roam, but suddenly they have an abundance of fine spices and bags full of liquorice root. Twiggy asks them no questions, though, she's happy that she makes such a large profit. The dwarfs wont deal in gold, so Twiggy pays them with meats, eggs, and grains."

"So, it would be unusual for a man to simply toss a liquorice root to a goat?" I said.

"Unless he was *very* attached to the animal, or was able to grow the root himself. It would be comparable to you tossing a diamond to someone in the mortal world. It would be unheard of, unless you owned a diamond mine or had taken leave of your senses."

CHAPTER THIRTEEN

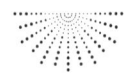

*M*aeve gave me a stern glare, her eyes dancing with emotion — flickering between incredulity, hurt, and as her eyes bored into mine — anger. "Derek would do no such thing!" she said. "This is your grandmother's doing! She's always harboured hatred for Derek. She's put thoughts into your head!"

Heading straight back to the boat after leaving Twiggy's shop, and piecing together snippets of information as we walked, we'd summoned Maeve as soon as we had formed a viable explanation for why we suspected Derek of being involved in the disappearance of the witches. Maeve wasn't taking it well, convinced we had misinterpreted the information in Barney's notebook.

Granny sighed. "I've done no such thing."

"The story you summoned me to listen to is a wild one indeed," said Maeve. "I find it hard to believe. Derek has been loyal to me for centuries."

Granny took a hard-boiled egg from a dish and mashed it into a lumpy paste on a slice of buttered bread. A slice of ham topped off the open sandwich, and she chewed as she spoke. "My sister is with Derek!" she said. "Whether you like it or not, or think I'm biased, I happen to love Eva, and I want to know she's safe! Think about it, Maeve. Derek could easily be taking on the form of his younger self — a fine disguise, nobody would suspect he was as handsome as he was in the portrait hanging in your house. Everyone thinks of him as a tubby blond-haired idiot. I'm worried for my sister."

"As a lawman," said Barney, "I think Gladys's concerns are valid. You just told us yourself that he has a home on The Ridge of The Morning Sun, Maeve — the place liquorice grows. He had a tin of liquorice during the meal in Eva's garden, and you told us he enjoyed growing things from seed, and I must say, my honed policing instincts have always told me there was something off about him."

"Hilda warned us of a man with coal black hair," said Willow. "And Derek's hair *is* pretty dark in the portrait we saw of him."

"He has no boat, though," said Maeve. "Derek has never enjoyed water travel, he prefers to travel using magic. As a trusted companion, I have afforded him the ability to do so. Only a select few have the power of transportation. I cannot imagine Derek travelling by boat, he prefers to make a more dramatic entrance."

"That's a small part of the puzzle," said Barney. "Look at the bigger picture."

Maeve's eyes darkened. "And you think Derek was the intruder you found on the boat last night? I don't think so. I would sense his presence had been here, and I sense no remnants of his aura."

"He used powerful magic," said Mum. "He put a forcefield over his boat, it would be easy for a man with that sort of magic to disguise his aura."

Maeve shook her head. "Yet he took nothing from your

boat, and did no damage. Maybe it was a coincidence, maybe it was a wizard who wanted to know more about you. I've heard you've caused quite a stir in the city; young people are walking around with their britches around their thighs and making strange music with their mouths. People are talking about you. Maybe the intruder was simply curious to see a boat from the mortal world, and to find out more about who you are."

"Word would have had to have spread fast," I said. "We came back here straight from The Nest of Vipers. News of Barney and Boris's performance couldn't have travelled that quickly."

"Eww!" said Boris, from beneath the dinette table. "Rosie's been sick again, it nearly landed on my hoof, would somebody please put her outside? I'm trying to eat!"

Rosie had been unwell since we'd returned to the boat. We'd put it down to her eating one of the rotten fish which lay in a forgotten wicker basket on the dockside, happy that the rotting flesh would soon leave her system with no ill effects. Rosie was as protected from illness by magic in The Haven as much as the rest of us, but as we'd found out from Granny's happy herb hangover — the protection didn't extend to guarding us from the unpleasant after effects of what we were foolish enough to ingest.

Barney scooped Rosie up in his arm and carried her gently to her basket. He lay the poorly cat down, and placed a blanket over her as Willow knelt beneath the table and scooped up the cat's vomit in a paper towel. She emerged from between our legs with the paper towel close to her nose, her nostrils dangerously close to the yellow mess. "It smells odd," she said, standing up. She sniffed it again and bristled with excitement. "It smells of liquorice!" She hurried to the bin. "And I bet that twig she chewed up this morning smells the same!" She reached into the bin, the sounds of empty tins clanking as she searched for the chewed up remains of the stick we'd pulled splinters of from Rosie's gums. She stood up, holding the mushy mess wrapped in a paper towel. "As I thought," she said, sniffing it. "Liquorice! The man on the boat last night must have dropped it!"

"It's very toxic to cats," said Boris. "She'll be okay soon enough, though."

"Come on, Maeve," said Granny. "I know you don't want to consider it, but you have to! You've seen Derek with liquorice, which is a prized rarity which only grows where he lives, and now we find some on the boat the day after an intruder broke in! Derek must be involved — too many clues point toward him, and my sister is with him! She may soon be the seventh missing witch, and goddess only knows what he intends to do with those poor women! I've always said he has perverted eyes!"

Maeve looked between us. She formed an arch with her fingers and closed her eyes. "I'm still doubtful, but I will transport myself to Derek's home in the East and —"

"The east!" I said. "You told us that the writing on the stone near the castle you found said that the one with the true power would come from the east! It must be him!"

"A jewel was mentioned too!" said Granny, the worry for her sister not preventing her from buttering more bread. "Derek has a jewel on top of that pretentious staff of his! He'd better keep his staff away from Eva, or I'll snap it in two!"

Maeve stood up, urgency etched in her features. "You people must go and search for the depths. With a very heavy heart, I will visit Derek. I'll return when I have answers, and you must summon me should you discover answers. I feel my hold on The Haven weakening, and I fear that whoever has the women captive is planning something terrible."

A swirl of smoke marked Maeve's departure, and the rest

of us hurried from the boat, heading to the edge of town where Twiggy had told us we would find the spire of light, and possibly, the depths.

CHAPTER FOURTEEN

A gang of teenage boys, with their underwear on display, stood at a corner, attempting to beatbox. When Barney had finished signing autographs for them, they gave us directions to the spire of light, which we followed earnestly. The route took us down narrow alleys and wide roads, until after almost half an hour of walking, we approached the edge of the city, the buildings becoming sparser and with fewer people present.

"I must say," said Boris. "I'm really feeling it today. I've got a skip in my step and I'm brimming with energy!"

"It's the magic," said Granny. "You're beginning to feel it, Boris. You're from a magical family, remember — I'd hazard a guess that if you didn't have hooves at the end of your limbs, you'd be able to cast a spell or two."

"Well it feels remarkable," said Boris, sauntering ahead. "Almost like I've been on the brandy all day, but without the anger in my belly or the craving for a kebab."

Long shadows crossed our path as the sun dipped in the sky and evening approached, and soon we neared the stone bridge which spanned a small stream the gang of teenagers had told us to look out for.

"The spire should be on our right," said Barney, checking the map he'd sketched out in his notebook. "Among the trees. In a valley."

Barney led the way, following a well-worn footpath, the stone smooth from centuries of foot traffic. He craned his neck to see past low hanging tree branches and stepped over a fallen log, warning us to watch our step. The scent of crushed pine needles and earthy wet moss filled my nostrils, and the musical repertoires of song birds was a pleasant change from the harsh squawks of the seagulls which had made the dockside their home, leaving white deposits on the roof of *The Water Witch*, and stealing fish from the fishermen as they landed their catches.

Barney rounded another corner, and an ivy covered stone spire appeared through the trees, narrow at the top, and thickening as it disappeared into the ground, the base overgrown with bushes and thick grasses. Barney stopped. "Someone's coming," he said. "I can hear footsteps."

Three large trolls appeared around a bend in the path and stared at us. Dust clung to their leathery skin and worn out clothes, and they approached us with an air of distrust. "What do you lot want?" said one, his voice tired. "What are you doing here?"

I thought quickly. "We're here for work," I said. "The man with black hair told us to come. He said he had a job for us."

"You're too late," said the biggest troll, his eyes glowing amber. "The works done. It was finished yesterday, we're the last crew out, we did the final clean-up today. It was good pay while it lasted, but it's back to earning pennies working in the quarry for me." He looked at us in turn, a smirk curling his rubbery lips. "Anyway, what work did you expect to do?

AN EYE FOR AN EYE

None of you look strong enough to lift the metal we've been building with."

"We're the interior designers," said Granny, with a bow. "We've come to add the finishing touches."

"It could do with more than some finishing touches," said another of the trolls. "It's a miserable place, whatever it's for. I'm used to being below ground, but that room feels bad."

The third troll wiped his brow, smearing more dust across his forehead. "Any place with a hidden entrance and a password is bad news," he said. "I'm glad to be out of there, it gave me the chills."

"Hidden entrance?" said Granny. "Where is it?"

"The clue is in the name," said the first troll, "it's hidden, and if you'd been given work here you'd have been told where it was and what the password is. I smell a rat — you're not here to work, are you?"

"We are!" said Granny. "How dare you accuse me of fibbing, and the rat you can smell is the stink from your armpits. I can smell it from here."

"A feisty one," said the tallest troll. "Maybe we should tie them up and wait for the boss to come back, he told us to look out for busybodies."

One of the trolls took a step towards us. "He'll give us extra silver and liquorice," he said. "I vote we tie them up."

"You can try," said Mum. "I'll turn you into toads. You've already got the complexion, I just need to work on your size."

The largest troll laughed. "Magic won't work here," he said. "You're too close to the spire. Only the boss man's magic works here."

"The lead," said Barney. "But surely that would stop his magic working too?"

"The light giving jewel on top of the spire powers his magic," said the smallest troll. "It —" He let out a pained gasp as the biggest troll slapped him on the back.

"Will you stop talking and help me tie them up? We've said too much already."

Granny slipped a hand into her pocket. "If it's money you want, I've got plenty." She tossed the money pouch from hand to hand, making it jingle seductively. "How does three gold pieces each sound — for telling us where the entrance is and giving us the password."

The smallest troll's eyes glinted. *"Three?* Imagine what we could do with sort of money, boys?"

"How about we take *all* their gold and tie them up anyway?" said the nearest troll. "*And* get some silver and liquorice from the boss."

"You could try that," said Granny, "but even without magic, do you think we'd let you tie us up without a fight? The tall ginger man is stronger than he looks, and the goat has got a set of teeth which he'd love to get around your family jewels."

Boris bared his teeth and growled, and Barney flexed a thin bicep.

"I'm tired," said the smallest troll, covering his crotch with shovel sized hands. "I don't want to fight. Let's just take the gold and bugger off, I fancy a beer. We're never going to see the boss man again anyway. He won't know who gave them the password."

The leader relented with a frustrated sigh, which added an extra three inches to his barrel chest. "Okay," he said, "hand it over."

"Show us the entrance first," said Granny. "I wasn't born yesterday."

The troll bared his teeth in a hideous smile. "I can see that," he said. "You're wrinklier than my family jewels will ever be."

Boris growled again. "Don't you speak to her like that," he warned, saliva dripping from his teeth. "I'm feeling particularly fit today. I'll make short work of ensuring none of you ever father another… troll-let."

"Pups," said the troll. "We call them pups, but I get the picture. There's no need for threats of that magnitude. Come with us, we'll show you the entrance, then we can get out of here for good. I'll be glad to see the back of this place."

The trolls turned around and led us along the last stretch of footpath, taking us into a valley, until we stood in the shadow of the spire. The stone work looked centuries old, and the ivy which shrouded it grew from vines as thick as a man's arm. I craned my neck to look upwards, using a hand to shield my eyes from the low sun. "There's the jewel," I said, pointing at the baseball sized chunk of crystal at the tip of the tower. It glowed dimly, the light hardly visible in the beams of sunlight which poured through the tree canopy.

"You can hardly call it a light," said Willow.

"It glows brighter at night," said a troll. "Especially for the last week. We don't work at nights, but whatever the boss has being doing over the last six nights has made the jewel glow so brightly I can see it from the mountain I live on."

"What's the spire for?" said Mum. "It seems odd, out here on its own."

Barney pushed aside some foliage at the base of the spire. "This isn't all of the spire," he said, scooping some earth aside. "The rest of it is buried."

"That's not all that's buried," said a troll. "The spire is just one part of a whole mansion house, and there's other buildings down there too, lost beneath the ground."

"How do we get in?" said Granny, becoming impatient. "Show us the entrance or you won't be getting your gold."

The tall troll pointed at a large nondescript rock, its surface weather worn and smooth. "It's right there."

"Password?" said Granny, jingling the money pouch.

The troll opened his mouth to speak, but was silenced by

his friend, who shook his head. "Whisper it to her," he said. "Let her speak it. Maybe the boss man can tell who opened it — we don't want the blame if these lot cause him problems."

Granny held her nose as the troll placed his lips next to her ear. "No offence," she said. "But have you heard of mouth hygiene?"

Th troll grunted and whispered a short sentence. Granny looked at him. "It sounds very vengeful," she said.

"The boss seems like a vengeful man," said the troll. He held his hand out. "Gold."

"Not until I've seen it open with my *own* eyes," said Granny, stepping forward and gazing down at the rock. She cleared her throat. "An eye for an eye," she said, her voice loud and deliberate.

The rock trembled a little, the dry soil at its base shaking and a deep groan coming from within it — as if it had a voice. Granny took a step backwards as the rock twisted and turned, its hard form becoming soft and rubbery, until with a gentle hiss it slid to the side, revealing a gaping hole with a set of stone steps leading into the darkness.

"Amazing," said Barney.

"Gold," said a troll. "Now."

"It's a small entrance," said Granny. "How on earth do you get all the lead down there? It must be a real struggle."

"There is a river running below us," said the troll, his hand making a grab for the money pouch, which Granny expertly side stepped. "He brings everything he requires in by boat. The entrance is hidden by a waterfall on the opposite edge of the city, near the mountains."

"How do we close it after us?" I said.

"Repeat the password when you are inside and the entrance will close. Now give us the gold, or you *will* have a fight on your hands. I'm beginning to think your goat is all bleat and no bite."

AN EYE FOR AN EYE

Granny handed over the coins, carefully counting out three pieces into each troll's hand as they formed a queue before her. "Thank you," she said, as the trolls headed into the trees, leaving us to gaze into the void.

"I'll go first," said Barney. "I can see flickering light at the bottom of the stairs. There must be torches down there."

Cold creeping air rose from the entrance, musty and thick, and I swallowed hard. "It feels wrong," I said. "It feels evil."

"There's dark magic here, no doubt," said Mum. She licked her lips and frowned. "I can taste it."

My skin crawled as a soft voice came from the air behind me, the sound itself brushing the nape of my neck with warmth. I turned to see a shimmering shape, struggling to take form, and surrounded by trails of red smoke, swirling in and out of existence. "Hear me," came the voice again, distant and ethereal, with no real substance.

"Maeve?" I said. "Is that you?"

With everyone's attention on the apparition, it spoke again, distant and haunted. "It is me, Maeve. I cannot take form here, there is dark magic blocking me. I barely found you. The signals from the stones I gave you is weak. As am I. I bring bad news of Eva, Gladys."

"What news?" said Granny, her hand on her chest. "What's happened to her? What's happened to my sister?"

Maeve shimmered and faded, her shape barely visible, as if covered by a veil of muslin. "I went to Derek's home, and Eva is not there. There has been a struggle, and I fear for her safety. Derek's staff was tossed aside, the jewel which decorated it missing, as is he. I fear you were correct, I fear Derek has moved to the darkness. I fear for your safety, and I cannot help you… I cannot reach you."

"A jewel missing from Derek's staff, a jewel on top of the spire, and a jewel mentioned in the inscription near the castle you found, Maeve," said Willow. "What does it mean?"

The air popped and crackled, electric swirling among us, and Maeve briefly took on her solid form, her eyes scared and her voice urgent. "I have no answers, but you are our only hope. All of you. I feel darkness approaching. I fear for The Haven and everyone in it, I sense you are in the presence of great danger, but you must hurry, you must —"

Her words were cut off by an abrupt puff of red smoke, and Maeve was gone, a final shimmering of faint light the only proof she'd been there.

"You heard her," said Granny, rushing for the entrance into the depths. "My sister needs me."

"She needs *us*," I corrected, following her.

CHAPTER FIFTEEN

*B*arney had pushed his way past Granny, refusing to allow her to descend the steps before him, his face set with an urgency I'd never seen before. He was as nervous as the rest of us, and he had every right to be, without any magic of his own — although I'd felt my own magic draining from me with every step nearer to the spire we'd taken. We were unprotected, all of us mortal in a place where powerful and dark magic resided.

Barney led the way down the steps, and I followed him — so close that I could hear his breathing coming in heavy anxious puffs. Boris's hooves clicked on the stone steps behind me, and the narrow corridor darkened as Willow repeated the password Granny had spoken, and the entrance closed with an ominous thud.

We spoke in hushed tones as we descended the long flight of steps, none of us with the magic available to conjure a light, and each of us holding tightly to the clothing of the person in front. Soon Barney spoke, his voice calmer and his breathing less laboured. "I can see the bottom," he said. "There *are* torches."

Barney stepped onto the dusty ground at the base of the steps, and relief flooded me as I stepped behind him. The passage was much wider than the staircase, and the claustrophobia which had been building in me was washed away by the warm light emitted by the flaming torches which lined the walls of the passageway.

Musty air filled my nostrils, bringing to mind the smell of *The Water Witch* when I'd bought her; unloved and damp throughout. A cool breeze blew across my face and the nearest torch flickered. As my eyes adjusted to the darkness, crevices in the walls began to take shape, and as a torch burned bright as another breeze ran past it, the faded letters of a sign high on the wall came into focus. "It's a shop," I said. "A very old shop."

"We're in a buried street," said Boris. "Not a corridor."

Willow wiped her hand across a smooth part of the wall, and the surface below the dirt reflected the torchlight like a mirror. "Glass," she said. "A window."

Barney glanced above his head. "The tree roots are holding the roof up," he said. "I'm surprised these buildings are still standing with all that weight on top of them."

The tree roots *were* the roof. Gnarled and thick, and high above us, the old roots twisted into one another, forming a shelf on which the ground soil lay. Smaller roots hung in clusters like strands of long grey hair, and the occasional drop of water fell to the floor, pooling against the ancient walls of crumbling buildings. It must have taken centuries for nature to form the ceiling, and I wondered when the forgotten street had last seen daylight, or heard the singing of a bird.

"Which way?" said Mum, her head twisting left and right, ignoring Barney's architectural concerns.

"I think we should head towards the spire," I said. "I tried to estimate the distance we travelled along the steps. I'm

AN EYE FOR AN EYE

guessing we're thirty metres below ground level and the staircase was about two hundred metres in length." I pointed to the right. "The house with the spire must be that way."

Granny rushed ahead, taking a torch from an iron bracket on the wall. "Quickly," she said. "Something tells me Eva is here. I can sense her. I always could, even without magic."

Barney handed me a torch and took another for himself. Willow and Mum followed suit, and soon we resembled a mob of angry villagers walking the buried village streets. The only things missing were the pitchforks, and without magic we could have used them. Any weapon would have been better than nothing.

We cast long shadows as we walked, which dragged over the walls of derelict buildings and over the thick trunk of a long-rotted tree which stood in what had once been the front yard of a small cottage. The street widened and the cottages turned into larger houses. Smaller alleyways and streets led off the route we were following, and as we passed a turning to the left, my nose told me of a scent I was familiar with. "I smell the river," I said, "and diesel fumes. Derek must be here, and if he's got Eva, they must have come by boat. We should look."

"So much for Derek using magic to transport himself everywhere," Willow said. "Maeve was wrong about that, wasn't she?"

"He'd have to use a boat," said Mum. "It's possible for him to transport another person with himself, but that person has to be a willing participant in the magic. Eva wouldn't have come without a fight. He'd have had no choice but to bring her by boat. The same as the three witches the dwarfs saw tied up. I'm sure Derek would have liked to have magically transported his victims around The Haven, but no witch would have gone with him willingly."

"Don't use that word," said Granny. "*Victim*. It makes it sound so final, like there's already no hope for those poor people. No hope for my sister."

We headed down the side street, walking toward the smell of river and fuel, the light from my torch showing a very different surface below our feet than the one we'd recently been walking on. "Look," I said. "There's footprints everywhere."

"And gouges out of the ground as if heavy objects were dragged," commented Boris, his nose close to the ground. "It smells of trolls too. This is the route they used to transport the lead and building equipment. I hear running water too; the boat must be nearby."

He was right. The unmistakable sound of a fast running river was close. I took a few more steps and held my torch ahead of me. The red hull of a boat shone back at me, and we hurried toward it, not caring if anybody hostile was aboard the vessel, only caring about the safety of Eva and the other six witches. We reached the river quickly. The bank-side had obviously once been used as a docking point for boats, and rusty mooring posts dotted the stone quay — the red boat tied to one of them with a thick rope, looking out of place among the rotting dereliction of its surroundings. A rat slithered into the water as it heard us approach, its beady eyes reflecting the light of the torches, and its torpedoing body leaving a wake as it swam with the current.

"Only Derek and rats would feel at home down here," said Granny, lifting a leg as she prepared to climb aboard the boat.

Barney stepped in front of her. "No, Gladys," he said. "None of you have magic while we're down here, my police training makes me the only one equipped for this situation."

Granny gave him a smile and stepped aside. "Be careful,

Barney," she said, placing a hand on his forearm. "We all love you. You know that, don't you?"

Barney nodded and squeezed Granny's trembling hand. He leapt aboard with a smile in my direction, his long legs making easy work of climbing the hull wall, and his hair a vivid red under the torchlight. Granny was right. We did love him. I loved him, and the seriousness of our situation hit me in the gut with a surprise blow which made me gasp. "Please be careful," I said, as Barney climbed the ladder to the upper deck where the entrance hatch to the hold stood proud.

He nodded and lifted the hatch, the hinges creaking and the boat rocking as dark water sped beneath it. The boat wasn't big, but was large enough to carry the tonne weight of lead the dwarfs had sold Derek each time he had visited them. It was more than large enough to hide somebody in the shadows of the hold, though, but my senses told me the boat would be empty, they told me that we would find our answers below the spire with the jewel. In the long-buried house.

Barney held the torch above the hole, peering into the hold. "It looks empty," he said. "I'll make sure." He lowered himself into the hull, and a thud from inside, followed by muffled footsteps, told me he was safe.

Flame-light flickered on the hull, and a curling shape of gold caught my eye — the sweeping tail of a letter. I'd thought the boat was unnamed, but it was apparent that Derek didn't clean his hull very often. Layers of grime covered the boat's moniker, but with a few vigorous wipes of my sleeve I exposed enough of the painted letters to make sense of them. "*A Vision of Beauty*," I read aloud.

"He didn't name it after himself then," said Granny. "*The Ugly Bastard* would have been more appropriate."

Barney's movement through the boat was easily detectable by the sound of his footsteps, which echoed with an alien presence in the otherwise abandoned world we found ourselves in. Finally, his head emerged from the hatch, and he made his way slowly off the boat and onto the bank. "There's nobody aboard," he said, standing next to Granny, "but I did find this."

Granny's strangled whimper fed into the fear I already felt. The piece of fabric that Barney held was soaked in blood, the floral pattern typical of Aunt Eva's fashion sense, and the discarded chains he held in his other hand, bundled next to his torch, spoke of imprisonment.

"Eva," said Granny.

"There's not much blood in the boat," said Barney. "The fabric was caught on a nail, I think she cut herself as she pulled it free. I'd expect to see a lot more blood if somebody was… well… you know."

"Murdered," said Granny. "Just say what you mean."

"Can witches be murdered?" said Boris, pushing himself against Granny's leg in an attempt to comfort her.

"Of course," said Granny. "Especially down here with no magic, but even *with* magic a witch can be killed. The Haven only protects us from death by natural causes, not death at the hands of a psychopath."

"We should go," said Barney. "We'll follow the footsteps from the boat — I'm certain they'll lead us to the house with the spire."

CHAPTER SIXTEEN

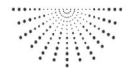

*B*arney was correct, as we'd all suspected he'd be. The footsteps and disturbed earth beneath our feet led us straight to the rusting gates of a large house, the hinges weakened by centuries of neglect, their wrought iron load tilted and twisted. The house loomed at the end of a driveway, our torches illuminating the old walls and roof. The spire we'd known we'd find thrust upward from the centre of the roof, vanishing into the tangle of tree roots which formed a dark, living sky.

"I feel Eva," said Granny, stepping through the gateway. "I know she's here."

The house was large, and dead trees formed a splintered landscape in what would have once been an impressive garden. Barney led the way along the rubble strewn driveway, the light from his torch picking out an old sundial and an ornate birdbath, both of no use in the dark and lifeless underground world.

"A light," said Barney, nearing the entrance, the wooden doors cracked and held open by rotted debris. "I see a light inside and I smell smoke too."

"Look," said Mum, taking a step backwards and lifting her torch.

Smoke drifted from a ruined chimney, torchlight turning it amber as gathered like a cloud amongst the roots, its tendrils spreading through the canopy.

"A fire," I said. "That answers any questions about anybody being at home."

"Maybe the kettle's on too," said Willow, the tremble in her voice betraying her attempt at seeming upbeat.

A floorboard creaked as Barney entered the house, and he glanced at us. "Be careful," he warned. "Stay behind me, all of you."

At the end of a long corridor, lined with stone sculptures and dusty furniture, the wall was painted a flickering orange from the light which poured from an open doorway. The fire. We ignored the sweeping marble staircase which loomed on our left, and followed Barney as he edged closer to the room, reaching down to pick up a length of wood and brandishing it as if it was his police nightstick. I grabbed a rusty length of metal, happy to feel its weight in my hand, and the rummaging scuffles behind me told me everyone else was arming themselves too. What I expected to do with a piece of metal against whatever dark magic Derek possessed, I didn't know, but as I gripped it tighter, its solid reassurance gave me some hope.

The crackle of burning wood grew louder as we approached the doorway, and I jumped in fear as torchlight picked out the haunted eyes of an old man in a portrait which hung on the wall next to me. Barney came to a stop a few feet from the doorway and looked over his shoulder, his eyes serious and his brow furrowed. "Boris," he whispered. "We're the only men here. We should go in first."

"Of course," said Boris, pushing past me and taking his

place next to Barney, like a strange breed of horned guard dog.

"Sexist," murmured Granny.

"Really, Granny?" I said. "Now?"

"Nerves," said Granny, squeezing my shoulder. "And I can't help calling it out *wherever* I see it. It's innate."

Boris nudged Barney's leg with a horn. "After you, copper," he said.

Barney gave me one last smile, and with Boris at his heels, stepped into the room. He was silent for a few moments, and then appeared again, his face less concerned. "It's empty," he said. "Come on."

The room smelt of burning logs, damp furniture, and soil. The large fireplace roared with a bright fire, and a pile of fresh logs stood next to the hearth. A chair and a table, both wiped clean, had been dragged in front of the fireplace — the only sign that somebody had benefited from the fire's warmth. The other furniture was as decrepit as the rest of the underground world. Dust covered everything, and wood had rotted while metal had rusted. Pictures still hung on the walls, their subjects lost beneath grime, some of them hanging at odd angles — ready to crash to the bare floorboards at any moment.

"He's been here," said Granny, gazing around. "Derek's been here, with my sister, and those other poor witches. I can sense him. I can sense evil."

Willow stood before a canvas on the wall, wiping the dirt from the oil paint with her fingers. "I thought so," she said, rubbing at some stubborn grime with a thumb. "I could make out a little of the painting under the dirt, look, its a boat. A red boat."

The paint was badly faded beneath the dirt. A large circular window sat high in the wall opposite the picture, and I suspected it had once allowed streaming sunlight into the room which had ruined the painting, instead of the roots which now searched and poked for a route through the broken glass and rotting frame.

"Who is it with the boat?" I said, leaning closer to the canvas, my nose almost brushing the old artwork. "Derek?"

The shape of a person next to the boat was hard to make out, and the paint had cracked where the face should have been. It was a man though, I was sure. Or maybe a woman.

"I don't know," said Willow, "but it's definitely the same red boat that Barney's just been on. I can tell by the shape."

"This place is really old," said Barney. "That painting is really old. How can it possibly be the same boat? It would have rotted by now."

"Magic," said Granny. "Come on, Barney, use that noggin of yours."

"I see something shiny," said Boris, peering beneath an old chair in a dark corner. "In the dust." He reached beneath the chair, using a hoof to drag the object towards him, dust rising into the air in billowing clouds which made him cough and splutter. "It's a piece of cloth," he said. "With little jewels on it."

The oval piece of cloth almost crumbled as I picked it up from the dust at Boris's feet, and two tiny jewels fell from their mountings. It took a few seconds to realise what it was I was holding, the two holes through which string or elastic could be threaded finally making it apparent. "It's an eye-patch," I said. "Covered in tiny jewels."

Footsteps thudded at the doorway, and Mum gave a frightened gasp as a figure shrouded by shadows walked into the room. "I wondered where that had got to! I lost it almost five hundred years ago, and to think it was under that chair all the time! Oh well, it matters not. I think the one I wear now is much nicer!"

"Hilda?" said Granny. "Is that you?"

The figure stepped into the light cast by the fire, and the bejewelled eye-patch she wore glinted in the orange light. Granny was right, it was Hilda. "Hello, Gladys," she said. "How nice of you to bring your family for a visit. I think we'll have a wonderful night together. I've been looking forward to today for a long time, a very long time indeed."

"What's going on?" said Granny. "Is Eva here?" And Derek?"

Hilda smiled. "Yes, Gladys, they're both here. I'm sure they'd love to see you. They're waiting patiently for you in my new room — the room that those dumb trolls built for me. I like to call it my burn room, but you might like to call it the death room, or the room of agonising pain, because that's what you're going to experience in there."

Mum lifted her hand, but no sparks danced at her fingertips. "What are you talking about, Hilda? What's happening here?" she said.

Hilda laughed, her whole body shaking. She looked at Willow, a smile on her lips. "You've cleaned my painting for me," she said. "How kind. That's me with *A Vision of Beauty*. A lovely name for a seer's boat, don't you think?"

Barney lifted the piece of wood in his hand, and I closed my grip on the length of metal I carried.

"You're not thinking of attacking a helpless old lady, are you?" said Hilda, her face twisting with anger. "I've got no time for fighting with you people. I think it's about time I took you all to my burn room, it's dark outside and tonight the jewel on my spire is going to glow brighter than it's ever glowed before."

Granny took a step towards Hilda, but one step was all she manged. Hilda lifted both hands and magic crackled at her fingertips. Sparks of red and blue danced in the air weaving between us, brushing my skin with a cold evil which made me shudder. Granny sank to her knees as if being pushed to the floor by a heavy weight, and Barney's spine arched as he was flung against a wall, his torch dropping to his feet where the flame was extinguished by a shower of Hilda's sparks, and the length of wood he'd armed himself with turning to dust.

"Impossible," groaned Granny. "How do you have magic and we don't?"

Hilda laughed again, her magic disarming and immobilising us all, the flames in the hearth growing brighter, lighting the room and warming the air. "I'll tell you everything when I get you all into my burn room," she said. "And I won't leave a thing out. My plan has taken centuries to bring to fruition and I'm dying to tell you all about it. I've had to bite my tongue for so many years, but tonight I can finally tell my tale! Tonight, I can shine as bright as the jewel on top of my spire!"

Torches fell from people's hands, and the metal rod I carried dropped to the floor, clunking as it hit the wooden boards. I tried to move, but invisible tethers of magic held me still, icy cold against my flesh, becoming tighter each time I struggled against them.

"This is such fun!" laughed Hilda. She waved her hand, green sparks flowing from her fingertips, swirling through the room and searching for targets. Willow gasped as sparks flooded her nostrils, and Boris grunted as his ears were invaded. A stream of green approached my face, the dancing lights forcing their way into my mouth, warming my throat and making me gag.

"A spell of total control," said Hilda. "You're all under my command. Now follow me, all of you, in silence. Eva and Derek are waiting for you, and Maeve will be along soon. It's going to be a good night!"

Hilda walked from the room and like obedient servants we followed her, taking one forced step after another, help-

AN EYE FOR AN EYE

less against the powerful magic which controlled us, and unable to speak.

"This way," said Hilda, walking ahead of us in the darkness, only her voice leading the way. "My burn room is where the ball-room once was; right beneath my spire. You're going to love it, I'm sure!"

CHAPTER SEVENTEEN

*H*ilda led us through the darkness, magic fizzing around us in brightly coloured sparks which occasionally lit up a sculpture or painting as we were led along corridors. Finally, Hilda ordered us to stop. A tall wooden door loomed before us, its brass knobs dusty and faded with time. "I had some memorable times in here," said Hilda, pushing open the door which groaned in protest, "but tonight's going to the best of them all."

Bright light burst from the open doorway, and my eyes stung as they adjusted to their new surroundings. We followed Hilda into a huge room, the walls, ceiling, and floors lined with sheets of dull silver metal. Lead. Lots of it, covering every surface, creating a room that was void of character, but full of dread. In the centre of the room, hanging from the metal sheet ceiling on a length of copper coloured wire, was the source of the bright light which flooded the room. A glass ball, the size of a melon, emitted a white light and tiny sparks of blue electric, which cut through the air like lighting, making a sizzling sound as they arced from the ball.

Below the sphere was a large round stone plinth on which was stacked a layered pile of wood, with a tall wooden stake protruding from the centre, the top of which stopped a few inches shy of the glowing ball. It was built in an identical manner to the pyre in the painting in Maeve's library, and icy tendrils of dread gripped my heart as I imagined what Hilda intended to do.

Next to the pyre stood Derek and Eva, both immobilised by the same magic that Hilda had used on us, only their eyes free to move.

"Join Derek and Eva," Hilda commanded. "Make a semi-circle around the pyre. I need you all to be able to see. The burning will begin when everyone's in place and the guest of honour arrives."

Unable to prevent my feet from moving, I shuffled into position, taking my place next to the pyre, with Boris on my left and Barney on my right. I used every available grain of inner strength I possessed, reaching inside myself for something that would help me break the magic which controlled me. Spells from Granny's book flashed before me, but I could do nothing to make one work, it was as if my body wasn't mine, as if I was peering out of the eyes of another person, unable to do anything to control my fate or the fates of the people I loved.

Panic surged through me in a powerful wave that made me nauseous, and I made eye contact with my sister, desperate to connect with somebody, desperate for somebody to tell me it was all going to work out fine, but Willow's eyes reflected my own fear, her pupils large and tears welling. I couldn't swivel my eyes far enough to the right to see Barney, but his rapid breathing told me he was scared too, and why wouldn't he have been? It was obvious that Hilda meant somebody great harm, and it was as equally obvious that she intended to make the rest of us watch the horror. Boris was a blur of white in my peripheral vision, but I managed to roll my eyes far enough to the left to tell he was staring at Granny, whose eyes were calm as she attempted to convey the same emotion to anybody who looked at her — trying her best to keep her family soothed.

Hilda stood to the side of the pyre, her bony hands held before her thin body and her eyes dancing with excitement. "I think it's time for the guest of honour to make an appearance," she said. Her hand moved across her body as she cast a spell, and the air next to her shimmered and hissed as Maeve slowly took form, her face lined with anxiety and her hands bound with a silvery thread. "What magic is this?" she said. "Hilda, what are you doing?"

Hilda looked at Maeve. "Am I to take your voice too, like I have the voices of everyone else present at this ceremony? Or will you remain calm? Listening to what I have to tell you?"

"I will remain calm," said Maeve, her eyes searching the room, trying to make sense of what was happening, looking for a way to escape. "Why are we here, Hilda? How am I here, and why do I have no magic, yet you so obviously do?"

It filled me with revulsion, and hatred for Hilda — knowing that we were going to be forced to watch Maeve burn. She'd been named the guest of honour, and I doubted that the moniker had been bestowed upon her for any less heinous reason. It seemed that for the second time in her long life, Maeve was to be burned alive, and we were to be the witnesses. Bile rose in my throat, and the acrid flavour of guilt filled my mouth, as I found myself hoping that should Maeve not be the only victim of Hilda's madness, I wished death upon Derek and not somebody I loved.

Hilda gave Maeve a long drawn out smile, the corners of her mouth curling with hatred as she prepared to speak. "You have no magic, Maeve, because I choose it to be that way. Anything that happens in this room is of my making. I

AN EYE FOR AN EYE

control you, all of you, and soon I will control your haven. In fact, my power is spreading as we speak, for the last six nights I've been feeding the jewel on top of my spire with magic, and as the jewel fed on its prey, my power has been spreading throughout this land, weakening you, and making it easy to transport you here against your will. Soon I will be the ruler of this dimension, and I fear I shall not rule it with such a …" Maeve made a growl of revulsion as Hilda took her hand and ran a finger over the soft skin. "… fair hand as you have," she finished.

Maeve's eyes dimmed, and her jaw muscles rolled as she clenched her teeth. "Six nights… six missing witches," she said. "What have you done, Hilda? What have you done to those poor women?"

Hilda's laugh echoed around the room, bouncing off the walls and ceiling, the lead dulling the high-pitched mirth. "They burned well," she said. "Their magic left them just as I predicted it would, deflected by the lead walls and targeted at my orb, feeding my jewel and spreading my power across the land. You see, you're not the only witch who releases a burst of magic when she slowly burns to death. It would appear that the pain causes all witches to do so. Call those six deaths practice runs if you will, I'm appreciative that they gave their lives — although they didn't go easily — but tonight is the main event, tonight is the night that I recreate the day you burned, Maeve — all those years ago, *and* recreate the stream of power which created this land. The power will be harnessed to me through my jewel, and then I shall finally enter the castle which you thought you had hidden so well. The castle that belongs to the one true ruler of The Haven. The castle which belongs to me."

"You would burn six witches so you could rule The Haven?" said Maeve. "If it must be that I am the seventh as it seems is to be my fate, then I will go without a struggle, but you must promise not to harm any of these other people. If you do not promise me that, then I shall fight my death with every ounce of power I have within me. I will do everything to make my magic work against you as I burn, everything in my power to foil your plan."

"How very brave," said Hilda, her voice low. "How very, very brave of you, Maeve, but I'm afraid that tonight is not your night. You shan't be tethered to my stake with flames melting the flesh from your bones, screaming as the heat boils your blood, and choking as the hot clogging smoke fills your lungs. No, that won't be you, Maeve, you are just here to watch — to know you are beaten, after all these centuries." She lifted a hand and extended a finger. She pointed at us, one by one, turning in a slow spin, her eyes glinting as they met mine, but passing me quickly, moving on to the next person. "No, tonight, I will be burning …" She stopped spinning and jabbed her finger at the intended victim. "Gladys Weaver!"

Granny's eyes dropped briefly, but quickly lifted in defiance and met Hilda's. As Granny winked at the woman who was to murder her, my gut twisted and my heart struggled to beat. Only the dark magic which held me in place prevented me from collapsing.

HILDA WAVED a hand in Granny's face, showering her with red sparks of magic. "You have your voice back, Gladys, and soon you will have your magic back, but not for long."

"You vile old bitch," said Granny. "I've never trusted you."

"Why are you doing this, Hilda?" said Maeve. "I thought we were your friends."

"The time has come," said Hilda, scraping a long fingernail over Maeve's cheek. "Finally. The moment I've been waiting for. The moment I've ran through my mind over and over again. I've often fantasised about how you were going to react when you realised who I really was, when you realised that you never escaped me, when you realised that you were beaten." Maeve shuddered as Hilda licked her face, her tongue sliding over Maeve's chin and across her lips. She drew her tongue back into her mouth and gave a satisfied sigh. "And now that moment is here, it tastes so much better than I ever thought it would. I taste fear on your flesh, I taste uncertainty, and I taste curiosity. You want to know why sweet little Hilda the seer has burned six witches and is about to burn another."

Maeve nodded, her eyes searching Hilda's face for answers. "I do."

Hilda took her eye-patch between two ragged fingernails and lifted it slowly, moving her face closer to Maeve's, her tongue flicking like a snake's, and her breathing ragged and excited. "Do you recognise me, Maeve? Do you remember my eyes? Do they scare you? One of green and one of brown — a gift from god, a gift given to me so I could search out your type and burn them where I found them!"

"It can't be," said Maeve. "*You* can't be!"

"But it is, and I am," said Hilda. "I am the Witch-finder General, although that title is redundant in this land of yours — finding witches is not hard, and I no longer wish to burn all of your type — ruling them would give me far more satisfaction, and if the truth be known, I've become quite fond of The Haven and *some* of its inhabitants. I'm hoping Gladys Weaver will be the last witch I am forced to burn, because to be quite honest, the smell of burning flesh is very hard to get out of the nostrils."

I strained at the magic that held me, but could do nothing. A sickening pressure built within me, and I knew that if

Maeve didn't possess the power to save Granny from the flames, then nobody did.

"Show yourself," said Granny. "If you are the Witch-finder."

Hilda laughed, the sound perverse and haunting, tinged with an evil which made Granny's eyes darken. Hilda's whole body shook violently, as if she were a marionette at the end of strings controlled by a psychopath. The air around her moved and whispered, vibrating in time with the pulses of energy which shook her. She lifted her face towards the ceiling, the old flesh on her chin shifting on the bone, as if being twisted into a new shape by an invisible hand. Gold and red sparks danced around her, and her voice deepened as she laughed louder, the very clothes on her thin frame changing as her shoulders widened and she grew in height. The skin on her hands crawled, and her long feminine fingernails shortened, like a cat drawing in its claws, until they were short and at the tips of thick masculine fingers.

"No," said Maeve.

"How?" said Granny.

In place of Hilda, a man stood before us, over six feet in height, a tall black hat on his head and a high necked white shirt beneath his dark clothing. He gazed around the room, his eyes, one green and one brown, studying us in turn. He lifted his hat in a macabre greeting, revealing long dark hair, and he split his mouth in a manic grin. "I *am* the Witch-finder General!" he shouted. "And tonight, I will burn one more witch!" He took a deep breath and looked around the room he'd built, pride evident in his expression. "First, though. Let me tell you all a story —"

"I don't want to listen to your stories," said Granny. "If you're going to kill me, get it over with. I don't want to hear one more word from your hateful mouth."

The Witch-finder bent at the waist, and put his face close

to Granny's. "I would advise you do listen, Gladys Weaver. It will make you understand why you should concentrate on burning well when I wrap you in flames, it will help you understand that if you struggle or fight my magic, that I will kill the remainder of your family, one by one, until I get the result I desire." He cast his eyes over the rest of his captives. "If anything, listening to me will buy your family some more time in your presence before they lose you for ever. It looks as if they love you very much, which will aid me immensely when you burn — you see, love is a vital ingredient which was missing from the last six burnings. Look, Gladys, look at the love they have for you — they all have tears in their eyes. Even that annoying goat is weeping."

Granny closed her eyes, not in defiance, but to hide the tears I'd seen glimmering in the bright light. She opened them again and started directly at the man she'd known as Hilda for so many years. "Tell your story if you must, Witchfinder," she spat.

CHAPTER EIGHTEEN

Like a motivational speaker on a stage, the Witch-finder clasped his hands behind his back and began pacing, the heels of his black leather boots clicking on the lead floor. "Where should I begin?" he pondered.

With a sigh, he lowered himself into a seating position on the stone plinth, using the logs piled high behind him as a backrest. "I know!" he said, raising a single finger. "I'll start at the beginning — as the old saying goes. I'd offer you all a seat, but I enjoy watching you standing, trapped by my magic. It makes me realise how powerful I've become."

"Nobody's as powerful as they think they are," said Maeve.

The Witch-finder smiled, a glint in his eyes. "So very true," he said, "and how very pertinent to the story I have to tell. You see, Maeve, you didn't conjure The Haven into existence because you were more powerful than any other witch. It was purely a matter of luck that I chose to build the fire I burned you on in the place I did."

"In the middle of my village," said Maeve. "With the people I loved being forced to watch me suffer."

"Indeed," said the Witch-finder. "In fact, this house is built in the exact spot your pyre was built on. In a different dimension of course, but on the exact spot. The spire is built directly where the centre of the fire would have been."

Maeve's demeanour had become calmer and relaxed, but I could tell by the fierce spark in her eyes that she was struggling against the powerful magic which swirled through the room. I hoped with every fibre of my being that she would find the strength within her to save Granny from the awful fate she'd been threatened with.

The Witch-finder gazed upwards, as if drawing on memories, his face serene — the complete antithesis of the panic which gripped me, clawing at my gut and quickening my heartbeat, forcing my breath from me in frightened gasps.

Granny looked at me, the message in her eyes one of calm, but with a hint of hope. I took comfort from her, concentrating on trying to access my magic — if Granny could muster hope in such a situation, then so should I.

The Witch-finder gave a low laugh and continued with his story, his words wrapped in a pride that forced me to focus on my hatred for him, willing myself to find my magic. "I found you easily, Maeve," he said. "When you turned that man into a toad for a day, as punishment for stealing eggs from you, some of the villagers couldn't wait to report you for being a witch. When the news got to me I came quickly, I hadn't burned a witch for almost a full month, and I was itching to smell roasting flesh again."

"Evil," said Granny. "That's what you are."

"On the contrary," said the Witch-finder. "I was on the side of good. God gave me a gift — the gift of seeing. My visions began when I was six-years-old, and my mother said it was my special eyes which made my skill possible. I'd already seen Maeve in a vision, but the tell-tale villagers made the job of finding her easier, and saved me a little time."

The orb above the pyre crackled and dimmed briefly, and the Witch-finder looked at Granny. "I am running out of time, as are you, Gladys. The jewel requires more magic." He stood up and began pacing again. "I will tell my story quickly, so as I can get on with the important business of burning you."

Granny laughed, a bitter outburst of defiance. "Do what you must," she said.

"As Maeve burned," said the Witch-finder, "surrounded by people who loved her, and the people who had betrayed her, I heard a strange noise... a throbbing hum the like of which I'd never heard before, and the ground vibrated beneath my feet. As the flames grew hotter and Maeve screamed louder, the sound grew in volume too, until Maeve vanished in a flash of light." He closed a fist. "One moment she was there and the next... she was gone. The villagers thought it had been God's doing of course, but I knew different. I'd seen a flash of light at the base of the fire, and heard the humming sound grow louder. I knew it was magic, but I also knew it hadn't all been of Maeve's doing — she'd been in too much pain to cast a spell that powerful. Of that, I was certain."

"I watched you smiling as I burned," said Maeve. "The anger I felt for you fuelled my magic."

"Oh, your magic had a part in in it all," said the Witch-finder. "But you had help. When the fire had cooled, I searched the ashes. I searched them for a day and a night, finally digging beneath the hardened ground, looking for the cause of the sound I'd heard." The Witch-finder looked upwards. "And what I found sits on top of my spire, where it has done for six hundred years, waiting for this day."

"The jewel," said Granny.

AN EYE FOR AN EYE

The Witch-finder nodded. "Indeed, the jewel. Luckily for me, I had another witch captive in the horse-drawn cage I travelled with — what I now know was an oriental witch, a beautiful prize I wished to give to the king. She was too important to burn — a witch from a foreign land had never been seen before. The king would have rewarded me handsomely."

"Did you make her suffer too?" spat Granny. "You vile creature."

"I would have, of course," said the Witch-finder. "But it wasn't to be. I required her help, and I promised to slaughter every man, woman, and child in the village if she refused to comply. The cage bars were made of lead — I knew, even all those years ago, that lead was a deterrent to magic, so I took a risk by releasing her, but she valued the lives of innocents above her own. She gave me the help I needed."

"How does *your* magic work in this lead lined room?" said Maeve. "I do not understand."

"My jewel is more powerful than any magic you have ever known," said the Witch-finder. "The orb above the pyre is connected to it, and only I am able to access it. The magic flowing from my jewel cannot be hindered by lead, for it is the very jewel that created The Haven, and I am joined with it as one. The lead prevents you weaker witches from accessing magic, and try as hard as you might, that fact will not change – you are powerless in this room, and you will be powerless against me outside this room when my jewel has been fully powered by magic."

"I don't —"

The Witch-finder interrupted Maeve with a wave of his hand. "No more time wasting. I must hurry." He sat down again and continued. "The oriental witch told me what the jewel was — a simple diamond which had reacted to Maeve's magic, amplifying its power and causing an opening to another dimension. This dimension. The dimension you call your own, Maeve. As you know, though — as is inscribed on the stone near the castle — the person with the one true power will rule The Haven."

"It mentions a jewel too…" said Maeve, her voice faltering, realisation spreading across her features.

The Witch-finder laughed. "Now you see — my power *and* my jewel!" He glanced to the side. "Now, where was I? Oh, yes! The oriental witch used magic to work out what had happened. She knew a dimension had been opened, and she knew that if I passed into that dimension carrying the jewel which had formed it, I would possess the very heart of the dimension, and when you possess the heart, you control the rest of the body. I would become magical, and rule this land."

"So why don't you rule The Haven?" said Granny. "You've been here for a long time. A very long time."

"She betrayed me," said the Witch-finder, dark anger lining his face. "As I passed into The Haven, through a portal she'd opened, she cast a spell and chipped a piece of diamond from the stone I carried. She kept that piece of diamond, and though it was only small, it dramatically reduced the power of the stone. The stone has provided me with magic in this land, but has never been powerful enough to afford me total control over The Haven…" The Witch-finder's tongue stroked his top lip, and he smiled. "…Until today."

He reached into his pocket and withdrew a jewel. He held it between finger and thumb, and inspected it, rolling it from left to right, the light from the orb reflecting off it, the sharp corners sparkling.

He placed it on the stone plinth next to him and straightened his collar. "When I arrived here, in The Haven, only a few days after Maeve, I already had magic, but I knew I wasn't as powerful as I could have been. I needed a disguise —

AN EYE FOR AN EYE

without strong magic I knew I'd be no match for Maeve, and it was highly doubtful that Maeve would have afforded the man who burnt her any mercy, so I used the power of the stone to shift my shape into the opposite of what I'd been. Instead of the handsome young man you see sitting before you today, I took on the shape of a grizzled old woman. The only problem was my eyes. I could only control their colour temporarily, for minutes at a time, so I came up with the idea of an eyepatch. It fitted my new persona perfectly, and as I still had my gift of visions, I became Hilda, the seer. It was perfect, and worked a treat, and what fun I had lifting my eyepatch occasionally, taunting Maeve when I was in her presence, but knowing the colour of my eyes could shift at any moment. The risk gave me such a wonderful feeling of excitement!"

"All the time we spent together," said Maeve. "To think that you fooled me for centuries makes me sick."

"Oh," said The Witch-finder. "Don't be too hard on yourself. I did begin to enjoy myself here, and I valued people's friendship too. When I first arrived in The Haven, I built this house, placing my jewel at the highest point, spreading its power, trying to take control of the land. As other witches fled the justice of the mortal world and found their way to The Haven, more people built homes near mine until there was a village.

I became popular in the village, using my gift of seeing to help people. After a century, I almost forgot who I really was, and when this village was hidden by a landslide, I moved to the east and began a new life, befriending people like yourselves and spending my time enjoying my boat and growing herbs, spices, and the best liquorice in The Haven. I enjoyed my life, and *nearly* forgot about my desire to control The Haven, until I had a powerful vision, almost fifty years ago, and now that vision is about to come true." He stood up, and took Granny's hand in his. "It's almost time for you to burn, Gladys."

"So, it was you all along," said Granny. "You were the dark haired man the dwarfs spoke of, and you were the man on Penny's boat."

"Of course," said the Witch-finder. "And my visit to the boat was very important for helping today's events go smoothly, Gladys."

"Why?" said Granny. "You didn't take anything."

"Oh, I did," said the Witch-finder. "You see, when we all sat together in Eva's garden, eating her mediocre food, I'd already burned four of the six witches — one a night, but I simply couldn't get enough magic into my jewel to make my plan work. Those witches just weren't powerful enough. When I saw you, surrounded by your family, I realised something of great importance. I realised that when I'd burnt Maeve, she'd been watched by people who loved her.

Love is a very potent magic, as you know, and I understood that as you were the eldest and frailest of your family, the love for you would be immense. As your family watch you burn, their love for you will enhance your magic and help power my jewel. As for what I took from your granddaughter's boat — well, to make sure your magic is deflected off the lead walls and collected in the orb above the pyre, there needs to be some of your essence inside it. I made a potion from the hair of each of the other six witches, and I thought it prudent to do the same for you."

"My hairbrush," said Granny. "I knew I'd packed it."

The Witch-finder nodded. "Indeed, and the potion helped draw you here, guiding you to clues and leading you too your demise."

The Witch-finder looked to his left, an eyebrow raised. "Derek is gesticulating wildly with his eyes, perhaps he wishes to speak." He flicked a hand, releasing sparks. "Speak,

AN EYE FOR AN EYE

Derek, but make it quick. When my jewel brings down the spell surrounding the castle of the one true ruler, and I take residence, then you'll have plenty of time for an audience with me, but for now, make your words count."

"Burn me!" said Derek. "I'm powerful. Don't burn Gladys. Not in front of her family. It's barbaric!"

I tried to twist my eyes in their sockets, but couldn't swivel them far enough to see him. Derek was willing to sacrifice himself to save my grandmother, and I couldn't even look at his face.

"Oh, Derek," said Granny. "I misjudged you. I'm sorry."

"It's a brave gesture," said the Witch-finder. "But there's not enough love in the room for you, Derek. Your magic just won't work."

"I'm sorry, Gladys," said Derek, "for anything I ever did to upset you."

"You just be good to my sister when you all get out of here," said Granny. She looked at the Witch-finder. "They will all get out of here, won't they?"

Granny's eyes darkened as the Witch-finder cupped her frail chin in his hand. "I give you my word that if you go to your death willingly, and the magic works, then I will harm no one. I won't need to, I will control this world. If you struggle, though, and my magic fails. I will burn your family one by one until the magic *does* work."

Granny nodded. Her fate accepted.

"Wait!" said Derek. "Why did you take the jewel from my staff?"

The Witch-finder scowled. "I know you're wasting time, trying to preserve the life of Gladys for as long as possible, but I *will* answer your question. The vision I spoke of having fifty years ago was unclear. It showed me that I needed to burn witches, and it showed me that I needed to come back to my buried home and build this room of lead beneath it.

The vision showed me the spell protecting the castle being broken, but it did not show me everything. Do you remember my vision at Eva's home, Derek?"

"I do," said Derek. "You spoke of a great power, and you spoke of a man with hair as black as coal."

Hilda had also spoken about a blossoming romance, and I shed a tear as I thought of Granny's love for Charleston. She would go to her death having never told the man she loved how she felt.

"That was foolish of me," said the Witch-finder. "I didn't mean to speak so candidly. I was excited you see, and when I become excited I speak my visions freely. I saw a vision of myself in this room, and I saw great power, I couldn't help myself, the words escaped my mouth. They did no harm though. My plan is working as expected. Nobody suspected me."

"What were you excited about?" said Derek. "What made you speak so freely?"

The Witch-finder picked up the small jewel from the stone plinth. "I was excited about the jewel in your staff, Derek. I had another vision as we sat at that table, one I kept to myself. I saw that the owner of the piece of diamond the oriental woman stole from me, was in that garden. Nobody else had a jewel like yours, Derek. The jewel that was set in the top of your staff *had* to be the missing piece, and when I place it beneath the fire Gladys will die in, I will have recreated Maeve's burning perfectly — the love for her, the pain, *and* the jewel beneath the blaze."

"But that jewel —"

The Witch-finder silenced Derek with a wave of his hand. "You too, Maeve," he said, taking her voice too. "The only sounds I wish to hear are the anguished screams of Gladys Weaver as she melts."

AN EYE FOR AN EYE

"You'll never be forgiven," said Granny. "You know that, don't you?"

"I neither expect or wish to be," said the Witch-finder. "I need no forgiveness. I will be immortal i this land, and I will rule this land. I care not for the forgiveness of any of my subjects.

He reached inside Granny's dress, eliciting a shout from her. "Burn me to death all you like, but never touch me without my authority!"

"I'm not trying to violate you, Gladys. I'm looking for the dementia cure which Maeve gave you. I need your magic working correctly while you burn, otherwise I may as well be burning a mortal. You won't be able to use your magic in this room, but with dementia still afflicting you, your magic will never leave your body, however hot I make the flames."

"It's on a chain, around my neck," said Granny. Realisation dawned in her eyes, and she stared at the floor to the left of me. "Charleston," she said. "When I take this cure, you'll be released from the body of Boris. The spell that trapped you in the goat was cast in the mortal world, the lead in this room won't stop it from being reversed. You must tell my son that I love him, and tell him never to come here —"

"Silence!" said the Witch-finder, taking the cork from the small glass vial which contained the cure.

Granny ignored him. "And, Charleston — I want you to know that I lov—"

The Witch-finder silenced Granny with magic, and her eyes dimmed, all hope leaving them. She stared ahead of herself, blankness on her face, as the Witch-finder forced the vial between my grandmother's lips and poured the contents down her throat.

A crackling sound next to me and a rush of warm air on my legs told me that the spell trapping Charleston in Boris's body had been reversed. Charleston would wake in Granny's guest bedroom, knowing what was happening in The Haven, unable to help us, and aware that he would probably never see any of us again.

Desperation fuelled more tears, and I wished I could move an arm to wipe them from my cheeks. I wanted to appear brave. I wanted to *be* brave, but the only sensations that coursed throughout my body were those elicited by fear.

The Witch-finder took Granny's hand in his. "Look," he said, glancing to my left. "It's a simple goat again. Perhaps I'll keep it as a pet, it can keep my lawns trimmed when I move into my castle."

Tears ran freely down Granny's cheeks, and she did as she was told when the Witch-finder gave her what would likely be the last instruction she would ever follow. "Get onto the plinth, Gladys. Your pyre awaits, as does your martyrdom."

CHAPTER NINETEEN

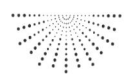

My whole body ached as I fought the spell which held me captive. The panic and perseverance in Willow's eyes showed she was doing the same. I didn't need to be able to see everybody to know they would be fighting too, even Barney, whose heavy breaths grew louder as Granny climbed onto the plinth and took her place on the pyre.

With Granny's back against the stake, and her legs knee deep in wood, the Witch-finder waved a hand. The spell forced Granny's hands behind her back, and she gave a grimace of pain as her hands were tied to the pole with a strand of silvery magic.

The Witch-finder gazed at his victim, a sickening pride in his smile, and a casualness in the way he spoke which made me shudder. "Have your voice back, Gladys. I'll need to hear your screams."

Granny looked at us in turn. "Don't mourn me in sadness," she said. "And don't remember me as I am now — helpless and tied to a stake, remember me as I was for all the years you knew me before this moment, because as horrible as this moment is — it's only one of the millions of beautiful moments I've lived through with all of you. I give my life freely to ensure none of you will be harmed."

"Yes, yes, very nice," said the Witch-finder. "Very sentimental." He bent at the waist and slipped the jewel he'd stolen from Derek's staff beneath the pile of wood. He muttered something under his breath, and flames appeared at his fingertips. "Now, if you've finished saying your goodbyes, I think it's time we got going. This fire is not going to light itself."

"Willow, Penny," said Granny, speaking quickly. "A woman couldn't have asked for kinder, nicer grandchildren. I love you both, deeply. You've both brought immeasurably joy to my life.

Barney, look after Penny — you're a fine man. I know you'll do good by Penny, and I hope you tell your children that their great grandmother loves them, wherever she is.

Eva, I was wrong about Derek, cherish him and cherish yourself. I love you.

Maggie, my second born, take care of yourself, my dear, dear daughter. You were always there for me, and I appreciate you more than you will ever know.

Maeve, thank you for everything, and I trust you will eventually beat The Witch-finder and rule The Haven again."

Flames flew from the Witch-finder's fingertips, and the hope I'd been holding onto that somehow one of us would be able to save Granny, evaporated in a surge of wretched despair.

The flames took hold quickly, wood crackling as it burnt, the smoke being drawn into the orb above the pyre.

Every muscle in my body fought at the magical bonds which held me, my emotions becoming a tangled mix of anger, fear and desperation. Time seemed to slow in my mind, but the flames that worked their way closer to

AN EYE FOR AN EYE

Granny's legs did not. As the first lick of heat touched her papery skin, she let out a whimper — the sound a cold blade of hopelessness which pierced my heart.

Memories of Granny flooded my mind as flames wrapped her legs in heat, her whimpers becoming loud shouts as she gave way to inevitable panic. I remembered her showing me and Willow how to make cup-cakes, the three of us laughing as we gave Granddad the single cake we'd flavoured with salt instead of sugar.

I remembered her teaching me how to read, using magic to bring the pictures in the book alive, and never getting frustrated when I couldn't pronounce difficult words. I remembered a beautiful woman, a kind woman, a complicated woman, but a woman I loved. A woman I loved deeply.

Heat spread from the fire, warming my neck and hurting my skin even at the distance I was from the flames, and I tried not to think of the temperatures Granny was experiencing.

As the flames licked at Granny's neck, and her screams mingled with the manic laughter of the Witch-finder, a surge of white light blinded me momentarily, and I had what was only my second vision since I'd discovered I possessed the power of seeing.

It seemed that the lead in the room prevented me from using magic, but it couldn't stop a vision — and even as I watched Granny's face disappear in flames, her screams becoming less intense and her magic visibly pouring into the orb above her head — I became calm, knowing that everything was going to be okay, but not knowing how or why.

The Witch-finder's cackling mirth grew louder as the orb above the fire grew brighter, and Granny became silent, her body hidden by flames, and her magical essence leaving her in beautiful strands of gold and amber which rose from the flames and filled the orb.

My vision faded, but I'd seen all I needed to see – Granny alive, and happier than I'd ever seen her — and I was certain that it was to happen in the *very* immediate future — as certain as I was that the Witch-finder was going to live out his immortality in misery, and not ruling The Haven as he had envisioned.

Willow's eyes had deadened, and I wished I could tell her everything would be okay, but she stared at the flames, lost in her despair.

A loud grating of metal was the first sign that something was not right with the Witch-finder's plan. The sound reverberated through the room, the floor trembling beneath my feet, and a heavy pounding making the walls shake violently.

The orb above the fire flickered, and the bright white light changed — slowly at first, whites becoming blues, then purples, until it throbbed with an angry red which cast the room in a scarlet glow.

The Witch-finder stepped backwards, his face lit with the dancing oranges of the flames, but concern replacing the glee which had emanated from him as Granny had suffered.

"What is this?" he shouted. He looked at Maeve. "Is this your doing, witch?"

Maeve's eyes remained expressionless, and the Witch-finder span on the spot as one of the lead walls groaned, it's surface bubbling and melting as if a great heat was forming behind it, forcing its way through the metal.

Molten lead dripped in a waterfall of silver, pooling on the floor at the base of the wall, and the dim glow of a light beyond the wall became visible, becoming brighter as lead spat and bubbled in its path.

"What is this?" shouted the Witch-finder, stepping backwards. "Who dares do this?"

White light filtered into the room, piercing the scarlet light cast by the orb, and parting the lead wall like the petals of a flower, spreading the metal until a perfect circle was formed. Brilliant blue light filled the hole, a dark shape appearing in the centre, its form becoming clearer as it approached, until it became apparent what it was — the silhouette of a person.

"Who are you?" shouted the Witch-finder. "Tell me!"

The silhouette stopped moving, and a loud vibrating voice filled the room — distant and warped by magic, but unmistakable as to whom it belonged. "Gladys, I'm here, and I love you too!" it boomed. "I have since the day I met you."

CHARLESTON HUANG STEPPED into the room, a closed fist held before him, blue light pouring from the ring on his finger.

"Everything's going to be okay," he said, confidence oozing from him. "I promise."

Light poured from his ring in a powerful stream which wrapped itself around the Witch-finder and thrust him upwards, pinning him against the ceiling, where he remained, silent and unmoving.

Charleston turned his attention to the fire, guiding a stream of light into the flames. The crackling of burning wood gave way to a melodious humming which changed in pitch and tempo as the flames rose and fell, becoming a dancing kaleidoscope of colours, the oranges and reds mixing with pinks, blues, and yellows, until there were only flames of white and blue.

The heat from the flames gave way to a gentle breeze which cooled my face, and I gazed into the fire, screaming inwardly as I caught a glimpse of Granny's charred lifeless face.

Charleston stood next to the fire, his dark eyebrows

narrowing as he concentrated, the light from his ring flowing into the cold blue flames.

Granny's face was hidden once more, and the flames grew taller, beginning to spin, twisting and turning, moving closer to the stake in the centre of the fire, until they wrapped Granny's body in light, enveloping her in a shimmering beauty which I instinctively knew was good magic. A healing magic.

"It's okay," murmured Charleston, his body rigid. "You're okay, Gladys."

Flames transformed into beams of twisting light, which shattered the orb above the fire and spread throughout the room in a sudden rush of power which filled me with a sense of good – a sense of love.

"Nearly there," said Charleston, the light from his ring brightening as my magical bonds weakened.

I collapsed to the ground with a gasp as the Witch-finder's magic finally failed, and struggled to my feet, rushing towards the pyre. "Granny!" I shouted.

Barney joined me, dragging me into his arms, his hand on my head. "Penny," he sobbed. "I tried to get free. I tried so hard. I couldn't move."

"I know," I said, my tears wetting his shirt.

Willow and Mum hugged, and Boris the goat bleated in panic, galloping in circles around the room until Charleston waved a hand, sending sparks cascading over the animal's back, calming it.

"Granny!" I shouted again, knowing she would be okay, but needing to see her – the urgent desire twisting my gut and closing my throat as I sobbed.

Charleston's ring glowed brighter, throbbing on his finger, and the stream of light pouring from it stopped abruptly. The blue light surrounding Granny began to fade, and her face became clear, her skin complete again, and her eyes bright. Her voice came softly at first, her words incomprehensible, but as the light slid down her legs and across the burnt wood, evaporating into the ether, she cleared her throat and smiled. "Hello everybody," she said. "That was a bit of a palaver, wasn't it?" She looked at Charleston. "Oh, you're here. I was under duress when I said what I did. Ignore me, it was the ramblings of a silly old lady about to meet her maker."

Charleston reached up, easily plucking Granny from the pyre and placing her at his feet. He drew her close and planted a soft kiss on her blue hair. "Don't worry, Gladys. I've wanted to hear those words come from your mouth for a long time. I love you too."

Granny's shoulders shook, and the sound of her gentle sobs were muffled by Charleston's chest as he pulled her close.

Charleston gazed around at the rest of us. "Are you all okay?" he asked.

When he was happy we were unharmed, he looked at Maeve. "I have the power to transport you all out of here," he said. "The spell guarding the castle has fallen, I can sense it. I will send you all there, where you can wait for me. Gladys needs to recover, and I'm sure you would all like to get out of this terrible place. Will you look after them until I get there?"

"Of course," said Maeve. "It would be my pleasure… Charleston Huang."

"Where are you going, Charleston?" I said.

Charleston looked at the ceiling, from where the Witchfinder gazed down at us, his eyes glazed, and his body rigid. "I'm not going anywhere. I'm going to deal with him once and for all. I'll be along as soon as I'm done. I'm sure you'll all have questions for me."

"I'll stay with you," I said.

Charleston shook his head. "No, you should —"

"I want to," I said.

"If Penny's staying, I'm staying," said Barney.

Charleston nodded. "Okay," he said. He waved a hand, and red smoke enveloped everybody else, including Boris. With a shimmering of air and a loud popping sound, they vanished.

I looked up. "What are you going to do with him?" I said.

"You're not going to kill him, I hope," said Barney. "I know I don't hold jurisdiction here, but the death sentence seems wrong."

"I'm not going to kill anybody," said Charleston. "Even though he's responsible for the death of six witches here, and only he knows how many in the mortal world." Charleston gazed around the room. "I have a fate far worse than death in mind for him. I only wish we could have saved those six women, but he burned them to ash, there's nothing I can do. Gladys was lucky I got here when I did, with her heart intact I was able to regenerate the rest of her body, any longer and it would have been all over for her. Maybe then I'd have been considering the death sentence, as hypocritical as that sounds."

"It's not hypocrisy," said Barney, smiling at me. "That's love."

Charleston waved a hand, and the Witch-finder fell from the ceiling, sprawling at our feet, groaning in pain. "He'll never know love," said Charleston.

The Witch-finder gazed up at us, the eyes he was once so proud of, now dull and scared. "What will you do with me?" he said.

Charleston looked around the room and with a flick of his fingers cast a spell which closed the hole he'd made to enter the room. "This room will be your prison," he said. "For two hundred years. Then I will reconsider."

"No," said The Witch-finder. "Kill me."

Charleston shook his head. "No, and I'll cast a spell preventing you from harming yourself, and removing your need for sustenance. You'll live here, in the dark, with no requirement for food or drink. You're going to pay for what you did, Witch-finder."

"No! You can't do that to me," begged the Witch-finder. "I'll go insane being alone for that long. It's crueller than death!"

Charleston smiled. "Oh, you won't be alone, not all of the time." He gazed into a corner, and made a gentle beckoning motion with his hand, as if calling a frightened animal. He lowered his voice, and spoke softly and slowly. "Make yourselves shown. Your suffering is over, you can walk among us now."

Nothing happened for a few moments, but suddenly the air burst into life with tiny orbs of light. Zipping left and right like a swarm of bees, they joined with one another, forming larger and larger orbs, until the transparent shapes of six women took form.

"What are they?" I said, knowing the answer, but not believing it could be true.

"Ghosts," said Barney.

"Yes," said Charleston. "Ghosts walk in this world, and the mortal world. They rarely make themselves seen, but in this case, I think they'll enjoy the exception. They are free to leave this room as they wish, but I'm sure they'll spend a lot of time with their murderer."

"No!" said the Witch-finder. "Kill me, I beg of you!"

The six ghosts approached us, pushing cold air in front of them, and hovering a few inches from the ground. They smiled at us, their silvery bodies undamaged by flames, and their clothes intact.

One of them came closer, cold air swirling past us as she moved. "Thank you," she said, her papery voice out of sync with her lips, arriving a second after her mouth had moved. "Thank you for searching for us, it was not to be that you would find us in time, but we appreciate you trying, and we thank you for allowing us to take our revenge. You should leave now, we don't wish to frighten you."

"I wish you well," said Charleston, "and I'm sorry we couldn't save you."

"No!" screamed the Witch-finder, pushing himself along the lead floor, his boots sliding as they searched for purchase. "Please! Not this!"

Red smoke clouded my view as Charleston prepared to transport us from the room, but I could still make out one of the ghosts rushing from the corner, a scream pouring from her mouth, deafening in the metal lined room.

She approached the Witch-finder and her face transformed. Flesh hung from her bones, and as Charleston cast the spell my nostrils filled with the sickly aroma of burning flesh, and the blood curdling scream of the Witch-finder followed us for a few seconds after we'd left his self-constructed prison.

Charleston's spell set us down at *The Water Witch*, and I rushed on-board, scooping Rosie from the bow decking and holding her close to my chest.

"I thought we'd pick up your boat on the way." said Charleston. "Maeve said something about a lake at the castle — I'll have us there in a jiffy. I don't know about you two, but after all the excitement, I could kill for a brandy and a nice fat cigar!"

CHAPTER TWENTY

*C*harleston had transported us to the perfect spot on the lake, landing *The Water Witch* with hardly a ripple on the glass smooth surface to show the boat had appeared from thin air, and was not sailed into position.

Grassy banks filled with mature trees and teeming with wildflowers made a beautiful mooring, and after securing the boat, the three of us made our way up a steep pathway leading to the castle.

The huge building held a commanding position above the lake, its many turrets and towers reminding me of the fairy tales I'd read as a child. I'd not have been surprised to see a knight in shining armour appear around a corner, or spot a damsel in distress in one of the highest windows.

Boris the goat had been put out to pasture in the main courtyard. He had a whole lawn to himself and a trough full of fresh water which he lapped from as Charleston approached him. "I'm sorry if I filled you with Brandy and cigar smoke," Charleston said, kneeling next to the animal's head, "but Gladys assured me you were protected by magic, you'll suffer no ill effects."

Boris nudged Charleston's hand with his snout and gave a gentle bleat.

"I don't think he cares," said Barney.

"It'll be strange speaking to you, as… you, Charleston," I said. "It'll take some getting used to."

"Call me Charlie," he said. "And treat me how you treated me when I was a goat. I enjoyed it, it's been the best time of my life."

"Look," said Barney, pointing skyward. "Up there."

"Coooeee!" shouted Granny, leaning between the turrets of a high tower. "We're up here, King Charleston, and we've conjured up a feast fit for a king… and his queen! There's brandy too, and some beautiful cigars!"

Charleston laughed. "We'd better get up there," he said. "*Queen* Gladys demands our attention."

Long spiral staircases and narrow corridors led us through huge halls and past open terraces, until we finally found the high balcony the feast was waiting for us on.

Derek and Eva sat together, giggling as they sipped glass goblets of red wine, and Willow and Mum picked at the food on the long wooden table, Willow opting for grapes and cheese, and Mum choosing hunks of roast beef which she slathered with mustard.

Maeve stood up as we made an entrance, her smile as bright as the sun and her hair blowing in the breeze. "Here's the hero of The Haven!" she said, clapping. "Charleston Huang!"

Mum, Willow, Derek and Eva joined in the applause, but Granny rolled her eyes. "Don't be so daft," she said, flopping into the large wooden chair at the head of the table. "It'll go to his head! Stop that clapping, a brandy is all he'll want!"

"Granny!" I said. "Two hours ago, you were dead — burnt to a crisp on a fire. Charleston saved you — he brought you back to life, of course he's a hero!"

Granny poured brandy into a glass. "I didn't say he wasn't, I *said* it would go to his head." She lifted the glass and thrust it towards Charleston. "Here you go," she said. "Get your laughing gear around that, and then you can tell us all how the heck you passed from one dimension to another, through a metal wall, and brought a dead woman back to life... then you can have a cigar."

CHARLESTON SIPPED HIS BRANDY. "I felt different since I arrived in The Haven," he said. "I felt stronger every day — more healthy, you know?"

Granny patted his hand. "I know, dear," she said. "It was the magic in the air."

Charleston nodded. "And as we approached the spire of light I brimmed with energy — I realise now it was the magic from the jewel on the spire, but I just thought it was the fresh air. When we got underground though, the feeling passed. I felt like a normal... goat again."

"The lead," said Maeve.

Charleston sipped his drink. "Yes, the lead."

"Then how on earth did that ring of yours manage to slice a hole in the lead?" said Granny. She looked around the table. "They've filled me in on what happened while I was... on fire, and then dead. It sounds like you made quite the entrance."

"The moment that vial containing the cure touched your lips, Gladys," said Charleston. "I was back in my body. In your guest room. I thought I'd gone blind at first, but I remembered you'd put a light shade on my head to help me blend in. When I'd removed that, I knew something had changed within me." He looked at his hand. "The diamond in my ring was glowing and vibrating, and I knew everything —

I mean I could *see* everything — the history of the diamond in my ring, and what I had to do with it — how I could use it to save you all and deal with the Witch-finder."

"How?" sad Maeve. "Tell us."

Charleston looked out across the scenery. The lake, far below us, sparkled in the sun, and the balcony we were gathered on, built on one of the castle's highest towers, gave us a view as far as the horizon. "It began with my ancestor," he said. "The oriental witch the Witch-finder spoke of."

"Of course," said Willow.

Charleston smiled. "When she cast the spell, which chipped the diamond in my ring from the stone the Witch-finder carried into The Haven, her magic tangled with the magic of the Witch-finder, and she stole a vision from him, one which was meant for the Witch-finder, but one he never saw. Luckily for us, or today may have ended very differently."

"A vision of what happened in that lead room?" said Mum.

Charleston nodded. "And everything that came before it. My ancestor was not a seer, and that was the only vision she ever had. She did what the vision told her to do. She entered The Haven, travelled to the west, and conjured this castle into existence. Using the stone to cast the spell which guarded it, and ensuring that only the stone could break the spell. A key if you will."

"And she wrote the inscription on the stone," I guessed. "And when she wrote the one true ruler would come from the east, she meant the far east in the mortal world!"

"Exactly," said Charleston. "From China, to be precise. When the castle was built, she left The Haven, knowing the stone must never again travel to this land until the day it was needed… today. She saw that a man would bear the ring, and would only come when needed, and I'm the first boy in the

Huang bloodline. Every generation of witch the stone was passed down to was told they must never bring it here, and they must only visit The Haven on occasion, never arousing the suspicion of The Witch-finder. They knew he was here, and they knew he was in disguise, but not *what* disguise. He could have been anyone — they needed to stay away — they couldn't risk the Witch-finder finding them out."

"So they sacrificed their immortality in The Haven to die in the mortal world and keep the stone safe," said Granny. "No wonder none of your ancestors are here Charleston. They all gave their lives knowing that one day you would need the stone to save The Haven from the Witch-finder."

Charleston nodded. "Indeed, and they couldn't tell anyone, not even Maeve, because the vision *had* to come to fruition. They couldn't risk changing the future. Of course, I didn't know I was a witch until the day *you* told me. My grandmother had decided to take the secret to the grave — giving up on the vision for reasons known only to her, but fate brought us together, Gladys, as you said it had, and it seems that fate had a very good reason for doing so."

Willow, Granny, and I had found out that Charleston came from a magical family when we'd discovered a photograph of his grandmother.

Granny had recognised her as a witch she'd once known, and told Boris that she'd chosen to die outside The Haven -- although Granny had wrongly surmised the reason she'd given up her immortality was that Charleston's grandmother was ashamed of her witch heritage.

Charleston's grandmother had never informed her own daughter that she was a witch, and without being able to practice and develop her magic, Charleston's mother would have remained ignorant of the fact that she had magical powers.

Charleston had never known he came from a magical

background, until Granny had told him, and I was beginning to believe Granny was correct when she had blamed fate for bringing Charleston into her life – fate had made sure that the vision had come true and The Haven had been saved.

"Your grandmother was trying to save you," I said. "She knew the vision said a man would bear the stone, and you were the first boy to be born in the bloodline. She didn't know if you would die saving The Haven or not, so she chose to keep you safe by ending the vision with her death. Her love for you came before her promise to ensure the vision came true."

"And the safety of the people in The Haven," murmured Charleston. "I don't know what to think of her actions."

"But why didn't she destroy the stone?" said Willow. "With the stone still in the family, it was possible the vision would always come true, were she told anyone else or not."

"A guilty conscience," said Charleston. "When I was eighteen, I received a parcel from a lawyer containing the diamond and a letter from my grandmother. The letter said that she hoped I would know what to do with the stone one day. I had it mounted in a ring and never really thought about it again until today. I think the letter was her way of telling me, *without* telling me."

"It all sounds a little sexist to me," said Granny.

"What's sexist about it?" I said. "Did that fire scramble your brains?"

Granny wriggled her fingers in my direction, and smiled. "Careful with the insults. I've got my magic back, remember!" She reclined in the large wooden chair. "I'll tell you why it's sexist. Charleston's family refused to bring the diamond to The Haven for centuries, even choosing to die in the mortal world so the stone wouldn't get into the wrong hands. Waiting for a *male* witch to be born, who would eventually save The Haven? *That's* sexism if ever I've seen it."

AN EYE FOR AN EYE

"The vision told them it would be a boy," said Willow. "I'm not sure visions can be sexist."

Granny smiled. "Everything can be sexist, my dear." She stood up, and clapped. "Now, who's up for some exploring. If I'm to be the queen of this castle, I think I should get to know it a little better, and work out how many servants I'll require."

"You're not a queen, Gladys," said Charleston, "and I'm not a king. There'll be no servants. As far as I'm concerned, The Haven is still Maeve's, and if she wants this castle, she may have it."

"I'll hear of no such thing," said Maeve. "You deserve this castle, Charleston Huang, and you deserve to live here as a kept woman, Gladys Weaver."

"Careful, Maeve," said Barney. "Gladys is a feminist, remember? She doesn't want to be kept by a man." He smiled at Granny. "Your lectures have paid off," he said. "I think I understand feminism!"

"No, Barney," said Granny, with a frustrated sigh. "That only applies to men like accountants, plumbers, or garbage collectors. A feminist wouldn't be kept by a man like *that*, of course not, but when a king takes you as his queen, you throw your principles out of the window and embrace your sugar daddy."

"I'm not a king," said Charleston. "And you're not a queen."

"Lord and Lady?" said granny.

Charleston smiled, the lines around his mouth tightening and his eyes twinkling. "Okay. Lady Weaver it is."

"Really," said Granny. "You land a catch like me and you don't put a ring on it? It's Lady Huang, or nothing!"

"Are you proposing?" said Charleston. "Or are you expecting me to get on one knee?"

"You can forget all about that romance stuff with me! I

don't go in for it all that nonsense, but if you want to see my hammer and sickle, my finger had better have a band on it."

"Granny, enough!" said Willow. "Nobody wants to see your tattoo."

Granny winked at Charleston. "I'm game for marriage if you are?"

Charleston took her hand in his and kissed it gently. "Of course I'm game for it," he said. "I love you, Gladys Weaver."

Eva stood up. "I love a bit of… romance — if that's what you can call it — as much as the next person, but I'm tired. It was nighttime in Hilda's sunken village, but it's turning to dusk here a few hours later, I think I'm suffering from what mortals call…"

"Jet-lag," said Derek. "We're in a different timezone."

"Bedtime it is," said Granny. "At a conservative estimate, I'd say that this castle has sixty-four bedrooms, so take your pick."

"I'm sleeping on the boat," I said.

"Me too," said Willow. "I want to snuggle up with Rosie."

"Me too?" said Barney.

"Of course," I said. "You can cook us breakfast in the morning."

" I want a room with a four poster bed, please," said Mum. "And an en-suite."

WITH THE CASTLE a silhouette against the starry sky, on the hill above us, Willow, Barney, and I sat on the roof of the boat, sipping wine and listening to music. Rosie sat next to us, swatting moths, and purring whenever one of us gave her any attention.

Willow gave in to fatigue first, giving a loud yawn and stretching her arms towards the moon. "That's it," she said.

AN EYE FOR AN EYE

"I'm going to bed. I've had enough excitement to last me a lifetime."

Barney and I followed her off the roof, and said goodnight as she closed her bedroom door with another loud yawn. Barney began transforming the dinette furniture into a bed for himself, but I held my bedroom door open. "Come on," I said. "I watched my grandmother die and get resurrected today. I don't want to sleep alone."

With Barney's legs bent at the knees, he managed to fit on the mattress next to me, and with my arm across his chest and my head on his shoulder, the last sound I heard was a distant owl, before I drifted off to sleep quickly, feeling calmer and safer than I had in a long time.

THE NEXT MORNING, after breakfast, Willow, Mum, Barney, and I stood on The Water Witch, waving at the shore.

Granny and Charleston stood side by side waving back at us, with Boris squeezed between them, eating a mouthful of grass.

Derek, Eva, and Maeve had already left, and Charleston and Granny had insisted we had breakfast in the great hall with them, dining on croissants, fruits and berries, and pancakes with wild honey.

Maeve had willingly handed over control of The Haven to Charleston, telling him she'd never seen magic so powerful as the magic he now possessed, and as she'd said, six-hundred years was a long time in the same job. She fancied a change.

Charleston and Granny were making changes. They were staying in The Haven, living in *Huang Towers*, as Granny had named it overnight — and sleeping in separate bedrooms until such time Charleston had made an honest woman of her. Granny had told us that it would be prudent to go hat shopping in the next few weeks, as she wasn't going to be wasting any time.

I steered the Water Witch towards a bridge which spanned one of the four rivers leading off the lake, and with a final wave and shouted promise to Granny and Charleston that we'd be back soon, I opened a portal and gave the engine some power, aiming the bow at the centre of the glowing gold light, looking forward to getting back to Wickford, and happy I was surrounded by people I loved.

The End

ABOUT THE AUTHOR

Sam Short loves witches, goats, and narrowboats. He really enjoys writing fiction that makes him laugh — in the hope it will make others laugh too!
You can find him at the places listed below - he'd love to see you there!

www.facebook.com/samshortauthor/

www.samshortauthor.com

sam@samshortauthor.com

Printed in Great Britain
by Amazon